The Matchmaker Murders
(Season One)

Death at the Double Date
Murder at the Movies
Poisoned at the Picnic

by

CATHERINE GIBSON

Copyright © 2024 Mira Gibson

Cover Design: Book Cover Zone

Mystery Royalty

mysteryroyalty.com

All rights reserved.

ISBN: 979-8-9901812-2-9

This is a work of fiction. Names, characters, places, and incidents either are the product of the author's imagination or are used fictitiously. Any resemblance to actual persons, living or dead, events, or locales is entirely coincidental.

THE MATCHMAKER MURDERS (SEASON ONE)

DEATH AT THE DOUBLE DATE
(The Matchmaker Murders, Book One)

CHAPTER ONE

AUTUMN WINDS NEARLY stole my fluffy, knit hat. One strong gust after the next tore through the playground behind Walnut Mountain Middle School where I was supervising recess with my friend and fellow teacher, Esther.

A group of boys were kicking a ball around and hollering no matter who scored. There was a jungle gym nearby where girls practiced dance moves and flipped around the bars. Some of the kids liked to huddle to stay warm, while others burrowed against the walnut trees and read books.

"You introduced them only two months ago?" Esther asked me, referring to a recent romantic match I had made.

Matchmaking was my hobby.

Frail as a winter bird, Esther was bundled up from head to toe to keep cozy. Barely a year had passed since she had beaten cancer. Her soft, feathery hair was still growing in and she hadn't yet gotten her weight up, which was why she dressed in layers upon layers and wore a coat, hat, scarf, and mittens whenever she went outside.

"Yup," I answered. "I first met Edgar in the summer. I believe I introduced him to Gloria in early September, and they immediately hit it off."

"Wow," Esther remarked with a hint of longing in her voice. "After two months, he knew he wanted to marry her?"

"Older men move fast. Edgar is in his fifties and so is Gloria for that matter."

"He's a Christian?" she double-checked.

I tried not to let my doubts show as I told her, "Edgar has

started to attend church when he has time. Given his love for Gloria, I believe he'll come around."

A faraway look came over her. "That's all I want at this point."

"Really?" I said, somewhat surprised.

Esther had been solely focused on her health for as long as I had been friends with her. Granted, our friendship had formed when she had received her life threatening cancer diagnosis. I had found her crying in the teachers' lounge and when she had opened up to me about the diagnosis, we became best friends, right then and there. I had invited her to church after that. From then on, we had developed a routine of praying for one another, trusting the Lord, and oftentimes venting about the unfairness of life. Perhaps prior to cancer, Esther had wanted to meet the right man and get married, but had put that dream on hold. But if that was true, it was news to me.

Frustrated, she went on, "This town is too small. There are hardly any men, much less good, Christian men with values."

"I've never heard you talk like this."

Esther sighed. "I don't mean to sound jealous, but when I heard that Gloria had gotten engaged, it just made me feel like time is running out."

"Time is hardly running out, Esther," I reassured her. "You're barely in your thirties."

"I'm thirty-five, but I think we both know that's beside the point," she said, as worry clouded over her. On both her mother and her father's sides of her family, no one had lived past the age of forty due to cancer. Deep down, Esther lived in a constant state of anxiety that her breast cancer could return. "The fact of the matter is that I could go at any moment, and what if I do before I find love? Time *is* running out."

One of the bigger boys sent the kickball flying and it accidentally bonked little Peter in the side of his head. Peter was nestled under a walnut tree with his nose in his book, but glanced up to figure out what had hit him.

"Are you okay?" I shouted to Peter, who was all glasses and imagination.

"I'm okay!" he said as he found the kickball that had bounced off into the leaves, eager to return it to the bigger boys.

"I don't mean to sound sour," Esther went on. "I'm happy for Gloria, and I'm far from surprised that Edgar proposed to her. I mean, *of course* Gloria got engaged. *Of course* Edgar proposed to her. *You* introduced them, so *of course* they got engaged!"

She let out another sigh then perked up.

"Congratulations, by the way," she said, bucking up and trying to sound positive. "Mrs. Matchmaker has made another match."

Over the years, I had made nearly a dozen successful matches that had resulted in marriage, and I hadn't even meant to.

"Plus, you have the perfect marriage," Esther went on. "Your parents have the perfect marriage. I'm sure Alan's parents have the perfect marriage—"

Alan was my husband.

"And then there's me," she vented, shaking her head but stopping herself from saying more.

In a sense, Esther had been holding herself back from living life to the fullest out of fear that the other shoe could drop at any moment.

But that was no way to live.

And she knew it.

We had prayed about this many times.

"The right man for you is out there," I promised, as I began mentally running through the single men I knew who might be a good match for my friend. No one immediately came to mind except for a handful of men who worked with my husband at the police station, but none of them were Christian, though a few swung into church during the holidays. "Walnut Mountain may be a small town, but the world is a big place. You just have to have faith."

She mustered a hopeful smile.

"Don't worry, Esther," I told her. "Mrs. Matchmaker is on the job!"

"Really?"

The recess bell rang and all of the children across the playground, field, and edges of the forest began jogging towards the back of the brick schoolhouse where they collected at the rear door and slowly funneled inside.

Esther and I trailed into the building behind the children. There were assigned cubbies along the walls of the vestibule. As the kids peeled out of their coats, hats, and mittens, and grabbed their school books, I followed Esther into the teachers' lounge where we did the same, in a manner of speaking.

I hung my long coat on the rack next to Esther's and tucked my knit hat into one of the pockets, but decided to keep my thick, knit scarf around my neck to ward off the chill that was known to draft into my classroom.

Esther was discreet as she quickly swapped her warm winter hat for a fashionable sequin chemo cap that she liked to wear inside. Her dark hair looked like wispy feathers, though the growth was patchy.

I cared deeply for Esther and whenever I glimpsed her delicate scalp through those feathery tufts of hair, I felt my heart swell with motherly love.

My own hair was relatively short. The day Esther had started chemo a year ago, she had been very disturbed at the idea of losing her hair, and even more disturbed at what she would look like as it grew back. Focusing on her hair had kept her from worrying that she might not make it. So, to put her mind at ease, we had brainstormed all the different growing-out hairdos that she could try, and we used my long, auburn hair to test out the different styles.

Three interesting haircuts later, I had looked like a tomboy, but today my bright red hair was chin-length and cut bluntly in a "bob" style I happened to like. The hairstyle had also worked out well for Halloween at the school. I had thrown on one of Esther's sequin chemo caps, wore a dress with fringe, and had called myself a 1920s Flapper.

I had looked so stylish, in fact, that Esther had said I could keep the chemo cap, and to this day, I wore it whenever I was at the school with her.

Once Esther's head was completely covered with her sequin cap, and mine was too for that matter, we made our way out of the teachers' lounge—Esther looking like a bohemian goddess while I trailed beside her, feeling a bit flapperish.

The corridors of the small schoolhouse began to clear as children found their classrooms.

Mine was across from Esther's, but before we parted ways, another teacher stopped us.

"Hey, Chemo Club!"

It was Samantha.

I cringed.

Samantha wasn't my favorite.

Esther and I touched eyes, dreading the encounter with

Samantha as she approached, beaming her thousand-watt smile that I didn't trust.

She offered her usual backhanded compliment when she reached us, "Cute hats! If I get one, can I join the club?"

Samantha was obviously being snide. Not only did she have no intention of chopping off her long, flowing, thick, blonde locks to show emotional support for Esther, she had never bought a sequin chemo cap to "join our club," which would have been easy enough. Despite this, she greeted Esther and me every day with the "Chemo Club" joke as if we wouldn't notice she was mocking us.

That being said, our responses were always polite. We tried to be as gracious as possible, even though it was extremely difficult to pull off.

"It's not a club, Samantha," I said dryly.

"Oh, I know!" she laughed, as she brushed her long hair off her shoulder and glanced down her nose at Esther. "I'm just kidding! I wanted to catch you two before the staff meeting that's scheduled for later this week. What are your thoughts on the issues?"

I had only one issue and I was looking at her, but I chose to hold my tongue.

Samantha barrelled on, "I hope you will fight alongside me! This school is hardly progressive, and I would really like to integrate progressive ideologies into the core curriculum so that the students are trained to be mindful of the critical social dilemmas that face our country in this modern day. As you know, our children are the future, and it's so important that they think—"

"Samantha," I interrupted as kindly as I could when I sensed Esther bristling beside me. Esther hardly appreciated how Samantha's push for progressivism often trampled all over our personal boundaries and insulted our religious beliefs. "I'm not sure that as a Language Arts teacher, I would really have much to say about your proposed changes to the curriculum."

"Me neither," Esther chimed in. "The mathematics I teach is hardly a place for social justice."

"I beg to differ, Esther," said Samantha. "Just because I'm the only *social studies* teacher doesn't mean I should be the *only* teacher who cares about the modern-day *social* issues that face our children."

The school bell rang a second time, indicating the start of class.

"Think about it," she told us before turning on her very high heel and swaying her way up the corridor and into her classroom.

"I have nothing nice to say," Esther grumbled under her breath.

I was thinking the same thing.

"She's young and idealistic," I allowed.

"She's disrespectful. All that 'Chemo Club' stuff."

I shot Esther a tender look, screwed my face up with an air of humor, and said, "As if we would actually let her into the club."

✝

BY THE TIME I LEFT Walnut Mountain Middle School a few hours later, having taught my students the importance of correct grammar and syntax all afternoon, dusk was quickly gathering across the pale blue sky.

I waved goodbye to Esther with my mittened hand, as I drove out of the small parking lot and onto School Street.

Making my way through the heart of Walnut Mountain in order to get to the cabin that Alan and I had called home for a little over twenty years, I cranked up the heat and thought about what I should wear to the double date tonight.

My husband, Alan, and I were going to meet Gloria and the man I had set her up with, Edgar, to celebrate their recent engagement at the fanciest restaurant in town, Fancy's.

I couldn't wait!

I wouldn't have much time to throw myself together once I got home. Alan had promised to meet me at the restaurant at 5 pm sharp, and I wanted to look my best without being late since Alan didn't know Edgar and had always felt awkward around Gloria.

Even though I had been with Alan forever—we had met in middle school, fell in love in high school, and had gotten married shortly after graduating—I still felt full of butterflies at the thought of seeing him.

Esther had been right about my parents and their perfect marriage. They had gotten married right after high school, and so had my grandparents on both sides of my family, though sadly all of my grandparents had since passed away. My parents lived on the far side of Walnut Mountain where three creeks forged into a mighty river. Bears liked to snack on the berries around their property, which was why we all had to be extra careful during the springtime to keep from getting mauled.

I saw my parents regularly at church and also made an effort to swing by at least once a week.

In all my life, it had never occurred to me to leave Walnut Mountain, and I was grateful that my husband, Alan, felt the same.

Our small town had a big heart, and as far as I was concerned, the town provided everything a person needed. We had one coffee shop called Morning Glory, which the newly engaged, Gloria Davis, happened to own. One gas station, one church, one library, and one post office, all nestled on the same intersection in the center of town. Charming Diner served casual diners while Fancy's provided a fine-dining alternative when folks felt like getting dressed up and holding their pinkies in the air.

Walnut Mountain contained a strong Christian community that I felt privileged to be a part of, and though there was a growing liberal community here as well, our politics had never clashed so much that we couldn't get along.

Aside from the occasional pickpocket during the summertime fairs or a group of teenagers who found their way into their fathers' liquor cabinet and caused a bit of trouble around town, Walnut Mountain saw virtually no crime, which made me feel much better about Alan's line of work, being the police officer that he was.

At the cabin, I wasted no time tearing through the closet I shared with my husband in search of the most figure-flattering dress I could find.

I honestly couldn't wait to see him. I hadn't dined with Alan at Fancy's in ages. It was almost a shame that Gloria and Edgar were going to be there, but then again, celebrating their engagement was the entire reason for the double date. I hoped Alan would treat me affectionately. Even though I was forty years old, I felt as giddy as a schoolgirl just thinking about it!

I was looking forward to the next chapter of my life with Alan. I wanted to have a baby—it wasn't too late, it wasn't! I wanted to get pregnant and be a mother and watch Alan embrace his new role as a loving father. I was already fantasizing about staying home with a newborn and possibly even taking a few years off from working at the middle school so that I could pour all of my love, wisdom, and attention into our child—I wanted that new life so badly, I could taste it!

But faith and patience would have to come first.

That's what I was focused on. Exercising my patience and

growing my faith, and trying with all my might to become a better version of myself, even though it oftentimes seemed that the harder I tried, the worse I became...

I wasn't one for wearing makeup, but this was supposed to be a fancy celebration so I dabbed on a little eyeshadow and used mascara to help my brown eyes appear huge and feminine. Next I ran a damp comb through my choppy, chin-length hair to straighten the tangles. I used a full-length mirror to give myself the once-over, and when I determined that I looked alright, I raced out the door so that I wouldn't be so much as one millisecond late for Alan.

When I arrived at Fancy's not twelve minutes later, I spotted Alan at the bar before I even reached the hostess' stand at the front of the twinkling, French restaurant.

I felt the color rise in my cheeks just seeing my husband standing at the long bar counter. He wore a dark suit and was easily the most handsome man in all of Vermont.

The hostess was kind enough to take my coat and escort me to my husband.

"Did you order a stiff drink?" I teased, feeling nervous.

"Penny," he warned.

Alan didn't drink.

I felt shy and said, "I'm just making conversation."

"Mrs. Matchmaker!" Gloria exclaimed from the front of the restaurant, having just stepped in from the cold with her austere fiancé, Edgar Swaine. "Oh, and look! Mr. Matchmaker is here, too! Right on time!"

Believable or not, Alan's last name really was 'Matchmaker,' which made my hobby of matching people with their soulmates rather serendipitous.

"Come Edgar!" she sang as she dragged Edgar along.

Alan stiffened beside me, and I knew him well enough to understand he was already dreading the entire evening.

I offered him a sympathetic smile, but he didn't look encouraged.

"Alan, thank you for being here," I breathed.

He nodded curtly, but kept his attention on Gloria and the scene she was starting to make at Fancy's as she crossed the restaurant like an opera singer making a *big* entrance on stage.

In fact, everything about Gloria was *big*.

She had big hair, a big hourglass figure, and an even bigger personality. She didn't so much speak as sing, which worked well at church where her loud voice and humongous presence could help her praise the Lord like no other. She sang with the Worship Team every Sunday.

To the untrained eye, Edgar might appear to be the polar opposite of Gloria. He was a serious man who barked when he talked and always seemed upset. But he was an attorney and what attorney wasn't abrasive?

Gloria and Edgar actually shared a lot of common ground, which was why I had thought of Gloria the second I'd met Edgar last summer at a small-town apple stand in Pennsylvania. I had been on my way home from a Christian Conference and Edgar had just won a legal case in court. We had gotten to talking and the next thing I knew, I had set him up on a blind date with Gloria.

After the initial pleasantries at the bar, during which Edgar shook Alan's hand and ordered a scotch for himself and a glass of wine for Gloria, the hostess escorted us to our reserved table in front of the large picture windows that Fancy's was known for. The windows overlooked gorgeous views of Walnut Mountain—the twinkling heart of town, which dark mountains loomed over. Tonight, the moon was high in the night sky.

"Can I get you two some cocktails?" the waitress asked my husband and I since we were the only ones without drinks.

"No, thank you," said Alan, as we all got comfortable around the table. "We'll have water instead."

"Are you sure?" Gloria asked us. "We're celebrating!"

Gloria wiggled her fingers in front of my face, showing off the huge diamond engagement ring that Edgar had surprised her with not a week ago.

"You can always call a cab!" she pushed and I glanced at my husband to respond, but he was hiding with his nose in a menu. "No reason not to get loose! I'm fifty-five and have never felt more alive! Right, babe?"

Edgar frowned and complained about the drafty windows.

"Really, water will be just fine," I maintained.

"Hi, Tom!" Gloria sang across Fancy's the moment she spotted Thomas Ford, the Worship Team Leader, from church.

I glanced over my shoulder and gave Tom a smile, even though it was a bit sad to see him dining alone. As I glanced around, I noticed a few other members of our congregation were at Fancy's, including Milton Cranston, Esq. of Walnut Mountain Legal. He looked like he was attending an important business dinner.

The waitress pushed off to get water for Alan and me at the bar.

"Penny, I can't thank you enough for introducing me to this man!" sang Gloria as she clutched Edgar's arm and pulled him in for a quick smooch. "How did you know we would be perfect for one another?"

"I'm not sure I can put my finger on it, to be honest," I told them with a shrug. "I'm pretty good at reading people, and as different as you both are, I could tell you would get along. Plus, you both share a love for music."

Alan asked, "Do you play an instrument, Edgar?"

"Saxophone," he barked. "But I never had the time to get especially good."

"Oh, stop, Edgar!" sang Gloria. "You're excellent! He plays all the time and I sing along!"

Gloria careened into Edgar, simply overjoyed with herself, and slammed another kiss on his face, while Alan and I exchanged an awkward glance.

Alan's blue eyes twinkled in the candlelight, and I wished he would kiss me to compete with Gloria and Edgar, but our waitress returned with a bread basket and ruined the mood.

She set the bread basket down, but it was too close to the edge of the table for Edgar's liking.

When the waitress began collecting our appetizer orders, jotting each item down on her notepad, Edgar didn't trust her competency and insisted that she read the list aloud so that he could make sure she hadn't messed it up.

In general, Edgar was intimidating and not especially kind during his interactions, which was why I had looked much deeper than his personality to figure out whether or not he would make a good match for Gloria.

Underneath it all, Edgar had a strong sense of moral values, and measured everything and everyone against what was right... and what was *correct*, which was why I had high hopes that he would one day make a devout Christian.

But the downside was that, in the meantime, he had no problem telling people when they were wrong, which quickly annoyed Alan during the course of our meal.

I considered Edgar a work-in-progress. His saving grace was

that he was passionate about upholding the law and making sure that injustices were exposed and prosecuted. But he was a terrible dinner companion. Luckily, Gloria could live with Edgar's barking, abrasive personality.

"Have you set a wedding date?" I asked as our waitress placed our desserts in front of us.

"No, no, no!" Edgar balked. "We asked for *raspberry* drizzle on the chocolate cake! This is clearly drizzled with *caramel*."

"I'm so sorry, Sir," said our waitress, who by this point was on the brink of tears.

"If only you had properly written it down!" he complained.

Gloria sang, "Happy accident! I love caramel! Edgar, it's fine!"

"Are you sure?" he asked, unconvinced.

"I like caramel, too," I said, while Alan glared at Edgar from across the table.

Edgar complained, "There have been so many errors this evening…" He pushed his chair back and stood. "I'm going to negotiate with the restaurant owner to get our bill reduced. We shouldn't have to pay for our waitress's imbecile shortcomings! Excuse me."

"He always *has* to be right, which can be irritating," Gloria admitted, albeit with affection, as Edgar stomped through the restaurant in search of the owner, a French man named Jacques Vique. "But the fact of the matter," she went on, "is that Edgar *is* always right. Who can argue with that?"

Alan looked like he might say something, but in the end, he chose to hold his tongue and I loved him fiercely for it.

Gloria and I resumed small talk about her wedding plans, and as we chatted, I sensed Alan growing uncomfortable beside me. His attention wandered and he soon stared out the huge window. On the other side of our reflection was a beautiful view of Walnut Mountain and the twinkling heart of town.

As I continued to speak with Gloria, I suddenly realized that Edgar had been gone awhile. I glanced across the restaurant, but I didn't find him speaking with the owner of Fancy's any longer.

I glanced at Alan next. He seemed a million miles away. Gloria continued to elaborate the details of the wedding ceremony that would take place in the springtime at our modest church.

I was reminded of my own wedding and how deeply happy I had been the day Alan had said 'I do.'

Without warning, I felt emotions rise up in my chest. Suddenly, my face felt hot and my eyes stung, remembering how overjoyed I had felt on my wedding day.

My God, that was so long ago. I had only been a child, really, at nineteen years of age.

But I had chosen my life partner wisely.

Alan was my soulmate, absolutely, no question.

Returning his attention to the conversation, Alan touched eyes with me and immediately noticed something was wrong.

I blinked the tears away when he quietly asked me if I was okay, trying not to interrupt Gloria's story about her first date with Edgar.

"I think I should excuse myself for a moment," I whispered.

"Penny, are you sure you're okay?" Alan asked me.

"Penny?" Gloria said, catching on that I was becoming emotional.

"I'm just so happy for you, Gloria. These are tears of joy," I promised. "I just need a minute in the ladies' room."

Pushing away from the table, I got to my feet as soon as I could. I wanted to rush through the restaurant and dive into the privacy of the ladies' bathroom, but that would've drawn unwanted attention to myself, so instead I deliberately walked slowly, making my way in-between the tables. I came into a short hallway that led to both the men's and ladies' bathrooms.

I was about to spill towards the ladies' room door and let the tears out, when an odd sight on the wooden floor stopped me.

Seeping out from the crack under the door of the men's bathroom was…

Blood?

It couldn't be.

But, was it?

I was so stunned and confused by the sight of dark, sticky-looking liquid on the floor that I could barely think straight. It was like my brain had stopped working. I couldn't make sense of the blood-like substance or why it was oozing out from the men's room, until I gently pushed open the bathroom door to see where it was coming from.

There on the floor of the men's room was Edgar Swaine.

Lying in a pool of his own blood.

He was dead.

CHAPTER TWO

I COULDN'T GET THE image of Edgar Swaine's dead body out of my mind.

All of Fancy's was in an uproar of horrified confusion.

My husband, Alan, had taken charge of the scene since he was the only law enforcement officer at the restaurant. He had cleared everyone away from the bathroom area and blocked off the short hallway so that none of the diners would be able to venture into the crime scene where poor Edgar remained sprawled across the cold floor. Alan had also called the police station to report the death, but investigators had yet to arrive.

Gloria looked catatonic for the most part. She was slumped beside me at our table. A mile-long stare had come over her, and other than the initial scream she had let out upon seeing her dead fiancé on the bathroom floor earlier, she hadn't made a peep. Highly unusual for a woman as flamboyant as Gloria.

The other diners remained at their tables, as well, because Alan had forbidden them to move. He had also ordered the waitstaff to stay put, but the owner of Fancy's, Jacques, wouldn't listen. Every time Alan turned his back or dove into another phone call, Jacques slipped from the dining room and disappeared into the kitchen.

Our waitress, who had been on the brink of tears thanks to Edgar's harsh, unrelenting attitude throughout our celebration dinner, was seated on one of the bar stools. I studied her from across the restaurant. I had since learned that her name was Hailey, and Edgar must have really offended her, because she did not look torn up about his mysterious death one bit.

No one knew what had caused Edgar's death, other than the fact that with so much blood spilled, Edgar obviously hadn't died of natural causes.

To think that he was dead was surreal. The sight of him lying on his back on the men's room floor had seemed *wrong*. His eyes had been open and he had looked furious about the fact that he was no longer alive.

I shook the image out of my mind and stared blankly at the warm scotch Edgar had ordered not two hours ago. The tumbler was within reach on the table...

"Penny?" Alan said, as he intentionally moved Edgar's scotch to the far side of the table away from me and sat down. "The police are finally here."

I glanced up and saw a handful of uniformed police officers entering Fancy's, just as Gloria burst into tears and began wailing.

Alan went on, "I would like to get you home—"

"What about Gloria?"

"The police may send her home, too, after they ask her a few questions. They understand that she will be in better shape tomorrow to speak with them, once her shock has worn off."

"Do the police need to speak with me?"

"I've spoken with you and that's enough," he said. "I've noted the time that you discovered Edgar and the sequence of events leading up to your discovery of the body. And everything that took place after that. Right now, I need to get you home."

Alan urged me to my feet, but before leaving the table, I turned to Gloria and hugged her.

"I will pray for you," I told her softly. "Please call me if you need—"

"Penny," Alan warned.

"A moment, please, Alan," I said, frustrated. I promised Gloria, "I'll come by tomorrow, first thing."

"Penny," he pushed, rushing me, not that it was necessary.

On my feet, I clutched my purse to my chest, as Alan took me by the arm and led me past the investigating police officers and through the restaurant to the coat check.

"I don't want you getting overwhelmed, Penny," he explained, speaking in a low, authoritative tone. "You know what I mean. I'll see to it that Gloria gets home safely."

The coat check girl was with the rest of the Fancy's waitstaff near the bar, so Alan entered the coat check alcove, found my coat, and helped me into it. Once I had buttoned up, we left the anteroom and stepped outside into the chilly night.

A harsh wind cut across the street. Alan tensed up, his shoulders rising against the cold. With his hand on my lower back, he guided me along the sidewalk. His jaw clenched and a determined glimmer filled his eyes.

He told me, "I think it would be best if I drove you to your parents' house—"

"Don't be silly—"

He stopped walking and confronted me.

"Don't lie to yourself, Penny. You can't be alone. You just saw the dead body of a man you knew. You're not going to be able to handle the psychological effects of what you saw in there unless you're with loved ones. Who knows how you're going to react to the fact that one minute Edgar was alive and the next he wasn't. You don't know the long term effects of seeing a friend of yours dead on the floor, having been murdered—"

"Edgar was *murdered?*"

"Since I can't come home with you, you have to go to your parents."

"But—"

"I have to help investigate what has happened," he informed me, steering me towards the parking area where his pickup truck was parked.

He opened the passenger's side door for me and helped me up into the truck.

"You can't be alone," he repeated before he shut the door.

As soon as he climbed in behind the wheel and started the truck, I asked, "Will you come to my parents' house once you're done helping the police tonight?"

He let out a sigh, and didn't respond until he had gotten to the first stop sign at the center of town.

"I don't know when I'll be done investigating and I wouldn't want to wake up the whole house." Before I could object, he added, "I'll give you a call tomorrow to check in. I want you to take the day off from school tomorrow, Penny, and if Principal Longchamp will allow it, I think you should take the rest of the week off."

"My students will get behind."

"For once, Penny, worry about yourself. Please."

"Alright, Alan. I'll see," I said, feeling put off.

"I'm warning you. Do not take Gloria's grief upon yourself. You can't fix this. You can't heal Gloria or make this situation right, do you understand? Please, take care of yourself."

He didn't say much after that, and I knew better than to combat him or defend myself. He knew me too well and had gotten to know how I tended to self-destruct whenever I put everyone else first.

Deep down, Alan cared about me, and seeing that he did gave me hope.

My parents lived in a two-story cabin where the only source of heat was three wood-burning stoves. I could smell the sweet scent of chimney smoke as Alan angled his pickup truck down their long, winding driveway.

Soon the cabin came into view through the walnut trees. The windows were aglow with amber light, and all the little lights that my dad had installed across the lawn outlined the walkway and Mother's garden.

We rolled to a stop, but Alan didn't turn the engine off. He didn't even put his truck into Park.

"When will you call tomorrow to check in?" I asked, already feeling abandoned.

"I won't call too early and wake you up, if that's what you're worried about."

"I'm not worried about you calling too early."

"Goodnight, Penny."

Finally, he met my gaze. His blue eyes were dark in the low light, and for a moment he looked like a stranger.

The portico lights over the front door of the cabin flipped on, and a second later, my father stepped outside, wrapping his robe around himself tightly.

I popped the passenger's side door open, and as I climbed out, Alan told me:

"I love you."

I turned and met his gaze. "Then forgive me."

✝

THE NEXT MORNING, I woke before dawn. My bedroom

smelled of cedar, cinnamon, and spices. I felt snuggly and warm under the covers, but my nose was cold and I knew the chill in the air would take some getting used to.

The closet was full of my clothes, which was a testament of how often I stayed with Mom and Dad. My bedroom had a small bathroom and Mom kept the towels fresh.

I took a quick shower to warm my bones, threw on a woolen dress, thick tights, and a big sweater, layering up as much as I could, and then made my way downstairs where my mother was shoving wood into the stove in the living room to heat up the house.

"Help yourself to coffee," she said, as she fit another piece of wood into the stove, embers sprinkling around her gloved hand.

"Thanks!" I called out, already in the kitchen. I poured myself a mug, splashed cream in, and gulped a few sips down. "I'm heading off!"

My mother appeared in the open doorway. Her hair was white and wavy. She was wearing her around-the-cabin clothes, a Christian cross necklace, and a worried look on her face.

"Please don't look at me like that," I said with a sigh. Sitting at the table, I laced up my boots and gulped my coffee.

I had already talked to her last night. I hadn't withheld anything from either of my parents. They were just as concerned about me as my husband was, but I was concerned about Gloria and everyone else in this town who was going to be horrified once they heard a man had been murdered at Fancy's.

"You're still staring at me, Mother."

"Don't you think you ought to heed your husband's advice, dear?"

"I *did* heed his advice."

As I wrapped my knit scarf around my neck as many times as it would go, my mother reminded me, "Alan would like you to stay here and take it easy."

"I'm not made of glass."

"Penny—"

I sprang to my feet, threw my coat on, and slung my purse over my shoulder.

"Alan told me to stay here last night. I stayed here last night. Alan told me to take today off from work, and that's what I'm going to do. Alan told me to—"

"What do you always do when you're stressed out?" she

challenged me.

She wanted me to say it.

But I refused to dredge up the past.

Instead, I snapped, "If everyone would just trust me and have a little faith, I would really appreciate it."

"Please don't leave mad—"

Too late.

I was already out the door.

My car was parked in the driveway, thanks to Alan. I knew the keys would be in the ignition because I knew my husband better than anyone else in the world. He had driven it over in the middle of the night so that I wouldn't feel stranded today.

Alan was the best.

He lived by a higher set of laws than most people, even compared to other Christian men. Above all else, he was committed to doing the right thing, not in man's eyes, but in God's eyes alone. He took the 10 commandments seriously. He lived up to them each and every day. He understood what it meant to be a good husband, and that was how he treated me, whether I deserved it or not…

…which was why, at times, I found it very difficult to be his wife.

He was too good for me.

I wasn't good enough, because oftentimes I fell short of God's perfect and holy standards.

I had never known Alan to fall short of anything, and I thought that was why, at times, he felt that being my husband was more than he could bear.

Once the car warmed up and the frost had cleared from the windshield, I drove into the heart of Walnut Mountain.

The sun pierced between mountain peaks, washing Main Street in golden light.

Gloria's coffee shop, Morning Glory, sat on the corner. Morning Glory offered bagels, breakfast sandwiches, and an assortment of freshly baked pastries. This morning, its huge sign rattled in the strong winds.

I parked my car along the curb and climbed out.

The building itself had two stories. Gloria lived above the coffee shop in an apartment, though as far as I understood, she had been in the process of moving the majority of her belongings into the new house that Edgar had bought in Walnut Mountain. Given her Christian faith, however, Gloria was not planning on officially moving in with Edgar until they were married.

I didn't expect to find Gloria in Morning Glory when I breezed in through the glass entrance door to grab a cup of coffee. I thought I would knock on her apartment door and discover her slumped on her couch upstairs with bags under her eyes.

I also didn't expect to find Alan in the coffee shop that morning. But there he was, with three police officers, clustered around Gloria and questioning her about the events that took place last night. The questions they asked about Edgar Swaine sounded cold-hearted.

Alan wasn't wearing his policeman's uniform, which was odd.

Instead, he wore regular blue jeans and his winter jacket with some warm flannel layers underneath, which was how he usually dressed when he went hunting with my father.

There were a handful of customers waiting in line for the young barista behind the counter to take their order. The barista's name was Dex and he attended church regularly. I had also taught him Language Arts some years back at Walnut Mountain Middle School.

I might have gone unnoticed long enough to sneak out—obviously, this was a bad time and I wouldn't be able to comfort Gloria if my husband started chastising me—but Dex hollered, "The usual, Mrs. Matchmaker?"

Suddenly, all eyes were on me, including Alan's, and I shrank.

"The usual would be great, Dex, thanks."

Alan looked a strange mix of surprised and furious to see me, but Gloria was relieved. She broke free of the police and sang, "Penny!"

"How are you holding up?" I asked as we made our way to one another.

She grasped my hands and stared up at me with worried eyes.

"I just want to be left in peace, but the police want me to go to the station."

I touched eyes with Alan.

Gloria shouldn't have to go to the station. She was in mourning. But I couldn't see why Alan would put her through any *unnecessary* measures. If Alan needed to question Gloria at the police station, then I trusted that he had his reasons.

"I'll come with you," I decided.

Alan advanced on me in an instant. The other police officers gathered around Gloria again and began explaining what needed to happen next.

Alan informed me, "You aren't coming with Gloria to the station, and that's final."

"Why aren't you wearing your uniform?"

Alan answered my question like an afterthought. "I was promoted to detective."

"That's fantastic news!"

"You can't come to the station with Gloria," he repeated, as he ushered me towards the door.

But Dex stole our attention, waving my small coffee and bagged bagel in the air—"Here you go, Mrs. Matchmaker!"

Alan doubled-back, collected my order, and brought it to me.

"I told you to stay with your parents."

A thought popped in my head. "Did you *apply* to become a detective? Or did Pepperdine promote you out of the blue?"

Chief Pepperdine, or Sergeant Pepper as the station house cops liked to call him, was the head honcho at the Walnut Mountain Police Station.

"I applied—"

"You didn't tell me. When did you apply?"

"Penny—"

"I'm really happy for you! We should celebrate!"

He shot me a warning look, took me by the arm, and escorted me through the glass door, bringing me into the bright, morning sunshine.

"I'm in charge of a team of investigating officers, Penny. Edgar's murder is huge."

"Who would've murdered Edgar?" I wondered, then quickly realized, "He was awful to so many people…"

"I have a lot of responsibility and Walnut Mountain hasn't seen a murder since the late 1800s. This is a big case for me."

"I'm so proud of you for being promoted!"

I was overjoyed for him and could not contain myself.

"Can you please do me a favor and stay out of trouble, as well as out of my way?" he asked.

It stung—hearing him talk as though I was some kind of burden.

"I only came to check on Gloria."

"Which I asked you not to do."

"No, you told me to take care of myself," I reminded him,

"which I'm doing. Look, a healthy breakfast and everything." I shook my bagged bagel in his face.

He hissed through his teeth, "Go back to your parents' cabin, Penny, before you accidentally overwhelm yourself and—"

"I can't sit around and do nothing, Alan, I'll go crazy!"

"Your parents will keep you busy—"

"I have to keep my regular schedule if I want to stay sane," I insisted, putting my foot down.

One of the police officers, Jeremiah, who had never gone to church even though I had invited him countless times, poked his head out of Morning Glory and asked Alan:

"Should we exercise the warrant for upstairs now?"

I felt my eyebrows shoot up to my hairline and I hissed at Alan, "You got a warrant to search Gloria's apartment? Why?"

Alan barked at his police officer to hold his horses, and I was stunned. Alan had never barked at anyone. His stern, take-charge attitude intrigued me, however, and my husband suddenly looked even more attractive.

He returned his attention to me and compromised, "If you think you can handle keeping a regular schedule, then fine. But don't do too much, Penny, I'm warning you."

"I'm glad you're warning me," I agreed. "And I promise, I won't do too much."

He sighed. "Are you going to the school?"

As hard as I tried, I could not suppress the giddy, guilty smile that was coming over me. But I wasn't smiling for any other reason than the fact that being around Alan, even if we were arguing, was my favorite place to be.

✝

ONE THING I HAD learned over the years, during this Christian walk, was that I was not in control. This wasn't to say that I didn't have control over my choices or my actions. I did. But it was to say that I understood I played a small, important role in a very big story that I was not the author of. Whenever I *forgot* that my purpose was to be pleasing to God and to be of service to his greater plan, I faltered. Significantly.

This was the primary reason I had to go to Walnut Mountain

Middle School that morning. It had been the reason I had felt compelled to swing by Morning Glory and check on Gloria. I had to focus on helping others and stay busy by making myself available to my friends. I had to be of service to others in order to serve the Lord.

Otherwise…

I didn't want to think about 'otherwise.'

Alan didn't necessarily understand this about me, yet his perspective was valid. From where he was standing, it looked to him as though I served others to the point of exhaustion, became overwhelmed, and backslid to the point of…

I didn't want to think about that either.

Walnut Mountain Middle School was sleepy and quiet by the time I arrived at a little before 7 am in the morning. The big yellow school buses had yet to pull up to the brick building and drop off children. At this hour, the buses were still growling through the farthest reaches of our small, rural town, collecting kids.

Principal Garth Longchamp was in the teachers' lounge.

I hung my coat and fluffy, knit hat on my assigned rack, and sat down at one of the tables with my bagged bagel and cream cheese sandwich.

"Good morning, Garth," I said before taking a big bite.

Garth Longchamp had been the principal of Walnut Mountain Middle School since I had attended nearly three decades ago. He was a crotchety, withered man who wore bow ties and had no intentions of yielding to Samantha's progressivist crusades.

"Morning, Penny," he said, as he glanced at me briefly over his spectacles. He returned his attention to the morning paper, flipped a giant page, and asked, "Edgar Swaine was murdered at Fancy's yesterday evening?"

"Very unfortunately," I said. I took another bite of my bagel, washed it down with sweet, creamy coffee, and added, "His fiancée is devastated."

"You're talking about Gloria?" asked Esther from the coat rack area, having just come in from the cold. "I heard the news this morning on the radio while driving in."

Esther quickly slid her winter hat off of her delicate head and pulled on a beautifully embroidered chemo cap. She pulled up a chair beside me and looked at me with empathy in her huge eyes.

"Killed at the restaurant?" she breathed.

I nodded at Esther, touched eyes with Principal Longchamp, and told the tale of what I had seen, from Edgar's dead body on the floor to the chaos that had followed.

More teachers piled into the lounge. The science teacher, Matthew, speculated on the cause of death, though no one really knew what had done Edgar in. Samantha breezed in, looking sun-kissed and gorgeous, yet grave about the recent murder.

"Who do you think could have done such a thing?" she wondered.

All I could guess was, "Someone who was at the restaurant. Someone who hated Edgar. Someone who was bold enough to go into the men's bathroom to kill him. I assume it was a man, but who can be certain?"

Esther asked, "Who was at the restaurant, Penny? Can you recall?"

The question got me thinking, but the school bell rang, indicating a five minute warning for the start of First Period, which prevented me from naming names out loud.

However, as the day unfolded, I tried to recall as many faces from last night as I could.

Was everyone a suspect? That didn't seem right. Certainly Gloria wasn't suspicious. She hadn't left her chair all night. That being said, I had been surprised to see her at Morning Glory earlier. I certainly wasn't suspicious, and I doubted that our traumatized waitress would've taken revenge against Edgar for having berated her for her mistakes during dinner. Edgar had argued with the owner of Fancy's, Jacques, but that hardly seemed like enough to motivate him to kill.

I huddled next to Esther during the outdoor recess after lunch. We bounced some ideas around concerning who might have killed Edgar and how. Esther had only met Edgar once or twice at our church. Hardly anyone in Walnut Mountain knew Edgar. In fact, I probably knew Edgar better than anyone else in our small town with the exception of Gloria, of course.

I decided that I would stop in on her as soon as school let out, since I hadn't really been able to talk to her or comfort her earlier that day with all the commotion in the coffee shop.

As soon as the final bell rang at 3:30 pm, I did precisely that.

The drive from School Street to Morning Glory took less than five minutes. The leaves of the trees lining the streets were turning shades of red, orange, and yellow. Shopkeepers had decorated their storefront windows and entrances with pumpkins, colored gourds, and other autumn decorations. Residents strolled down the sidewalks while others sat on park benches and enjoyed the crisp air and waning sunshine.

When I swung the glass entrance door of Morning Glory's open, Dex greeted me with a big smile.

"Afternoon, Mrs. Matchmaker! The usual?"

From behind the counter, Dex pushed his shaggy, boyish hair out of his eyes and waited for an answer.

"I came to see if Gloria was back from the station yet."

"She is, but she told me to only call her if there's an emergency."

"She's upstairs?"

"I think so," he said.

"What pastries do you have left?"

After buying more sweets than I knew what to do with, I headed out into the chilly air. Dusk gathered across Walnut Mountain as I walked around to the rear of the building. The entrance door that led up to Gloria's apartment was right in front of her parking spot. Her car was there, as well as other vehicles. The door was never locked, so I pulled it aside and started up the stairs.

I hadn't climbed more than five stairs when I heard Gloria's voice clear as a bell from deep within her apartment beyond the landing.

"Are you crazy? Get out of town! You should not have come here!"

She sounded distressed.

I froze.

Who was she talking to?

I guessed her apartment door was open, because I was able to hear a man respond.

"You shouldn't be alone right now—"

"That's not for you to say," she snapped. "My God! You think I want anything to do with you?"

"When I saw you at Fancy's last night—" said the man.

"I don't know what game you're playing, but it's time to quit and leave town!"

The argument sounded intimate, and whoever Gloria was arguing with had been at the restaurant last night...

Their voices fell. I strained to hear what they said next, but their argument had dropped into hushed whispers.

I crept up another step and then another, easing my way up the stairs.

Gloria said something like, "I don't know what you did, but you better leave Walnut Mountain," but I couldn't be sure those were her exact words.

The man responded with a deep, raspy voice, but most of what he said was muffled. I thought I heard him say "justice" and "fate" but my mind may have been playing tricks on me.

Heavy footfall neared the upper landing and my heart punched up my throat.

I raced down the stairs as quietly as I could, just as the man stomped out of Gloria's apartment and crossed the landing.

I didn't want to make a peep so I slipped through the door and didn't close it after I spilled out into the parking lot.

Dusk had turned to darkness outside.

I leapt away and tucked myself between a pair of parked cars, as the man stomped out of the building. When he reached the parking lot, he pushed the door closed behind him, shoved his hand into the front pocket of his jeans, and produced a set of keys.

All the while, I spied him from the shadows. He had salt-and-pepper hair and was dressed like an aged rock 'n roller. A real bad boy type, yet far past his prime. If I had to guess, I would have said he was in his early sixties, but his posture was erect and his figure appeared trim.

As he turned for the only Mustang in the lot, one of the building's overhead lights illuminated his face and I got a good look at him.

I was certain I had seen him at Fancy's last night.

Certain.

When I finally went upstairs to check on Gloria, long after the mystery man had driven off in his faded red Mustang, I didn't ask her who he was.

I didn't ask her anything.

I felt on edge.

How well did I really know Gloria?

CHAPTER THREE

MY CHURCH, HOPEFUL HEART MINISTRIES, was situated across from the gazebo in the center of Walnut Mountain. In a lot of ways, the entire town revolved around the church. This was no accident. Centuries ago, when American settlers had laid down their roots in Walnut Mountain, Vermont, this humble church was the first structure they had built. All the other shops around town had come after. And since the white church sat atop a little hill, its steeple could be seen for miles around.

Members of our congregation who loved Gloria made their slow, mournful way into Hopeful Heart. Unfamiliar faces belonging to Edgar's extended family entered the church as well, and began unbundling their coats and scarves in the vestibule where the pastors greeted them with quiet condolences, consoling hugs, and somber handshakes.

Everyone was dressed in black, including myself.

Edgar had never been married and didn't have any children, but among his relatives were his siblings and their spouses and children who had all reached adulthood.

The vestibule was a bit crowded, so once I removed my coat, I made my way into the sanctuary. The pews were filling up. Parishioners clustered around Gloria near the pulpit. A black veil covered her face.

I wondered if Gloria was *hiding* behind her veil… or hiding *something*.

Who was the man with the red Mustang that she had been arguing with?

Glancing around the church, I didn't see the guy, which made sense considering that Gloria had essentially told him to get lost. After he had left that night and driven off in his Mustang, I had gone up to check on Gloria as planned. She hadn't acted like herself, which had raised my suspicions. But then again, how was a woman supposed to act after her beloved fiancé had been murdered?

I hoped Alan would arrive at the funeral on time. I felt naked without him. He had explained to me, however, that investigating Edgar's murder was going to demand all of his time. Even still, I didn't want to be alone.

The sweet voice of my friend, Esther, stole my attention from Gloria, who I had been watching like a hawk.

"How are you holding up, Penny?"

"I'm alright. Keeping busy," I told her.

Working the day after Edgar's murder had been a bad idea, but it had also been a Friday, so having the rest of the weekend to myself was a saving grace.

"What about you?" I asked her even though she hadn't really known Edgar.

"I feel terrible for Gloria," she said as she discreetly touched the side of the sleek, black chemo cap she was wearing on her head. There was a tuft of hair poking out in front of her ear, which she tucked under the cap. "Did you hear he was stabbed?"

"He was?" I whispered. "I didn't know."

Esther looked up at me with big, concerned eyes and nodded.

"Alan didn't tell you?" she asked. When I shook my head, indicating that he hadn't, she questioned me even further. "Really?"

I felt embarrassed, but tried not to let it show.

"Alan was promoted to detective and even though I'm his wife, it would be wrong of him to divulge to me the details of an ongoing investigation," I explained, hoping I was right.

"Alan is a detective now?" she asked, brightening. "That's great news."

"I'm very proud of him."

Her optimism drooped. "A detective of what, exactly?"

"Other than Edgar's murder?"

"Is he a *homicide* detective?"

"You mean, *permanently*?"

Esther frowned. "I hope no one else gets murdered... Why else would the police need a *homicide* detective *permanently...?*"

"I'm not sure," I said as the possibility took root in my mind. "But even if someone else is murdered, Alan is not going to be able to tell me about it. Why did you ask, though? He didn't tell *you*, did he?"

"No, not at all. I heard from Gloria that Edgar was stabbed."

"From Gloria?"

She hadn't mentioned anything to me when I had checked in on her.

Esther nodded, "Yesterday morning at Morning Glory she told me."

"She's been working?" I said, stunned. "She should have Dex handle the coffee shop while she mourns and recovers."

Again, I studied Gloria from across the sanctuary then glanced around the congregation to see if the mystery man had come to the funeral.

"Penny?"

"Hmm?" I returned my attention to Esther.

"Are you sure you're alright?"

I didn't like it when people doubted that I was fine, especially when they were right and I was lying. But considering all that had been going on, and going *wrong*, in my life, I knew I wouldn't be able to open up to Esther without breaking down.

There would be nothing more selfish than having an emotional breakdown and drawing attention to myself when my problems were not about Edgar and his murder and the devastation that was sweeping through Walnut Mountain as a result. Instead, my problems were due to my own shortcomings and therefore a matter for the Lord to straighten out. Not that I wanted Esther to know any of that. The last thing I wanted to be was a burden to my friends.

I told her as honestly as I could, "I'm as alright as I can be, considering Edgar's murder."

At the front of the sanctuary, Pastor Peter tapped the microphone on the lectern and greeted the congregation in a somber tone. Behind him, the Worship Team played harmonious chords.

As the Worship Team leader, Thomas Ford, conducted the band and Pastor Peter began the funeral proceedings with the Lord's Prayer, parishioners took their seats in the pews and bowed their heads.

I followed Esther into the nearest pew and just as I was about to sit down, Alan surprised me.

My husband had arrived!

He took hold of my hand and kissed me on the cheek.

"You made it!" I whispered.

He wasn't dressed in a suit, which told me he wouldn't stay long.

"I have about an hour," he said as we cozied up next to one another on the pew.

Esther leaned forward and smiled at Alan to say hello.

Alan took my hand in his, keeping up appearances for anyone who might glance our way.

Tears welled up in my eyes. I lowered my head and allowed my emotions to quietly spill out.

I was so tired of pretending.

Esther consoled me.

She had no idea why I was crying.

✞

LEAVING THE FUNERAL without my husband felt miserable, but Esther had accepted my invitation to have apple cider over at my parents' house after the Service, and I was looking forward to her company.

She needed to go home first to change out of her gloomy funeral dress, but said she would meet me at my mom and dad's cabin in a half-hour.

I gave Esther a squeeze and she left the church. Then I approached Gloria, who was standing with her own family, as well as Edgar's, in the church vestibule so that loved ones could offer condolences on the way out.

"Gloria, I'm so deeply sorry for your loss," I said, as I pulled her into a hug.

"I know you are, Penny," she breathed into my ear.

I released her and tried to look into her heavily made-up eyes, but the thin, black veil over her face was difficult to see through.

"I understand the importance of keeping busy," I told her. "But I don't want you to spread yourself too thin, Gloria."

"I have to keep working and keep going," she said, "or else I'm going to fall apart."

"I know the feeling," I assured her. "But you don't have to go it alone. Please let me know how I can help. I can even come over and cook dinner or tidy up or do your laundry. Anything."

She appreciated the offer, gave me another hug, and promised she would be in touch.

The November sun shined pale and white, as I left the church. There was a chill in the air that cut through my coat and stung my bones. I hunched my shoulders against the wind, wishing I had worn a thicker scarf, and started off for my parked car.

On the other side of the gazebo that sat smack-dab in the center of the town square, something red caught my eye.

The particular shade—faded red, like a brick—immediately reminded me of the Mustang that Gloria's mystery man had climbed into three nights ago.

I broke away from the fray of funeral goers who were also heading towards their parked cars. When I got to the one way street, I waited for oncoming traffic to roll by then jogged across, as a mean gust of wind beat against my back and pushed me along.

I walked around the white gazebo, which was a huge octagonal structure where honky tonk bands played in the summertime, and came to another one way street where little shops lined the block.

Sure enough, parked in front of the Walnut Mountain Library was the same faded red Mustang I had seen at Gloria's.

I glanced around, feeling suddenly self-conscious. I didn't want the mystery man to catch me snooping around his car. But I found it curious that he was still in town after Gloria had insisted he leave Walnut Mountain and never come back.

As I neared the Mustang, I noticed the license plate—1KLRF8—and slowly read the license plate number out loud to myself, carefully pronouncing each number and letter.

"One killer fate."

My heart started racing.

How dreadfully ominous!

Again, I looked around to make sure I wasn't being watched.

I wasn't.

Pretending to bumble around my purse as if I was trying to find some important item, I walked up to the side of the Mustang, slowed my step when I reached the passenger's side door, and purposefully dropped my keys on the ground.

I used picking up my keys as an excuse to peer into the Mustang on the way down and also on the way back up.

There was some everyday trash inside—empty water bottles, scattered candy wrappers, and a balled up tee shirt. In the backseat, there was what appeared to be a small amplifier and a nest of tangled electrical cords.

A band flyer rested on the passenger's seat, and I got a really good look at it once I had returned my keys to my purse.

The band featured on the promotional flyer was called Jail Bird and apparently they were going to play a show at the only bar in town, Heartbreakers.

I never went to Heartbreakers. It was a dive bar, filled with all kinds of seedy types, though from time to time, the younger members of our congregation met there for an early drink or a date. Having a bar in town wasn't a bad idea, but the place attracted residents from the surrounding towns, and not all of them were the kinds of characters I would want to associate with. That being said, the police officers that Alan worked with loved Heartbreakers, and patronized the bar whenever bands played on the weekends.

According to the flyer, Jail Bird was scheduled to play at Heartbreakers *tonight*.

"Penny Matchmaker!"

"Ah!" I startled terribly and turned on my heel to find Thomas Ford, the Worship Team leader, keying into his car, which was parked right next to the Mustang.

"Pardon me for frightening you!"

Tom was chipper for his old age, though at the moment he was as downtrodden as anyone else who had attended Edgar Swaine's funeral.

"That's okay, Thomas," I said, clutching my chest and willing my heartrate to subside. "I suppose I'm a bit jumpy knowing that the newest member of our congregation was killed."

He shook his head at the shame of Edgar's death and then awkwardly indicated that I was blocking him from the driver's side door of his car.

"Excuse me for being in the way," I said, slipping around him to make room. "Lovely music selection, Tom. Very thoughtful. I really enjoy the songs you put together for the church."

"Thank you, Penny," he said as he opened his driver's side door and climbed in. "You have a blessed day now."

"You, too."

I watched him drive off, turned on my heel with my keys in hand, and started briskly for my own car that was back at the church.

I didn't want to be late for Esther.

✝

"IT MIGHT BE NOISY here the next few mornings," my dad warned me the moment I got to my parents' cabin.

The house smelled of cinnamon and warm apples. I decided to keep my coat on, as I entered the living room where a crackling fire was burning in the wood stove.

"I have a contractor coming to help me with the new storm shutters," he explained, keeping at my heels as I crossed through to the sliding glass door that led to the rear deck. "He wants to come at first light, Penny, but we can start on the other side of the house."

"Start wherever you would like to start," I said, as I assessed the table and chairs that were on the deck. "I've been getting up at 5 am anyway."

"What are you looking for, dear?"

My father, Lucas Hawkins, was a workhorse at heart. He had retired years ago but hadn't slowed down one bit, and there wasn't a day gone by that he hadn't fixed or renovated something here at the house, at the cabin where I lived with Alan, or at the church. I had gotten my fiery red hair and steadfast attitude from my father.

At the moment, he wanted to know why I was distracted by the cold, uncomfortable-looking patio furniture.

"Esther is on her way, and I thought it might be nice to sit outside while the sun is shining."

Dad planted his meaty fists on his hips and had himself a good, hard look around. A determined frown came over him, and a moment later, he had an entire battle plan.

"I'll get the portable fire pit going. We've got thicker cushions in the attic that will fit on the patio furniture, and once we pile wool and flannel blankets on the chairs and get a few tiki torches in the mix, we should be able to get the area warm and cozy for Esther."

I smiled and gave my dad a hug.

"It's nice to have you home, Penny."

"It's just temporary," I told him.

He urged me back, gave me the once over, and then we got to work, putting the deck in order by the time Esther rang the doorbell.

My mother was happy to see Esther, as she entered the cabin, looking as soft and snuggly as a baby goose.

"It's nice to see you, Dottie," said Esther to my mother, as I ushered her through the living room.

"I've got warm apple cider on the stove," she told us and Esther said she would love a mug.

Dad mentioned we could keep the sliding glass door open if we liked for additional warmth. He had completely transformed the deck. Esther set down the tote bag she had brought and got herself settled under a heap of blankets on one of the chairs. The portable fire pit crackled at her feet.

I joined Mom in the kitchen, poured two steaming mugs of apple cider, and placed them on a carrying tray with a plate of cookies.

As I walked slowly and carefully, my mom said, "I'll bring the whole pot out once I make a bit more."

"You're just trying to get me to stay forever," I said with a wink as I slipped out of the kitchen.

I heard her say, "You better believe it," and the thought made my heart sink a little.

I didn't want to stay with my parents forever.

I wanted to be at home with my husband.

As I eased out onto the deck and set the carrying tray of apple cider and cookies down on the table next to Esther, she asked me:

"You're not *living* here, are you?"

"Oh, no," I said, letting out an awkward laugh. "No, I'm just here for..." I had to think fast to fabricate a legitimate reason that wouldn't make Alan look callous. "Well, I guess I don't know how long. You see, with Alan's big promotion, he really needs his space to solve Edgar's murder. We both thought it would be best if he had the cabin to himself at least for a few days."

"You're such a good wife, Penny."

"Oh, hardly," I said, brushing her compliment aside as if I was humble and not internally cringing at how profoundly wrong she was. "Giving each other space is what makes our marriage work."

"Your marriage works *so* well," she said, in awe of my

relationship with Alan.

In reality, Esther was in awe of a lie. Of course, Alan and I hadn't been living this lie for very long. For years, we had enjoyed a strong, happy marriage. But the happiness we shared had recently begun to slip through my fingers like sand. The harder I tried to clutch what we once had in my fist, the faster those grains spilled out of my grasp.

"I want a marriage like that so badly," she went on as she reached for her tote bag and pulled out a bottle of red wine. My stomach dropped. I couldn't take my eyes off the wine. "When I saw how happy Gloria was after Edgar had proposed to her, it was like I suddenly realized I've been walking around with a giant hole in my heart. And don't get me wrong, I'm devastated for Gloria. But Edgar's shocking death has made me all too aware of how short and precious life is. I mean, the cancer could have killed me. It didn't. But what if something else comes along?"

"You can't live in fear that you're going to die," I gently reminded her.

"You're absolutely right, Penny. I *can't* live in fear. I have to *live*. My Mr. Right is out there somewhere," she declared as she found a bottle opener in her tote bag. "Do you like Merlot?"

Staring at the wine, I didn't know what to say.

I loved wine.

I couldn't take my eyes off the bottle she had brought, I loved Merlot so much...

My mother breezed out onto the deck with a steaming pot of apple cider in her gloved hands.

"Dottie, can I trouble you for a pair of wine glasses?" Esther asked my mother, who stopped dead in her tracks when she saw the bottle of wine in Esther's hands.

My mother went pale.

She didn't look me in the eye.

She didn't look at me at all.

Tempering her response, she said, "I believe I have wine glasses in the kitchen."

"Thanks, Dottie!"

My mom placed the pot of apple cider on the table, turned on her heel, and disappeared into the house.

I finally let out the breath I hadn't realized I was holding, but when my mom returned with two long stem wine glasses, every muscle in my body tensed up all over again.

"You're the best, Dottie! Want a glass?" Esther asked.

"No, thank you," she said politely.

When she entered the house, she closed the sliding glass door behind her and didn't come out again, she was so furious.

Esther was practically bursting at the seams, her hopes were on fire in the best possible way that she would find Mr. Right. As she poured two glasses of wine for us, she mentioned her recent prayers and how she was committed to living life to the fullest from now on.

I listened to her. I nodded and responded. I promised that I would be on the lookout for her Mr. Right, as well.

All the while, in the back of my mind I thought about the Jail Bird flyer I had seen on the backseat of the mystery man's Mustang, and I thought about Heartbreakers bar and how I had never set foot inside the place.

The entire time I spent with Esther on the rear deck of my parents' cabin, I didn't touch the glass of wine she had poured for me…

…even though gulping down Merlot was all I wanted to do.

CHAPTER FOUR

NIGHT HAD FALLEN. I had survived dinner with my parents. My mother hadn't said a word to me about Esther's wine—which I hadn't drunk, by the way—but somehow that made her quiet disapproval even worse.

I was now sitting in my car and staring at Heartbreakers.

I had parked in the dirt lot in front of the bar nearly ten minutes ago.

Chilly air seeped through the vents of my car, which told me I ought to go inside already, but I was worried.

Located on the outskirts of town, Heartbreakers bar sat on a rural county road, but was otherwise tucked in the woods. Having once been a barn, Heartbreakers loomed over the landscape. The huge sign above the door—a red, broken heart—glowed, casting pink light across the parking lot.

Motorcycles were lined up in front of the wide entrance door. Outside, seedy types smoked cigarettes and flirted loudly with one another. Muffled music boomed from inside the bar.

Jail Bird was playing.

I had every reason to believe I would find Gloria's mystery man in Heartbreakers. What, precisely, I planned to do about that was up for debate at this point, but in the short term, part of me believed that if I could uncover the truth about who had killed Edgar, then Alan would forgive my shortcomings and I would be released from the purgatory of my parents' custody.

Taking one final moment before venturing in, I folded my hands, bowed my head, and prayed for guidance, protection, and deliverance from temptation.

I opened my eyes, made sure the Christian cross pendant of my necklace was resting flat against my chest, and climbed out of my car.

When I entered the bar, I was immediately confronted with a world I wasn't used to. The thud of the band's music punched into me without ceasing. It was too crowded for my taste. The smells of spilled beer and crisp cold air reached me, as I instinctively made my way to the long bar counter that spanned the full length of the floor. I tried to regain my bearings even though I felt like I was on autopilot.

Why had I made a beeline for the *bar*?

The scene was chaotic and I felt unnerved.

I needed to think.

I wanted a drink.

"What'll it be, sweetheart?"

I turned to find the bartender looking right at me.

"What? Me?"

"Yes, you, honey. What can I get you?" he asked.

I couldn't lie to myself. I had been thinking about taking the edge off ever since Esther had presented that bottle of Merlot earlier at my parents' house.

"A water," I said before quickly amending my order. "Actually, I'll have a cranberry seltzer, please."

Bartenders worked for tips, after all, and I didn't want to annoy him by asking him for water, which was free.

"Vodka cran?" he shouted over the loud music.

I almost didn't correct him.

But then I did.

"No, just cranberry juice with seltzer, if that's alright."

"Virgin. Got it," he said.

As he turned to make my non-alcoholic drink, I let out a rocky breath and swallowed the lump that had formed in my throat.

It wasn't smart to come here.

I found cash in my purse and told the bartender to keep the change, as soon as he gave me my drink, after which I got as far away from the bar as I could.

People were dancing in front of the live band that was playing honky-tonk music. I came to the edge of the dancefloor and claimed a vacant table that wasn't too close to the speakers.

The table was tall and round, the kind meant for standing and not sitting, which explained why there weren't any chairs around it. I was too nervous to sit down anyway, so I rested my cranberry seltzer on the table and eyed the band, Jail Bird.

There he was.

Gloria's mystery man.

Rugged, wearing a tee-shirt and jeans under the hot lights, the mystery man strummed an amplified acoustic guitar and sang his heart out. His looks might have faded since his youth, but he carried himself with the kind of bad boy charm that never really went away.

The other members of the band had the same rock 'n roll swagger, aged yet attractive. The mystery man, the bass player, and a man playing an electric fiddle, all tapped their feet in rhythm with the sharp drummer in the back, really getting into the crescendo of the song.

A few beats later, the band brought the swelling music to an energetic end, and Gloria's mystery man said:

"That was, *I Would Kill For You If You Asked Me To,*' an original song I wrote for the love of my life."

My eyebrows shot up to my hairline. I glanced around, as everyone clapped and whistled, oblivious to what had sounded to me like a blatant murder confession.

"We'll be back to play another set in fifteen," he said.

He flipped off his microphone and set his guitar on its stand, as classic rock music came through the house speakers, playing quietly and barely competing with the conversations throughout the bar. The rest of the band tucked their instruments away and followed Gloria's mystery man to the round table next to mine.

I took big, nervous gulps of my non-alcoholic drink, mustering up the courage to do something.

What exactly, I didn't know.

"Not a bad crowd," said the man who had been playing the fiddle. He clapped his hand on the mystery man's shoulder and gave him another compliment. "Man, Hank, I thought playing at a bar in Walnut Mountain would be a waste of time, but this is quite a turnout. Look at all these people! And they love our music!"

"We might be able to stick around for a few more days," said Gloria's mystery man in response, whose name was Hank, apparently. "I can talk to the owner to see if he'll pay us to play a few more shows."

The fiddler thought that sounded good and asked his bandmates, "I'll grab us a pitcher of beer?"

I tried not to stare at him, as he squeezed past me, making his way through the crowd to get to the long bar counter.

"You really want to stick around Walnut Mountain?" asked the drummer as Hank pulled on a leather jacket, having cooled off.

"You know I do," Hank responded.

Ideas quickly formed in my mind, validating my suspicions about Hank the mystery man and Gloria.

What I couldn't fathom, however, was why in the world Gloria would allow herself to get mixed up with a man like Hank.

But then again, everyone had a past. The other night, Gloria had told Hank to stay away from her. She obviously didn't want her past coming back to haunt her. Who would? But by then it had already been too late. Edgar had been stabbed to death.

I was willing to bet Gloria was afraid of him. Had she told Alan about Hank?

If she had, I doubted Hank would be at Heartbreakers tonight playing with his band... Or maybe he would...

"We would make more cash playing Industry City, and you know it," the drummer challenged.

As the fiddler returned with a pitcher of beer and a stack of plastic glasses, Hank agreed with his drummer, "There are a lot of high-paying venues in Industry City."

"I say we play Walnut Mountain until they're sick of us," argued the fiddler, having caught on to the topic of conversation.

As they debated whether or not to stick around Walnut Mountain, I studied Hank.

There was a twinkle of optimism in his eye and something told me it had to do with Gloria. He bristled every time his drummer pushed to leave town. Yet he relaxed and let out a deep, booming chuckle every time another bandmate complimented Walnut Mountain.

I had my shortcomings, Lord knew I did, but one thing I was darn good at was reading people.

Written all over Hank's sexy, weathered face was an ulterior motive for staying in Walnut Mountain, and his motive had nothing to do with playing honky-tonk at Heartbreakers.

Cautiously, I drifted over to them with my drink in hand.

The drummer noticed me first and probably thought I wanted to flirt.

I smiled and asked, "What made you decide to call your band 'Jail Bird'? You sounded great, by the way."

Hank told me, "Jail Bird is a name we dreamed up when we were kids. We started playing over forty years ago."

"No kidding?"

"Glad you like our music."

"I noticed quite a theme in your songs," I said, carefully scrutinizing Hank's reaction and reading his every muscle twitch and the ways he shifted his stance.

Growing slightly uncomfortable, he replied, "Oh?"

"Killing for love," I pointed out. "Two of your songs were about how you're willing to do anything for the love of your life, including kill."

His relaxed facial expression hardened, and my heart began racing.

The drummer turned away. I couldn't tell if I had offended him or if he was more interested in refilling his beer glass.

I needed to keep the conversation polite and complimentary. If I crossed a line, he would know I suspected him of Edgar's murder, and yet if I didn't provoke him at least a little bit, then the truth wouldn't surface.

So I added, "Killing for love is very Shakespearean."

"That's classic rock for you," Hank agreed. "Hundreds of songs have been written about love and murder."

"Art imitates life," I suggested.

He didn't appear to appreciate the comparison.

"Did you hear about the recent murder?" I pushed.

His entire countenance darkened.

"I wonder if there was a love triangle no one knew about," I boldly added, "and I wonder if it resulted in death."

Hank glared at me through his eyebrows, and I sensed that if we hadn't been surrounded by a crowd full of potential witnesses, he would have lunged at me.

I had crossed a line. Hank seethed, working very hard to keep from losing control, as upbeat rock 'n roll music played softly through Heartbreakers and his bandmates joked around behind him.

As intimidated as I was—I felt rattled right down to my toes—I kept going in the hopes that I would strike a nerve and the truth would come out.

"But then again," I went on, "if the murder was some kind of solution to a twisted love triangle, the killer would end up with his love… wouldn't he? And I see no evidence of that…"

Hank was staring daggers at me.

I stared right back at him.

There wasn't a shred of pleasantries between us.

He knew exactly what I was implying.

But then, from out of nowhere, Gloria burst through the crowd, threw her arms around Hank, and sang:

"Great show, babe! Did ya miss me?"

✝

GUILT WAS WRITTEN all over Gloria's heavily made-up face.

"Penny?!"

"Hello, Gloria," I said, as she slowly released Hank and stepped out from behind him. "I'm glad to see you're feeling better."

Her wide eyes locked on me.

"I realize this probably looks really bad," she admitted.

"To say the least."

Gloria was wearing a low-cut blouse, a short denim skirt, and a look of intense remorse on her face.

It had only been this morning that she had stood in our church and had accepted the deepest condolences from the entire congregation for her beloved fiancé's murder. And here she was, not ten hours later, all dolled up and having the time of her life, *and* calling Hank *babe*.

Perhaps Edgar Swaine hadn't been so beloved to Gloria after all.

Hank yelled at me, "You think it's your business what Gloria does with her life?"

"Hank, please!" Gloria shouted.

She let out a hard sigh next and asked him to excuse her, but he wrapped his arm around her instead and told me, "Nothing can keep us apart."

"Please, Hank, please," she begged.

Finally, he backed away and joined the rest of his band at the neighboring table, leaving Gloria and me to speak privately.

Gloria eased towards me and I could tell that she desperately needed me to be understanding.

"I met Hank back when I was living wild," she explained. "This was decades ago, Penny."

"I'm not concerned with 'decades ago,' Gloria, I'm concerned that your fiancé was killed and three days later, you've gotten back together with some old fling."

She cringed. "I know how this looks."

"Do you?" I hotly returned.

"Listen, Penny, I loved Edgar, I really did. But Hank was my first love. Now that he's back, I can't fight fate."

I stared at her in disbelief and hissed, "What if Hank stabbed Edgar at Fancy's? That's not called *fate*, Gloria, that's called *motive*!"

"Hank didn't do it."

"How do you know?"

"I saw Hank at the restaurant—"

"You *saw* Hank at Fancy's the night of the murder?!"

"He didn't leave his table the entire time that Edgar was running around the restaurant and yelling at people. When Edgar went to the men's room, Hank was still at his table."

"You had your eyes on Hank the whole night?" I asked, doubtful.

That night Gloria had been celebrating and kissing Edgar and singing out in her grand Gloria fashion about how happy she was.

"He didn't do anything to Edgar," she maintained.

Everything about her demeanor was genuine, and I believed that she wholeheartedly thought Hank was innocent. But I wasn't so sure. At all.

"You asked him to leave town," I said, confronting her about the argument I had overheard.

"Excuse me, when did I do that?" she snapped, folding her arms.

"The night after Edgar was murdered."

She turned cross. "You were *spying* on me?"

"I came to check on you," I said, taken aback. "I didn't expect to overhear you two, but Gloria, it sounded to me like you were afraid of him and you wanted him to leave town!"

"Penny," she warned as if she was putting her foot down with me. "I am fifty-five years old. I've never been married, I don't have any children, and I refuse to die alone. I was more than happy to spend the rest of my life with Edgar, but someone killed him—"

"Yeah," I agreed. "Hank did."

"—Hank wants to be with me," she said, speaking over me. "I have every intention of being with Hank, period."

"He might be dangerous."

She snapped, "Plenty of people wanted Edgar dead. He wasn't very nice."

"He was a work-in-progress!"

"Yeah, well, now he's *not* a work in progress, because he's *dead*, and I'm not going to mourn for him forever!"

"Clearly!"

Hank joined Gloria, wrapped his arm around her, and gave her a kiss on the cheek.

"Time to play another set. You want to sing lead on the first song?"

"You betcha!" she exclaimed, looking as thrilled as a schoolgirl in love.

She shot me a strange look then took center stage as the rest of the band collected their instruments and got ready to play more honky-tonk music.

I felt beside myself. Angry and confused, I glanced down at the non-alcoholic drink in my hand. It was half empty.

The band kicked into high gear, playing an upbeat song. Gloria belted out one lyric after the next, as a sense of surrealism gripped me.

I glanced over my shoulder to see if the bartender was very busy at the moment...

What was I doing here?

I sipped my cranberry seltzer then glanced at the bartender again.

He wasn't helping any customers at the moment...

I should leave.

But why?

I didn't want to go back to my parents' house. I would much rather go home to my own cabin, but I didn't really want to be there either if Alan wasn't going to come home.

It had been three months since Alan had left our cabin...

...since Alan had left *me*.

Three long months.

Agonizing months.

He had been staying in a motel.

It was killing me.

Again, I eyed the bartender through the crowd, as Gloria sang a joyful duet with Hank and people danced, full of uplifted emotions and malt liquor, like I wanted to do and be and feel…

I closed my eyes to keep from eyeing the bartender and the bottles behind him.

I felt trapped.

I had to get out of there before I did something I would regret.

But when I opened my eyes and started for the exit, I saw Alan charging through the crowd with four uniformed police officers at his heels.

I froze, wide-eyed and mesmerized by the sight of Alan barrelling across the dancefloor as his police officers fanned out.

The drummer faltered. Hank strummed a sour note and stopped singing. Gloria backed away, stunned. The cops were coming straight for her.

No one in the band knew what to do and soon everyone in the bar was watching the scene, as the police apprehended Gloria!

"Gloria Davis, you're under arrest for the murder of Edgar Swaine," Alan announced.

As he proceeded to recite Gloria's Miranda Rights, Hank tried to shove the cops off of Gloria, which quickly turned violent. The drummer threw himself into the mix, but that didn't stop Jeremiah, one of the police officers, from handcuffing Gloria and hauling her through the crowd at Alan's directive.

Gloria shouted, "Penny! Help me, I didn't do it!" as Officer Jeremiah escorted her past me.

Alan heard her, loud and clear.

He locked his sights on me, and I had a heart attack when I realized my husband had just caught me in a bar with a drink in my hand.

This *really* did not look good.

✝

ONCE AGAIN MY HUSBAND was driving me to my parents cabin in the dead of night.

"My drink was non-alcoholic," I told him. "You can breathalyze me."

"I'm not going to breathalyze you, Penny."

The glow from the dashboard of the truck illuminated his handsome features. His jaw was clenched and he was gripping the steering wheel so tightly that his knuckles were white.

"I didn't go to the bar to drink," I said.

"You shouldn't have gone to the bar at all."

Alan knew that I was telling the truth and hadn't been drinking. He had tasted my cranberry seltzer back at Heartbreakers and had even sniffed my breath. But he really wasn't happy to have found me there.

"I'm not a child," I breathed. "Please drop me off at home. I don't want to go to my parents' house."

He didn't respond and he also didn't take the winding road that led to our cabin. Instead, he turned in the opposite direction.

I decided not to push it. I stole another glance at my husband. He was deep in thought, and I hoped he wasn't trying to figure out the quietest way to divorce me.

"Why did you arrest Gloria?" I asked. "Why not Hank? He's in love with Gloria, you know. He could have killed Edgar in order to have Gloria all to himself."

Alan touched eyes with me, and I felt a zing of excitement shoot through my body.

Returning his attention to the dark road ahead, he told me, "I can't discuss the investigation with you."

"If you arrested Gloria, what are you still investigating?"

"I can't discuss it."

"Is the investigation going well?"

He glared at me, but it only lasted a moment.

After he took another turn, we drove in silence down the long, winding road that led to my parents' cabin.

He pulled to a stop in front of the house, and unlike last time, he shifted the pickup truck into Park and removed his foot from the brake and his hands from the steering wheel.

As he took a moment to collect his thoughts and find the right words to say to me, I promised him:

"I stopped drinking. All that stuff is behind me."

He locked eyes with me and said, "I don't trust you."

I was taken aback, but managed to respond, "How very damning of you, Alan."

He stared at me for another long moment, looking hurt and furious and also like he might kiss me.

"I want to have a baby with you and start a family, Penny. I've set my heart on it—"

"Me, too," I interjected. "I want that, too."

"I need to be able to trust you."

"You can," I assured him, but he wasn't convinced.

"I need to be able to trust that you can live your life sober."

"Alan," I said. I swallowed to clear my throat, not liking how defensive I was starting to sound. "It's not like I have some big problem—"

"You have to give up alcohol for good," he insisted.

"Yeah, I know, but it's not like I've ever had an actual *problem* and I don't like you treating me as though you married some kind of embarrassing, fall-down drunk."

He stared at me in horrified disbelief.

"You haven't, Alan," I insisted, feeling horrified myself. "I'm not an alcoholic!" I tried not to feel offended. "I *want* to start a family. I have no problem giving up my occasional drink. This whole thing is no big deal. I don't think you should've moved into a motel over it, and I don't think I should have to live with my parents just because you think that Edgar's murder is going to cause me to start drinking."

The way he was looking at me, like I was living in some kind of delusion, broke my heart.

"I think it's great that you have no problem with putting alcohol behind you. But make no mistake, Penny, your drinking is a major problem, and until you show me that you can live your life sober, you're not going to be the mother of my children."

"I know that," I snapped.

Tears welled up in my eyes but I blinked them away and popped the passenger's side door open to make my escape.

Alan captured my arm with his strong hand, pulled me back into the truck, and kissed me.

I melted, feeling his warm lips pressed against mine. I missed him like crazy. I missed his scent and his voice and his smile, which I hadn't seen in ages.

I could've sat in that idling truck all night, kissing him.

But I didn't.

And before I knew it, I was all alone in the childhood bedroom

THE MATCHMAKER MURDERS (SEASON ONE)

I had grown up in, and my husband was long gone.

CHAPTER FIVE

THE BIGGEST PROBLEM regarding my drinking problem was that, frankly, it wasn't much of a problem.

I didn't drink every day. I didn't even drink once a week. Oftentimes, months passed by and having a drink wouldn't even cross my mind.

Whenever I chose to enjoy a glass of wine or a seasonal ale, it was usually due to a social engagement like the one that had occurred after Edgar's funeral when Esther came to my parents' house.

I rarely overdid it. I had never driven drunk, or embarrassed myself or my husband.

Sure, from time to time, I had gotten a little out of control, but that generally resulted in me crawling into bed and passing out. Meaning, on those isolated incidents, I had been at home in our cabin in the first place. No harm had been done, and I was my bright-eyed-bushy-tailed self the next day.

That being said, there was one time not so long ago that I really *had* overdone it...

I hadn't meant to. It had been unintentional—an *accident*—and it had also caused an accident...

I couldn't let myself think about it. The past was behind me. It's not as though anyone had gotten hurt, and I wished everyone would just forgive me already and forget about the one time I had made a mistake.

Alan didn't drink. He had never touched the stuff. The Bible commanded him to stay sober-minded at all times, and he lived up to those instructions without fail. His highest aim was to choose goodness with every decision he made. He was no stranger to sacrificing momentary pleasures in order to gain long-term rewards for a better future. For Alan, that was what living righteously was all about, and I loved him for it.

Simply giving up alcohol wouldn't be hard to do, and I agreed with Alan. I shouldn't drink. There was no sense in clinging to the occasional glass of wine. I certainly didn't *need* to reserve the option to enjoy a drink if and when I became a mother.

Alan and I were on the same page in that regard.

But we weren't on the same page in terms of who I was.

Alan believed I was an alcoholic, and I wasn't. I simply wasn't, and I felt severely judged by him whenever he insisted that I had a problem!

I drew in a deep breath, forcing air into my lungs to help calm my racing mind, as I patted myself dry from the shower I had taken.

I dressed quickly, putting on a knee-length skirt, a thick sweater, knit tights, and a colorful scarf, and told myself that it was only a matter of time before Alan would trust that I truly had given up drinking, not that I had a problem, and would come home.

It wasn't right that he had been living in a motel, leaving me all alone in our cabin. It wasn't right that he had suddenly decided my parents ought to babysit me. For God's sake, I was forty years old!

I forced some more air into my lungs and told myself not to get worked up, then I threw on my boots, grabbed my purse from the white wicker desk in my room, and started for the kitchen where I was sure I would find a pot of fresh coffee as well as my disapproving mother.

We had already gotten into it thanks to my dear friend Esther and her bottle of wine, so I didn't expect much drama when I entered the kitchen, but that was predicated on the fact that my mom didn't know I had gone to Heartbreakers last night. She thought I had been working things out with Alan.

"Morning, Penny," said my mother.

She was seated at the round kitchen table, nursing a mug of steaming coffee, and engrossed in the newspaper.

"Thanks for making coffee."

"Gloria was arrested last night," she said, lifting her nose from the paper. "Alan arrested her?"

"I'm just as shocked as you. Gloria obviously hadn't gone into the men's bathroom at Fancy's to stab Edgar. She hadn't left her chair. I don't know what in the world Alan is thinking."

"My Lord," she said, as she shook her head and folded the newspaper, having had enough bad news for one morning. "I can't imagine what it was like for Gloria to spend the night in jail."

Thinking of Gloria, I lost my appetite for coffee.

"Would you join me in prayer, Penny?"

Of course, I would.

I sat down next to my mother, placed my mug of coffee aside, and took her hands in mine.

Closing our eyes and bowing our heads, we prayed for Gloria. We prayed for Alan, asking the Lord to guide his steps as he investigated. We prayed for Edgar's family, and we prayed that the killer would be brought to justice, see the light, repent for the sake of his own salvation, and live righteously for the rest of his life in prison.

My mother extended the prayer, praying for me, for my marriage, and for my shortcomings.

As I listened, I fought a sting of resentment that was burning through my chest.

I hated being subtly judged by my mother while she prayed for me out loud.

But my mom was right. Alan was right. If anyone was wrong, it was me.

I had shortcomings that only prayer, and the Lord, could fix.

I told myself to be humble and to have faith. My actions, in the long run, would speak louder than words. I had already explained myself, and no one had believed me. But no one would be able to deny the good fruit that I would surely produce as time went by. Soon everyone would see that it didn't bother me one bit to decline wine, spirits, liquor, and cocktails, and life with my family would go back to normal...

...like how life used to be this time last year when I would wake up in Alan's arms with the morning sunshine on my face...

...and have pancake breakfasts with Alan on lazy Saturday mornings...

...holding hands with him in church and discussing the sermon afterwards while strolling through the heart of town...

...and going for hikes with my handsome, outdoorsy husband up Walnut Mountain and the other mountains that surrounded our quiet corner of Vermont.

With time, patience, and faith, I would weather this storm and before I knew it, my old beautiful life with Alan would be restored.

"Amen," said my mom, having finished the prayer.

I was about to say, "Amen," myself when the deafening shriek of a chainsaw startled me.

"That must be your father's contractor!" she shouted over the noise.

"Wow, that's really loud!" I said, yelling.

The ear-splitting shrieks were coming from right outside the kitchen windows.

Mom and I bundled up and ventured out into the chilly morning as first-light pierced through the mountains.

We rounded the side of the cabin to find my burly father and a contractor slicing wood on a saw-horse.

"Lucas!" my mom shouted over the sounds of the chainsaw that the contractor was angling through another panel of wood.

Dad got the contractor's attention by waving his arms and yelling, "Daniel! Daniel! Whoa!"

"What!"

"Whoa, Daniel!" yelled my dad as he indicated they had company.

Daniel straightened up, coming into his full height, powered-down the electric chainsaw, and set it on the saw-horse.

"Did we wake you?" Dad asked.

As my parents' conversation turned into a bit of an argument over the fact that, apparently, Dad needed to measure and cut brand-new storm shutters for the cabin instead of just fixing the old ones, I introduced myself to Daniel and shook his hand.

"Sorry about the noise," he apologized, as he pulled the protective goggles he was wearing from his face and smiled good-naturedly. "The project shouldn't take me more than a few days, then I'll be out of your hair and the cabin will have proper storm shutters for winter."

I guessed Daniel was in his early-to-mid thirties. He had boyish good looks, light eyes, and dark hair.

"No need to apologize," I told him, but my mother begged to differ.

"This was supposed to be a little fix it job," she pointed out, "not a major production!"

"Really, Dottie, there's no getting around it," my dad argued. "Our current shutters are purely decorative."

Mom wasn't pleased that my father hadn't consulted her, but she knew when to pick a battle, and when to back down.

Regaining control over her emotions, she told Daniel that it was nice to meet him, and then she and I returned to the front of the house where my car was parked, Alan having once again magically deposited my sedan in the middle of the night.

"I know I shouldn't complain," she complained, "but we don't need storm shutters. Your father hired Daniel to be charitable, and that was very kind of him, but I don't see why he decided to make a big project out of our shutters."

If my mother had a personality flaw, it was that she couldn't tolerate change. Any kind of change. Change disturbed her. Even changing the cabin's shutters was too much.

She folded her arms against the wind, shook her head at the situation, and added, "We already donate to the church and if your father has any hopes of *fully* retiring, we need to start pinching our pennies."

I doubted Dad had any real plans of fully retiring.

"Was Daniel out of work or something?" I asked as I opened the driver's side door of my car, eager to head into town and start my day.

"Yes, for about six months."

"But there are plenty of construction projects in the county."

"Daniel was battling cancer so he couldn't work," she told me. "He survived and he's doing better than ever, health-wise. But it's still taking him some time to get back on his feet."

☦

"AS OF TODAY, Walnut Mountain Middle School is the *only school* in the county that hasn't incorporated Social Justice & Equity into the *core curriculum*," Samantha informed Principal Garth Longchamp and all of the staff that had gathered in the teachers' lounge for the meeting. "I shouldn't be the *only teacher* here who thinks this is a major problem."

Contempt was written all over Samantha's pretty face as she cut her eyes from one teacher then the next.

The science teacher, Matthew, was the first brave soul to respond.

"Couldn't you use the curriculum materials you would like in your social studies classes? You don't need our permission. I don't see what's stopping you."

A bookish man who loved to play chess and believed that the Bible supported science and vice versa, Matthew pushed his glasses up his nose and wondered why Samatha was appalled at his question.

"This isn't about *me*," she balked as she tossed her flowing, blonde hair off her shoulders, limbering up for the argument at hand. "This is about *us*. All of us. We all have to agree to teach this very important ideology *in all of our classes*, or else the entire world will never overcome the horrible injustices that exist!"

"Samantha, please calm down," said Principal Longchamp, as Esther and I exchanged a worrisome glance.

"I *am* calm," she protested.

"You're yelling," he pointed out.

"I'm very passionate about the issues, Principal Longchamp," she insisted as she began passing out glossy pamphlets. "Here's some information that details the direction we should take to end inequality. Other schools throughout Vermont have had a lot of success with this very program."

Principal Longchamp frowned as he unfolded the pamphlet Samantha had given him.

"All I ask," she went on, "is that you guys read the information and visit the website to see how easy it is to incorporate these socially equitable ideologies into your classes. *Even mathematics*, Esther."

Esther shrank beside me in her chair and frowned.

"Then perhaps we can vote at the next meeting," Samantha suggested.

"Hold your horses," said Principal Longchamp.

"The curriculum materials are within the budget," she promised him, anticipating the reasons for his objection.

The school bell rang, announcing that First Period would start in five minutes.

Esther and I got up. She slung her tote bag over her shoulder. She was wearing an orange chemo cap today, which she adjusted to make sure her feathery hair wasn't poking out. I was wearing a chemo cap, as well, but my auburn, chin-length hair framed my face.

"I really wish she would mind her own classes and leave the rest of us alone," Esther muttered, sharing Matthew's sentiment.

"Samantha has to be the champion of social change," I quietly sympathized as we made our way out of the teachers' lounge and through the corridor towards our classrooms. "It's not enough that she teaches as she sees fit. She needs everyone else to teach as she sees fit, too."

"As if her teaching methods are better than ours," said Esther, shaking her head. "I don't see how the mathematics I've been teaching has inadvertently perpetuated inequality..."

"Hey, Chemo Club!" Samantha barked.

When we turned around, Samantha wasn't wearing a snide smile on her face like usual. In fact, she looked downright furious.

"You didn't back me up in there. What gives?"

After all I had been dealing with recently, I was short on patience. "Samantha, sorry to break it to you, but we happen to have problems with a lot of the progressive ideologies you presented mainly because they have nothing to do with educating children and everything to do with brainwashing them—"

"Are you bigots?" she asked both of us, point blank.

I resented the accusation.

"What?" I said, taken aback.

She raised her eyebrows, folded her arms, and stared at each of us, *hard*.

"There are *a lot* of problems with Christian doctrine, you know," she stated. "*A lot*."

Esther screwed her face up, offended.

Not only had Samantha lost her mind, she was just getting started.

"*Good people* don't refuse to teach *children* the importance of Social Justice & Equity."

Esther lost her temper. "Are you saying that Penny and I aren't good people?"

"I'm saying that if you *think* you're good people just because you're *Christians*, you're *wrong*. You should *prove* that you're good people by *agreeing* with this very important social justice ideology that our children need to embrace now more than ever!"

"You know what, Samantha," I said, exasperated. "We showed up for your meeting. We heard what you have to say, and we gave our opinion."

"Your opinion is wrong."

Esther growled, "Opinions can't be wrong!"

Samantha stared down her nose at Esther and snapped, "Read the pamphlet. Learn something, and evolve."

With that, Samantha turned on her very high heel and started off for her classroom.

"I know what you're thinking," I told my friend. "But we can't think *that* way about Samantha without making her right."

Esther pushed her shoulders back, held her head high, and agreed, "Love your enemies."

"Not that it's easy," I acknowledged.

"At times like this, it feels like the hardest thing in the world to do."

✞

I MANAGED TO GET through the school day well enough, though my thoughts often turned to Gloria and how uncomfortable she must be locked up in jail.

What in God's name had Alan been thinking when he had arrested her?

Was Alan's judgment less sound than I had always assumed?

After all, he believed I was a raging alcoholic and I hardly ever touched the stuff...

Was it possible that my perfect husband might not be so perfect?

The more I thought about the rift between Alan and me, the more determined I felt to clear Gloria's good name. Whether that meant I was motivated by the thought of fighting *for* Gloria, or *against* my husband, was up for debate. All I knew was that Gloria hadn't done it, and Alan was crazy to think she had!

As soon as school let out, I drove to the police station which was located a block from the gazebo in the center of Walnut Mountain.

After parking, I climbed out of my car and a stiff breeze gusted at me sideways. The sequined cap Esther had given me wasn't going to cut it in this cold, so I exchanged it for my fluffy, knit hat and turned for the brick police station.

Suddenly, Hank was towering over me, having appeared from out of nowhere.

"Ah!" I clutched my chest to steady my pounding heart, but with my car at my back, I was trapped.

"Your husband is the detective who arrested Gloria?" he said, seething with anger.

"Back off!" I ordered and my loud voice startled both of us.

Hank eased away from me.

"I don't know why my husband arrested Gloria," I admitted. "He should have arrested *you*."

"You think I wouldn't gladly trade places with her?" he barked.

It was then that I realized how much he truly did love Gloria. His angry eyes grew round and a look of hopelessness crashed over him.

That didn't mean he hadn't killed Edgar. But it did mean that at least for this moment, we were on the same side.

"I'm going to see if there's a bail I can pay to get Gloria out of there," I told him.

"You think I haven't tried that?"

"Alan stopped you from bailing her out?"

Hank raked his thick fingers through his salt-and-pepper hair, unable to fathom the nightmare that had become his life.

"She still hasn't seen a judge or had a bail hearing yet," he said, his expression turning forlorn.

I glanced at the police station. Alan was somewhere inside. The kiss we had shared in his truck last night surged to mind. I wanted to see him, even if it meant having another fight.

Fighting with him would be worth it if there was any chance his frustrated emotions would compel him to pull me in for another kiss.

But I could see that Hank was suffering and at a loss for what to do with himself, he was so disturbed by the fact that Gloria had been arrested when he hadn't.

"Come on," I said, thinking fast on my feet. If Hank couldn't bail Gloria out, I wouldn't be able to either. "Let me buy you a coffee."

"Is it okay if my brother, Ronnie, comes along?"

CHAPTER SIX

HANK'S BROTHER, RONNIE, was the drummer of Jail Bird, I realized when he pulled up in the faded red Mustang I had seen around town.

In the waning light of day, Ronnie looked as innocuous as anyone from Walnut Mountain. The deep creases in his forehead and cheeks didn't cast menacing shadows as they had seemed to in Heartbreakers bar.

His window was rolled down and his arm hung out, hugging the door. He did a bit of a double-take and recognized me from the other night.

Hank told him to park and join us for coffee.

"Morning Glory is right around the corner," I added, inviting Ronnie to come.

He raked his thick fingers through his hair in a manner similar to his brother, and for a moment I wondered which one of them was older. I couldn't immediately tell.

Ronnie addressed his brother instead of me. "We've got too much equipment in the Mustang. I don't want to leave the car out of sight."

"Walnut Mountain is perfectly safe," I told him with a friendly smile.

"Yeah, it's safe, unless you count the fact that some old dude was murdered," he said darkly before shifting his attention to Hank. "I'll meet you at the coffee shop if you insist on going."

With that, he carefully steered the Mustang into the street and drove off.

"Ronnie is a bit on edge," Hank explained as we started down the sidewalk.

The tree lined street twinkled with strung lights, which turned on as dusk gathered across the sky. Given the time of year, all of Walnut Mountain became dark by the late afternoon, but I didn't mind. I liked how cheerful our little town could look thanks to the strings of white lights, glowing lamp posts, and bright storefronts that illuminated each block.

"He wants to get the hell out of Walnut Mountain," Hank went on. "Ronnie has never felt comfortable in small towns where everyone knows everyone else. He prefers big cities where he can remain anonymous, so-to-speak."

As we walked, I glanced at him time and again, studying his demeanor. Hank knew he looked guilty. The pressure I had put on him at the bar was probably nothing compared to how the police viewed him.

"But I'm staying," he continued. "I'm not about to leave Gloria while she sits in a jail cell."

We turned the corner, coming onto Morning Glory's block, and were met with hard winds head on. The coffee shop was a few doors down, but we slowed our pace.

"Her bail hearing is scheduled for Monday morning," he mentioned. "I can get her out if Jail Bird plays enough shows at Heartbreakers."

The red faded Mustang was parked curbside in front of the coffee shop. Ronnie climbed out, locked the car, and waited for us to catch up.

I asked Hank, "Why come back into Gloria's life now? You met each other so long ago…"

A faraway glimmer filled his eyes and a grin formed on his face.

"I met Gloria when we were both in our late twenties. I was playing a show and there was this vivacious woman—Gloria—in the front row of the crowd, singing and dancing and clapping her hands, larger than life. I couldn't take my eyes off her. This was a big concert. You have to understand that Ronnie and I were a big deal back in the day with Clank."

"Clank was the name of your former band?" I asked, as I crossed my arms against the wind and glanced at Ronnie who was smoking a cigarette on the sidewalk up ahead.

"You've never heard of Clank?" Hank seemed surprised. "Most

of our songs were on the radio. We were huge."

"I was raised in the church," I mentioned with a shrug as if that might explain why I had never heard of his big-time rock band.

"Anyway," he went on, "after the show, I had one of my roadies invite Gloria backstage. I really wowed her and we had a hell of a night."

I could imagine Gloria in her youth, and I wasn't surprised to hear that she had gone through a wild phase.

"Of course, back then I had been too dumb to recognize a truly great woman when I saw one. The rock 'n roll lifestyle can lead a man to think women are a dime a dozen, what with groupies throwing themselves at you night after night. I guess you could say I'm the type of fool that didn't realize what I had lost, romantically speaking, until I heard that Gloria was engaged to be married."

As far as I could tell, Hank fancied himself a bad boy. He had probably bedded a lot of women in his day, having impressed them with his rock 'n roll swagger and ability to command a crowd of fans with his music. Men like Hank struggled to grow up and settle down. In a sense, it was tragic. These types of men acted as though they were eternally twenty years old, playing show after show, enjoying women with no sense of commitment or responsibility, and hopping from one city to the next. Then one day, they woke up in their early sixties and realized they were washed up and alone.

Hank had heard Gloria was going to get married to a successful attorney with wealth and clout, and the information had jarred him awake. He had taken a long, hard look at himself, and he hadn't liked what he had seen—an old man trying to live a young man's life. He had convinced himself that he could rechart the strange course his life had taken by picking up with Gloria where he had left off nearly thirty years ago.

I understood the logic, but I didn't respect his selfishness.

Hank had ambushed Gloria, confused her mind, tempted her to leave Edgar, and thrown a wrench into Gloria's otherwise wholesome relationship with Edgar.

Hank admitted all of this to me as we spoke on the sidewalk.

"Listen, Penny, when I came to win back Gloria's heart, I didn't come to steal her from the upstanding life she had created for herself, and I didn't come to corrupt her morals. The moment I saw that she had changed, I wanted to prove to her that I could change, too."

"What do you mean?"

"I started cleaning up my act. Gloria cares about things like going to church and reading the Bible, so I told myself to care about those things, too," he explained.

"I thought you arrived at Walnut Mountain only a few days before the murder," I questioned, but he was already shaking his head at that.

"No," he said. "Jail Bird played Heartbreakers a good six months ago. That was when I reconnected with Gloria and learned she had become a Christian. She didn't want to see me at all based on the fact that I hadn't grown up one bit over the years. But she was single at that time, six months ago, so even though I went my way and left her in peace, I used the time to transform myself into the kind of man I thought she would want to be with."

Hank shared his revelations with me, and as he opened up, he became less two-dimensional—less of a bad boy caricature—in my eyes. But that wasn't necessarily a good thing. The more he explained himself and how he had begun to rearrange his life to be good enough for Gloria, the easier it was for me to suspect him of murder. After all, Gloria hadn't chosen Hank. She had stuck with Edgar without wavering, right up until the night he had been killed.

"I'm not going to lie," he said the moment we realized that Ronnie was growing impatient. "I'm glad Edgar is dead. But I didn't kill him."

He let that hang in the air between us and I didn't know what to say.

Should I believe him?

Or should I nurse my suspicions and keep digging?

It wasn't until we entered Morning Glory that I finally believed Hank, and the reason I believed him had nothing to do with any of the explanations he had provided during our slow walk to the coffee shop. Instead, believing him had everything to do with Jacques Viques, the owner of Fancy's.

As soon as Hank, Ronnie, and I entered Morning Glory, I noticed Jacques seated at one of the round tables. He offered Hank a somber hello when he saw him, and greeted me, as well.

They knew each other?

While Hank joined his brother, Ronnie, at the counter where Dex was managing the early evening rush who wanted hot chocolates and heated brownies, I approached Jacques to find out how he was doing.

Jacques stood, gave me a hug, and said, "Alan is making my life a living nightmare."

"Oh, no."

"My restaurant is still a crime scene. He won't let me open. He comes nearly every day with the police. I can't afford to lose this much business."

"He hasn't been interrogating you, has he?" I asked, concerned that my husband might have gone off the deep end. Was no one at the precinct keeping Alan in check?

"No, no, nothing like that," said Jacques to my great relief. "Alan knows I was talking with Hank at the restaurant when Edgar went into the men's room. I'm not a suspect."

So that was why Jacques had just said 'hello' to Hank…

They knew each other from the night of the murder.

But that meant…

If Hank was Jacques' alibi, then Jacques was Hank's alibi…

The aged rock 'n roller hadn't committed the crime.

✝

AFTER HAVING COFFEE, which wasn't the most pleasant experience thanks to Ronnie's cold, foreboding attitude, Hank offered to give me a ride back to my car that was parked at the police station, but I declined.

I needed to walk and clear my head, and I also needed some time to myself to figure out whether or not I should go into the police station and talk to Alan.

Talk to him about what, exactly?

I wasn't sure and that was part of the reason why I decided to take a long stroll through the heart of Walnut Mountain despite the frigid chill in the air.

The biggest thing on my mind should have been the puzzling mystery of who had killed Edgar since Hank hadn't taken his life that night.

But the love story that Hank had told me had only brought to mind my own love story with Alan. I deeply hoped our love story wasn't finished.

I remembered the very first moment I had seen Alan. This was a lifetime ago when we had both shown up for our first day at Walnut Mountain Middle School. Alan had been the sensitive boy who protected the littlest children from the older bullies on the playground. I had been the red-headed tomboy who spent recess climbing walnut trees.

By the time we had entered high school, Alan had grown into a sharp, athletic young man who loved me fiercely and refused to look at other girls. I had given up my overalls and blue jeans, as well as climbing trees, and began to develop a relationship with God. But that wasn't all that had developed inside me during those years.

Back then, I had also begun to notice an edge of anxiety in my gut, and unless I was spending time with Alan, the dark feeling would become too much.

He had stuck with me, and I hadn't always been at my best.

Alan was the only man I had ever been with and the only man I had ever loved. He wasn't just my husband. He was a part of me that I couldn't function without. And nothing beat those twinkling blue eyes of his, or his dark hair and woodsy style. I was as in love with him today as I had been the day he had challenged me to race him up one of the walnut trees at the middle school.

That day, he had let me win.

But today, I had no idea how to win with him.

Sometimes I wondered if we were even playing the same game, or if we had drifted off into separate worlds without realizing.

I shook the thought away and discovered that I must have made a wrong turn. I had meant to take a shortcut across Church Street to get to the police station, but it looked like I was on Lake Way, a scenic road where most of the town's professional offices were located.

If you needed an accountant, a dentist, or an attorney, Lake Way was where you went.

It wasn't the end of the world that I had gotten off course. I could simply take the pedestrian bridge that connected Lake Way with Main Street and I would arrive at the police station in no time where I had parked my car.

I passed the dentist's office then the accounting firm, both of which were winding down for the evening. But when I came to the law firm, I noticed the entrance door was wide open even though the place was totally dark.

I peered through the large picture windows that lined the front of the commercial space. Inside, the cubicles and furniture had been removed—stripped bare. The place was completely vacant except for a few work ladders and bags of trash.

Stepping back, I looked up at the awning and was shocked to discover the strange law firm name that was printed in bold-faced letters.

"The Law Offices of *Swaine*, Downes, & Sons?" I muttered, reading the awning out loud. "What?"

For as long as I had lived in Walnut Mountain, this particular address on Lake Way had been occupied by Milton Cranston's firm, Walnut Mountain Legal.

Walnut Mountain Legal handled everything from civil lawsuits to divorces to corporate disputes. My dad had hired Milton Cranston a few years back to draw up some contracts for his construction side business, and Alan had also worked with Milton based on Dad's glowing recommendation. This was last year after Alan had sold his old pickup truck and the buyer had tried to sue us because the truck hadn't run as smoothly as he thought it should. Milton had handled the lawsuit beautifully and we won without ever having to go to court.

But as I stared up at the awning that was flapping in the cold winds, I couldn't comprehend why Walnut Mountain Legal's familiar name wasn't where it always had been.

The Law Offices of Swaine, Downes, & Sons.

Swaine, as in, *Edgar Swaine?*

What in the world?

My mind struggled to understand what I was learning, but the unthinkable slowly dawned on me.

Edgar Swaine had not only brought his law firm to Walnut Mountain, having picked up his entire life from Pennsylvania and deposited it down in Vermont to be with Gloria. But it appeared as though he had also *replaced* Milton Cranston's law firm, Walnut Mountain Legal? Or...

Could Edgar have driven Milton out of business?

Why else would Edgar's law firm name be printed on the awning? And why else would the offices that Milton Cranston's firm had occupied for decades suddenly be gone?

There came a clatter from deep within the dark, vacant law offices.

I stepped through the entryway that had been left wide open.

"Hello?" I called out, as my eyes adjusted to the darkness.

I was hesitant to venture into the vacant space where Walnut Mountain Legal had once provided professional services to the residents of this small town. I certainly didn't want to trespass and get myself into trouble. At least there were people out on the sidewalk. A few employees from the neighboring accounting firm were locking up shop, and a cluster of dental hygienists were discussing dinner plans farther down the block.

"Is anyone in here?" I called out, inching deeper into the vacant offices.

In the back, a custodian spilled out of the closet with a broom and dustpan in hand. He wore a blue janitor's jumpsuit and a weary expression on his face that told me he was a sad combination of annoyed and exhausted.

"I'm so sorry to disturb you," I said. "But as I was strolling along Lake Way, I was very surprised to see that Walnut Mountain Legal is gone? Do you know where they moved to?"

"Don't worry, they're moving back in," he told me as he neared the wall where I was standing and flipped on the lights. "I cleared this whole place out and now I have to bring everything back."

"Where did Milton Cranston's firm Walnut Mountain Legal go?" I asked, trying to put the pieces together mentally.

"Into a storage unit on the other side of the lake."

"Into a storage unit?" I questioned. "Was he moving locations?"

"I have no idea."

"What about Edgar Swaine's law firm? It's no longer moving in?"

"I hung the Swaine awning," he offered, "but Milton Cranston hired me the other day to move everything back into the offices. I'll take the new awning down tomorrow."

"Why would Milton leave in order for Edgar to replace him, but then it fell through?" I asked, thinking out loud.

"Lady, all I know about Edgar Swaine is that someone stabbed him to death at Fancy's and now I have to put everything back exactly the way it was."

CHAPTER SEVEN

"I HAD TO SWING BY the cabin," I told my mother, cradling my cell phone to my ear and keying into my cold, dark house.

"How long are you going to be?" she asked, and I could imagine what she was thinking.

I closed the cabin door behind me and flipped on the lights, as I explained, "I need to use the internet."

My parents house had many comforts, but a solid internet connection wasn't one of them.

"I'm not sure I'll be back in time to have dinner with you and Dad."

"Is Alan there?"

I had never actually confided in my mother the full extent of how badly my marriage was going. She didn't know that Alan had been living in a motel in the neighboring town. I didn't feel like getting into it with her right now. Not when Milton Cranston's law firm, Walnut Mountain Legal, was weighing heavily on my mind.

"Alan is investigating a murder, Mother!"

"So, that's a 'no'?"

"I'll be home before you know it," I promised, as I crossed hardwood floors to get to the wood-burning stove in the living room. The place was freezing. "Don't wait up."

"Penny—"

"See you soon!"

I ended the call and ventured through the cabin, heading up to the second floor and veering into the office I shared with Alan that would one day become our first born child's baby room, God willing.

It was then that it hit me—the hard emotions.

This beautiful home we had built felt empty.

I prayed that wouldn't be the case for long, as I fought to regain control over my feelings.

At the moment, focusing on what had happened between the two attorneys, Milton Cranston and the late Edgar Swaine, was all that mattered... Or at least that was what I told myself, as I grabbed my laptop computer and headed back down the stairs.

"Brrr..."

When I returned to the living room, I set my laptop computer on the wooden coffee table in front of the couch and opened the glass door of the wood-burning, cast iron stove. Beside the stove was a firewood rack filled with chopped logs, and beneath the rack were a stack of old newspapers and a box of matches.

If I used more than one small log, then I would be stuck here all night since Alan and I had a rule not to leave the cabin until the fire had completely burned out. Accidental house fires were hardly rare around Walnut Mountain during the cold months, and Alan and I were determined not to become a statistic.

Once I got a little fire going, I shut the glass door and sat down on the rustic lodge couch. There was a flannel throw draped over the back of the couch, but I figured I would warm up soon enough thanks to the crackling fire, so when I wriggled out of my coat, I opted not to pull the flannel throw around my shoulders.

I opened my computer on my lap, clicked the Google shortcut, and decided that the first thing I needed to know was whether or not Milton Cranston's law firm, Walnut Mountain Legal, had been acquired or had officially dissolved.

If Milton's firm had been acquired by The Law Offices of Swaine, Downes, & Sons, that would have made Edgar Milton's new boss, which I doubted Milton would have enjoyed. He was just as grumpy as Edgar. But that scenario wouldn't necessarily breed murder.

On the other hand, if Edgar had somehow bullied, sued, or intentionally destroyed Milton's law firm, in order to become the sole legal practice in Walnut Mountain, that would have made Edgar the competition... and Milton's *enemy*.

Could Milton have killed Edgar as a result of his business being destroyed?

I used the Vermont State Secretary website and clicked on the Division of Corporations tab, feeling bizarrely grateful for Samantha and her pushy insistence that all the teachers at Walnut Mountain Middle School had to understand local and state politics to truly comprehend the systemic sexism therein. Earlier this school year, Samantha had lectured the teachers, including me, about the shameful lack of women-run businesses in the county, which she blamed on politicians. During her rant, she had referenced the Division of Corporations web page in an attempt to prove her point.

When I had heard her out that day, I believed she had jumped to conclusions, and solving the problem of sexism wouldn't be so simple as voting for one political party over the other.

At the moment, however, I could've kissed her for the fact that she had drilled into my head the importance of using the Vermont State Secretary website, a resource that was now proving handy.

While I wasn't using the website to research businesses for the purposes of only patronizing the ones that adhered to the highest social standards, which was what Samantha had wanted us to do, I did discover a clue.

About a month ago, Edgar Swaine's law firm—Swaine, Downes, & Sons—did some fancy filing to essentially move their corporation from its original state of Pennsylvania to Vermont. The Vermont-incorporated business, according to the State Secretary's website, cited the address on Lake Way where Walnut Mountain Legal, Milton's firm, had been located.

This matched up with what my two eyes had told me earlier this evening.

After a bit more digging, I learned that Edgar had *bought* the commercial space on Lake Way, and after even more digging, visiting one website then the next, my stomach started growling with hunger, but I couldn't stop.

I was deep in the annals of Google images dating back to the late 70s.

My attention locked on an old black and white photo of a row of smiling young men dressed in university graduation caps and gowns. The two young men standing in the center looked an awful lot like Edgar and Milton.

"No, way," I breathed, as I clicked on the image and was redirected to an old newspaper article. "They attended law school together?"

Captivated, I read the full article, which had been published in May of 1979 by the Harvard Gazette, Harvard University's newspaper.

Edgar Swaine and Milton Cranston had graduated from Harvard Law School at the top of their class along with the five other young men who were featured in the graduation photo. The article didn't go into further detail about Edgar and Milton, but rather focused on the bright futures of all the graduates.

I leaned back on the couch and glanced up, resting my eyes from the laptop screen, as I mulled over the long history that existed between Edgar and Milton.

Had they been friends? Or had they been rivals from the start?

And had their long history culminated in murder?

I was so engrossed in deep thought, pondering the longstanding connection between the attorneys, that I didn't hear the sound of a key scraping into the front door.

I practically jumped out of my skin, however, when Alan stepped into the cabin.

"Penny?"

On my feet, I set my laptop computer on the coffee table and explained, "I had to get a few things. I didn't expect to see you. Are you staying here tonight?"

As he entered the cabin, closing the door behind him, he replied, "I wasn't planning on it."

"I wasn't either."

"I have to get a few things myself," he said as he came into the living room, his boots striking the hardwood floors. He neared the wood-burning stove, stooped, and used the poker to stir up the embers and kindle the flames. "I should also do a load of laundry."

"I can put a wash on," I offered.

He returned the iron poker to its stand next to the stove and stood.

Light from the fireplace caused his blue eyes to glimmer, and I felt tension rise between us the longer we looked at one another without saying a word.

I thought he might be upset with me for having come to the cabin alone, but when he broke the silence between us, I was reminded of how much he truly did care about me.

"Gloria's bail hearing will happen some time Monday. There's no reason to worry she won't be granted a reasonable bail. I don't want you to worry about her."

"But you arrested her."

"Penny, you don't understand police tactics," he warned. "How are you holding up? Are you stressed? Overwhelmed?"

He wanted to know if I was going to resort to calming myself down with a drink or two, but he was polite enough not to go so far as to ask me outright.

If I opened up to him about how I was really doing—I missed him terribly and felt like my world was free-falling towards oblivion—I knew I would break down.

"Did you know that Edgar was in the process of moving his law firm to town?"

He held his gaze on me for a moment, and for some reason, I had to cross my arms.

One of the things that drove me nuts about Alan was that I wasn't able to read him as well as I could other people. I blamed his good looks. He was so handsome, it was distracting.

He neared me and said, "I asked you how you were doing."

"I'm fine," I said, unsure about how he wanted me to react.

How well could I possibly be doing when the romantic match I had made for Gloria had ended in murder and she was sitting in jail as a result?

How could I be alright when my husband had abandoned me in the name of upholding his own high moral standards?

"I walked by Lake Way earlier and Walnut Mountain Legal was gone," I told him. "Apparently, Edgar's firm was about to replace Milton Cranston's firm. Do you find that suspicious?"

Alan stroked my arms, running his large warm hands over my sweater.

He locked eyes with me and removed the sequin cap from my head, as firewood crackled in the wood-burning stove.

Feeling my auburn hair between his fingers and drinking in the sight of the longing and confusion that was written all over my face, he gently said:

"I miss you."

Before I had a chance to respond—I had missed him like crazy!—he pulled me in and kissed me.

"Penny, this time apart from one another is for the best." He kissed me again then said, "The Lord has been strengthening me and growing my faith during these past few months, and I know he's doing the same for you. When we come back together, we will be stronger and better than ever before."

✟

THE FOLLOWING MORNING, I arrived at Hopeful Heart Ministries with my parents and entered the little white church just in time for the Sunday Service morning worship songs.

Esther glanced over her shoulder and smiled at me from one of the pews in the middle of the sanctuary. She gave me a wave, indicating that she had saved a spot for me.

I whispered to my mother, "I'm going to sit up front with Esther," and made my quiet way to Esther, who scooched over for me, making room.

Esther looked lovely in a colorful knit dress and feathered chemo cap.

"Should we move down for Alan?" she asked me.

My heart sank.

"He's wrapped up in the investigation," I whispered, knowing I was telling the truth but feeling as though I had just lied.

I would have loved Alan to join me this morning. I would have loved to have stayed at the cabin with him last night, instead of parting ways after one load of laundry and a great deal of kissing and fighting and more kissing.

Esther gave my hand a sympathetic squeeze and we turned our attention to Pastor Peter as he greeted the congregation and led the parishioners in prayer.

I folded my hands and bowed my head, but didn't close my eyes.

Glancing around the church, I spotted Milton Cranston sitting next to his wife, Rose, across the aisle and two pews ahead.

Milton's white hair was combed neatly. He wore a three-piece suit and held the bowler hat he usually wore in his hands. Nothing about his attire indicated that Edgar Swaine had run him out of business, but I knew that appearances could be deceiving.

His wife, Rose, wore a flowery dress with a thick shawl draped over her shoulders.

From the sanctuary pulpit, Pastor Peter concluded the prayer and the entire congregation replied in unison:

"Amen."

As the sermon began, I studied Milton and recalled how I had seen him at Fancy's the night of Edgar's murder. Milton had been dining with business associates, or so it had seemed to me that evening. I hadn't taken notice of where Milton had been when Edgar had disappeared into the men's bathroom. Could Milton have excused himself from his associates, slipped into the men's room, and stabbed Edgar Swaine?

If only Alan had confided in me about the murder weapon. All I knew was that a knife had been used to kill Edgar. But what kind of knife? It wasn't like a person could walk around comfortably with a knife in their pocket... unless it was small and sheathed.

Milton Cranston looked so unassuming and innocuous, though. He wasn't a particularly tall man, and he didn't seem like he could kill with his bare hands like that. If anything, Milton had a scrawny build and the decades had worn him down. He couldn't even really sit up straight thanks to the slight hunch in his elderly posture.

After the Service, when parishioners mingled in the sanctuary to discuss the finer points of Pastor Peter's sermon while others gathered around the coffeemaker in the vestibule and visited with one another, I found Milton and Rose Cranston chatting with the Worship Team leader, Thomas Ford, near the pulpit where Tom had just packed up his sheet music, hymnals, and modern worship song booklets.

I hung back for a moment, not wanting to be rude and interrupt their conversation about the hymns that had been sung during the Service.

"Mrs. Matchmaker!" said Tom with a hearty smile. "How do you do this morning?"

I smiled and nodded. "Very well, thank you. Good morning, Mr. and Mrs. Cranston."

Rose offered me a reserved smile, but Milton wasn't nearly as friendly. He twitched his nose and looked me up and down.

Daring to find out what had become of his law firm, I asked, "I only realized the other day that Walnut Mountain Legal moved from Lake Way, Mr. Cranston, to make room for Edgar Swaine's firm."

Tom seemed curious about that. But if I wasn't mistaken, Rose's gaze turned into a glare. Her tight smile faltered and she told Tom:

"Milton's law firm has been, and always will be, on Lake Way.

Right, dear?"

Milton cleared his throat and explained, "We've been undergoing renovations."

My suspicions might have subsided if Milton had provided a straightforward story about his long-standing and mysterious relationship with the late Edgar Swaine, but he hadn't even tried to explain himself.

He had lied...

According to the janitor at Lake Way, Milton wasn't renovating. He had moved his business into a storage unit...

The fact that Milton was lying to me made him seem far guiltier than I had originally imagined.

Rose didn't like the tone of the conversation. She changed the subject, asking Tom about how he went about selecting modern worship songs.

I wasn't finished with Milton yet. I could tell he was hiding something. He wouldn't look me in the eye, and yet he wasn't paying attention to his wife. I could practically see the gears turning in his fast-working mind.

Was he trying to figure out how to throw me off his scent?

"I was under the impression," I pushed, "that Edgar Swaine's law firm had taken over the commercial space on Lake Way. It lent the impression that Edgar had perhaps put you out of business."

Milton squared his brittle shoulders at me and snapped, "I can assure you, Mrs. Matchmaker, that my law firm is very much in business."

"Then why was a new awning put up with Edgar Swaine's name on it?"

Milton had to try very hard not to lose his temper. He clenched his jaw and his weathered cheeks turned red. Through gritted teeth he asked me, "What are you implying?"

"Forgive me, I didn't mean to offend you," I said, feeling intimidated. Milton Cranston might have been small in stature but he had no problem with straightforward confrontation. I, on the other hand, felt my heart race and hands tremble. "I was just curious about the fact that your law firm had left Lake Way."

"I told you," he warned, "we moved out temporarily due to *renovations*."

"I see," I said in a small voice.

"Oh, Penny!"

That from Esther. She was waiting for me on the far side of the sanctuary where people were flowing out into the vestibule.

"Excuse me," I said to Milton. "I hope you have a blessed day."

As I turned to go, he caught my wrist and warned, "Don't stick your nose where it doesn't belong."

The hairs on the back of my neck stood on end, but Milton released me before either of us could make a scene.

I walked briskly up the aisle and met Esther in the vestibule.

"What was that about?" she asked, having seen the strange confrontation between Milton and myself.

"It was nothing. He's done some legal work for my dad in the past, and I guess that makes him feel entitled to take hold of my arm."

Esther didn't like the sound of that.

"It was nothing, really," I promised as we made our way outside into the sunshine of the crisp autumn day. "Can I interest you in lunch?"

"I have to finish up some lesson plans for this school week," she said, declining the invitation. She let out a sigh and shook her head. "Sometimes I feel like I have to run as fast as I can just to keep from sliding backwards."

I gave her a hug. "You and me, both."

Back at my parents' cabin, my mother and I had barely put lunch together when the deafening shriek of a chainsaw disrupted our otherwise peaceful afternoon.

Mom groaned and closed her eyes.

"Is that Daniel, the contractor?" I shouted.

"Who else?" my mom replied, shouting over the loud, electric saw as it shrieked through another wood panel.

"He's working on a *Sunday*?"

She shrugged, threw her hands in the air, and shouted, "Storm shutters!"

I was surprised that Dad would allow anyone to work on the Sabbath. Our family hailed from a long line of Sabbath-keepers, and while we didn't always uphold the commandment perfectly, we certainly had never bought, sold, or *worked* on the sacred day.

I shouted, "Maybe I'll invite Daniel in for lunch so we can eat in peace!"

In the foyer, I bundled up. Then I opened the door and started around the side of the cabin.

Daniel was working in the backyard just shy of the rear deck, while my dad chopped firewood nearby.

"Yoo-hoo!" I called out, getting Daniel's attention with a wave.

He straightened up, turned off his chainsaw, and peeled the protective goggles from his light eyes.

"Am I making a racket again?" he asked, flashing me a boyish smile that I believed Esther might find very attractive.

"It's understandable," I allowed good-naturedly, as I glanced at his left hand. No wedding ring. "I wanted to know if you would like to join us for lunch?"

"I don't think I've ever turned down lunch, but I promised your father I would have these storm shutters finished by tomorrow."

I frowned at my dad who had taken notice of my conversation with Daniel.

"I'm sure my father won't mind if you take a few minutes to eat."

My father started over and called out, "What's for lunch?"

"Go in and find out!" I told him.

Dad veered across the yard and disappeared around the side of the cabin, leaving me and Daniel to follow after.

"I hope you don't mind, but my mother mentioned you recently survived cancer?"

Daniel slowed his step. A glimmer of determination, as well as a shadow of fear, filled his otherwise handsome face.

"I did," he said.

"A dear friend of mine survived cancer as well," I told him. "Her name is Esther."

He seemed interested.

I asked him, "Are you seeing anyone special?"

CHAPTER EIGHT

DURING OUTSIDE RECESS at the school, Esther and I avoided Samantha like the plague, as she cornered teachers and students alike, pressuring them to agree that society, as well as Walnut Mountain Middle School, was in dire need of social reforms.

Esther and I found a cozy spot near the jungle gym where the harsh autumn winds wouldn't reach us, nor would Samantha—we were tucked out of view. Boys competed with one another on the monkey bars to see who was the fastest, while most of the girls stood huddled beneath the largest walnut tree behind the schoolhouse. They played hand-clap games with mittened hands.

The skies were bright, but the air was frigid.

"My dad hired a contractor to install new shutters at my parents' cabin," I said, easing into the topic. "His name is Daniel, and I think you might like him."

A subtle look of trepidation surfaced on her face, which surprised me.

"Really?" she asked.

"I had a chance to speak with him and get to know him a little bit," I explained, sensing that Esther was curious, but also hesitant. I decided to lead with the details that she would be most impressed with. "He's your age—thirty-two—and he's very fit."

"I'm a bit older than thirty-two," she said, correcting me, as skepticism filled her eyes.

"A few years difference is nothing," I said, feeling excited about the match. I knew from experience that people first wanted to know how attractive their potential match was, so I began to describe Daniel. "He's really cute, and he's tall. He has kind eyes and dark hair, and boyish good-looks. You might find him very handsome."

Worried, she crossed her arms and a downtrodden look came over her. She gnawed her lip. Whatever she was thinking about wasn't good.

I had more encouraging news to share with her. "Daniel attends church fairly regularly, but he's Catholic. Hopefully that won't be a dealbreaker for you. I believe his faith is solid—"

"My hair is still growing in," she quietly reminded me, as she tucked a feathery tuft under the brick-red chemo cap she was wearing. "It's patchy in areas."

"Your caps are lovely," I told her. "There's no reason you should have to take them off."

She shook her head and I could tell that she was contemplating the unlikeliness that anyone would find her attractive.

"I should probably get my weight up before I meet anyone," she said as if debating with herself. Then, she let out a heavy sigh of defeat and murmured, "The double-mastectomy." She shook her head, "I can't meet anyone. What was I thinking?"

"Esther, you're young and beautiful—"

"You think that because we're friends," she said, full of doubt that an attractive man would see it that way.

"Daniel is single, and he's looking for someone special to share his life with," I assured her. "He knows that real beauty is more than skin deep. I spoke with him at length, Esther. I might not know everything about him, and people certainly do have their secrets, but from what I can tell, he's an upstanding Catholic man who's trying to lead a life that's pleasing to the Lord. Would you be willing to meet him?"

"I hope you didn't tell him about me," she blurted out, her eyes widening.

Confused, I said, "I thought you wanted me to help you find a good man."

"Well, I do, but..."

She couldn't quite put into words what she wanted to express.

"I hope you didn't make me sound..."

Struggling, she trailed off and sank into deep thought.

This wasn't the first time I had encountered a woman who wanted to meet Mr. Right and yet harbored deeply seeded fears in her heart that she would be rejected, or worse, sabotage herself.

"If you meet him, I think you'll discover you have a lot in common," I said, but the sudden look of horror on her face told me that I had made some kind of unforgivable error.

"Oh, Penny, you didn't tell him that I had cancer, did you?"

I froze.

"Did you?" she pushed.

I couldn't understand why Esther was getting so upset.

"You did, didn't you?" She groaned, cringed, and groaned again. "You told him I had breast cancer?"

"I'm so sorry—"

"I want a *normal* life, Penny. I don't want some guy guilted into dating me because he thinks I'm a charity case—"

"I didn't make you out to be a charity case, Esther, I promise—"

"I don't want to be pitied by anyone, certainly not a man, and when people find out about my cancer, all they do is pity me—"

"Daniel also beat cancer."

She held all of her horses, stopping dead in her worrisome tracks, and stared at me for a very long moment, after which she said:

"He did?"

✝

DIRECTLY AFTER SCHOOL, I drove to the police station with every intention of paying Gloria's bail so that she wouldn't have to spend another night in the precinct jail.

Her bail hearing had gone well earlier that day. As far as I understood, the presiding judge had been courteous and fair, though the actual bail amount was more than I had expected.

I entered the police station, a small brick building with simple architecture, and neared the front desk where Officer Charles Abel was standing post. Everyone knew Charles as "Chuck," but I knew him as the police officer who was most likely to attend church on Christmas Eve and Easter.

"How are you, Chuck?" I asked when he politely greeted me from the other side of the front desk.

"Very well, Mrs. Matchmaker," he said, as he gave me a nod.

"Alan has really shaken up the department for the better."

I didn't know what to make of that.

"I can see if he's around?" he offered.

I was tempted to take him up on it. Alan had been drifting in and out of my thoughts all day. But unlike his reaction to finding me alone in our cabin, I doubted he would be very pleased to learn I was planning on bailing Gloria out of jail.

"Actually, I'm here for Gloria Davis," I explained. "I heard her bail was set and I'd like to get her out of here."

"I can process that for you," he said, as he turned his attention to the computer behind the desk. "I'm not sure she'll be ready to go, just yet," he added. "She's meeting with her new attorney."

"Oh?" I didn't realize Gloria had a *new* attorney. I hadn't even realized she had an *old* one. "Do you think they'll be very long?"

Officer Chuck sort of winced as if giving me an accurate estimation would be tricky.

"It's hard to say. Milton tends to work slowly and methodically whenever he meets with a new client, or so he warned us—"

"I'm sorry," I interrupted. "Did you say that Milton Cranston is meeting with Gloria?"

"Yup."

"Milton Cranston of Walnut Mountain Legal is Gloria's *attorney?*"

He glanced up from the computer and said, "He's some kind of angel, if you ask me. He came right over after church yesterday and offered to represent Gloria free of charge, which is the only reason the judge was so favorable to her this morning at the bail hearing. Let me tell you, if Gloria had used a public defender, I doubt she would've been offered bail at all."

For better or worse, jumping to conclusions or not, I was convinced that Edgar's law firm, its very presence in town, had threatened Milton's. Edgar's murder had benefited Milton, evidently, because now Milton's law firm would remain at its location on Lake Way.

And now Milton Cranston had volunteered to defend Gloria?

What if Milton really was the killer? What if his ulterior motive was to provide Gloria with such a poor legal defense that she would take the fall for the crime that he committed?

How horrible!

"You look alarmed," said Officer Chuck.

"I'm just chilly."

The police station itself wasn't large and it definitely wasn't typical. Other than a shallow entryway before the front desk counter, there was only about one hundred square feet of hardwood floors that contained a handful of desks. Beyond those, there was a short hallway that led to only one interview room and a single jail cell where Gloria had been kept for a number of days. Chief Pepperdine's office was located at the back of the station, too. At the moment, his office door was closed and I could hear the faint sounds of a verbal argument happening inside.

From where I was standing, the jail cell was out of view, but I imagined Milton Cranston was seated in the cell with Gloria and using deceit to gain her trust.

I felt eyes on me and when I looked up, Alan was storming out of Chief Pepperdine's office and had locked his sights on me.

He pressed his mouth into a hard line, annoyed to find me there.

Officer Chuck finished typing and I proceeded to pay the bail amount, as Alan started through the station.

I thought Alan might greet me with a kiss since he was in the habit of keeping up appearances around town and hiding the fact that our marriage was crumbling, but he didn't make it all the way to the front desk.

Chief Pepperdine shouted after him and they began arguing all over again.

"Don't mind them," commented Officer Chuck. "Alan has been butting heads with Sergeant Pepper, but it's been for the best. Growing pains, as they say."

"Ah," I replied, smiling at Chuck's use of Pepperdine's cute nickname.

But the argument between my husband and the Chief didn't sound like healthy growing pains. It sounded like Pepperdine didn't agree with how Alan had been handling the murder investigation.

Alan cut his eyes towards me, stealing a glance, before the Chief pulled him into his office at the very back of the station once again.

"I'll let Gloria know you've gotten her bail squared away," Officer Chuck told me.

I thanked him and patiently waited for him to return with Gloria.

When he did, Milton Cranston was in tow, trailing behind them.

Milton's countenance drooped the moment he saw me standing at the front desk. I could tell he didn't want Gloria spending any time with me. He knew that I suspected him of having something to do with Edgar's murder. And he knew that I knew he knew.

"Remember, Gloria," Milton advised, as he pulled Gloria aside before I could give her a hug. "We are not out of the woods yet. Do not discuss any aspect of the investigation with *anyone*." He glared at me then returned his attention to his client. "I'll be in touch. Try to stay positive, and remember, don't talk to *anyone*."

"Thank you so much, Mr. Cranston!" she sang out, pulling him into a big fat hug that he hardly wanted. "You're a lifesaver!"

Milton grumbled his way past me without saying hello, and Gloria brightened, threw her arms open, and exclaimed:

"Penny! You bailed me out!"

We hugged. I urged her back so that I could get a good look at her. Other than her eyes looking a bit pale and her cheeks lacking color since she wasn't wearing her usual makeup, Gloria seemed upbeat and in good health.

"What are friends for?" I said, "Come on, you can stay with me at my cabin and recuperate from the whole, horrible ordeal."

✝

THE WOOD-BURNING stove was crackling and my cabin smelled of buttery herbs. Gloria and I had just finished eating a delicious dinner, and after leaving our dishes in the sink, we sat down in the living room with the spiced cider I had whipped up, using my mom's family recipe.

The color had returned to Gloria's cheeks.

She had kept her cell phone within reach during the entire meal and now that we were settling on the living room couch, she placed her cell phone on the wooden coffee table, face up.

"When are you expecting Alan home?" she asked as she brought her steaming mug of spiced cider to her mouth.

My stomach twisted at the thought of being dishonest, but I didn't want my friend—*any* of my friends, or *anyone* I knew, for that matter—to catch wind of my rocky marriage. It was painful enough that my parents knew as much as they did.

"He's going to stay with one of his police buddies tonight,

either Jeremiah or Chuck."

"Really?"

"Well, as you know, I'm a witness because I was the one who found poor Edgar. Since Alan is the lead detective, it's really for the best that we keep our distance from one another while he investigates."

"I see," she said, even though she seemed puzzled.

"Trust me, you won't have to worry about Alan putting you on edge while you're here. He really isn't coming to the cabin tonight. I can't imagine what possessed him to think that he should arrest you. My God, I'm so terribly sorry, Gloria."

"It's not your fault," she said in a small voice. "I'm just grateful to be out of that jail cell."

"Milton Cranston is going to provide your legal defense?" I asked, cautiously wading into the conversation I most wanted to have with her.

"The Lord answered my prayers, Penny, you have no idea," she said, full of optimism. "The judge likes him, and he isn't charging me a dime."

"That's what Officer Chuck told me earlier," I allowed, good-naturedly. "You trust him?"

"Milton?" she asked. "Of course. Why wouldn't I?"

I cradled my steaming mug of spiced cider in my hands, trying to find the right way to put my concerns into words.

"What, Penny?"

"Milton had history with Edgar. He was at the restaurant that night..."

Gloria screwed her face up and a strange-sounding laugh rolled out of her.

"Lord, you don't think Milton killed him, do you?"

She already thought I was crazy, so I kept going. "Edgar was in the process of moving his law firm to Walnut Mountain. What if Milton feared that Edgar intended to run Milton's practice either out of town or into the ground? They went to Harvard together. They have a long history, Gloria. I don't know if it's a good idea to trust Milton with your legal defense."

"I'm going to stop you right there, Penny," she warned. "Milton Cranston is a godsend, period. Edgar would never try to run him out of town—"

"Have you been to Lake Way recently?"

Ignoring my point, she asserted, "If you should be concerned with anything it should be that Alan has been an utter disaster as a detective."

My jaw dropped.

"Arresting me, when it was blatantly obvious to everyone that I did not go into the men's bathroom that night—my God, I was sitting right next to you!—was a very foolish move on Alan's part. I'm surprised Chief Pepperdine hasn't fired him yet, frankly."

"I'm very sorry that Alan arrested you," I snapped, "but I'm sure he had his reasons."

Gloria's cell phone vibrated on the wooden coffee table and she didn't waste a second checking to see who had texted her.

"His reasons," she muttered, snorting a laugh, as she composed a responding text message. "What's the address here?"

I told her, then I resumed defending my husband and his unorthodox investigative tactics, not that I knew what they were.

"Alan probably arrested you as part of a larger strategy to flush out the real killer."

She shot me a glare. "Alan thinks *I'm* the real killer."

"No, he doesn't," I insisted and hoped to high heaven I was right. If I wasn't, and if Gloria was right, that would mean that Alan *had* lost his mind and probably *would* be fired...

I couldn't bear the thought.

"Listen, Penny," she said, after composing and sending another text message. "If I were you, I would try to talk some sense into Alan before he ruins his reputation and loses his job."

I hardly appreciated the backhanded advice. Alan was the most moral, ethical, and level-headed man I had ever known. I doubted any decision he made could damage his reputation. He was idolized. Alan did no wrong.

Headlights cut through the living room windows as a vehicle pulled into the driveway outside.

Gloria popped up.

"That's Hank."

"What?"

She padded through the living room and started bundling up in the foyer, as I hurried after her, feeling wildly confused and hurt and horrified.

"You're leaving? With *Hank*? Gloria!"

"Please don't lecture me, Penny—"

"The timing of your relationship with Hank is very suspicious!"

"Don't—"

"My God, Gloria! You wonder why Alan arrested you? Not two days after your fiancé's murder, you've found a new lover!"

"I said, don't, Penny!"

Hank honked just as Gloria threw the cabin door open and started for the faded red Mustang that was idling in my driveway.

"You better not skip town now that I've paid your bail, Gloria!"

She climbed into the passenger's seat without responding.

Unbelievable.

I watched as Hank pulled the Mustang around and drove off.

Returning inside, I slammed the door behind me.

My mind raced, but I couldn't catch hold of a single idea long enough to make sense of it.

Infuriated, I felt overwhelmed and out of control.

Did Gloria not care about her future or her fate? Was she not concerned for her own wellbeing? It didn't matter to her that she looked guilty? How could it not matter to her that her new attorney might be setting her up to take the fall?

I felt like my brain was on fire, as I started through the cabin and took the stairs two at a time until I reached the second floor.

The next thing I knew, I was rummaging through my bedroom closet, shoving dresses and skirts aside to clear a way to the floor where a row of slouchy boots sat behind stacks of old boxes that I had asked Alan countless times to sort through and throw away.

I reached into one of my knee-high boots and felt the cool glass bottle that I had hid months ago.

I pulled the bottle out and held it in my hands.

Amber-colored liquor sloshed around.

I could almost taste it—Irish whiskey.

On my feet and with the whiskey in hand, I rounded into the bathroom, threw open the cabinets beneath the sink, and found the flask of vodka I had been keeping in an empty box of tampons.

I raced throughout the house, collecting alcohol bottle after alcohol bottle I had stashed in secret places over the months and years.

Soon my arms were full and I was out of breath.

In the downstairs kitchen, I placed the bottles on the counter and they clattered, rolling around.

I wanted to scream or punch a wall or slap myself across the face for the fact that I desperately craved a drink. I wanted to guzzle all of it—the whiskey, the vodka, the gin, the old red wine that had probably turned to poison by now.

But instead, I began dumping liquor down the sink drain, one bottle after another, until there wasn't a drop left.

"I don't have a drinking problem," I insisted under my breath. "Anymore."

CHAPTER NINE

I SWUNG INTO MORNING GLORY early the next day, feeling grateful for my sobriety and the optimism that came with it.

I could have drank last night, but I hadn't. I could have guzzled booze to keep my fears at bay, but I had chosen the opposite. I could have given into the craving, but instead, I had poured all temptation down the drain and driven to my parents' cabin where I had gorged myself on Mother's warm apple strudel and listened to Dad tell tales in front of the fireplace about the importance of faith and true love, both of which he had found the day he had met my mom.

The coffee shop was bustling with early risers who needed a cup of joe to get a jump on their busy day.

I could use a strong cup as well, but buying a coffee wasn't my primary reason for coming to Morning Glory.

I felt horrible about the tiff I'd had with Gloria, and I needed to apologize and clear the air.

Dex was working behind the counter, helping one customer after the next, and though Gloria was also behind the counter arranging freshly baked pastries, her attention was focused on Hank, who was seated at the nearest table.

"Morning, Dex," I said when it was my turn to order.

"Can I get you the usual, Mrs. Matchmaker?"

"That would be great, Dex, thank you."

As Dex began collecting a coffee and toasted bagel with cream cheese for me, Gloria turned with a tray of warm donuts in her hands, keeping busy. She had obviously taken notice of me, but didn't acknowledge me. I guessed she was still sore about our many disagreements last night.

"Gloria?"

"I'm really busy, Penny," she said as if she didn't have the energy to deal with me.

Hank shifted in his chair, bristling at the sight of my attempt to speak with Gloria, which told me she had probably vented to him about me at length. I couldn't blame her for it if she had. I thought Hank might try to interrupt me, but his brother Ronnie returned from the bathroom, sat down, and resumed whatever conversation they had been having, which gave me a chance to reconcile with my friend.

"I want to apologize," I said, which got her attention.

She wiped her hands on her apron, as I formed the right words to say.

"I was out of line to judge you. I'm sorry. It's not my place to judge you. There is only one judge, our Lord, and even though I *am* concerned for your welfare, it isn't for me to rationalize my opinion and try to convince myself that I'm in the right. I'm not. I'm in the wrong. Your relationship with Hank is your business. Would you please forgive me?"

I should have also had the humility to tell her that I was wrong for questioning Milton Cranston's motives and for planting a seed of doubt in Gloria's mind, but the fact of the matter was that I didn't think I was wrong about that, and the best I could do at the moment was simply not address my opinion of Milton.

Gloria considered my apology, sucked in a deep, fortifying breath, and exhaled, letting the bad feelings go.

"Of course, I forgive you, Penny. You're not the only one who overstepped her bounds last night. I shouldn't have said what I did about Alan."

"Water under the bridge," I told her, as Dex neared the counter with my coffee and bagged bagel. "Thanks, Dex."

"No problem, Mrs. Matchmaker," he said before pushing off to help the next customer.

"You don't have to worry about Milton Cranston, either," she went on, as she tucked her hair behind her ears and glanced at Hank, who was fully engrossed in our conversation.

Seated beside him, Ronnie looked annoyed and a tad gloomy that his brother wouldn't give him his full attention.

Gloria went on, "Milton is more of a civil attorney, so he decided that Edgar's partners should represent me since they have a lot of experience representing criminals."

Gloria cringed at the notion that she was a criminal, but I was too preoccupied with the new information.

"Are you telling me that Edgar's law firm has merged with Walnut Mountain Legal?"

Why else would Edgar's partners represent Gloria at Milton Cranston's suggestion?

Furrowing her brow, Gloria looked at me as though my curiosity would eventually lead us into another fight.

"I'm not trying to be nosy," I told her, but she didn't believe me.

"Yes, you are."

"I thought the two law firms were rivals," I explained.

"I thought you just told me you weren't going to rationalize your opinion. Wouldn't that mean you're also not going to rationalize your meddling?"

"I'm not rationalizing my meddling," I lied. I was, but only mentally.

A merger between Walnut Mountain Legal and The Law Offices of Swaine, Downes, & Sons changed the big picture, but might not have altered Milton's culpability. But then again, it could have. There was only one way to find out.

"I know how you think, Penny," she said. "I've known you for years."

"I should head out so I'm not late for school," I said. I offered her a genuine smile and added, "Your friendship means a lot to me, Gloria. I'm not going to jeopardize it."

She narrowed her eyes on me, sizing me up. "I feel the same way."

She didn't trust me.

But who did?

As I left Morning Glory, I felt eyes on me and knew that Hank and Ronnie were glad to see me go.

I gulped down hot, creamy coffee, climbed into my parked car, and blasted the heat as soon as I started the engine. The clock on the dashboard indicated that I had more time than I thought, so instead of turning onto School Street, I headed towards Lake Way where I hoped to find answers.

Milton Cranston and the late Edgar Swaine had known each

other since law school.

By all appearances, it had looked as though Edgar had replaced Milton's business, which could have motivated Milton to murder Edgar at Fancy's.

But could Milton have really harbored ill will towards Edgar's law firm if Milton was now working with Edgar's associates, Downes & Sons?

The professional offices that lined Lake Way looked cheerful this morning in the sunshine. Walnut trees lined the street, their turning leaves offering bright splashes of color to the brick buildings.

I found a spot in front of the law firm and immediately noticed the brand-new awning.

Walnut Mountain Legal: Cranston, Downes, & Sons, Attorneys at Law.

"That's quite a mouthful," I said to myself as I chewed the last bite of my bagel and climbed out of my car.

As I neared the glass entrance door, I could see paralegals and attorneys inside. The office furniture had been returned, and for all intents and purposes, it looked as though business had never been better.

Call me cynical, but I found the whole thing suspicious.

I was about to pull the glass entrance door open and enter, but my heart jumped up my throat when I spotted my husband, Alan, speaking with the receptionist inside.

Acting on instinct, I quickly turned and started down the sidewalk so that he wouldn't catch me, but I moved too quickly and collided with a young, well-dressed man who was carrying a briefcase and a lot on his mind.

"Oh!"

"Pardon me," he said, taking a step back. "I wasn't paying attention."

"Not to worry," I told him with a smile.

The young man wore a camel-hair coat and a suit underneath. He had a clean-cut look about him and smelled faintly of designer cologne.

"I'm used to hustling through a big city," he explained. "I didn't mean to bump into you."

"You're new to town?"

He nodded. "Just arrived from Industry City to work at the newly branded Walnut Mountain Legal. The name's Downes,

Gregory Downes. My father and I used to work with Edgar Swaine."

I shook his gloved hand.

"It's nice to meet you," I said. "I'm sure I speak for all of Walnut Mountain when I say, we're glad to have a law firm in town. When I passed by here the other day and saw the offices empty, I was a bit worried."

"Oh, that, yes," he said as a weird smirk came over him, memories of a recent difficulty clouding his mind perhaps. "Well, what does the Bible say? The biggest battles will unite the worst of enemies?"

The Bible didn't say anything like that.

"What verses are you referring to?"

He shrugged, "I'm probably misquoting… The good news is that our law firm will offer Walnut Mountain the best legal services in all of Vermont for criminals charged with murder."

Why in God's name would we need that?

"So, there was a merger?" I asked.

"Oh, no, no," he chuckled and shot me a wink. "My father owns the firm. Don't let the sign on the door fool you."

"Your father…?"

"Jeffrey Downes, Esquire."

"Would Edgar Swaine have owned the firm instead, had he lived?"

"As a partnership with my dad," he allowed.

"But Milton Cranston isn't part owner of the new firm?" I asked.

Again, Gregory chuckled and shook his head. "Milton has been deferring to our firm for years. He knows his limitations, and he also knows his place now that we are all working together under the same roof."

"Are you referring to his limitations concerning criminal trials?" I asked, Gloria's case having come to mind.

Our sleepy, little town didn't see a lot of crime, if it saw any crime at all.

"Is that why Milton won't be at the helm of representing Gloria Davis? Because he lacks criminal defense experience, and your father doesn't?"

"Well, yes. In fact, Edgar and my father have represented a number of criminal defendants, a few of which had even lived in

Walnut Mountain."

Gregory rattled off a few cases that involved former residents of Walnut Mountain who had committed crimes in other counties of Vermont, which explained why I hadn't heard about them.

Then he added another layer of information that I found fascinating.

"Edgar Swaine, God rest his soul, was able to bring an invaluable perspective to the criminal defense strategies at Swaine, Downes, & Sons thanks to his prior experience as a prosecuting attorney. For decades, Edgar worked for the state and put countless bad guys behind bars. The last case he tried as a criminal prosecutor really exhausted him, and that's when he decided to work with my father and make a *real* living as a defense attorney."

I nodded, "Yes, I knew he had worked as a prosecutor. He loved upholding the law."

"Edgar Swaine was no one to mess with, that's for sure."

Suddenly, my husband spilled out of the law offices with Milton Cranston.

"Please excuse me," I said, distracted. I didn't want Alan to catch me there. "I really must be going, but it was so nice talking with you, and I wish you well with your business."

"See you around," he said with a wave as he turned for the building.

I slipped down the sidewalk, briskly walking away from Alan and Milton before either could question what I was up to.

☦

BY THE TIME I arrived at Walnut Mountain Middle School, I was nearly late for First Period, but I had to use the bathroom thanks to the Morning Glory coffee I had drunk earlier.

I didn't even stop at my coat rack in the teachers' lounge to unbundle. I made a beeline for the ladies' room on the far side of the teachers' lounge, entered the nearest stall, and relieved myself as soon as I sat down.

"Holy moly!"

The ladies' room door swung open and I heard the distinct sounds of high heels clicking across the floor. The sounds of a running faucet came next, and when I emerged from my stall, I found Samantha washing her hands and looking rather pale.

"Where's the rest of the Chemo Club?" she said, referring to the fact that Esther wasn't with me.

Ordinarily, I would have taken issue with Samantha's snide attitude, but she didn't sound snide.

She sounded raspy and looked ill.

"I'm sure Esther is in her classroom already," I said as I washed my hands at the neighboring sink and kept my eye on Samantha in the mirror.

She turned her faucet off, clutched the sides of her sink, and looked as though she might get sick.

"Are you okay?"

"I would be *okay*, Penny, if my fellow teachers would *support me* in my effort to improve the fabric of society by *properly educating* our students."

It was hard to like Samantha at times like this.

But when she keeled over, all I could think to do was help her.

"What's wrong, Samantha? Are you going to be sick?" I asked as I braced her.

"I have a splitting migraine," she groaned. "It's a stress migraine because no one at this school supports my altruistic initiatives."

Trying not to roll my eyes, I suggested, "Come, sit down."

I steered Samantha towards the handicap stall and eased her down onto the closed lid of the toilet.

"My head hurts so bad, Penny, I feel like I'm going to puke."

I pulled a trash can in front of her just in case and asked, "Would you mind if I prayed for you?"

"All I need is for the Advil I took to kick in…"

I frowned.

"…But fine," she agreed. "If you think it will help."

As the sound of the warning bell rang, marking the start of First Period, I placed my hands around Samantha's head, holding her temples, and asked the Lord to take away her pain.

I was careful with the words I chose to use, as I prayed out loud for Samantha. I prayed for her migraine to subside. I prayed for the Lord to fill her with peace and tranquility, and I prayed that the underlying cause of Samantha's migraines would be brought to light so that she could address the issue and be healed of her distress permanently.

When I trailed off and finished the prayer with, "Amen,"

Samantha said:

"Your warm hands are helping. It doesn't feel like my eyeballs are going to explode anymore."

"Hallelujah," I said.

She blinked her eyes open.

I released her head and took a few steps back.

She turned her head side to side and smiled up at me.

"The pain is gone," she said brightly.

"Really?"

Praise the Lord!

"The Advil must have kicked in," she decided, pleased with herself as she hopped up and breezed past me. "Gotta get to class! Later, Penny!"

I was left standing alone in the ladies' room, shaking my head at Samantha but feeling more connected to God than ever.

After I taught all of my classes throughout the day, I convinced Esther to follow me back to my parents' cabin to meet Daniel, the Catholic contractor who had also survived cancer.

When we arrived at the cabin, Daniel's pickup truck was parked in the driveway and I could hear his chainsaw slicing through wood.

Stark, golden sunlight cut through the mountains in the distance, as I stepped out of my parked car and waited for Esther to join me. She had parked behind me, but hadn't climbed out. After a moment of waiting, I realized she wasn't going to. Seated behind the wheel, Esther looked worried, her sequined chemo cap perfectly framing her pretty face.

I rounded to the passenger's side of her car and climbed in.

"I'm not ready, Penny."

"Even to simply say 'hello'?"

She glanced at me, looking defeated.

"Esther, you can do this."

"But what if he's disappointed? What if he envisioned some kind of gorgeous bombshell when you told him about me? What if he rejects me the moment he sees me?"

"What if he doesn't?" I countered. "What if he wants to get to know the real you?"

"Then in a lot of ways that would be even more frightening," she admitted.

"I'm good at this," I reminded her. "How many successful matches have I made?"

"More than I can count," she allowed but quickly added, "with the exception of Gloria and Edgar."

"Okay, so *one* match ended in murder, but that doesn't mean yours will," I teased.

She swallowed the lump in her throat.

"Love takes courage," I said. "The Bible warns us not to be fearful and unbelieving. Be courageous, Esther, and believe that you deserve love."

A brave smile formed on her face and she looked to me for strength.

"You can do this," I told her. "And so long as you do, it will be worth it, no matter what happens."

She inhaled deeply, pressed her mouth into a determined line, and climbed out of the car. I did the same and we headed into the cabin just as dusk closed in, darkening the golden skies.

We unbundled and got situated in the comfy living room to the sounds of Daniel's chainsaw shrieking through wood panels outside and my mother's grumbling complaints under her breath as she busied herself in the kitchen.

A moment later, the chainsaw went quiet.

Esther tensed up in anticipation.

My dad crossed the deck outside, nearing the sliding glass door with Daniel at his heels.

Esther froze. Her eyes widened, and she sat up very straight as my dad came into the living room with Daniel.

The moment Daniel saw Esther, he was taken with her. I could tell. His light eyes went white all around and the corners of his boyish grin lifted.

As casually as I could, I offhandedly said, "Oh, Daniel, good you're here. This is my friend, Esther, who teaches with me at Walnut Mountain Middle School."

Esther's cheeks turned pink and she was on her feet in no time to shake Daniel's hand.

"It's so nice to meet you," she breathed.

"Likewise," he replied, his voice sounding deeper than I had remembered.

As my father disappeared into the kitchen and my mother got into it with him all over again concerning the storm shutters and why this project wasn't finished yet, I watched Daniel and Esther.

They were still shaking hands and gazing deeply into each

other's eyes.
>   Neither wanted to let go.

CHAPTER TEN

NOT ONLY DID ESTHER and Daniel hit it off, they both stayed for dinner.

Esther was shy and quiet around Daniel, yet her character shined through. Daniel asked her about herself, and Esther answered his every question. I could tell they liked each other. Daniel remained polite and gentlemanly. He never pried, but when he opened up about himself, his faith, and his recovery from cancer, Esther related to him genuinely and shared as much as she felt comfortable sharing about her own survival.

It was truly sweet.

As Esther and Daniel bonded throughout the course of our meal, my parents often glanced at one another, held hands, and smiled as if the budding romance between Esther and Daniel reminded them of themselves from years ago.

I tried not to feel like a third wheel, or a *fifth* wheel, but sadly, I was the odd woman out.

The conversation around the table shifted from discussing Hopeful Heart Ministries, which Daniel had been very curious about, to the topic of my knack for matchmaking.

"Really?" asked Daniel, impressed by the high praise that Esther had just given me. "You've made nearly a dozen matches that ended in marriage?"

"It's hard to believe," I admitted, as I sat all alone on my side of the table, hardly a living example of romance.

My mother explained, "Penny has always had a gift for reading people, and being able to deeply and intuitively understand what people really want and need. She can tell when two people will complement each other."

Esther and Daniel touched eyes and smiled in silent agreement that I had done a good job matching them, as well.

"Amazing," said Daniel, as he looked at me in awe. "So, where is your husband?"

My heart sank. I tried not to let my upbeat attitude falter, but I could feel a bitter knot of envy twist in my stomach. I wanted Alan to be here with me now. I wanted him to look at me like Daniel had been looking at Esther and like my father had been looking at my mother all night. I couldn't answer the question of where Alan was, and it killed me.

My father must have sensed my anxiety. He was well aware of the difficulties in my marriage, as was my mother, so he explained to Daniel how my husband had just been promoted at the police station and was solely in charge of investigating the recent murder.

"I'm very proud of Alan," I added as Dad went on.

Esther must have perceived my disappointment about Alan's absence. She sympathized and said, "Hopefully, he'll catch the killer soon, and won't have to be at the police station so much."

My smile drooped. If only Alan's absence was due to the investigation. I tried not to let my fears show any more than they already were, as my mother began overcompensating by insisting that time spent apart helped to strengthen marriages in general.

The doorbell chimed, but my mom didn't slow down one bit.

As she continued detailing the importance of little marriage breaks, which I was sure no one was buying, my dad got up from the table to see who was at the door.

"Mom, it's not like Alan and I are taking little breaks," I interrupted, terrified that she was going to let it slip to Esther that my marriage was in temporary turmoil. "He's very busy with the investigation."

"There is nothing shameful about taking breaks," she argued, but she was only making the situation worse.

I wished she would stop talking before everyone caught on to what was really happening in my personal life.

Confused, Esther asked, "Penny and Alan aren't *separated*, are they, Dottie?"

My mom began making a face that would've answered the question outright, and torn me to pieces in the process.

But then a miracle occurred.

My father returned to the dining room with Alan.

"There he is!" Esther exclaimed. "Hi, Alan!"

"You weren't just talking about me, were you?" he asked good-naturedly, and everyone around the table chuckled.

My mother hopped up to make him a plate, as my dad welcomed him to sit in the empty chair next to mine.

My handsome husband peeled his coat off and draped it around the back of his chair. He sat down beside me, wrapped his arm around my shoulder, and gave me a kiss on the cheek. I smiled from ear to ear the entire time.

After kissing my cheek, he whispered in my ear, "You talked to Gregory Downes?"

I froze.

Quietly, I said, "Is that a problem?"

"Why else would I be here?" he whispered and then leaned back in his chair.

He kept his arm around me. He ate dinner and laughed with us. He played the part of the perfect husband.

But once we finished dinner, he asked my parents, Esther, and Daniel to excuse us, and led me upstairs into my childhood bedroom where I had been staying ever since Edgar was murdered.

Alan closed the door behind him.

The room was softly lit from the nightstand lamps.

Suddenly, tension rose between us, but it didn't necessarily feel romantic.

"Did you think I wouldn't notice you talking to Gregory Downes this morning?" he asked, speaking in a low tone.

I could tell he probably wanted to yell at me, but he wasn't willing to risk everyone downstairs overhearing him.

"I didn't realize I wasn't allowed to talk to Gregory Downes."

"Please don't get cute with me, Penny."

"Walnut Mountain Legal amalgamated with Edgar Swaine's law firm—"

"Yeah, I know."

"You don't find that suspicious?" I challenged.

"I don't need your help investigating—"

"I'm not saying that you do, Alan, but I found out a few things that might help—"

He let out a laugh that I didn't find funny.

"Don't laugh at me."

"Laughing at you, darling, is the best scenario," he barked. "I could have you arrested for tampering with an investigation, do you realize that?"

"Oh, yeah, that would go well for you," I blurted out. "I bet Chief Pepperdine would be really impressed if you arrested *another* innocent woman."

"Penny, I'm warning you," he asserted. "You're walking on thin ice."

"If anyone is walking on thin ice, Alan, it's you! Considering some of the decisions you've made, like arresting Gloria, who obviously had nothing to do with Edgar's murder, you could get fired!"

"You have no idea what it takes to catch a killer—"

"Maybe not, but I'm certain it shouldn't involve wasting time with Gloria! My God, Alan, she was right next to me at the restaurant!"

"It was her knife!"

A moment passed before his shocking statement reached my brain.

"What?" I asked, unable to comprehend the information.

"The murder weapon belonged to Gloria," he said, frustrated with himself. He raked his fingers through his thick, dark hair and paced away from me, taking a lap around the bedroom. "I shouldn't be telling you this."

"What do you mean the murder weapon belonged to Gloria?"

"It was her switchblade knife—"

"So, it was a *switchblade?*"

"She admitted it was her knife!" he went on. "The thing was found at the crime scene and it has her name engraved on it!"

"But she didn't kill him, and Hank has an alibi. He was talking with Jacques, the owner of Fancy's—"

"You think I don't know that?"

"It wasn't Gloria!" I snapped.

"I agree she didn't stab him," he snapped right back. "But she could be an accomplice to murder. I have to keep the pressure on her until she cuts a deal and tells me who the killer is."

"She's not an accomplice," I insisted.

He stared at me for a long moment.

Then he said, "I'm aware that the investigation isn't going great and that Pepperdine has half a mind to demote me to my former position as a police officer, if not fire me altogether. Believe me, I'm aware."

Alan took another lap around the bedroom. His fists were planted on his hips. His brow was furrowed, and his muscular shoulders looked full of tension.

Alan advanced on me, took my face in his large hands, and kissed me.

As he pulled me in, pressing against the length of me, he pulled the sequin chemo cap I always wore off my head and ran his fingers through my hair, controlling the rhythm of our deep kiss.

"I need my wife," he growled, ready to devour me.

But there came a gentle knock at the door and my mother called out, "Dessert is ready, you two!"

Alan searched my eyes, as I shouted over my shoulder, "We'll be right down!"

"I have to get back to the station," he said.

"Now?"

"I need you to listen to me, Penny. I'm your husband. When I tell you not to poke around and when I tell you not to get in the way of my investigation, you know that you have to listen to me."

He was right so I nodded in agreement. But I knew I wouldn't be able to stop.

"If you want to help me," he went on. "Then *this* is what I need."

He squeezed my hips.

"But I'm willing to wait for it," he added. "I'm willing to wait until everything between us is right."

Even though Alan had to leave for the station house, he had a slice of pie with me in the living room. Dad had rekindled the fire in the wood-burning stove. Esther and Daniel looked cozy on the loveseat, and my parents canoodled on the couch.

Alan and I ate our dessert in silence on the other side of the room.

Someone who had wanted Edgar Swaine dead had gotten their hands on Gloria's knife, but who in the world could have done that?

Who had the ability to steal Gloria's knife?

Alan turned to me and whispered, "Can I take you out to dinner tomorrow night?"

"Are you asking me out on a date?"

✝

I WAS THRILLED that my husband had asked me out on a date!

Thrilled might have been too small a word.

Ecstatic!

I could barely sleep all night, the anticipation of Alan wining-and-dining me was too great!

The next day, my excitement was unbearable. All I wanted was for the day to pass by quickly, but instead, every class I taught at Walnut Mountain Middle School unfolded so slowly that I felt like I was being tortured.

Esther was in high spirits. At the lunch hour recess, she gushed about Daniel and could not stop thanking me for introducing them.

Finally, I had something to gush about, as well.

"Alan is taking me out to Fancy's tonight!"

She couldn't quite understand why I was over the moon at the thought of a date with my husband, but she remained encouraging nonetheless.

"Lovely!"

"It's just that he's been working so hard," I explained in an attempt to smooth over why I was acting like a love-addled teenager. "I feel like I haven't seen him in months."

"But the murder was only a week ago," she pointed out.

"Oh, you know what I mean."

"Fancy's opened? The police left for good?"

"Yup," I said, grinning from ear to ear.

I was already fantasizing about what I should wear to seduce my husband and ensure that we would both end up in the same bed tonight.

My mood was so good, in fact, that not even Samantha was able to bring me down when she tried to harass Esther and I between Third and Fourth Periods about her social justice agenda.

An hour later, school officially let out for the day, and I was practically jumping out of my skin to get back to my cabin and freshen up for the date.

When I did, I decided to throw on a cranberry-red, scoop-neck dress that flattered my figure. I dolled myself up with make-up and picked out an autumn shawl that matched my purse. All the while, I fantasized about where the romantic night might take us. I loved seeing Alan in a suit… and I loved seeing him in-between the bed sheets even more…

I felt giddy just thinking about it!

When I parked at Fancy's, night had fallen and the exterior of the restaurant twinkled with strings of little white lights.

Inside, the hostess greeted me and asked if I would like to wait at the bar since Alan had yet to arrive.

"Can I be seated at our table?" I countered.

The hostess apologized and explained, "We only seat complete parties."

Waiting for Alan at the bar was out of the question, so I told the hostess I didn't mind standing in the anteroom and stepped aside.

The owner of Fancy's, Jacques, breezed by the anteroom and turned on his heels when he saw me.

"Mrs. Matchmaker! Welcome! How are you this evening?"

"Very well, thank you," I said, as Jacques quickly helped me out of my coat. "I'm glad to see you've been able to open up again."

"You have no idea how relieved I am," he said, as he hung my coat in the coat check area. "Wonderful timing, Mr. Matchmaker!"

I glanced over my shoulder to find Alan entering the restaurant.

He locked eyes with me and grinned.

Just as I had hoped, he was dressed in a dark, tailored suit, and he was cleanly shaved, looking as handsome as ever.

Jacques collected Alan's coat and told the hostess that he would escort Alan and me to our reserved table.

Jacques spoke to us over his shoulder as he walked us to one of the cozy tables near the large, picture windows that offered charming views of Walnut Mountain and the mountains surrounding the heart of town.

As we sat down, Jacques asked Alan, "How soon before the killer is caught?"

Alan bristled and tension filled his shoulders, but he tempered his response, trying not to let the extreme pressure he was under show. He mentioned that the investigation was moving forward at a clip.

I wondered if that was true, as Jacques waved our waitress over.

It was Hailey, the same waitress who Edgar had brought to tears the night of his murder.

"Enjoy your evening," Jacques said before bowing out and

allowing Hailey to take over.

She greeted us and began reciting the specials.

As she did, Alan and I touched eyes. I liked how he was looking at me—like he couldn't wait to get me alone and have me all to himself.

Our waitress, Hailey, struggled to remember the last entrée special. She pursed her mouth, racking her brain, but quickly gave up and pulled a notecard out of the sleek, black apron she wore.

"Tagliatelle pasta with black truffle sauce," she read aloud.

"That sounds delicious," I said.

Alan told her what he and I would like to drink—sparkling apple cider—and she started off through the restaurant.

He offered me his hand. I placed my hand in his on the table.

"It never ceases to amaze me," he began, "how good you are at making matches. If I hadn't known better, I would have thought your friend Esther and Daniel had been together for years. I love what a big heart you have, Penny."

"Thank you," I breathed.

"How is your sobriety coming along?"

I chose my words very carefully. "I'm glad to put drinking behind me. Really, Alan, I haven't thought twice about it, and I've been doing great."

"Thank God," he said, relieved. He gave my hand a squeeze. "Your father made it seem like—"

"My *father*?"

"Lucas and I talk, you know," he reminded me as though I should be well aware of the fact.

"What did my father say?" I blurted out, hating how defensive I sounded.

"Calm down, Penny, it's not like he betrayed you. I asked him how you were doing."

"And?"

"And he mentioned that you haven't told your friends that you're an alcoholic. He's concerned that it's an indication you're still being secretive. I think it would be best if you told people. That way, everyone can help you stay on track."

Alan might as well have slapped me across the face, and I couldn't even begin to mentally process how furious I felt at my father.

"Please don't look at me like that," he said.

I pulled my hand out of his and continued to stare at him.

"Everyone loves you and cares about you," he added. "I love you and care about you, and I miss you."

"I had high hopes for tonight, Alan. I didn't think you would choose a restaurant to attack me."

"I'm not attacking you."

"I think you are."

He sighed and glanced across the restaurant. I thought he might argue that no one could hear us, but when he didn't return his gaze to me, I realized that something had stolen his attention.

On the far side of the restaurant, Officers Jeremiah and Chuck were charging into Fancy's. They spotted Alan. As my husband stood, the police officers made a beeline for him.

"Sorry to interrupt, Detective," Officer Jeremiah said, "but we couldn't reach you on your cell."

"I must not have felt it vibrate," he said.

"There's been a development."

"I'm right behind you," Alan told them, as he absently patted his suit jacket.

He pulled his wallet out of the inside pocket of his suit jacket and tossed cash on the table.

"I'm so sorry, Penny," he said. The police officers crossed through the restaurant, wasting no time to return to their squad car and chase down whatever development had surfaced. "I'll meet you at the cabin when I'm finished investigating tonight."

"You will?"

"We need to continue this conversation, no matter how late."

He stooped and gave me a kiss on the cheek, then darted through the restaurant after his police officers, leaving me alone to ponder whether or not I would ever get my husband back and restore our marriage to how it used to be before Alan had become fixated on blowing my drinking way out of proportion.

The waitress, Hailey, swung by with two long-stem flutes of sparkling apple cider on a tray.

I was beyond tempted to order a stiff drink, but decided to channel my sour emotions towards figuring out how to seduce my husband so that he would no longer see me as a problem wife that he needed to fix.

I must have looked either horrified or furious or terrified, because Hailey asked me if I felt alright.

"The last time I was here, I found a dead man in the bathroom," I said, darkly answering her question.

"It isn't easy being here after what happened to Edgar Swaine," she agreed to my surprise, as she set the flutes down on the table. "They say, never meet your heroes…"

Huh?

Edgar had berated Hailey so badly that night that Hailey had needed to bite her lip to keep her mouth from quivering…

"What hero did you meet that night?" I asked, confused.

"Edgar," she said. When it was obvious I didn't understand, she clarified, "I had always thought highly of Edgar Swaine and looked up to him. I thought he was my knight in shining armor. But he turned out to be a jerk."

She shook her head and let out a sigh.

"He was so nice to me when I was a little girl," she went on. "He promised to get the bad guy who had attacked my father, and he kept his promise."

She had my full attention now.

"This was back when Edgar was a criminal prosecutor?"

Hailey nodded. "My dad got stabbed. I was barely five years old at the time. My dad used to manage a big-time rock band called Clank. But the band thought that my dad was stealing money from them. I don't know if that was true, but the drummer stabbed my dad to death because of it. My mom was devastated. The only thing that kept us going was Edgar Swaine. He was more than an attorney. He became like a family friend throughout the trial."

Jacques swooped in and politely asked Hailey to attend to her other tables. Fancy's was filling up.

Before leaving me, she added, "Edgar didn't deserve what he got, even though he had turned into a rude, cruel old man."

As she started through the restaurant, I mentally put the puzzle pieces together.

Clank was Hank's former band—the one he had played in before he formed Jail Bird.

The drummer of Clank had stabbed Hailey's father and Edgar sent him to prison as a result?

Could the drummer have come to Walnut Mountain to kill Edgar out of revenge?

I had a solid guess as to who the drummer was…

But I wanted to be certain.

CHAPTER ELEVEN

EATING DINNER AT FANCY'S was the furthest thing from my mind.

I found my cell phone in my purse and speed-dialed Alan. As the call rang and rang, I clamped my phone between my ear and shoulder, and counted the cash that Alan had left on the table.

Considering we had ordered two sparkling apple ciders that neither of us drank, I tucked a twenty-bill under my water glass for Hailey, pocketed the rest, and rushed through the restaurant.

When I got to the coat check, Alan's outgoing voicemail message started playing.

"Alan, give me a call. I'm heading to the cabin." I was about to add that I thought I knew who had killed Edgar, but I held my tongue. "Come as soon as you're done investigating. Love you!"

I hung up, slid my cell phone into my purse, and as soon as the coat check girl handed me my coat, I threw it on and was out the door.

As I drove through the darkened back roads of Walnut Mountain, I commended myself for the simple voicemail message I had left Alan, and for the fact that I had not mentioned anything about Hailey's father who had been stabbed to death by the drummer of Clank. Alan had been irritated enough with me for poking around Walnut Mountain Legal and speaking with Gregory Downes. Besides, I needed to put the pieces together and make absolutely certain that they fit before I brought anything to Alan's attention.

I needed a strong internet connection…

My gut told me that Hank's brother, Ronnie, was the killer.

But it wasn't until I ran into my freezing cabin, having parked at a hurried angle out front, and got online that I confirmed my suspicions.

I opened my laptop and clicked the Google browser. One Google search of "Clank" later, and I was staring at old photos from the early 90s. Hank looked like a much younger version of his bad boy self, and his brother, Ronnie, was just as recognizable, holding drum sticks in just about every photograph I came across.

Toggling out from the Google Images view, I scrolled through web page headlines until I found one that appeared to address why the band had broken up.

"Can Clank Survive the Clink?" I murmured under my breath as I read the headline out loud.

The article itself confirmed the details that Hailey had told me at the restaurant. Hailey's dad, the manager of Clank, had been accused of stealing tour income, and during a heated debate one night after a show, Ronnie had lost control and stabbed the manager in front of witnesses that included Hank, the band, and a handful of groupies. Gloria, however, hadn't been among them.

Ronnie had insisted on a trial, which spoke to his extreme arrogance as a rock star. He had actually thought that a jury would be so starstruck that they wouldn't send him to prison. He had been wrong. Edgar Swaine prosecuted during the trial and had also fought hard to ensure that Ronnie would get the maximum sentence.

I leaned back on the couch where I had been sitting and reading about Clank.

It wasn't hard for me to imagine that Ronnie could have gotten his hands on Gloria's switchblade knife. Though it wasn't totally obvious how he could have kept it throughout the years. Of course, once Ronnie had gotten out of prison, he could have found the old knife among Hank's things. Those kinds of details were happenstance.

What I found most interesting was that another article noted the date when Ronnie had been released from prison on parole for good behavior. The article itself was about Jail Bird, the new band that the brothers had formed.

I wished Alan would hurry home. I was dying to text him that I knew who the killer was, but I didn't want to act impulsively.

Instead, I set my laptop computer aside, kneeled in front of the wood-burning stove, and started filling it with chopped wood, kindling, and newspaper.

I struck a match, and as the flame crackled and fizzed, I tapped it under the crumpled newspaper balls I had shoved under the wood.

Soon a fire began devouring the wood in the stove. I closed the glass door and watched the flames for a moment, enjoying the warmth.

Behind me, the front door of the cabin creaked open.

Alan!

I sprang up to my feet, expecting to find my handsome husband walking in through the door.

But when I turned, I came face-to-face with the killer.

Ronnie stood in the dimly lit entryway of my cabin.

I hadn't thought to lock myself in when I had gotten home earlier.

He was glaring right at me.

Terror shot through me. My heart pounded so hard in my chest that I could feel my pulse throbbing in my ears. I thought I might faint. My legs felt like jelly, but I didn't fall over.

I mentally screamed at myself to run, but I couldn't see a way out with Ronnie blocking my path to the door.

"I think you know why I'm here," he said in a tone that made my blood run cold.

I swallowed the lump in my throat, but my voice was like wind over reeds. "My husband will be home any minute."

"The homicide detective?" he questioned, snorting a laugh as if he knew all about Alan. "He's not going to come here. Each night, he goes to a motel near the highway on the other side of town. And in terms of the investigation, he doesn't know what the hell he's doing…"

Ronnie took one step then another, crossing the hard wood floors towards me.

"But *you* know what you're doing, don't you, Mrs. Matchmaker?"

"I don't know anything," I breathed, my voice trembling.

He narrowed his dark eyes on me. "Oh, I think you do," he sneered. "I think you're trying to solve the murder. I think you're trying to exonerate Gloria, but you see, Gloria needs to go to prison for what happened to Edgar."

Again, I swallowed hard, choking down another lump that had formed in my throat.

"Gloria didn't kill Edgar," I breathed.

"You just can't leave well enough alone, can you?"

While I inwardly prayed for the Lord to be my protection, I told him, "I can leave well enough alone. I don't want any trouble. Why don't you leave town? I won't say a word to anyone about anything."

I hated to learn there was a coward inside me.

If Ronnie wanted to leave town, he would have been gone by now.

Deep down, I feared the reason he had come after me tonight, and it had nothing to do with me promising not to tell anyone that I knew he had killed Edgar Swaine.

Mustering every shred of courage I had, I desperately willed myself to sound strong and asserted, "Get out."

Ronnie flicked his wrist, opening a butterfly switchblade in his hand.

He must have really liked switchblade knives!

Oh, God!

He took another step towards me...

...then another.

Ignoring my trembling voice, I said, "Forgiveness could have set you free, Ronnie."

He stopped and cocked his head.

"You did your time. Why couldn't you just move on? Why did you have to execute revenge against Edgar? Why did you seek him out and—"

"I didn't seek him out!" he yelled, startling me.

I had struck a nerve.

A big one.

"I *had* moved on! I was happy drumming with Jail Bird! I was adjusting to life on the outside! I thought I had gotten past the rage I felt towards Edgar for putting me in prison! But when I saw what Edgar did to Hank, I couldn't let it go!"

"What did Edgar do to Hank?"

"Edgar stole his girl!"

"Gloria? But Hank and Gloria had broken up decades prior," I pointed out.

"Hank never stopped loving her. He came to Walnut Mountain

and tried to win her back six months ago. But *you*," he seethed, spitting each word out of his mouth. "*You* introduced Gloria to Edgar. If it hadn't been for *you*, Gloria would have taken Hank back, and I wouldn't have become obsessed with Edgar!"

"I didn't know about their history," I stammered, hotly defending myself. "I didn't know anything about Hank."

"Seeing my brother heartbroken like that…" he trailed off, shaking his head. "When I saw Edgar Swaine at Fancy's… When I saw what a monster he could be, even to Gloria… After what he had done to me and after what he had done to Hank… The first chance I got…"

"You killed him," I supplied. "You waited until your brother was engrossed in a conversation with Jacques, the owner of the restaurant, and you followed Edgar into the men's bathroom and stabbed him to death."

"See how much you've figured out?" he said, sneering. "That's why I can't let you live."

"Don't!" I warned when he began approaching me again. "Stay where you are! Don't you take another step towards me!"

Darkness filled his eyes and he ceased to look human, as he advanced on me.

I tore through the living room, darting around him, desperate to escape or die trying.

Just then, my husband, Alan, stepped into the cabin and casually called out for me:

"Penny, I'm home!"

Alan was shocked when I spilled into his arms, a tangle of panicked terror he couldn't quite make sense of until he saw Ronnie in hot pursuit, holding a knife in his balled fist.

Thinking fast, Alan urged me aside and charged at Ronnie with his fist cocked back.

He delivered a strong blow to Ronnie's jaw, used his other hand to capture the killer's wrist so that Ronnie couldn't stab him, and punched him in the nose.

As Ronnie stumbled backwards, Alan quickly withdrew his handgun from the holster he wore under his coat.

"Don't move," Alan warned him. "Unless you want me to shoot."

CHAPTER TWELVE

THE FOLLOWING SUNDAY, Hopeful Heart Ministries had more people in attendance than I had seen all year. It seemed as though everyone's faith in the goodness of the world was now restored thanks to Alan. Everyone in Walnut Mountain knew that he had caught the killer and had saved my life in the process.

"How did you know it was Ronnie, Hank's brother?" Esther asked Alan after the Service.

We were all gathered in the church vestibule and chatting—Esther and her new man Daniel, my parents, and Alan and myself.

Gloria was still in the sanctuary with Hank, talking to Pastor Peter. The couple had a lot to contend with, and even more to heal from, if they wanted their relationship to rise above the long, dark shadow that Ronnie had cast over it.

Alan drew in a deep breath and was thoughtful in his response.

"I had my suspicions based on the connection I discovered between Ronnie and Edgar, who had put him in prison years ago. But the more I investigated, the clearer it became to me that Ronnie had actually killed Edgar Swaine in a twisted attempt to protect his brother's heart. For Ronnie, it was all about ensuring Hank's happiness with Gloria. Revenge was just an added bonus."

Impressed, Daniel asked, "Is that why Ronnie went after Penny?"

Alan and I glanced at each other, while Daniel cracked a quiet joke about Esther's old flames and how he hoped none of them would come after him.

She elbowed him in the ribs. "Don't make me admit that I haven't had boyfriends before you came along."

Everyone chuckled except for my mother who hadn't yet emotionally recovered from the fact that Ronnie had tried to attack me. She was still deeply disturbed that the killer had followed me to the cabin that night, and though she remained extremely grateful that no real harm had come to me, she was also very upset with me. In her mind, if I had gone to my parents house after leaving Fancy's, I wouldn't have found myself in harm's way.

"Killing Edgar wasn't enough," Alan went on to speculate. "Since Penny had also played a role in keeping Gloria and Hank apart, Ronnie shifted his obsession to Penny."

My mother frowned, but I was the only one who noticed. She blamed me, which wasn't the only thing she blamed me for. She thought my crumbling marriage was my fault, too… Maybe she was right.

Alan hadn't touched me since I had spilled into his arms that night, fleeing from Ronnie, and he wasn't being affectionate with me now, as he explained Ronnie's psychology and the deeply seeded issues that had motivated him to kill.

I was hopeful Alan and I would move back into our cabin and pick up where we had left off three months ago before he had moved into a motel. But apparently, the aftermath of catching a killer came with so much paperwork that he was practically sleeping at the police station, or so he said.

"But I can hardly take all the credit," said Alan. "There was a big development in the case the night I saved Penny. A potential witness had come forward. The individual was at Fancy's that night and saw Ronnie dart out of the men's bathroom, after which Ronnie left the restaurant. The behavior was strange enough, and the timing was uncanny enough, that when I heard about it, I had to drop everything and speak with the witness."

"This was during our date," I added. "Alan and I were at Fancy's and about to dine, and Officer Jeremiah interrupted us to steal Alan."

Alan gave my hand a little squeeze, intentionally touching me with affection for the first time since he had grabbed me and kissed me in my parents' cabin.

"Truth be told," said Alan. "The reason I drove home to our

cabin wasn't because I had a hunch Ronnie might be there. It was because I had decided that I needed to put Penny first that night. I shouldn't have raced out of Fancy's to chase a lead. The investigation could wait until morning, I thought."

"Thank God," my father said, blown away. "That was divine providence, son."

"I agree, Lucas," said Alan.

"If the Lord hadn't placed in your heart the decision to put Penny first... I don't even want to think about what might have happened that night," my father added.

"I don't either," I said.

"Who was the witness?" Esther asked, and we all perked up, highly interested in the answer.

"I probably shouldn't share this, but since we're on the topic of divine providence and the Lord influencing people's hearts for the greater good..." Alan leaned in and quietly told us. "It was our very own, Thomas Ford."

"The Worship Team leader?" asked Daniel, who had only just met Tom for the first time before the Service.

Alan nodded. "He was at the restaurant that night, and even though he saw what he saw, he told himself to think long and hard before he came forward, because he didn't want to bear false witness against his neighbor, so to speak. It would have been a different story if Tom had witnessed the murder, but all he saw was an unknown man rushing out of the men's bathroom. Moment's later, Penny found Edgar dead on the floor. For Tom, he was really terrified of doing the wrong thing. Pointing a finger of blame at an innocent man based on a coincidence would have been the wrong thing, but ultimately Ronnie wasn't innocent and in the end, Tom did the right thing by coming forward."

"Praise God," said Daniel. He gave Esther a squeeze and asked if she wanted to head out.

I hugged them both, and hoped Alan would invite me to do the same.

But he didn't. Alan checked his wristwatch and said, "I need to get to the station house."

He offered his goodbyes and didn't kiss me on the cheek before he crossed through the church vestibule and headed out into the sunny, frigid afternoon.

It was then that I realized the solved murder hadn't brought us together. My husband and I were as estranged as ever.

As parishioners disbursed, leaving Hopeful Heart Ministries to enjoy the rest of their day, my mom ushered me aside to speak privately.

Her face looked forlorn and heavy. I thought I knew what she was going to say, and I didn't want to hear her opinions about my marriage or about how she wanted me to permanently live in my childhood room at my parents' cabin, or worse, crawl back into her womb where I would be forever safe from both the world and my inner demons.

But my assumptions were wrong.

"If anything had happened to you, I don't think I could bear it."

"Mom, I'm fine. Ronnie didn't even scratch me—"

"Please, Penny," she interrupted, her emotions running so high that I suddenly realized she might explode. "You can never do that again, do you understand? Never again disobey your husband when he tells you—"

"Mom—"

"Penny," she warned, turning stern. "Alan told you not to investigate and you didn't listen. You could have been killed just like your grandmother."

I froze and stared at my mother for a very long moment.

No one in the family *ever* spoke of what had happened to my grandmother, Mable.

No one had ever found out who had killed her...

...and the unspoken sentiment in our household was that discussing Grandmother Mable wasn't allowed.

My mother looked me square in the eye and said, "You remind me of her more and more each day, Penny, and that isn't a good thing."

THE END

THE MATCHMAKER MURDERS (SEASON ONE)

MURDER AT THE MOVIES
(The Matchmaker Murders, Book Two)

CHAPTER ONE

WINTERTIME WAS FAST approaching, and all of Walnut Mountain twinkled with the cozy charm of the upcoming Christmas holiday.

In the heart of town, a decorated Christmas tree stood next to the gazebo. Shopkeepers strung festive lights around their storefront windows and hung wreaths on their doors, and there was a nativity scene displayed in front of Hopeful Heart Ministries, which my dad had carved by hand and set up for all the residents to enjoy.

As wonderful as the little shops were, having been transformed by the Christmas spirit, the talk of the town happened to be exclusively focused on Walnut Mountain's brand-new movie theater, Christian Cinemas.

Located a block south from the library, Christian Cinemas had popped up overnight. One day in early December the commercial lot had been vacant, but then the next week, a two-story movie theater had been constructed, and everyone in town was suddenly living in an anxious state of excitement for the grand opening, including myself.

The grand opening was tonight. There was one film listed on the marquee—Keep Christ in Christmas. Though I had never heard of this particular movie before, I bought tickets in advance and dressed to look my best, deeply hoping that my husband, Alan, would manage to steal away from his important work at the police station and join me.

As I drove my sedan around the corner, coming onto Main

Street where Christian Cinemas glowed up ahead, I couldn't believe the crowd that had formed in front of the theater.

Bundled up in winter coats and puffy hats, people huddled in tight clusters along the sidewalk. Some of them even spilled into the road, and a lot of them were holding signs and shouting profanities at the families who were attempting to enter the movie theater.

What in the world?

By the grace of God in heaven, I found a parking spot, pulled my fluffy hat down over my ears, and climbed out into the crisp night air.

That was when I really heard what the crowd was chanting in unison.

"Stop discrimination in Walnut Mountain! Stop discrimination in Walnut Mountain!"

It was a protest.

The large group was protesting… the movie theater?

"Stop discrimination in Walnut Mountain!"

When I reached the sidewalk, I pressed through the crowd and uttered, "Excuse me," whenever the protestors didn't realize that I needed to squeeze by.

"Penny!"

"Esther?"

Beyond an angry cluster of college-age students, none of whom I recognized, was my best friend, Esther. She was practically being swallowed by the protestors.

Luckily, Daniel was with Esther. I had matched the two a month ago and they had been going strong, in love, ever since.

Daniel protectively warded off the pressing crowd as he began ushering Esther towards me.

Before Daniel and Esther reached me, one of the protestors—a furious-sounding woman—shouted at me from behind, "This movie theater should be for *everyone*, not just Christians! This discrimination has to stop now!"

I glanced over my shoulder, preparing to confront the woman about her hysteria—obviously, *anyone* could attend the grand opening and watch the movie if they wanted to!

My jaw dropped when I saw who had been yelling at me.

"Samantha?"

"Penny?" said Samantha, my fellow middle school teacher.

She didn't seem all that surprised to find me here. She knew I was a Christian. Frankly, I wasn't all that surprised to find her protesting here either, considering my familiarity with her aggressive crusades for social justice. Her pretty face pinched into a determined frown and then she started yelling again:

"This movie theater should play movies that aren't designed to exclude non-Christians!"

Oh, for God's sake!

Finally, Daniel and Esther spilled towards me.

"You okay?" asked Esther, as Daniel opened the glass entrance door of the movie theater for us.

Ducking inside for safety, I said, "A protest was the last thing I expected to encounter tonight."

Esther agreed and added, "Matthew was the last person I expected to find among the protestors."

"Matthew is protesting the movie theater?" I asked. "Matthew, our science teacher?"

"He's out there with Samantha," she told me.

"But Matthew is a Christian," I said, puzzled, as I glanced through the glass entrance door, looking for Matthew among the protestors.

Sure enough, there was the bookish science teacher standing near Samantha as her beautiful, blonde hair flapped in the cold winds. He couldn't take his eyes off her.

"He's infatuated with her," said Esther.

"Unbelievable," I grumbled.

The interior of the lobby was regal with red carpeting, lofty ceilings, and gold-framed mirrors lining the walls.

Patrons greeted one another, bought popcorn and candy, and tried to make light of the hostile protest that was threatening to spoil the evening.

I knew almost everyone in the lobby. I spotted Gloria Davis and Hank Houston, who had rekindled their romantic flame last autumn after the man I had matched Gloria with was murdered. Pastor Peter was here, as well, and as I glanced from face to face, I realized that the majority of our church congregation had come. I caught sight of my parents, Dottie and Lucas Hawkins, too. They were filtering into the main auditorium along with the other moviegoers.

My mom waved at me, and I smiled and waved back.

Daniel asked Esther if she wanted popcorn. She told him she

would be right along, and then she asked me:

"Is Alan coming?"

My heart sank, but I kept a stiff upper lip and said, "If he does, I'm sure he'll just slip into one of the seats in the back."

"So, we shouldn't save him a seat?"

"Let's not worry about it. He's at the precinct and there's a low chance he'll show up."

"Popcorn?" she asked as she turned for Daniel.

"Sure."

As Esther joined Daniel in the concession line, I told myself not to feel down about my rocky marriage. Alan and I were just going through a rough patch. We would get through it!

Feeling suddenly warm, I pulled my fluffy hat from my head and removed my winter coat. My chin-length, auburn hair crackled with static electricity. I smoothed my hand over my head, which barely helped, so I found the stylish chemo cap that Esther had given me long ago and snugged it down over my head, making sure my hair framed my face and my earrings dangled properly.

"Penny Matchmaker!"

I would recognize that deep, booming voice anywhere. It belonged to Bobby Harder, the man responsible for the brand-new movie theater.

A former male model turned basketball coach, Bobby was 34 years old and resembled a Greek god. Towering at 6'5", he had a chiseled face, rippling physique, and boyish sandy-blonde hair. He also had a healthy love for the Lord, which was his most attractive quality, in my opinion.

Years ago, I had set Bobby up with a beautiful woman named Rachel, who had also retired from the modeling industry and given her life to Christ. The attractive couple now spent their days volunteering at the church—Bobby was the Christian youth pastor basketball coach and Rachel worked as an administrative assistant to Pastor Peter. As fulfilling as volunteering was, Bobby understood that if he wanted to start a family with Rachel, he would be wise to open his own business. Hence, the sudden and spectacular appearance of Christian Cinemas in the heart of Walnut Mountain.

"Congratulations, Bobby!" I exclaimed, as I threw my arms open and hugged him.

"I'm so glad you made it!"

"Where's your gorgeous wife?" I asked, looking around the

lobby for Rachel's jet-black hair and inky eyes. The woman was impossible to miss.

"She was feeling a bit under the weather," he mentioned as though his wife's absence from the big night pained him. "Let me walk you to your seat. I hope all the commotion outside didn't disturb you."

As we crossed the lobby and came into the dimly lit auditorium where the film Keep Christ in Christmas would soon play, I spoke quietly, asking him, "Could you call the police to get the protestors to leave?"

"Unfortunately, I did, but there's nothing they can do. The protestors obtained a permit from the county. This is quite a world we live in. As soon as those people learned that the purpose of the movie theater would be to screen Christian films, they began sending me threatening letters about how I should change the name of the theater and how I should promise to play non-Christian movies, too." Bobby let out a booming laugh and shook his handsome head. "Agreeing to their demands would have entirely defeated the purpose of my business."

"Of course, it would have," I strongly agreed. "Not to mention, you don't see Christians protesting at regular movie theaters, even though those theaters never play Christian movies except around Christmas time, and those movies tend to be about Santa and shopping."

"I think you're going to really love this film," he said when we reached the row where Esther and Daniel were seated. "It's actually a documentary."

"Oh?"

"It features twelve theologians and twenty-four historians who each go into painstaking detail to explain the cultural developments associated with the western Christmas holiday tradition. All throughout, there are interviews with experts who interweave highly spiritual information about how our modern-day holiday traditions reflect the symbolism of Christ's mission."

I felt the urge to yawn, but I fought the impulse and said, "Fascinating."

Bobby smiled brightly, gave me a little squeeze, and started up the aisle. He soon joined his friends, who were also lovers of Christ and basketball. He sat among them towards the back of the theater.

Bobby Harder really was the nicest guy in the world.

I took my seat next to Esther and she whispered, "Isn't Bobby the nicest guy in the world?"

"I was just thinking that!"

Daniel leaned around Esther and chimed in, "Bobby really is the nicest guy in the world!"

"I couldn't agree more!" I said, as the dim overhead lights went dark.

The silver screen flickered, and soon the documentary film began to play.

Deep down, I knew that Alan wasn't going to make it to the movie tonight, and his reason had nothing to do with working at the police station or his new, demanding position as the lead detective of the precinct.

He didn't want to see me.

Perhaps I was being too pessimistic about it. Alan wanted to see me, but not until I had transformed into an improved version of myself. What was so puzzling, however, was that I felt strongly that I already had. I no longer touched alcohol, which was Alan's only issue with me. I considered the problem entirely solved, but he didn't, and because of it, he was still living in a motel on the outskirts of town.

It broke my heart.

But even worse than his refusal to live with me was the fact that he didn't approve of me living at our cabin alone. Alan wanted me to stay at my parents' house. He wanted me to announce to my friends, colleagues, and loved ones that I was an alcoholic, which I refused to do, and he also wanted me to start going to AA meetings, which was totally unnecessary and downright ridiculous if you asked me.

I, on the other hand, wanted my life back! I wanted my husband to come home and for my marriage to heal from my past mistakes. I wanted to have a baby and start a family with Alan. I was ready to take on the world with Alan by my side! But he didn't trust me, and I couldn't seem to claw my way out of the damning pit he had thrown me into, no matter how hard I tried.

I couldn't seem to concentrate on the documentary film. My eyelids felt especially heavy. The room was so warm and cozy. Esther was nestled next to me like a baby goose, and when I glanced down at her, I realized she had closed her eyes. Her head rested on Daniel's shoulder.

I gave myself permission to close my eyes. As I listened to the very boring theologians in the documentary drone on and on about the intricate symbolism of pine cones and fractal mathematics as they related to the transfiguration of Christ, I became more and more sleepy.

The next thing I knew, the bright overhead lights startled me awake.

Had I fallen asleep?

The movie was over, and I realized that I wasn't the only one who had conked out.

The other moviegoers began murmuring and chuckling to themselves at the fact that they had all fallen asleep.

As they collected their coats and began making their sleepy way out of the auditorium, I turned to find Bobby sleeping in the seat next to me.

He must have been running around so much during the documentary in order to tend to movie theater business that he had lost his seat near his basketball friends. The theater house had certainly filled up. Perhaps the empty chair beside me had been the only one available when all had been said and done.

"Psst, Bobby," I whispered, giving him a nudge.

Esther and Daniel were to the left of me and the entire row beyond them needed to get out.

Bobby was fast asleep and didn't stir when I nudged him again.

"Bobby, wake up. The movie is over," I said, speaking loudly.

He didn't rouse from sleep whatsoever.

I turned to Esther and said, "What should I do? I don't have a blow horn."

"Oh dear, look Penny," she breathed, pointing to Bobby's throat.

There were pink, horizontal marks across the front of his neck.

I suddenly realized that Bobby's chest wasn't rising and falling. He wasn't inhaling and exhaling. He wasn't *breathing*. His face looked stiff and his eyes weren't completely closed.

I gasped.

I didn't want to believe what my eyes were telling me.

Esther said, "Penny, I don't think Bobby is…"

"Alive?"

Trembling, I pressed my fingertips against the side of his throat, hoping I would feel a pulse.

But there wasn't one.
Bobby Harder was dead.

CHAPTER TWO

THERE WAS VIRTUALLY no information about who might have killed Bobby Harder at the grand opening of Christian Cinemas last night, but one thing was clear. Bobby had been murdered in the seat beside me, while I had slept like a log. The horizontal marks across the front of his throat had been an indication that Bobby may have been strangled with some kind of rope or cord from behind, but that was purely my speculation.

What *wasn't* purely speculation was the fact that another man had been murdered in Walnut Mountain.

I couldn't believe it.

Neither could Esther, Daniel, my parents, and everyone else who had attended the movie.

Alan had arrived swiftly with the police once Daniel had called the precinct to report the unimaginable crime. He had taken command of the scene, but had quickly discovered that *all* the moviegoers had fallen asleep. Because of this, Alan had begun interviewing the protestors.

Suspecting that one of the protestors had taken Bobby's life made more sense than anything else, considering how beloved Bobby was in general. He had no enemies. He had never even gotten into a serious argument, as far as I had ever heard. He truly had been the nicest guy in the world.

Devastation was in the air. I could feel it, as I drove through the winding back roads of Walnut Mountain with a hot casserole on the passenger seat of my sedan.

Though the entire congregation at Hopeful Heart Ministries was certainly devastated by the news of Bobby's murder, no one had been shattered to the degree that Rachel Harder had.

In the blink of an eye, Rachel had gone from being a happy wife to a weeping widow, and I didn't want her to be alone, which was why I had gotten up before dawn to bake her a casserole, among other comfort foods, not that any home cooked meal could ever really console her.

Bobby and Rachel Harder lived in a two-story New Englander house with large picture windows, a wide front porch, and three brick chimneys. In a lot of ways, their home was just as photogenic as they were, especially this time of year thanks to the Christmas wreath hanging on the front door and the light fixtures glowing in every window.

The lawn and stone walkway were dusted with a thin layer of snow, but I doubted the driveway would be slippery.

After parking and climbing out of my car with the casserole in my mittened hands and a reusable shopping bag stuffed to the brim with comfort foods slung over my shoulder, I started up the stone walkway.

Bobby had always kept the lawn manicured and the house well-maintained, but something was different about the property. I slowed my step, trying to put my finger on what was different about the place, and then I realized what it was.

There was a black, wrought iron fence wrapping the perimeter of the property. The fence didn't span the front of the house separating the width of the front lawn from the road, however.

The wrought iron fence seemed to span only on the side perimeters of the property, and follow across the rear boundary, not that I could see that far.

With nothing but woods on either side of the Harders' home, I wondered why Bobby and Rachel had installed such a serious-looking fence.

If memory served me, the neighboring home on the west belonged to Pastor Peter and his wife, but their actual house was tucked so deeply in the woods, I couldn't even see it. On the other side of the Harders' property was a wooded expanse that eventually led to a creek.

It occurred to me that if Bobby and Rachel had been hoping to have a baby, the fence would effectively protect their child from wandering off and drowning in the creek. Figuring that Bobby had a good reason for putting up such an ominous fence, I told myself not to be nosy and continued up the walkway, crossed the front porch, and used my elbow to ring the doorbell.

A moment later, the door popped open and there stood Rachel looking unfathomably gorgeous despite the fact that her eyes were pink and puffy from crying all night, and her nose was red. She wore a fluffy sweater over her pajamas and a pair of slippers, as well as a bleary glimmer of surprise on her otherwise gloomy face.

"Penny, I'm so glad you're here," said Rachel before blowing her nose into the wads of tissues she clutched in her hands. "Please, come inside. You must be freezing."

"The casserole is keeping my hands warm," I said cheerfully, as I followed her into the house. "I'm so sorry for your loss, Rachel."

"I don't see how anything like this could have happened, Penny," she said. When we reached the kitchen, she threw her hands in the air and blurted out, "Bobby was the nicest guy in the world!"

"I can't imagine who would have wanted him dead," I agreed.

Rachel pushed her jet-black hair out of her eyes and took the casserole pan from me, and as I unpacked the comfort foods I had brought in the reusable bag, she tucked one item then the next into the refrigerator or pantry depending, and left the rest on the counter.

"You didn't have to go through all this trouble," she told me in a small voice.

"It's the least I could do. Plus, I wanted to come by and offer my support."

I removed my winter coat, mittens, and hat, getting comfortable.

Rachel was so beautiful that she didn't so much look like a widow who had just lost the love of her life, but rather like a movie star playing the role of one. Standing at 5'10", she glanced down at me with her huge, inky eyes, shook her head, and breathed:

"I don't know what I'm going to do without him."

"I think taking it one day at a time, or only one hour at a time, is the way to go."

"Your husband is investigating?" she asked, suddenly hopeful.

"I have full faith that Alan will catch whoever did this," I promised her. "He caught Edgar Swaine's killer last month."

"Did he mention anything to you about the protestors he talked to?" She blew her nose and tears welled up in her eyes. "Does he have any suspects yet? Any leads?"

I hadn't seen Alan since the movie theater last night, but all I had learned from him was that he strongly felt I should stay with my parents again. Of course, I had refused.

"I'm so sorry, Rachel, no. He didn't mention anything to me, but he really can't."

She nodded, understandingly. "Whoever did this must be one of those aggressive protestors, don't you think?"

"As a matter of fact, yes, that is what I think," I agreed. "Unless... Did anyone hate your husband?"

"I've been asking myself that very question all night, but no one comes to mind. Everyone loved Bobby. Everyone at Hopeful Heart Ministries loved him, and I mean *everyone* from Pastor Peter and his wife to all the boys that Bobby coached basketball. Plus, Bobby had his basketball buddies who would die for him, they loved him so much. We haven't even lived in Walnut Mountain that long."

"Only five years or so, right?"

"Something like that," she said, taking a moment to do the math. "I was living here about two years before you introduced me to Bobby, and the rest is history. I don't see why anyone from Walnut Mountain would want to kill my husband."

"That's why I agree that it could have been one of the protestors. Honestly, Rachel, I didn't recognize a lot of their faces."

"You didn't?"

I shook my head. "I really don't think the majority of them were local. Sometimes these political groups are state-wide and highly organized. They go from town to town. They try to make it seem as though a ton of residents are protesting, when in reality, it's all optics."

I chose not to mention my two colleagues from Walnut Mountain Middle School who had been at the helm of the protest as far as I could tell. I planned to talk to them, anyway, even though I doubted either of them could have taken Bobby Harder's life just because they objected to the religious purpose of his movie theater.

Treading as sensitively as possible, I asked Rachel, "Could anyone from Bobby's past have done this? Anyone from the modeling industry?"

She began racking her brain. Her dainty eyebrows knit together and her shapely lips narrowed into a thoughtful line. But soon she began shaking her head.

"I didn't know him from the industry, and since we got together, he's never mentioned much from his modeling days. But if I remember something, I'll let you know."

I told her that if she did, I would pass the information on to Alan, and then I insisted that she have a seat while I made coffee and toasted the blueberry muffins I had brought over.

All the while, I puzzled over who might have killed Bobby.

Yes, one of the protestors could have slipped into the movie theater and strangled him to death from behind, but I had a hard time believing that the killer's motive had to do with the protest itself. Taking Bobby's life seemed deeply personal, and the only way I could fathom a protestor killing Bobby was if the protestor also wanted Bobby dead for personal, and not strictly political, reasons.

Once the coffee was ready and I had toasted and buttered two blueberry muffins, I sat down with Rachel and we talked about everything from the upcoming Christmas holiday, to the Christmas pageant play I was directing at the church, to the ways in which I could emotionally support her throughout the holiday season. Rachel didn't want to be alone, but she also didn't know how she would carry on with life as usual. She wasn't sure if she could continue to volunteer at the church, and I assured her that Pastor Peter and the rest of the church administration would of course understand if Rachel needed to take time off, either temporarily or permanently.

"Bobby was my rock!" she exclaimed, popping up from the table and flinging herself towards the kitchen counter where she immediately dropped to her knees.

"Rachel?"

She threw the cabinet doors open and pulled a cardboard box out, which caused the bottles within to clank against one another.

"I've been struggling with my faith!" she cried, as she rose to her feet and shoved the cardboard box onto the kitchen table in front of me. "I've fallen off the wagon more times than I can count, and Bobby has always been there to help me get back on track!"

"Oh my," I breathed as I peered down into the box that contained twelve bottles of hard liquor. There was vodka and whiskey and gin and... the list went on. Most of the bottles were half empty. "Rachel, I had no idea."

"I don't know what I'm going to do without him, Penny! I'm an alcoholic!" she cried, collapsing onto her chair and burying her pretty face in both hands. "Bobby knew, but he had so much faith in me! He always said that I'm a *recovering* alcoholic, and that so long as I choose not to drink each day, I will strengthen my resolve. But he's gone now, Penny! Who is going to remind me each morning that I'm strong, and that I can face the day sober?"

I didn't know what to say. I deeply empathized with her. My own husband hadn't been killed, but I didn't have him to cheer me on every morning and remind me not to drink. I felt closer to Rachel than ever, and yet, I didn't dare admit to her that I was in the same boat. After all, how could the blind lead the blind and expect not to fall into a pit?

Rachel sobbed into her hands. I rubbed her shoulder and told her that it would be okay.

She lifted her puffy eyes and used a small voice to ask me, "Would you take it?"

"The box?"

"Please, Penny. If I have it here, then I'm just going to drink it. You can keep it all or dump it out, whatever you want. I just can't have it in the house or else I know I'll spend the rest of my life drunk."

"Yes, I'll take it. I had no idea…"

She wiped her eyes and sniffled. "No one had any idea, not even Bobby until a few months ago." She offered me a little, ashamed smile and shrugged. "Alcoholics know how to hide their addiction. Look at all these bottles. I had hid them throughout the house so Bobby wouldn't know."

Rachel might as well have been telling my story, and I suddenly felt less alone.

"When he found out about my *problem*," she went on. "I didn't have the heart to tell him about all the alcohol I had stashed around the house. I waited for him to go to coach basketball, and that's when I collected all the bottles. Oh, but Penny, I couldn't throw the bottles away or dump the booze down the drain!"

She wailed and sobbed into her hands all over again.

Rubbing her shoulder, I said, "There, there."

"I hid the box in the garage! There hasn't been one day that has gone by that I haven't thought about this box of booze! And then last night, when Alan came here to tell me the horrible news, I brought the box back inside!"

I empathized so greatly that I felt my heart might burst.

"Thank God, I didn't drink any of it," she added. "But I know I will unless you take it away."

"I will," I promised, as I gave her shoulder a loving squeeze and peered into the cardboard box at all the shiny bottles and the thick liquid of varying colors inside each one. "Stay strong, Rachel. One day at a time. You can do this."

"You're right," she said, sucking in a sniffling breath and becoming determined. "I can do it, and I *will* do it… for Bobby."

"For Bobby," I agreed, feeling mixed emotions—a twinge of guilt that I didn't fully understand, and a swell of excitement that warmed my chest.

After I bundled up, Rachel walked me to the door. I carried the box in my arms, so she opened the door for me.

"Thanks so much for stopping by, Penny, I really appreciate it."

"I'm here for you," I reminded her with a smile. "Please don't hesitate to reach out if you need a friend, no matter what time of day or night."

She bucked up and returned a smile, and I started down the walkway.

I placed the cardboard box full of alcohol in the trunk of my car and then climbed in behind the steering wheel. It took a moment to get the engine warmed up, but once it was, I backed out of the driveway.

No sooner than I had turned onto the road and shifted my sedan into Drive, a rusty pickup truck swung into Rachel's driveway and came to a screeching halt.

The driver jumped out of his idling truck and stomped his way up the stone walk and across the porch. He looked to be in his early 40s and had an angry expression on his rugged face.

I didn't recognize him from church or around town, but he had the same working class appearance as most of the Walnut Mountain residents. He was short and stocky, and wore a red plaid coat, blue jeans, and work boots.

He used a meaty fist to pound on the front door, and when Rachel answered, he immediately started yelling at her.

I couldn't hear what he was saying. The idling engine of my car was too loud, but the confrontation that was unfolding on the porch between Rachel and the angry man concerned me enough that I was about to climb out of my car to see what was going on.

But a moment later, Rachel crossed the porch and pointed at something. It looked like she was trying to reason with the man by offering explanations. He planted his fists on his hips, nodded, and eyed whatever she had pointed at.

I let out a rocky breath.

They knew each other, and whatever they were discussing was none of my business.

I drove off and tried not to worry about the uneasy feeling that was rising in my gut.

CHAPTER THREE

"YOU DON'T HAPPEN TO have my order ready to go, do you?" I asked Gloria with a smile as soon as I got to the counter.

Morning Glory, the local coffee shop, was bustling with early risers who needed their caffeine fix before tackling a big day of Christmas shopping.

"The muffins finished baking only a moment ago, and Dex is packing them up for you," said Gloria as she pushed her big hair from her shoulders and patted the powdered sugar off her hands, which caused little white clouds to billow from her apron. "I can't believe what happened to Bobby Harder last night."

"That makes two of us," I said, as she worked behind the counter, pouring coffee into to-go cups and sliding them into a carrying tray. "I stopped by Rachel's a bit earlier and let her know that the entire congregation is here for her."

"That was kind of you, Penny," she said. A somber look washed over Gloria's expression and she asked, "Alan is investigating?"

Gloria didn't have much faith in Alan in terms of his ability to investigate a homicide. When Gloria's fiancé, Edgar Swaine, had been murdered, Alan had believed Gloria was responsible, and had even arrested her. The opinions she had formed in her mind about Alan based on that weren't good to say the least, and she and I had gotten into quite an argument about it.

I could tell that she didn't want to open old wounds, but she was obviously concerned that if Alan was on the case, then Bobby's killer might not be caught. Her concern was written all over her face.

"Yes, Alan is in charge, and as far as I know, he worked all night and into the wee hours of the morning, interviewing everyone who attended the movie and everyone who was near the theater."

"He certainly tried to speak to me, but what could I say? That documentary put me right to sleep!" she said.

"You're not the only one. Alan certainly has his work cut out for him. If that film hadn't been so dreadfully boring, he would have at least a dozen witnesses at his disposal."

"If that film hadn't been so dreadfully boring," Gloria countered, "then I doubt the killer would have chosen to murder Bobby at the movies."

"You make a good point."

"If you ask me, Penny, you were the one who got to the bottom of things as far as catching Edgar's killer. Alan wasted so much time suspecting innocent people—"

"Oh, I don't know that he wasted *so much time*—"

"You might not agree, but I feel compelled to tell you that if Alan wants to find out who killed Bobby Harder, he could use your input as he investigates," she maintained, her tone full of conviction.

I had to laugh at that. "Alan would hardly appreciate my input. My goodness, Gloria, I don't want to insult him. Plus, I don't have the slightest clue as to who strangled Bobby."

Gloria's big eyes went white all around. "He was *strangled?*"

"You didn't know?"

She shook her head, horrified, and then came to her senses. "All I'm saying is that, you have a knack for sleuthing."

"I appreciate the compliment, but right now, it's far more important that I focus on *directing* the church's Christmas play and leave the *investigating* to my husband."

She brightened and asked, "How *is* the Christmas pageant coming along?"

I sighed. "I've never directed a play before. My only saving grace is that I know how to work with kids."

"I'm sure it will be great!"

From the back of the kitchen, Dex muttered a string of curse words loud enough for us to hear.

Gloria shouted over her shoulder, "You alright back there?"

"Fine!" he called out. "Be right out!"

Gloria made a face and shook her head.

Dex grumbled, "Unbelievable," and Gloria narrowed her eyes thoughtfully.

"Maybe I should check on him," she told me, excusing herself.

"Take your time."

She left the tray of to-go coffees on the counter in front of me. I found mine and took a sip, all the while feeling on edge about the box of Rachel's liquor that was still in the trunk of my car. I reasoned I would deal with it when I got home after church.

Moments later, Gloria and Dex emerged from the back, Gloria carrying a to-go bag full of freshly baked muffins and Dex carrying the heavy burden of whatever was on his mind.

"Here you go, Penny," she said, handing me the bag. "Have a great day, and we'll see you soon!"

I stepped aside, making room for the next customer, and carefully picked up the to-go tray of coffee.

Behind the counter, Dex was too distracted by whatever he was peering at in his hands to hear Gloria ask him if he had mixed batter in the back like she had asked him to do earlier.

"Earth to Dex?" she teased.

"Hmm?"

She rolled her eyes and started for the back, having completely given up on him.

When Dex muttered under his breath, I couldn't contain my curiosity.

"Is there something wrong?"

"There's a lot wrong," he complained, lifting his green eyes. "The government should stay out of people's paychecks."

I gleaned that Dex had been eyeing his paystub and didn't like how expensive the tax withholdings had become. He had recently switched from working at Morning Glory part-time to working full-time in a salaried position, and was now facing the harsh realities that came with understanding that the more money you made, the greater the tax withholdings.

"Welcome to adulthood," I teased. "Could you get the door for me?"

As Dex rounded out from behind the counter and walked me to the door, he vented, "Have you looked into where our tax dollars are going these days? I have. I shouldn't have to pay for other people's insanity."

I chuckled, in part because I agree, but also because life experience had taught me that there were more things outside of my control than within it.

"I'm going to vote libertarian from now on," he declared, as he opened the door for me. "What this state needs is as little government interference as possible."

"Amen," I said in wholehearted agreement, as I stepped out into the blustery winter morning.

✝

THE DRIVE FROM Morning Glory to Hopeful Heart Ministries took longer than usual thanks to the tray of to-go coffees on the passenger seat. I took each turn carefully, and soon I arrived at the church.

As I pulled my car around, coming into the parking lot, I noticed Pastor Peter outside kneeling in the snow not too far from the life-sized nativity scene that my father had built recently. The pastor was stacking stones, one on top of the next, making what appeared to be a little pillar.

I parked my car and made careful work of carrying the tray of coffee and the bag of warm muffins with me as I walked to the front of the church where Pastor Peter was now dusting the snow off his knees and marveling at the stone pillar he had constructed.

"Morning, Pastor Peter!"

"Good morning, Penny," he said, staring down at his work.

"Coffee?" I asked, offering him one of the to-go cups as I neared him.

He used the cup to warm his hands and took a few gulps, as I suddenly realized what the stone pillar reminded me of.

"Didn't Jacob build a stone pillar in Genesis after he had a vision of God?" I asked.

Impressed, Pastor Peter told me, "Yes, and a few chapters later, after Jacob wrestled with the Angel of God all night, he built a stone pillar to mark the spot, too."

I studied the pastor for a moment, contemplating the significance of the stone pillar he had stacked here in front of the church.

Pastor Peter was a mild-mannered man in his early 50s. Today he was wearing a thick sweater and corduroy slacks. I wondered how Bobby's murder might be affecting him, if the very next day he was re-enacting a story from Genesis.

Trying to come across light and upbeat, I asked him, "Did you have a vision of the Lord last night, Pastor Peter?"

He smiled and seemed to sink into deep thought as he took a quick sip of his coffee.

"Something like that," he allowed, falling into even deeper rumination.

He didn't say more and I didn't ask, as we both stared down at the stone pillar. Each stone he had used was roughly the size of a deflated basketball, and the pillar stood no taller than three feet.

"I don't want to be late for rehearsal," I said softly.

As I turned on my heel, Pastor Peter said, "Oh, Penny?"

"Yes?" I replied, turning to face him once again.

"To the modern-day world, God's justice looks like evil."

I felt my smile falter, and the hairs on the back of my neck stood on end.

Considering Bobby's murder and the fact that Pastor Peter had been at the movie theater last night, his weird statement sent a chill through my bones that I couldn't easily shake.

I tried to smile, found my voice, and said, "I'll keep that in mind."

He nodded and returned his attention to the stone pillar he had built.

I wasted no time heading inside the church where I hoped the warm air and Christmas spirit would ward off the dark feeling that Pastor Peter had given me.

My assistant and stage manager, Ashley, must have seen me through the windows, because as soon as I crossed the vestibule, she was ready to help.

"Let me get that for you!" she exclaimed, as she took the tray of coffee from me before my wrist could give out. "I'm so glad you're here. The kids are being impossible!"

A twenty-year old college senior, Ashley was home for the holidays and eager to gain any theatrical experience she could since she was a theater major concentrating in theater management and administration.

Ordinarily, she was cute as a button and twice as perky, but today she seemed frazzled.

"What's going on?" I asked as I set the bag of muffins on the narrow table in the vestibule and removed my winter coat.

"I tried to get them started with 'duck, duck, goose' as a morning game to play while the other kids gradually arrived."

"Good," I said encouragingly. We had gone over how to keep the children occupied when they first arrived for rehearsal since their parents tended to drop them off during a wide, twenty-minute window. Playing 'duck, duck, goose' was one of the games we came up with. "Are they not getting along?"

Ashley sighed in such a manner that caused her petite figure to slump into a defeated hunch. "The older kids immediately objected to the game, complaining that the game itself implies that ducks and geese are not equal."

I burst out laughing.

Ashley frowned.

"This isn't funny," she grumbled. "What the heck is going on at their school that has caused them to be suspicious of simple children's games. As if playing 'duck, duck, goose' was a training program for injustice…"

My colleague, Samantha, and her severe social justice ideology came to mind, but I kept that to myself. Instead, I took off my winter hat, covered my head with a sequin chemo cap, and mentioned, "We should get started in a few minutes anyway, but if you tell me who the instigators were, I can have a quick talk with them beforehand."

Ashley used a quiet tone of voice to name the specific children, as we entered the fellowship hall, which was across from the sanctuary.

Like a good stage manager, Ashley had arrived a half-hour ago and moved all of the tables to the back of the room so that we would have plenty of space to rehearse the Christmas pageant. Unfortunately, this meant that the children had all the room in the world to run around and act crazy, which they were at the moment.

There were twelve kids. Their ages ranged from seven to thirteen, though most of them were my middle school students and therefore about eleven years old or so.

"I don't know how you do it, Penny," she went on, rolling up her sleeves as we neared the center of the room and prepared to wrangle the children. "The public school curriculum has been introducing a lot of whacky concepts, and these kids are mentally soaking it up like sponges."

"I'm careful about what I say to my students and how I say it," I explained.

"Even when the government hands down radical course material?"

"It's not as radical as you might think."

Ashley didn't seem convinced. "I think the government should stay out of the schools and let teachers do their jobs. I mean, my God. Thanks to the government, Timmy thinks that ducks are a marginalized group of second-class bird-citizens that have been oppressed by geese for far too long. He actually thinks the game 'duck, duck, goose' was created by insensitive humans to mock their plight!"

I had to chuckle at that.

Ashley muttered under her breath, "The government should stay out of *everything*, as far as I'm concerned."

Huh.

I studied Ashley as she brooded over the ulterior motives and perhaps-nefarious objectives of the state education department. She was pretty and virtuous and only a few years younger than Dex...

I wonder...

Ashley clapped her hands and whistled loudly, starting the arduous task of getting the kids' attention. I shouted over their cackling laughter, asking everyone to stand in a circle so that we could hold hands for our pre-rehearsal prayer.

Once the children were properly gathered and holding hands, I prayed on behalf of the group, and as we always did during each prayer, we went around the circle and shared what we were grateful for today.

When it was my turn, I thanked the Lord for blessing me with the opportunity to serve him by directing the Christmas pageant, and I shared that I was grateful for each and every child that was here with me today...

...which was true, but it wasn't the whole truth.

I was grateful for the fact that working with the kids at church was distracting me from how lonely I had been feeling ever since Alan had moved into a motel.

I didn't want to be alone on Christmas.

And I knew that if I wasn't here directing the Christmas pageant, I would definitely spend my downtime alone at the cabin trying desperately not to drink.

✞

AFTER REHEARSAL, ASHLEY brought the kids down to the vestibule and waited with them until their parents arrived to pick them up, while I put the fellowship hall back in order, which involved returning our pageant props to the designated closet and dragging the tables where they belonged.

With the room organized for the afternoon Bible study group, I made my way into the vestibule where Ashley was waving goodbye to the last child.

"Great work today," I told her.

Ashley found her coat and began bundling up. "Thanks," she said, sounding a bit defeated. "I feel like all I'm doing is sitting there and not doing much."

"Things will get rolling once the children learn their lines," I assured her, becoming a bit distracted.

My dad, Lucas, was in the sanctuary with Pastor Peter. I spied them through the open doorway. Dad was using an electric screwdriver to assemble the Christmas pageant set that the children would soon rehearse on. Pastor Peter stood over him with his arms folded, and they seemed to be having a disagreement of some kind.

Arguing to any extent wasn't like Pastor Peter. I had always known him to be agreeable to a fault. Yet, there he was, shaking his head and barking at my father about wood shavings, splinters, and the birth of Christ.

Why was the pastor behaving so strangely?

"When do you think the set will be ready for the kids to rehearse on?" Ashley asked me excitedly when she noticed what had stolen my attention.

"You know, I'm not sure," I said.

"Hopefully, the kids will have plenty of time to memorize their blocking by rehearsing on the performance stage."

I was tempted to simply ask my father when he expected to be finished putting the scenery together, but I hesitated, feeling slightly wary.

I wouldn't go so far as to say that my dad had betrayed me, but I felt uncomfortable, and frankly upset, that Alan and my father had gotten in the habit of talking about me behind my back, a fact that Alan had let slip to me last month. Apparently, my dad had told Alan that I hadn't yet announced to the world that I was an alcoholic. Alan agreed with him that I should. I didn't think it had been fair of my father to act like a spy and report information about me back to my husband.

But was this a big enough transgression to make a stink over?

Probably not, which was why I hadn't confronted my dad about how his secret conversations with Alan made me feel.

"Whoa," Ashley breathed, her gaze having locked on whoever was now entering the church vestibule. She whispered, "Hottie alert," and elbowed me in the ribs.

I turned to find my husband breezing through the entryway and looking like a wind-kissed mountain man who could set a girl's heart on fire.

Dressed in a winter coat that hugged his muscular arms and a pair of blue jeans that hugged everything else, Alan raked his fingers through his thick, dark hair and locked his blue eyes on me.

Ashley whispered, "Do you know him?"

"That's my husband, Alan."

Her jaw dropped, and as he approached us, a huge, dopey grin formed on Ashley's face.

Using no preamble, Alan asked me, "Have you seen the pastor?"

I hadn't seen Alan in weeks, and finding Pastor Peter was the only thing on his mind when he ran into me unexpectedly?

"He's in the sanctuary with my dad," I told him.

"Hello!" said Ashley, so delightfully anxious to meet Alan that she was unable to control the volume of her voice. "I'm Penny's stage manager, Ashley."

"Alan Matchmaker," he said, introducing himself. "But everyone calls me Detective Match," he added, which surprised the heck out of me.

Detective Match?

That was new...

"Detective?" she asked, thoroughly impressed. "What kind of detective?"

"Homicide," he said curtly.

The moment he spotted Pastor Peter through the open doorway, he excused himself and crossed into the sanctuary.

"What a hunk!" said Ashley. Her cheeks flushed red, she felt so flattered to have shaken Alan's manly hand. "I would kill to be with a guy like that! What a cool name, 'Detective Match'."

I frowned. "His last name is *Matchmaker*... He must be having an identity crisis," I muttered under my breath, annoyed.

But soon annoyance gave way to overwhelming curiosity as I watched Alan confront Pastor Peter on the far side of the sanctuary.

Did Alan suspect the pastor of having murdered Bobby Harder? Was that why Pastor Peter had been acting so strange?

CHAPTER FOUR

WALNUT MOUNTAIN MIDDLE School was blanketed in a thick layer of snow on Monday morning. The little brick schoolhouse looked picturesque. Even the Christmas decorations the children had hung outside were dusted with white snowflakes.

Snow crunched under my boots, as I made my way towards the building with a warm to-go cup of coffee in my mittened hands.

This was the last week of school before the winter recess, and I already sensed it would be challenging to keep my students focused when all they would want to do is bounce off the walls in thrilled anticipation of the Christmas holiday while imagining the presents they hoped Santa would bring.

Entering the teachers' lounge, I shoved my mittens into the pockets of my winter coat, and when I reached the coat rack, I began unbundling and getting organized, as snow melted off my boots.

I wasn't the first teacher to arrive. Janice and Harriet, who taught art, were quietly conversing near the coffeemaker. Principal Garth Longchamp was seated at the largest table. He poured himself over the local newspaper he was reading, which had printed a front-page story about Bobby Harder's murder.

With my purse over my shoulder, I gulped my Morning Glory coffee and found Esther at one of the small round tables near the windows.

Esther wore a slouchy knit beanie on her head that matched her cranberry-colored dress. She locked eyes with me as soon as I sat.

She leaned forward and discreetly whispered:

"Have you seen Matthew and Samantha?"

"No, why?" I whispered as quietly as possible.

Esther was interrupted from divulging whatever news had rattled her when Principal Longchamp stood from his table and asked, "Ready, Esther?"

"Of course!" she told him with a smile. She whispered to me, "Let's talk after school. I have to see Garth now." A frustrated look came over her. "A handful of my students didn't pass the pop quiz on long division I gave them last week, and I might have to spend the lunchtime recess tutoring them."

"Oh no!"

"It's *that* time of year," she calmly explained as she gathered her tote bag and coffee. "Once we resume classes in January, I'm sure my students will do just fine, but for now I need to figure out how to get them to concentrate well enough to pass the next math quiz I have planned for the middle of this week."

"Garth will have good ideas," I said to encourage her.

"I'm counting on it," she agreed as she stood up.

She crossed the teachers' lounge and met the principal near the entryway, and they left together, heading for his office.

The warning bell rang throughout the schoolhouse, indicating that classes would start in five minutes. I gulped the rest of my coffee, collected my purse, and pushed my chair in as soon as I stood up.

Just then, Samantha and Matthew strolled into the teachers' lounge bringing the cold from outside with them and giggling like a pair of lovestruck teenagers.

Matthew's glasses fogged up as they hung their coats on the rack, and when Samantha noticed, she threw her head back, cackled to high heaven, and gave the firm wall of his chest a flirtatious smack.

"Silly!" she sang, as she shook out her long, flowing blonde hair.

"*You're* silly," said Matthew.

"You're both silly," I grumbled under my breath, making my way to the coffeemaker.

I refilled my to-go cup at the counter, all too aware that the chemistry between Samantha and Matthew seemed off, if not poorly timed. They had both been questioned by Alan regarding Bobby Harder's murder, and yet, here they were only a few days later laughing it up together at school.

I told myself not to confront either of them, but I ended up doing the opposite when I heard Samantha say:

"With Bobby out of the way, it's only a matter of time before *Christian* Cinemas becomes Walnut Mountain Movies and the residents of this town can breathe easy."

What?

I touched eyes with Matthew, who looked instantly embarrassed by Samantha's blatant lack of compassion.

I might have been able to hold my tongue if Samantha hadn't joined me at the counter to fill her thermos with coffee.

She angled her sharp green eyes at me, beamed a wide smile, and said, "Isn't karma wonderful?"

Pressing the lid on my to-go cup of coffee, I said, "What are you talking about?"

Matthew swooped in and told Samantha, "We don't want to be late for First Period."

She ignored him and responded smugly to my question. "Bobby thought he could exclude people from his movie theater, which was wrong of him, and now he's dead."

There were so many things I could've said to her, but I went with, "As far as I understand, the protestors are the biggest suspects at this point."

"The protestors weren't allowed in the movie theater," she countered, staring down her perfectly shaped nose at me. "Nor would any of us have wanted to go inside given the discriminatory film that was playing."

"Let's not be late for classes," Matthew said again, this time more urgently.

"You objected to the movie theater?" I challenged him just as the bell rang loudly, indicating that I should be standing at the front of my classroom right now.

As Matthew mentally formulated his response, Samantha flicked her gorgeous blonde hair off her shoulder, smirked at me, and said:

"Anyone who turns a blind eye to how offensive their business is deserves to die, and Karma with a capital 'K' agrees."

"Bobby wasn't killed by karma," I argued, losing my temper. "He was killed by someone who wanted him dead, and sooner or later, that person will face God's judgment as a result."

Samantha cackled to high heaven, turned on her very high heel, and swayed her way out of the teachers' lounge, leaving Matthew to make all kinds of excuses for her callous attitude.

"What has gotten into you, Matthew?" I demanded, interrupting his groveling explanations. "It's one thing to protest the movie theater, not that I understand why you would. But it's quite another to stand shoulder to shoulder with a woman who is literally laughing at the murder as though Bobby's death is good news."

"Wait, now, hang on, Penny—"

"Bobby Harder was the nicest guy in the world! He didn't deserve—"

"I agree. I don't think he should've been killed—"

"Your new girlfriend does!"

A weird grin came over Matthew as if the very thought of Samantha being his girlfriend thoroughly elated him.

"You're a Christian, for God's sake," I went on. "How could you protest a Christian movie theater?"

"Well, Samantha really opened my eyes—"

"Oh, I bet," I balked sarcastically.

"Hang on, now, Penny. I may be a church-attending Christian, but I happen to think that Christians shouldn't exalt themselves. Plus, I happen to like secular movies!"

"You happen to like the shape of Samantha's—"

We both startled at the sound of feedback blaring through the P.A. system. Principal Garth Longchamp's voice came through the speakers, as he made a quick announcement about the upcoming winter recess break.

"Do you know something about Bobby's murder?" I asked Matthew, point blank.

"I have to get to class," he said darkly.

By the time I reached my own classroom, I had formulated ideas about Samantha seducing Matthew into murdering Bobby Harder, and realized I wasn't far from losing my dang mind.

Complicating matters was how creeped out I felt every time I remembered that Bobby had been killed in the seat beside me while I had *slept*.

My students were behaving as chaotically as I felt, I discovered when I walked into the room.

I closed the door behind me and set my purse on my desk at the front of the classroom.

"Sorry I'm late, everyone!" I shouted. "Settle down, please, and take your seats!"

A group of boys was tossing a basketball between them. I crossed the room and intercepted it, as the rest of my students found their desks.

"Awe, come on!" complained Nathan, who was easily the most athletic boy at Walnut Mountain Middle School thanks to his astounding height and his parents' encouragement.

Nathan stood at 60 inches—or 5'—which was unusually tall for an eleven-year old boy. He was enrolled in the youth basketball program at Hopeful Heart Ministries even though his parents weren't Christian, and as far as I knew, he also played soccer and baseball when those sports were in season.

"You can play basketball during recess," I reminded him.

Nathan screwed his boyish face up and plopped onto his chair. He folded his arms in a huff and glared at me through his thin eyebrows.

"What's the use?" he complained. "With Bobby gone, who's going to coach us now?"

"Bobby was the best," another student said, his spirits plummeting at the realization that the man he had looked up to was no longer around.

A boy in the back added, "I want to grow to be 7-feet tall just like Bobby!"

"Bobby wasn't 7-feet tall!" Nathan corrected him, having spun around on his chair. "He was 6-foot-5!"

Nathan's eyes welled up with tears, and I felt my heart swell with sympathy for all of them who had lost the basketball coach they had loved.

At moments like this, all I really knew how to do was pray, but given that Walnut Mountain was a public school, I was prohibited.

So, I did the next best thing.

"Today, we're going to write about our heroes and compose paragraphs that explain why we love and admire those people. Doing this kind of writing is a great way to make sense of complicated emotions we may feel when our heroes and the wonderful people we look up to pass away."

✝

AFTER SCHOOL, ESTHER and I decided to meet in the heart of Walnut Mountain since she needed to do some Christmas shopping. This would be her first Christmas with Daniel, her new man, and she wanted everything to be perfect, from the present she bought him to the dinner she cooked.

We meandered side-by-side down Main Street where all the shops were twinkling with strings of white lights. Esther had good instincts about which stores to go into, and we otherwise window shopped as we went, admiring the festive window displays of each boutique we passed.

"I can't believe Matthew has gotten involved with Samantha," I said, as we paused on the sidewalk in front of a bookstore that also sold greeting cards. "I did not see that one coming."

"I wonder if they're really involved," she countered, lifting a single eyebrow. "I'm sure Matthew would like to be, but I think Samantha is just using him."

"Using him for what?" I had my suspicions, but I wanted to hear what Esther thought without my input.

"I believe Matthew was the one who did all the heavy lifting in terms of organizing the protest. He's trying to work his way into Samantha's heart. He doesn't realize that she doesn't have one."

"What kind of heavy lifting?"

"He built a website for her."

"A website?" I was puzzled.

Esther found her cell phone in the front pocket of her thick winter coat, pulled up the website she was referring to, and handed me her phone.

As I scrolled through the homepage of a website called, Walnut Mountain Warriors, Esther got me up to speed on what she had found out about the science teacher, Matthew, the social studies teacher, Samantha, and the murder at the movies.

"Matthew isn't just a science teacher. He also knows computer science, and not only did he build that Walnut Mountain Warriors website from scratch, he also invited other activists around Vermont to come to the protest at Christian Cinemas."

"I knew it," I said as I locked eyes with her. "I didn't recognize half of those protestors the other night."

"That's because a lot of them were from Burlington and other cities," she explained, leaning in and tapping on the LCD screen until the Join Our Cause web page opened. "The entire mission of

Walnut Mountain Warriors is to unite the 'social justice warriors' of Vermont in one place, Walnut Mountain."

"Why, oh, why would Matthew want to involve himself in this?" I asked even though we both knew the answer.

Love was a powerful motivator for both good and evil…

Not that a politically motivated organization was automatically evil, but as far as I was concerned, Samantha was.

I supposed I wasn't feeling especially Christian at the moment, but I couldn't get the sounds of her loud cackling out of my head. Bobby's murder had tickled her. There was something seriously wrong with that.

Even so, did I really think she had something to do with strangling Bobby?

"There's a men's boutique next door," Esther realized. "I have no idea what to get Daniel for Christmas."

"Let's check it out."

As we entered the store, the scents of black spruce, cedar, and other manly spices filled the air.

"What did you get Alan for Christmas when you two started getting serious after high school?" she asked me as we browsed around the men's colognes and a display rack of designer ties that I had never seen a single man from Walnut Mountain wear other than the attorneys who worked at Milton Cranston's law firm on Lake Way.

"My God, that must have been seven lifetimes ago…" I replied, drifting into nostalgic memories of my husband, our frisky engagement, and the heartfelt Christmases we had shared year after year throughout our youth.

"Daniel isn't really a 'cologne guy'," she said as she returned one of the bottles to the display rack. "I could get him a Bible, but that doesn't seem personal enough for some reason…"

"You can't go wrong with a travel-sized toolkit for his truck," I suggested. "Men can never have too many toolkits. Maybe a pair of comfy slippers for around the house?"

"Did you once give Alan a toolkit for Christmas?" she asked, double-checking as we made our way into the back of the store where electronics and other everyday accessories were located.

"I believe so. My mother certainly gives my dad some kind of toolkit every year, but Dad is easy. As long as he gets flannel pajamas and a coffee mug that decrees his domestic status—'King of the Castle,' 'Master of the Remote Control,' or 'I'm In Charge Once I Finish This Coffee,' he's happy."

"Lucas is hilarious." Chuckling, Esther perused the vanity mugs that were lined on a shelving unit, but none of them captured her blossoming relationship with Daniel. "Oh!"

I whipped around to see what had startled Esther and found Daniel emerging from the men's dressing rooms.

"Esther, darling," he exclaimed, as he gave her a kiss on the cheek.

Esther laughed, clutched her chest, and said, "You surprised me! What are you doing here?"

"What am *I* doing here?" he teased. "What are *you* doing in a men's store?"

She playfully shot him a sideways glance and promised, "Not Christmas shopping for you, that's for sure."

"Ha, ha," he said. "Penny, it's nice to see you. Happy holidays. How are those storm shutters holding up at your parents' cabin?"

"Great, as far as I know. Dad has been very happy."

Daniel turned serious and a glimmer of concern darkened his already dark eyes.

"How's the investigation coming along?" he asked. "Alan spoke to Esther and I briefly, but we couldn't tell him much since that documentary film put both of us straight to sleep."

I had grown accustomed to dodging these kinds of questions, so I replied with my usual response.

"Even though Alan is my husband, he really can't share with me the details of his investigation, unfortunately. That being said, I'm personally wondering about a few people..."

Daniel's eyebrows shot up to his hairline. Esther leaned in, and soon we were huddled closely enough that I could whisper.

"I believe a few people are suspicious," I began. Daniel and Esther were all ears. "First of all, no one can overlook the protestors. Though it pains me to consider that Matthew or Samantha, who Esther and I work with at the middle school, could have been behind Bobby's murder, I can't rule them out at this point. Even more bizarre is the fact that Alan came to the church the other morning to question Pastor Peter."

"He did?" Esther asked just as Daniel blurted out:

"Why would Pastor Peter kill Bobby?"

"Shh," I breathed. "I don't know why Pastor Peter would have killed Bobby, but I have to admit that the pastor has been acting very strange. The morning after the murder, I found him building a little stone pillar in front of the church and he seemed a million miles away mentally. But that's not what was so strange. He told me that morning that to modern-day people, God's justice resembles evil."

"What an eerie thing to say after Bobby's murder," said Esther.

"I couldn't agree more," I told her before sharing with them the last suspect who had been on my mind for days. "I stopped by to check on Rachel Harder the morning after the killing," I continued, "and as I was leaving, a man stormed up to her porch, pounded on the door, and confronted her about something. At first, I thought he was going to attack her, but after a moment, she seemed to know him and the confrontation became conversational. Still, I found it peculiar."

"Do you think it was a friend of Bobby's?" Esther asked, equally puzzled.

"I really don't know, but my gut instinct tells me that the guy had a real problem with Bobby. I don't see why a true friend of Bobby's would treat Rachel that way. Oh! And I almost forgot. There was a new fence at their house—"

"I bet I know who the guy was," said Daniel all of a sudden.

"Really?" I asked, surprised.

"Was it a black wrought iron fence?"

I felt my jaw drop. "How did you know that?"

"The guy was probably Vince Salisbury of Salisbury Landscaping and Fencing," he explained. "Vince drives a rusty pickup truck—"

"Yes!" I exclaimed. "That's the kind of vehicle he had!"

Daniel nodded and sank into deep thought. "I run into Vince from time to time at the hardware store. When I saw him last, he told me how he had installed a black wrought iron fence, but the customer stiffed him and wouldn't pay up even though Vince had finished the job and done good work. Vince was furious about it. His face turned beat red as he told me about it. He said if the customer didn't pay up, he was going to kill him."

CHAPTER FIVE

AS THE WEEK UNFOLDED, my curiosity about Vince Salisbury, the angry man I had seen confronting Rachel Harder, grew to intolerable heights.

According to Daniel, Vince was upset with the Harders for not paying him once he had installed their new black wrought iron fence. Vince had been mad enough to threaten to kill Bobby, maybe not to Bobby's face, but he had definitely vented to Daniel, stating in no uncertain terms that if Bobby didn't pay up, then Vince was *going to kill him*.

On the one hand, I knew that people who felt swept up in uncontrollable emotions could say all kinds of stuff they didn't mean. Just because Vince had blown off some steam, complaining to Daniel in the hardware store, didn't mean that he had actually taken Bobby's life.

But on the other hand, I wanted to know the full story. Why had Bobby stiffed Vince? As far as I knew, it wasn't like Bobby to refuse to pay a contractor. Doing so would be akin to stealing, and like my virtuous husband, Bobby had also committed himself to living up to the Ten Commandments.

So, why hadn't Bobby and Rachel paid Vince for their new fence?

What had Rachel said to Vince that morning to calm his rage, and why had she pointed in the direction of Pastor Peter's side of the property line?

Soon my curiosity became overwhelming.

I was unfamiliar with Salisbury Landscaping & Fencing, but discovered that the business was located in the neighboring mountain town of Corinth.

Having waited until Saturday to make the trip out to Corinth, I bundled up, picked a winding, scenic route to drive through the valleys of Walnut Mountain and into Corinth. Corinth was a quaint, one-horse town with Colonial houses and sprawling hills.

Vince's fencing business was tucked at the snowy end of a rural road, not too far from the heart of town. I knew they were open today with shortened hours. There were only a few parking spots out front, so I pulled into the one that was closest to the entrance.

The building itself was hardly bigger than a construction trailer. Outside stood a wide variety of model fences and I noticed excavation equipment lined up on the opposite side of the building. Most of the equipment was draped with tarps, though the winds and snowfall had exposed the machinery to the harsh Vermont elements.

As I entered the little building, a bell jangled overhead. The anteroom was small and warm, and I was immediately confronted with four boys of varying ages. I guessed the boys' ages ranged from five to twelve years-old, the eldest taking care of the youngest. There were school books open on the coffee table and floor in front of them.

"Hello," I said, greeting the boys with a smile.

All four of them began playfully shouting, "Dad! Customer! Dad, you have a customer!"

They *did* look like brothers, I realized. Their hair was reddish-brown and full of cowlicks. Freckles spanned their button noses, and they all wore denim overalls.

Before long, the angry man I had spied confronting Rachel emerged from the rear office and entered the anteroom, coming towards the business side of the front counter.

"Good afternoon," I said.

"What can I help you with?" he asked, as he tucked a pencil behind his ear.

Now that he was standing before me, he didn't appear half as intimidating as he had seemed at Rachel's. Though he was short with a stocky build, he looked strong and friendly. He wore a tee-shirt and blue jeans with a casual, button-down flannel shirt, and an old baseball cap on his head.

"Are you Vince Salisbury?" I asked, making absolutely certain that I was speaking with the right man.

"That's me," he said.

I had more or less mentally worked out how I would get him to open up, so I hoped for the best, and told him:

"I'm a friend of Rachel Harder's, and I'm here to resolve the dispute you have with the Harders, if possible."

Vince narrowed his steel-blue eyes on me and clenched his jaw, as if he wasn't sure I could be trusted.

"I understand that the Harders have an open invoice?" I mentioned.

"Are you here to pay for their fence?"

As I found my checkbook in my purse, I asked, "Could you tell me what happened?"

Since I hadn't answered his question, he studied me for a tense moment.

"How much is the balance that's due?" I asked, encouraging him to trust me and open up.

Resting on the counter was a file organizer, among other ad hoc office items—a mug full of pens and pencils, a stapler and a staple remover, and a snow globe and other tchotchkes.

He thumbed through the file folders until he found the right one, then slid the printed invoice on the counter in front of me.

I felt my jaw drop.

Apparently, quality wrought iron was more expensive than gold...

That being said, for a former male model like Bobby Harder who had made millions during the course of his lucrative high fashion modeling career, I doubted that the cost of the fence was what had influenced Bobby to withhold the payment.

"May I take this?" I asked, referring to the invoice. "I should consult with my husband..."

"Yeah, right," he muttered, sounding defeated. "Knock yourself out."

"Was Bobby disputing the price?" I asked.

Vince shook his head. "The guy said I didn't install the new fence on the property line correctly. The whole thing turned into a huge fight. You see, in order for me to get started, I asked Bobby to provide me with the land survey of his property."

"The land survey shows all of the boundary lines between

Bobby's property and the neighbors' properties?"

"Exactly. The survey wasn't wrong. I installed the fence perfectly. But Bobby thought that the western side of the fence was over the property line. The guy wanted me to *move* the western side of the fence about three feet *east*."

"Pick up and move the wrought iron fence *closer* to his house by three feet?"

Vince let out an exasperated-sounding laugh. "Can you believe it? Hey, I didn't put up a fight and I was more than happy to accommodate, even though Bobby was wrong about the property line. But I told him that he had to pay for the work that I'd done so far. Once he paid up, *then* I would come up with an estimate for the additional work. Well, he didn't think that was fair. He wanted me to move the western side of the fence at no charge and he said he wasn't going to pay me a dime until I did!"

"That doesn't sound fair," I agreed.

"No kidding."

"Plus, the western side of the property line is basically trees and not much else…" I said, thinking out loud.

The western property line was *also* the boundary line that separated the Harders' land from Pastor Peter's…

"Knowing Bobby," I went on, "there has to be more to the story."

"Yeah, there's more to the story, alright. Bobby Harder is a pretty boy with a cold heart who doesn't give a damn that without his payment, I'm not going to be able to give my boys a proper Christmas."

I didn't happen to agree with his impression of Bobby, but my heart filled with compassion for Vince and his sons. I was also struck with the fact that Vince was speaking of Bobby in the present tense, as though he hadn't heard that Bobby Harder had been murdered.

Or had Vince killed Bobby? Was he choosing his words carefully, speaking of Bobby as though he were still alive so that I wouldn't suspect him?

I folded the invoice and tucked it into my purse. "Give me a day. I would like to clear the debt, I just need to check with my husband since the balance due is more than I had anticipated."

Vince brightened, hope glimmering in his eyes. "That would be much appreciated."

I smiled at the boys on my way out and wondered how I was going to convince my husband that paying for a dead man's fence would be the right thing to do this Christmas.

✝

I HAD ONLY CHECKED on Rachel once during the week, so after leaving Salisbury Landscaping & Fencing, I returned to Walnut Mountain and drove straight to Rachel's house, figuring that I could cook lunch and ask her about the boundary line dispute that had arisen between Vince and Bobby.

There was a good six inches of fresh snow in Rachel's driveway, which told me she hadn't left the house or driven anywhere since it had last snowed.

I parked next to her car, which was also covered in a thick blanket of snow, and climbed out with my purse slung over my shoulder, the folded invoice tucked inside.

As I made my way up the icy walk and onto the porch, the steps of which hadn't been salted, I kept glancing over towards Pastor Peter's side of the boundary line where the black wrought iron fence stood, looking frosted with white snow and sparkling icicles.

I believed that Vince Salisbury had used the land survey and that the fence had been properly installed on the boundary line. What I needed to find out was what had led Bobby to believe otherwise...

I rang the doorbell and rubbed my mittened hands together, warding off the chill in my bones.

A moment later, Rachel opened the door.

"Penny!" she exclaimed, as she quickly ushered me into the warm house. "What a nice surprise!"

She was in much better spirits than the last few times I had seen her. Her cheeks were rosy and her eyes were clear. Instead of looking disheveled in sweatpants, she wore a tailored blouse and crisp slacks. Her jet-black hair was styled, and her overall appearance was the same as it used to be before her husband was murdered.

"You look well," I told her.

As we entered the living room, I complimented her jewelry and expressed how happy I was to see that she seemed to be in good spirits.

"I definitely look better than I feel," she confided as we sat down and I unbundled out of my winter coat and hat. "But I've committed myself to starting each day with praying and reading scripture. I ask the Lord to strengthen me and to keep me sober, then no matter what, I shower and get dressed to look my best. I've only been at it for a few days now, but having a routine like this helps."

"I know that the Lord will get you through this," I assured her.

She sighed. "I wish I could busy myself with making funeral arrangements, but the police won't release the body."

"Could you talk with Pastor Peter in the interim about when the church might be available for Bobby's funeral? I know the Christmas season is busy, but he should be able to tell you what dates the sanctuary will be available."

Rachel drew in a deep breath, and if anything, she seemed hesitant about the idea of giving the pastor a call.

"Aren't you close with Pastor Peter?" I asked since Rachel had been volunteering at Hopeful Heart Ministries for years, working as the pastor's administrative assistant part-time.

"You're right, Penny. I should give him a call." She smiled and reminded herself. "Baby steps."

I got the distinct impression that Rachel didn't want to reach out to the pastor.

I hoped now wasn't a bad time, but I found the folded invoice in my purse and tried to find the right words to say.

"You've been dealing with so much, Rachel… I sincerely pray that you'll allow Alan and me to help you…"

"With what?" she asked, her inky gaze falling to the invoice as I unfolded it.

"I had a chance to speak with Vince Salisbury, and I understand that there's an open bill. I'm sure Bobby meant to pay Vince, and since the murder, of course you completely forgot—"

"My God!" she blurted out. "Did Vince seek you out to complain about—"

"No! Not at all," I assured her, suddenly feeling as though I was making a huge mess of things. "My best friend Esther's boyfriend, Daniel, is a contractor who Vince spoke to. You know how small Walnut Mountain is—"

"I told Vince to be patient with me," she said, as she took the invoice from me and shook her head. "This whole thing has turned into a royal disaster, and now that Bobby isn't here, I feel paralyzed. I can't do anything until I get through the funeral, and I can't even do that until the police release my late husband's body!"

For all the composure that Rachel had achieved thanks to her daily routine, she completely fell apart and began sobbing into her hands.

"Rachel, please allow Alan and me to handle the bill so that Vince doesn't come here again to bother you."

She nodded and tried desperately to pull herself together.

"I just wanted to move slowly and carefully concerning Vince to make sure I was doing everything correctly, but with Bobby gone, I have to admit, I don't know what to do."

"If you don't mind my asking, what do you mean 'doing everything correctly'? Doing *what* correctly?"

She sighed as though there was so much on her mind, she had no idea how to squeeze all of the information into a single, coherent explanation.

After sighing again, she told me, "As I'm sure you know, Bobby hired Vince to install our new fence. Bobby flagged our property line where he wanted Vince to put the fence. But Vince didn't use Bobby's flagged line. Instead, he went to the county and obtained a copy of our land survey."

Contrary to what Rachel was now saying, Vince had told me that *Bobby* had supplied him with the land survey, but I kept that discrepancy to myself and continued to listen to Rachel.

"We didn't know that Vince obtained the land survey and disregarded Bobby's flags, mind you, until it was too late." She shook her head and muttered, "Men," then went on. "Vince used the property line from the land survey to install the fence without Bobby's permission, which was fine except for on the western side of the house. You see, Bobby had wanted that western side of the fence to be where he had placed the flags. Vince should have *never* taken it upon himself to use the survey map instead of Bobby's flags."

"Bobby was so upset about this that he didn't want to pay Vince?" I asked.

"Knowing Bobby, I truly believe he would have paid Vince eventually, but he felt that he should focus on rectifying the situation with Pastor Peter."

Intrigued, I leaned in and asked, "What does the situation have to do with Pastor Peter?"

"Pastor Peter and his wife are our neighbors to the west. Over the years, Pastor Peter has built a number of little stone pillars in-between our houses."

"The other morning, I found Pastor Peter building a little stone pillar in front of the church."

"He loves them," said Rachel. "Each pillar is spiritually symbolic, and as far as I understand, he builds one after he's had a dream about God or some other kind of holy and powerful experience."

"That was my impression, too," I agreed.

"Now, the pastor always believed that he was building those pillars on *his* property," she went on. "When Bobby referenced the land survey, prior to hiring Vince, he discovered that Pastor Peter had actually put the stone pillars on our property. He was over the boundary line by barely a few feet."

I gasped, understanding what had probably happened, and exclaimed, "Oh no!"

"Yes," Rachel said gravely. "Even though Bobby had flagged the yard so that the fence would be within our property and would not hamper Pastor Peter's pillars, Vince bulldozed over all of the pastor's stone pillars and installed the fence on the true boundary line."

"What a terrible misunderstanding!"

"I know, Penny, it was horrible. Bobby felt horrendous and he could not apologize to the pastor enough, and he also couldn't replace the stone pillars. They were religious symbols, you know? And therefore priceless and impossible to replace. But what made the situation so agonizing was that Pastor Peter refused to forgive and forget."

"Really?" I asked, surprised.

"No one was more shocked than Bobby. I mean, of all people, you would think that the shepherd of our humble congregation would be the first to demonstrate Christ-like forgiveness. Plus, Bobby was contrite and sincere in his apologies. But the pastor went nuts and saw red. He threatened to sue Bobby, and we didn't know if he was serious. What if he won a lawsuit or something? Anyway, Bobby wanted to sort the situation out with the pastor before he paid Vince. Whether or not that's fair, I suppose Christ will be the final judge. But Bobby didn't even get a chance to make things right because he was murdered at the movies."

Taking all of the information in and mentally digesting the full story, I had to ask myself:

Had Pastor Peter broken the sixth commandment and killed a man in cold blood for revenge?

CHAPTER SIX

HAVING ARRIVED AT Hopeful Heart Ministries for the Sunday Service early, I parked my car and approached Alan in the parking lot, as he climbed out of his pickup truck.

"Good morning, Detective *Match*," I teased. "Will you be joining us for the Service this morning?"

"Don't be insulted, Penny," he said, shooting me a look as we started for the church.

"I'm not insulted," I replied, even though I probably was. "However, I wonder. If I'm Mrs. *Matchmaker* and you're Detective *Match*, will people know that we're married?"

Alan didn't like the question. He stopped in his snowy tracks, as parishioners angled around us, heading up the walkway. He showed me that his wedding band was still on his finger.

"The question remains," I told him.

"I should be able to stay for the entire Service," he said, changing the subject as well as my mind.

I completely dropped the issue of his identity crisis and asked, "Really?"

We continued up the walkway, snow crunching under our boots.

"Why are you surprised?" he asked.

"I thought you would be busy with the investigation."

"I am," he allowed, mysteriously.

When we reached the entrance, my stage manager and Christmas pageant assistant, Ashley, quickly opened the door.

"Welcome!"

"Good morning, Ashley," I said and Alan resonated the

sentiment, though he seemed overly serious.

In addition to assisting me with the play rehearsals, Ashley also volunteered as one of the Sunday Service greeters.

My husband and I unbuttoned our coats in the vestibule, unbundling and quietly saying hello to the other members of our congregation.

As we entered the sanctuary, I said, "I need to ask you about a financial matter, Alan."

Pastor Peter stole Alan's attention, even though the pastor was standing near the pulpit at the front of the sanctuary where the partially constructed Christmas pageant scenery that my father had been working on was overlain with canvas drop cloths.

"Alan?" I whispered as we sat down in the pews.

I knew my husband well enough to understand that Pastor Peter was probably his primary suspect in the Bobby Harder case, but since Alan hadn't arrested the man, I gleaned that spying on the pastor was likely the reason that Alan had come to church this morning.

I suspected Pastor Peter, too, but my top priority was clearing Rachel's debt with Vince.

Did I think Vince was innocent? No, I didn't. He was on my own personal list of suspects. But that didn't mean he shouldn't be paid for services rendered. Vince had children, after all.

Alan gave me his ear but not his full attention, and to appease me, he took hold of my hand.

"Hmm?" he said to nudge me.

I should have been annoyed, but I loved the feeling of his strong, warm hand holding mine.

"Rachel Harder has an outstanding bill with a local contractor, and I would like to clear the debt," I told him in a whisper.

"Bobby's widow?" he asked, suddenly interested.

I looked up into his twinkling blue eyes and said, "Yes, Bobby's widow, Rachel. The invoice is quite expensive, Alan, which is why I thought to consult you…"

Anticipating that he would want to see the damage, I found the folded invoice in my purse and handed it to him. His handsome eyes went white all around when he saw the amount due. Then he made the same mental leap that I had a few days ago when I had learned about the debt.

"Can I keep this?" he said.

"Do you think it speaks to motive?" I whispered.

Alan shot me a glance that told me I had overstepped my bounds.

"Well, can I pay it, Alan? Rachel is dealing with enough chaos—"

"Penny," he warned.

"You know what, Alan," I blurted out, using a heavy whisper and all my strength to control my emotions. "Rachel is distressed and Vince is distressed, and God's mercy is such that he blesses even those people who don't deserve it. The Lord has moved my heart to want to—"

Alan shut me up with a kiss.

In the very same moment, Esther and Daniel settled in the pew directly in front of us. Esther breathed, "Awe," when she saw my husband plant a fat one on me. She elbowed Daniel to look at how cute we were.

"Leave a little room for the Holy Ghost," Daniel said, teasing us just as Alan eased off.

I touched my lips and couldn't remember what I had been so upset about.

Alan smiled at Esther, shook Daniel's hand, and as soon as the Sunday Service got underway, my husband leaned towards me and whispered in my ear:

"Pay the invoice, Penny. You have a big heart, and I love you for it."

After singing worship songs and bowing our heads for the prayer led by Pastor Peter, who had been keeping his eye on Alan as steadfastly as Alan had been keeping his eye on him, the pastor invited the congregation to the altar to accept the Holy Communion.

As a protestant church, Holy Communion wasn't offered every Sunday, but rather Pastor Peter offered this sacrament in conjunction with the Christian holidays, Christmas being the greatest of them all. Starting today, each Sunday leading up to the remembrance of our Lord's birth on the 25th, the congregation could take a sip of wine and eat a wafer, which represented the blood and body of Christ.

I made my way into the aisle, coming into the line that was forming to receive the Holy Communion from Pastor Peter at the altar. Alan kept behind me, and we inched along. I thought about all

I was grateful for and prayed inwardly in thanks for my husband's company this morning. Then it was my turn at the altar.

Pastor Peter took a moment to pour more red wine into the Holy chalice and offered me a sip.

As soon as the sharp aroma of wine hit my senses, I smiled. Pastor Peter lifted the chalice to my mouth and gently tipped the smallest sip of wine into my mouth, but by that point, it was already too late.

"Penny, no!" barked Alan.

I gripped the chalice with both hands and began gulping.

Confused, Pastor Peter tried to regain control, but I wouldn't release the cup. It was as though something animalistic and lurking deep within myself had come alive, and I couldn't stop gulping the wine until I had drained the glass, despite the fact that Alan was tugging on my arm from behind and the other parishioners looked on, horrified.

"She must be really thirsty," said one of them with a chuckle.

Another defended me, saying, "Far be it from any of us to deny her the blood of Christ."

"I'm so sorry," I breathed, finally releasing the chalice and realizing what I had done. Despite the sting of shame that burned through my chest, I already wanted more.

That being said, I knew to step aside and return to my seat, but as soon as I turned on my heel, Alan took me by the upper arm and hissed through his teeth:

"What the heck was that?"

"Are you going to take communion?" I asked him, as he escorted me back to our pew.

"I think you've had enough for both of us."

Furious, Alan deposited me on my chair. I felt glaring eyes on me and found my mother, Dottie, staring daggers at me from the opposite side of the church aisle.

Defensively, I told Alan, "You can't be mad at me for taking Holy Communion during the twelve days of Christmas."

"You want to bet?"

☦

I ASKED MY MOTHER, "Did Dad mention anything to you

about overhearing Alan speak with Pastor Peter the other day about the investigation?"

"Don't change the subject."

My mother was not pleased with me, having witnessed me guzzle the Holy Communion wine like an alcoholic in withdrawal.

Alan had left quickly after the Sunday Service. My father, Lucas, had gotten straight to work constructing the set for the Christmas pageant. And even though I only had about twenty minutes before I would have to meet Ashley and the kids in the fellowship hall for the play rehearsal, I let my mother, Dottie, talk me into having lunch with her outside on the snowy gazebo.

Mom had brought sandwiches and juice in a picnic basket. As cheerful as that might have sounded, the look on her face was anything but.

"Penny, you lost control of yourself at the altar for all eyes to see," she accused.

"So I got a little wrapped up in the Christmas spirit," I said, downplaying the situation. "This isn't the end of the world."

"I really don't like having to be blunt with you, Penny. You're an adult and I shouldn't have to tell you how to live your life—"

"No, you shouldn't," I agreed.

"But you are going to lose that man—"

"No, I'm not. How dare you?"

"I dare!" she asserted. "I dare, because I care. Alan needs to see that you are turning over a new leaf and making progress—"

"He *is* seeing that, Mother. I told you, I gave up drinking."

"It didn't look like you'd given *anything* up back there in the church."

"I've lost my appetite," I complained, placing my sandwich in its container, snapping the lid, and returning it to the picnic basket.

"You cannot touch alcohol," she informed me.

"I know that!"

"Not even for Holy Communion," she decided. "Next time, you'll have to abstain or perhaps Pastor Peter can use grape juice instead…"

There was no arguing with her, not unless I wanted my day to be ruined beyond repair, so I held my tongue as my mother thought out loud about all the ways in which she was going to control my drinking problem for me… not that I had one anymore.

"Are you finished?" I asked.

"No, Penny, as a matter of fact, I'm not," she replied indignantly.

That may have been the case, but I could tell that she had run out of steam.

She sighed and stared down at her sandwich, which she had barely taken a bite of. I thought she might cry. When she finally spoke, her voice wavered and tears welled up in her eyes. She didn't let them spill down her cheeks, though, as she said what she needed.

"I've been thinking about your Grandmother Mable, more and more, with each passing day."

This was the second time that my mother had brought up Grandmother Mable in conversation since I was a little girl. No one in our family talked about my mother's mother, Mable. It was too painful, and yet, my mom had broken her silence about Mable last month after Ronnie, the man who had killed Edgar Swaine, had almost taken my life.

"You remind me of your grandmother far too much, Penny," she said, shaking her head as a faraway look filled her glassy eyes.

"I can't help that."

My mom snapped, "Yes, you can."

I had no idea what had led her to believe that, until she began to open up about Grandmother Mable, sharing things with me that I had never known.

"I should have told you this long ago, Penny, but my mother was an alcoholic. Perhaps that's why I never liked the stuff." She touched eyes with me then looked away, as if the snowy scenery of Walnut Mountain would give her the strength to go on. "She tried to give it up, but ultimately, her addiction cost your grandmother her marriage. My father wouldn't stay with her, and after their divorce, Mable couldn't face our church congregation. That was why she moved to Paris."

"I thought Grandmother Mable moved to France to see the countryside and experience the city of Paris."

"That's what your father and I told you, because we thought you were too young to understand."

I felt compassion towards my mother, but at the same time, I wasn't my grandmother.

Dottie went on, "I have never stopped believing that if my mom could have overcome her addiction, she never would have been murdered in Paris."

"Mom, I'm not going to be murdered," I promised her.

"No?" she yelled, as the tears finally spilled down her cheeks. "Need I remind you that Alan saved your life last month? Your grandmother was quite the sleuth, did you know that?"

"No, I didn't know that," I said honestly.

"Well, she was! You're just like her, Penny, and I can't bear the thought of anything terrible happening to you!"

"Did Grandmother Mable ever solve a crime?" I asked innocently.

"Many," she said in a small voice, "and the last one got her killed."

✟

CONCENTRATING ON REHEARSAL wasn't easy after what my mother had divulged during lunch.

I often found myself spacing out and drifting into deep thought while the children struggled to remember their lines and stage blocking.

Ashley came through like a dream and took charge whenever I became distracted.

For some reason, it comforted me to know that I was just like my grandmother. Yet, whenever I allowed myself to grasp the magnitude of what that might mean, I felt spiritually swallowed, as if a dark curse was already in the throes of devouring me.

It grieved me to no end that my mother had conflated my practically non-existent drinking problem with the likelihood that I would be murdered at some point. I didn't think it was fair to make that leap, and yet, it caused me to wonder about the choices Grandmother Mable had made. Perhaps she had been tragically misunderstood. Perhaps her husband, my grandfather, had blown her drinking out of proportion just like Alan had done to me…

Suddenly, my mother's concerns made perfect sense and I really did feel scared for my future.

I didn't want Alan to divorce me. What if he did? No wonder my grandmother fled the country and tried to start a new life on the other side of the world. I would never want to suffer the kind of shame that Grandmother Mable must have felt after Grandpa left her…

"Penny?"

"Hmm?"

Ashley had put the fellowship hall back in order. The children were gone. She was bundled in her winter coat and hat, and I hadn't even closed my rehearsal binder that contained all of my director's notes.

"Are you feeling okay?" Ashley asked me. "I was happy to take the lead today, but you seemed really out of it."

"I must have had too much Communion wine at the Service," I said, as I collected myself. "Why don't you let me treat you to coffee at Morning Glory?"

She perked up. "That sounds nice!"

I turned off the lights and as we exited the fellowship hall and made our way outside into the snowy parking lot, I asked, "What's the dating situation like at your college?"

She laughed and admitted, "Not great, why do you ask?"

"You're a beautiful, young lady, and I was curious to find out if you were *looking*."

"For a guy to date?"

"For someone special," I clarified as we reached my car, which had accumulated a few inches of fresh snow.

I found my snow brush and ice scraper on the floor of the passenger side and began clearing snow from the front and rear windshields.

"Well, to be perfectly honest," she began, "I try not to think about how badly I would like to meet someone special. There are a lot of attractive guys at the college I go to, but they aren't attractive on the *inside*. Looks aren't everything, and I find it impossible to connect with the guys at school because they don't share my values."

Having dusted the snow from my car, I opened the passenger side door for Ashley and said:

"I think I know a guy you might be interested in."

Though Ashley was skeptical about meeting Dex in a romantic context, I could tell she was at least *curious*, as I told her about him and drove across town to Morning Glory.

Of course, Ashley had seen Dex here and there since she frequented the coffee shop, and since Dex wasn't always scheduled to work Sunday mornings, Ashley had caught sight of him at church once or twice.

That being said, she maintained that she wasn't easily impressed with cute, boyish looks and height, both of which characterized Dex.

"Feeling a connection is *everything*," Ashley insisted when we reached Morning Glory, and I couldn't agree more. "The guy has to be a Bible-reading, God-fearing Christian—"

"That certainly describes Dex—"

"*And* the guy has to be on the same page as me regarding the state of the world today. I'm not one of these Christians who's willing to bow down to the government in the name of 'tolerance.' The second the government began taking measures to remove God from the classrooms and telling teachers not to wear religious symbols, like Christian cross necklaces, the government lost my respect."

"You weren't even born yet when they removed God from schools…"

"Well, I was born angry about it."

"I think you'll discover that Dex feels the exact same way," I assured her as we made our way into the coffee shop.

"Really?" she said, delightfully surprised.

"Do you mind if I set you up?" I quietly asked.

Dex was working behind the counter, looking tall and tender-hearted in his apron.

"Oh, I don't know. I already feel embarrassed," she cringed, her cheeks turning bright and rosy.

"It'll be fine," I whispered. "I'm great at this." As soon as we reached the counter, I said, "Dex, have you met my wonderful stage manager, Ashley?"

The color rose in Dex's cheeks, as well, as he tossed his sandy-blond hair out of his eyes and said hello to the pretty young woman with me.

"It's nice to meet you," Ashley said bashfully as she shook Dex's hand.

"Hey, I think I've seen you around," he said, falling into a natural rhythm of conversation, which he kept up with Ashley even after I ordered coffees and croissants.

I stepped aside, giving Dex and Ashley a breath of privacy. Dex wowed the college-age girl with his charming personality, as he collected the baked goods we had ordered.

There were a number of customers seated throughout the

coffee shop, having stopped in to warm up in-between Christmas shopping and browsing the window displays along Main Street.

Just as I was about to turn back to Dex and Ashley, Pastor Peter stepped inside from the cold with his wife, a gentle woman by the name of Sharon.

Leaving Dex and Ashley and the flirtation that had ignited between them, I smiled at Sharon and complemented Pastor Peter for the lovely sermon he had given earlier.

"I've been checking in on Rachel," I added, shifting the conversation. "I was hoping she would start attending church again, but I think she needs a bit more time."

Sharon seemed sympathetic, but Pastor Peter's friendly demeanor drooped at my mention of the dead man's wife. I sensed more than saw his guard go up, which told me to probe and find out what truths lurked on the other side of his figurative walls.

"If I may be perfectly honest, I believe Rachel could be avoiding church because she's worried that you're upset with her."

"Who, me?" asked the pastor, but it was obvious he was only pretending to be taken aback. From where I was standing, he didn't look surprised by the insinuation whatsoever. "Why in the world would I be upset with her?"

Sharon tensed up, growing uncomfortable, but I didn't let that stop me from answering.

"Because of the misunderstanding with the new fence," I frankly reminded him. "She knows how upset you were at Bobby—"

"I don't know what Rachel told you, but she was wrong to speak ill of me—"

"She didn't 'speak ill of you'—"

"You're wrong to bring this subject up," he informed me. "It's none of your business."

"Why wouldn't you forgive Bobby?" I pushed. "Ruining your stone pillars was an accident, one which he had tried very hard to avoid."

"Come on, Sharon," said the pastor, as he guided his wife past me. "We don't have to take this."

"My husband questioned you for a reason, Pastor—"

Turning on his heel, he snapped, "You think I had something to do with the murder? I'm a man of the cloth, for God's sake!"

Sharon wrangled her husband towards the door, saying, "Let's go to Charming Diner instead, Peter. It's too late for coffee anyway."

"If anyone had reason to kill Bobby," he added, barely containing his displeasure with me, "it was that contractor. He's a widower, you know. He's behind on his mortgage and has children, which is the only reason I didn't move forward with a lawsuit against Bobby for having had his contractor bulldoze onto my property—"

Clearly, the pastor believed that his stone pillars *had* been within his side of the boundary line.

"—But what did Bobby do?" he raged on.

Sharon begged, "Peter, there's no sense in getting upset. Let's go to the diner!"

"Bobby left Vince and his children to starve, that's what he did!" he yelled. "And you have the audacity to imply I took Bobby's life? I'll have you know that Rachel's *impression* of the dispute between Bobby and me is strictly that—an *impression*—and I don't appreciate you insinuating that Rachel hasn't come to church because of something *I* did."

"Peter!" said Sharon, yanking on his arm.

Finally, the pastor listened to his wife and they left the coffee shop in a fit of high emotions.

I feared I had just caused a big scene, but when I glanced towards Ashley, I realized that she and Dex were causing quite a scene of their own.

"What do you mean, it's 'stupid' to support NGOs," Ashley hotly replied to whatever point Dex had just made from his side of the counter.

"They're just as bad as the government!"

"No, they aren't!" she cried. "NGOs are *'non'* government organizations! It's in the name!"

"Just because they aren't *run* by the government doesn't mean that the government doesn't *control* them," Dex argued, holding his head high.

"How can you call yourself a conservative and also refuse to acknowledge all of the Christian good that NGOs are doing in Third World countries?" she balked, exasperated at their profound difference of opinion. "There are *Christian* NGOs!"

"And those NGOs compromise their values and bow down to political pressure every time! They're total shills—"

"They're *not* total shills!"

"Wait til you get out into the real world, Girly!"

"What?!"

"Ashley!" I said, breaking up their argument. "I think we should go."

"Ya think?"

She looked red-faced and shaken as we collected our coffees and hot croissants, and I felt blindsided by how terribly their conversation had gone.

After we climbed into my car, I started the engine and cranked the heat, not that Ashley needed it. She was fuming with anger.

"Can you believe that guy?" she balked. "Who doesn't support NGOs?"

I wasn't totally clear on the disagreement, but I suspected that if I asked her about it, she would only get more upset.

Though I didn't fuel her fire with questions, Ashley continued to vent as I drove her back to the church where she had parked her car.

"I'm puzzled, Ashley," I said as I came to a stop beside her car. "I really thought you and Dex would hit it off."

She narrowed her eyes into a glare and determined, "He's one of those overly paranoid libertarian types who thinks everything is evil and won't give credit where credit is due! Those types of Christians are *impossible!*"

I thought she might punch the windshield, but instead she angrily shoved her croissant in her mouth and chewed until she calmed down.

Dex had really touched a nerve. I had never seen Ashley so passionate...

I apologized on Dex's behalf for having offended her, which almost set her off all over again, but she told me it wasn't my fault. Even though Dex was still on her mind, she refrained from launching into another tirade, thanked me for the croissant, coffee, and the ride, and climbed out of my car.

Once she had driven off, dusk gathered across the overcast skies, and moments later, darkness closed in.

I checked the clock on the dashboard and realized that I had a shot at catching Vince Salisbury at his landscaping and fencing business if I left now.

That being said, however, no one could have prepared me for

what I would find once I got there...

CHAPTER SEVEN

PASTOR PETER HAD POINTED his figurative finger at Vince Salisbury, and I honestly didn't know what to think. Both men had motives to kill Bobby, though neither of their reasons could ever justify taking a human life.

I pulled into the snowy parking lot of Salisbury Landscaping & Fencing, jumped out of my car with my checkbook in hand, and spilled into the warm anteroom where all four of Vince's sons were squirming around with school books, notepads, and pencils in their midst.

The boys seemed to be more focused on horsing around, as their father, Vince, was finishing up with some paperwork behind the counter.

"I'm so glad to catch you!" I exclaimed, out of breath as I came to the counter. "Good evening!"

Vince peeled his reading glasses off his nose in disbelief that I had returned as promised.

Cautiously optimistic, he asked, "You're here to pay the Harders' invoice?"

"I am," I said.

I opened my checkbook, plucked a black pen out of the mug on the counter, and began making out the check. Behind me, all four of the boys fell into humbled silence, perhaps having perceived from their father's shift in demeanor that something important and meaningful was taking place.

"I can't thank you enough," said Vince.

"No need to thank me. Consider it a blessing from God for

Christmas," I told him. "And please feel welcome to come to Hopeful Heart Ministries over in Walnut Mountain. We have a number of children's programs, and I'm sure your boys would enjoy our upcoming Christmas pageant."

I gave him more information and once I had filled out the check, I handed it to him with a smile, wished him Merry Christmas, and told him that I hoped to see him at the church.

Relieved that I had accomplished my mission, I turned on my heel and started for the door.

That's when I saw the rope.

Vince's youngest boy, who I guessed was about five-years old, was playing with a thin, white cord that couldn't have been longer than 3-feet.

I did a bit of a double-take and slowed my step when I realized that the middle of the cord looked slightly discolored...

A flashing image filled my mind of the pink horizontal marks I had seen across Bobby's throat after he had been murdered.

Was the diameter of the white rope cord that the boy was playing with the right size? Or did it appear too thick or too thin to have caused the marks on Bobby's neck as a result of him being strangled from behind?

Vince must have taken notice of what had stolen my attention and prevented me from stepping out into the snowy night, because he rounded out from behind the counter and nearly knocked me over on his way to snatch the rope from his son.

He didn't say a word or scold the boy. Instead, he began coiling the rope cord around his fist to ball it up, looked me dead in the eye, and said:

"Kids don't realize how dangerous rope cord like this can be. I didn't mean to plow through you like that."

"Not at all," I breathed, trying to seem as good-natured as possible and hide the fact that I felt deeply rattled. I swallowed the lump in my throat and said, "Goodnight."

The second I got to my car, I shoved my checkbook into my purse and found my cell phone.

With trembling hands, I dialed Alan. There was no time for text messages. I needed to speak with my husband right away. I might have just stumbled across the murder weapon, and who knew what Vince was planning on doing with it!

"Alan? It's Penny!" I blurted out as soon as I heard his deep voice come through the line.

"I've been meaning to call you," he interjected before I could tell him about my discovery.

In an instant, I was all ears. "Oh?"

"I've been talking with Pastor Peter—"

"Because you think he's a suspect?" I quickly guessed. "He might not be! I just found—"

"Penny! I'm talking about you and me."

I got my car started and fixed my gaze on the office windows. Though the blinds were down, I could see the silhouette of Vince collecting his boys. He was going to leave soon!

"Alan—"

"Pastor Peter agreed with me that it's a wonderful idea to start an AA program at Hopeful Heart Ministries."

I froze. My brow furrowed. What was he talking about?

"AA program?" I asked, horrified.

"Alcoholics Anonymous," he clarified, not that it was necessary. "I think it's important that you start taking this seriously and start going to meetings. You need a sponsor and you need to be held accountable—the whole nine yards. After what you did at the church—"

"That was nothing, Alan—"

"That wasn't nothing?" he barked.

"I called you for a reason!" I barked right back, changing the subject as effectively as I could. "Vince Salisbury is the killer! I found the murder weapon—the rope! You have to come quick!"

✝

NOT ONLY DID Alan *not* come quickly. He didn't come *at all*, but instead sent Officers Jeremiah and Chuck to investigate my claim.

By the time they arrived, however, Vince had locked up shop and driven off with his four boys and the murder weapon.

I tried to explain what the white rope cord had looked like, as I stood in the snowy parking area, shivering and pleading with the police officers to believe me.

I knew both men well enough to trust that they should respect my conviction, but to my surprise they lectured me on 'crying wolf' and the consequences of depleting police resources.

"I didn't mean to deplete police resources," I assured them.

"You implied that you had discovered rope that could have been used to kill Bobby Harder—"

"I did!"

"But you don't have it in hand," Officer Chuck pointed out as kindly as he could, though he obviously wasn't pleased with me either. "You haven't *found* anything, and yet two police officers have been pulled away from the station to follow up on your faulty claim."

"It's not a faulty claim," I maintained, but my voice sounded as small as I felt.

Officer Jeremiah added, "Do you have any idea how many contractors use rope?"

"Plus, kids play with rope all the time," said Officer Chuck, "such as jump rope…"

"Having rope isn't a crime," the first officer pointed out.

I tried my best to keep a level head, as I explained, "Alan knows that Vince Salisbury had a legitimate motive to take Bobby's life, which has everything to do with an unpaid debt. For that reason alone, I think that it would be worth it to check out the particular rope I saw inside that office. You should've seen Vince's face when he realized I—"

The police officers touched eyes with one another and I could tell they were exercising a great amount of patience.

Finally, Officer Jeremiah told me, "We'll let Alan know. Are you going to be able to get home okay driving in this snow?"

I said I would be fine and climbed in my car, which had accumulated a thick dusting of fresh snow.

I turned the engine on and freezing air blasted out of the vents. The next thing I knew, Officers Jeremiah and Chuck were brushing snow off of my windshield and windows, having grabbed their ice scrapers from their police cruiser.

They stepped aside and waved goodbye, as I backed out and got on the road, the light from my sedan's headlights illuminating the road and the winter wonderland of snow flurries that were coming down.

During the long drive home, I told myself that from now on I should keep my clues, hunches, and suspects to myself. Unless I had ironclad proof that a particular suspect was definitely guilty of murdering Bobby, I was going to have to learn to keep what I discovered to myself.

Alan might have been my husband, but he wasn't on my side.

I was starting to realize that it was possible he had actually been my enemy for a very long time.

✝

THE NEXT DAY, I taught at Walnut Mountain Middle School and spent the recess hour after lunch discussing Vince Salisbury and the rope with Esther, as we walked the perimeter of the playground to keep warm while supervising the kids.

More than anything, I wanted to vent about the unexpected blow Alan had delivered over the phone when he had mentioned the possibility of an Alcoholics Anonymous program starting at Hopeful Heart Ministries. He had gone so far as to discuss the idea with Pastor Peter. Had that been why Alan had been speaking with the pastor? The *only* reason? Surely, Pastor Peter was one of Alan's suspects… or had I made an assumption?

Esther thought the white rope cord was an interesting development, but Daniel hadn't passed on any more information to her about Vince. However, Esther had been poking around the Walnut Mountain Warriors website, as well as the protestors' favorite local hangout, which happened to be Charming Diner.

While I puzzled over Vince Salisbury and Pastor Peter as the most likely suspects, Esther seemed to be becoming preoccupied with the peculiar relationship that had been forming between Samantha and Matthew.

"Matthew has been acting very odd," she concluded. "He hasn't been himself since that movie theater was built, and if you ask me, his behavior has only gotten more bizarre since Bobby's murder."

After school, I gave Rachel a call to find out how she was doing and to see if she wanted to grab some dinner together, perhaps at Charming Diner if that was where the protestors liked to meet, not that I revealed that aspect to Rachel.

She was open to the idea, but first had to finish up what she had been working on at the movie theater.

"You're at Christian Cinemas?" I asked her, surprised.

"This movie theater was Bobby's dream, and I'm not going to let that dream die just because he did," she bravely said.

I told her that I would meet her there.

As I drove over to Christian Cinemas, I prayed to high heaven that the killer wouldn't target Rachel next if she decided to keep the movie theater open by screening Christian films.

Parking directly in front of the theater was easy. I pulled my fluffy knit hat down over my ears and climbed out of my car. Bitter-crisp air filled my lungs and snow crunched under my boots as I crossed the sidewalk, all of Main Street twinkling up with the Christmas lights of each shop's storefront display.

I approached the glass entrance door and gave the handle a tug, but the door was locked in its frame. A moment later, Rachel crossed the lobby and let me in.

"Sorry about that," she apologized. "You weren't waiting long, were you?"

"I just got here," I said, coming in from the cold.

Rachel threw her arms around me and gave me a great, big hug. "Vince stopped by first thing this morning and surprised me by plowing my driveway! That's how thankful he was for receiving the payment! Thank you, Penny! I don't think I know anyone who has a bigger heart than you do!"

"There's no need to thank me. I'm just glad to help. Like I told Vince, the Lord put it on my heart to clear the debt and I'm just grateful to be of service. Our church community is a family and if we don't lift each other up in service of Christ, no one will."

"I appreciate you. Come on in."

I didn't want to muddy up the red carpet with my snow-dripping boots, so I gave them a good stomp on the winter doormats before venturing farther.

"I'm just finishing up in the office," she explained as we walked through the lobby, passed the concession stands, and headed down a dimly lit corridor. "I don't want to put too much pressure on myself, but I've set my heart on reopening the movie theater immediately after the New Year. Bobby had already worked out the full screening schedule for the first quarter of January, February, and March, so it's really just a matter of making sure the staff can come back, and marketing the movies so that the business is successful."

Rachel breezed into the office, which was much larger than I had anticipated. There were two U-shaped desks in the far corners of the room and security surveillance monitors on the nearest wall, which I noticed as soon as I followed Rachel towards the desk she had been working at.

"Five minutes," she promised with a smile before returning her attention to the desktop computer she had been using.

I took a slow lap around the room, first checking out the surveillance monitors, none of which happened to be on.

"Do any of the security cameras capture the screening auditoriums?" I asked even though I could guess the answer.

If there was security footage of the movie theater where Keep Christ in Christmas had been playing, then Alan would've caught the killer by now.

"No, unfortunately," she said without glancing at me. As she continued to quickly type up whatever she was working on, she explained, "The security cameras are located in the box office and behind the concession stands. Bobby was more concerned with preventing employee theft than recording the patrons as they watched movies."

"That makes sense," I said as I came to the second desk that was covered with neatly organized stacks of paperwork.

Peering at each stack, I noticed that Rachel was greatly organized in her effort to make sense of Bobby's new business, as well as to stay on top of the financial matters that related to his death. Most people didn't realize how many forms needed to be filed once a loved one had passed away. The fact that Rachel wasn't still overwhelmed at home, but today looked polished and energetic, was an ongoing miracle.

I was about to cross the office and join her, but a contract on the desk in front of me caught my eye.

At the very top of the contract, printed in bold lettering, was the heading, 'Partnership Agreement.'

A bit farther down the page, after the contract date, were the two names of the partners who were entering into the contract together.

Those names were, 'Robert Harder,' i.e. Bobby, and Matthew Chapman.

Matthew Chapman?

Matthew the *science teacher* who I had been working with for years?

My heart punched up my throat as I eyed the partnership contract between Bobby and Matthew the *science teacher*... Matthew the *protestor*... Matthew the...

... *business partner* in Bobby Harder's brand-new movie theater? *What in the world?*

I was careful not to make a sound as I pinched the first page of the contract and flipped to the second page. The print was fine and dense, and there were more pages...

I glanced over my shoulder at Rachel who was in the process of shutting down the desktop computer, having finished whatever she had been working on.

"Ready to go?" Rachel asked me and I was startled.

"Sure am," I said.

I secretly slipped the partnership contract into my purse before I turned around to face her.

"I'm starving," she commented as she turned off the lights and we left the office.

"Me, too," I said, wondering all the while about Matthew Chapman and how he could have protested a movie theater that he partly owned.

✝

AFTER HAVING DINNER with Rachel at Charming Diner, I drove to my cabin and I would have been eager to start a fire in the living room, but as soon as I got home and stepped through the door, I smelled the warm scent of firewood crackling in the wood burning stove.

"Alan?" I called out, as I hung my coat on the rack and stepped out of my snowy boots.

I entered the living room. There was a strong fire burning in the stove. I thought I heard footfall overhead and glanced up. It sounded like Alan was in our bedroom, perhaps picking up more winter clothes from the closet.

I rounded towards the stairs and realized that my husband had also thrown a wash on in the laundry room. The telltale rumblings of the drier and faint scent of fabric softener wafted up the stairs as I made my way to the second floor.

I should have felt happy that my husband had dropped in unannounced, but my stomach was twisted in knots.

I hadn't gotten rid of the box of alcohol that Rachel had insisted I take from her.

Instead, I had slid it under the foot of the bed for reasons that even I didn't understand.

When I reached the landing, I again called out, "Alan?"

"In here!" he said and I found him where I thought I would—rummaging through the closet in the master bedroom.

Doing laundry and organizing sweaters and long johns on the bed must have caused him to work up a sweat, because he was down to a tee shirt and standing in his bare feet.

Feeling nervous about the hidden box, while also wrestling with waves of resentment towards Alan for sending his police officers the other night instead of coming to Vince's place of business himself, I folded my arms and said:

"I really wish you would text or call to let me know when you're going to be here."

"Vince Salisbury came into the police station today."

I was all ears. "To confess?"

Alan glanced over the winter clothes he had collected and stacked on the bed, and then sat down beside them.

"He brought the rope with him," he said.

"He did?" I was stunned. "The murder weapon?"

"At first, that's what I thought," he allowed. "But he insisted that he had nothing to do with Bobby's murder, and he said that he had brought the rope in as a gesture of good faith to prove his innocence. He also invited me to search his business office and his entire home, which we're in the process of doing right now as unobtrusively as possible."

"Interesting…" I took a moment to ponder the information. "But what if Vince really did kill Bobby, got rid of all the evidence, and because he 'cleaned up,' he wants you to search him, find nothing, and clear him as a suspect. What if it's all a strategy to get away with murder?"

"I considered that," he allowed. "But I have to tell you, his hands are clean, period. He didn't do it."

Alan held my gaze for a long moment. I might have realized that somewhere along the line my husband had become my enemy, but right now he was looking at me like we were best friends.

We had always been best friends throughout all our years together. Underneath it all, we had always been as close as a husband and wife could be. The way in which Alan was gazing at me was a reminder of that now, as he rose from the bed and took both of my hands in his.

"Penny," he said. "Vince was so moved that you paid the Harders' invoice, all he wants to do is to be as accommodating as possible. You're the reason he was able to buy Christmas presents for his children and get a Christmas tree. He got caught up on his bills and can breathe easy and make it through the New Year."

He kissed me and added:

"You're still the woman I married, and I'm grateful for you."

I ran my fingers through his dark hair, drank in the heavenly scent of his woodsy cologne, and pulled him in for another kiss.

I believed Alan. I knew in my soul that every word he had told me was true. Vince hadn't killed Bobby, and Alan had finally realized that I was the same person he had married and not a monster who needed to be caged.

Together, we made an absolute mess of the stacks of clothing Alan had organized at the foot of the bed.

Rolling around and making out like teenagers felt like a dream.

And like a dream, it didn't last as long as I would have liked.

Once Alan had ruined the mood by revisiting the idea of AA meetings at the church, he collected his clothing and laundry, and returned to the motel where he had been staying for the last four months, leaving me to finally read through the movie theater partnership agreement between Robert AKA Bobby Harder and Matthew Chapman.

Downstairs in the living room, I sat on the couch in front of the crackling fire and skimmed the first page of the contract.

In total, the agreement was twelve pages of very dense legal clauses.

I reached the last page of the contract and took a great pause.

On the bottom of the page, Matthew had signed his full legal name and dated his side of the partnership agreement.

Bobby had not.

What had stopped Bobby from signing his name to that contract?

And had the fact that he hadn't signed the contract to form a partnership with Matthew provoked Matthew to sneak into the movie theater and kill him at the grand opening?

CHAPTER EIGHT

"NATHAN, PLEASE STOP goofing around!" I shouted, struggling to gain control of the kids who were playing the Three Wise Men in the Christmas pageant.

With the performance coming up in mere days, the children didn't have a lot of time to memorize their lines and their stage blocking. Ashley had been rushing around the children as they rehearsed to properly position them and remind them of the exact wording of their lines. For the most part, we were making progress, but every so often, Nathan stole the show and derailed our efforts by cracking a joke or fooling around in some manner that the kids never failed to find hilarious.

Ashley prompted Nathan, and the eleven-year old boy proclaimed, "I have brought the baby gold!"

From where I was sitting, I gave Nathan two enthusiastic thumbs up and the kids continued with the rehearsal, the next Wise Men presenting the frankincense and myrrh to the plastic baby doll we were using as a prop.

My colleague, Matthew the science teacher, was weighing heavily on my mind, but I knew that if I continued to allow myself to get distracted while directing the play rehearsals, the entire Christmas pageant would be in jeopardy.

That being said, I was also becoming distracted by the urge to speak with Nathan's parents about his behavior, which had been getting worse since Bobby's murder. Nathan was one of my Language Arts students at Walnut Mountain Middle School. During class, he often flew out of control, acting like the class clown. The other students loved it, but I saw these comedic outbursts as cries for help. He had really looked up to Bobby and missed having him as the youth basketball coach.

"Can I treat you to a pastry at Morning Glory?" I asked Ashley once rehearsal was over.

The children had returned the tables to their places in the fellowship hall and were now filing out of the large room and into the vestibule where their parents were waiting if not sitting in their warm, idling cars outside.

The color rose in Ashley's cheeks and she turned cross at the very idea of setting foot in the coffee shop.

"Only if Dex isn't working," she snapped. "I can't stand him!"

"After one disagreement?" I asked as we helped the younger children button up their winter coats.

"It should have been only one disagreement," she agreed, shaking her head. "But I have foolishly gone back to Morning Glory a number of times. Every time, Dex has instigated a fight with me!"

As she composed herself for the sake of the children, I asked, "About what?"

"About anything he can think of, if you ask me," she hissed. "At first, he tried to resume the argument we'd had about NGOs. But since then, he has been antagonizing me about everything under the sun."

If I wasn't mistaken, I thought I caught sight of the corners of Ashley's mouth curling upward with a delighted smile. While it was clear that Ashley didn't appreciate Dex picking on her, I suspected that deep down she was intrigued by Dex and wanted him to express mature interest in her.

On a certain level, this was a cut-and-dry case of opposites attracting, and passions getting the best of both people, not that I was especially proud of Dex for his lack of maturity. He was a few years older than Ashley and should know by now how to relate to a young woman. But Ashley hadn't come into full maturity, either. Something told me they might still be a good match.

I expressed sympathy and suggested, "Perhaps you could treat Dex, not as he is, but as you would like him to be?"

She was unfamiliar with the concept. "What do you mean?"

"Try giving him the benefit of the doubt and not responding as though he's attacking you. But rather respond as though his comments and questions are intended to get to know you."

She cooled off a bit. "You mean, when he says something like, 'I bet you don't care whether coffee is Fair Trade or not,' I shouldn't automatically feel insulted? But that's impossible! Of course, I care that the coffee I drink is Fair Trade!"

"Ashley, I think he's purposefully trying to ruffle your feathers because he likes you, not because he dislikes you."

Contemplating the possibility seemed to hurt her brain.

After my second invitation to the coffee shop, she declined and walked the last child outside the moment the little girl's mother pulled up in the church parking lot.

The sounds of an electric screwdriver drilling a nail into wooden boards, which was coming from inside the church sanctuary, told me that my father, Lucas, was putting the final touches on the Christmas pageant scenery.

I peeked into the sanctuary, having buttoned my winter coat up to my chin and replaced the sequin chemo cap I always wore with my fluffy knit hat. Sure enough, there was my dad, standing with a toolbelt around his waist. He was on the beautiful set, his red hair as bright as the red flannel shirt he had on.

In a moment of pure honesty, I admitted to myself that I missed him. We hadn't really connected since I found out how he and Alan were in the habit of talking about me behind my back. I knew I had been blowing things out of proportion and turning a molehill into a mountain by harboring resentment in my heart. It had been easy to blame the busy Christmas season for why I hadn't had time to stop by my parents' house for dinner in weeks.

How long was I going to keep this up?

I didn't want to have a lonely Christmas, and I couldn't be sure that I was going to spend the holiday with my husband. Did I really want to freeze out my parents, too, and wind up all alone on the memorial of our Savior's birth?

I eased into the sanctuary and made my way up the aisle, marveling at the beautiful woodwork that my father had created. Instead of using childish paint colors, he had stained the wooden scenery and all of the hand-crafted fixtures he had made with handsome, glossy hues—mahogany, sedona red, and ebony, among other elegant shades.

"Penny, my goodness, I didn't see you there," he said when I stepped up onto the wooden stage.

"This is beautiful, Dad," I said, complimenting him as I ran my fingertips over the hand crafted wooden bench and the thatched nativity roof he had built.

He fit his electric screwdriver into a special holster on his toolkit and planted his hands on his hips, as we both took in the full sight of the scenery, which spanned the width of the transept crossing of the church, just shy of the altar.

"Thanks, Sweetheart. I have more sanding and staining to do tonight, but you guys should be able to rehearse in here tomorrow."

Since we were getting down to the wire, Ashley and I had scheduled rehearsals after school every day this week, as the Christmas pageant performance neared.

I was hoping to connect with my father, but before I had a chance to strike up a conversation about Christmas and ask how Mom and him were planning on spending the morning, he turned to me and said:

"Alan and I went ice fishing this past weekend."

"Oh?" I replied, sensing that my father wasn't about to tell me about the fish he had caught with my husband.

He didn't immediately come out with it. Instead, he paused, as if hesitant to broach a sensitive topic.

"Was it very cold?" I asked to fill the silence that had risen between us.

"Penny, Alan told me that he has been staying in a motel for months."

I could barely find my voice. "He shouldn't have said anything."

"Yes, he should have," my dad said sternly. He looked far from pleased. "Why didn't you tell me?"

"Because we're working it out. We have a right to privacy."

His face clouded with remorse. Pained, he said, "Isolation and secrecy isn't going to fix your marriage, Penny. You should have come to me and your mother for our wisdom and advice."

It was then that the magnitude of this conversation hit me. In an instant, I felt mortified, furious, and betrayed.

"Now, your mother and I saw you during the Service—"

"Mom already spoke to me about that, and she should have told you that I didn't mean to drink too much Holy Communion wine. You've got to let it go. It was no big deal—"

"You keep thinking nothing is a big deal, and that's the problem, Penny!" he barked. "Your husband is living in a motel, that's a huge problem, and you haven't been able to fix it yourself *for months—"*

"I don't have to listen to this," I snapped, turning on my heel and descending off the wooden stage. I shouted over my shoulder, "I'll give Mom a call about Christmas to work out the details!"

"Penny! I'm trying to help!"

I could have stopped dead in my tracks, spun around, and shouted, *How does humiliating me help?* But I didn't have the emotional strength to defend my own failures.

When I climbed in my car, I couldn't imagine going home, not when my rising, raging emotions were calling me to drink—ironically.

I still had Rachel's box full of alcohol to contend with in the bedroom of my cabin, so I started driving in the direction of Rachel Harder's house instead.

I didn't completely understand why, but I knew I would feel better in Rachel's company.

Maybe it was because, in a way, we had both lost our husbands.

Maybe it was because, in a way, we both desperately wanted to give up drinking, but weren't sure we could.

Or maybe it was because, in a way, if we both fell off the wagon together, then somehow it might not be as bad as falling off the sobriety wagon all alone.

I felt as though I was on the precipice of careening down a very dark abyss. Anxiety burned through my chest as I drove along winding roads, nighttime pressing in. The feeling reminded me of the hollow despair that used to come over me from time to time in high school. Back then, Alan had been the cure, but my husband was no longer available.

I knew where the dark feeling stemmed from—the anxiety that had begun to plague me when I had only been a girl in middle school.

It had all started after my parents had told me that my Grandmother Mable, who had moved to Paris, had been found murdered.

In that moment, the foundation of my entire world had shifted beneath my feet, and I had felt off balance ever since.

I pulled up Rachel's snowy driveway and spilled out of my car as soon as I had parked.

When I crossed the front porch and rang the bell, I knew I was in trouble.

The door opened.

"What a nice surprise!" said Rachel, welcoming me inside right away. It was a moment before she realized I had a long face. "Is something wrong?"

A lot was wrong. I wanted to drown my emotions in a bottle of wine, but I didn't tell her that.

"I need to ask you about Matthew Chapman," I said, surprising both of us.

"Matthew Chapman?" she asked as if the name wasn't ringing a bell.

If Matthew was going to go into business with Bobby, there was no way that Rachel hadn't met him. Why was she pretending she didn't know him?

"Matthew is one of the teachers I work with," I explained, "but as I understand it, Matthew was supposed to be a partner in the movie theater?"

Rachel folded her arms and challenged, "As you *understand* it? Today I realized that an important document was missing from the movie theater office. I went crazy trying to look for it. I told myself to think nothing of it, and I wouldn't have given it a second thought, except here you are."

She stared at me for a long moment and I didn't have an explanation.

"Did you steal the partnership agreement between Bobby and Matthew?" she asked me, point blank.

"Did you tell Alan that Bobby and Matthew were about to go into business together?" I asked, answering her question with one of my own.

"You think that's your business?"

"I think it's Alan's business as the lead investigator."

"Well, it isn't his business," she asserted. "It's no one's business, because Bobby never signed that contract. He never went into business with Matthew."

"Rachel, don't you see that Matthew could have killed Bobby for that reason. Matthew was at the protest that night, which tells me that he was so offended that Bobby didn't go through with the business deal, that he ended up fighting to close the movie theater."

Putting her foot down, she said, "Penny, it was wrong of you to steal from the office."

"I know that," I snapped. I found the partnership agreement in my purse and gave it to her. "I was wrong to steal, and I'm sorry. I was only trying to get to the bottom of what happened to Bobby."

She softened.

"Why didn't Bobby sign the contract?" I asked once Rachel had unfolded her arms.

"When Bobby first got inspired to open a movie theater, he was thinking of the endeavor as a money-maker, and he wanted the business to be as successful as possible. Meaning, it was going to be a secular theater. Matthew got involved at that point, also wanting to open a theater that played your typical blockbuster movies. But then Bobby realized that financial success wasn't what mattered. He didn't want to store up treasures on earth, as the scripture says, but rather to store up treasures in heaven. He decided that the theater should only screen Christian films, even if that meant that the movie theater didn't profit as much at the box office. Matthew didn't like that idea, and so their partnership agreement fell through."

We got comfortable in the kitchen, cooked dinner, and Rachel told me more about the business endeavor between Bobby and Matthew that never materialized.

I didn't end up drinking that night with Rachel, but it scared me how close I had come.

✝

DESPITE COMPLAINING OF an unbearable migraine for the better part of the week, Samantha was not about to let a good opportunity go to waste. Or at least that was my assessment of the situation when I saw her stand up in the teachers' lounge one morning and clap her hands together to get the attention of the entire staff, who were just trying to eat their breakfast in peace.

"Good morning, everyone!" she said, clapping her hands a few more times until the teachers quieted down. "There is a very important matter that concerns our entire community, and I would like your support!"

She turned to Matthew, who stood beside her with a clipboard in his hands, and nodded at him in an authoritative manner.

Esther and I were tucked at one of the smaller tables, nursing mugs of coffee. We exchanged a weary glance.

Samantha began explaining, "There is a discriminatory movie theater in the heart of Walnut Mountain. This movie theater is intentionally choosing film content that *excludes* residents on the basis of their religious faith, or lack thereof. To my horror, the movie theater is still in operation even though the primary owner is no longer alive. We must drive this bigoted business out of town!"

Matthew began going around the room, presenting the clipboard to each teacher, as Samantha went on.

"Please sign the petition to show your allegiance to this very important cause. If we collect enough signatures, I can present the petition to the county and hopefully compel Christian Cinemas to shut down for good!"

"The woman has lost her mind," said Esther in a grumbling whisper that only I could hear.

"No one is signing the petition," I noticed, as Matthew continued around the room, offering the petition to one teacher after the next to sign even though each was declining by shaking his or her head. "Hopefully, Principal Longchamp will remind Samantha that she's not supposed to solicit the teachers for their political involvement in non-academic matters."

"Garth could remind her one thousand times, but I doubt it would have an impact," said Esther. "I have to get to class."

I was on the same page, so we snuck away from our table and avoided Matthew. By the time he came around with the petition, Esther and I slipped out of the teachers' lounge.

As we made our way up the corridor, drinking hot coffee from our mugs, I mentioned:

"Vince Salisbury is off the suspect list."

"No kidding?"

I shared what I had learned about Vince, the rope, Alan's conclusion, and my agreement about his conclusion—that Vince Salisbury had not killed Bobby Harder.

"So, that leaves Pastor Peter and the protestors, or one of the protestors, on our list of possible suspects," Esther determined, as we neared our homeroom classrooms that were across from one another. "Considering Samantha's hairbrained obsession with shutting Christian Cinemas down, I honestly wouldn't be surprised if she murdered Bobby, or hired someone else to."

"More like 'seduced' someone else into doing her bidding," I countered.

Esther was quick-witted and guessed, "Not Matthew…"

"Matthew and Bobby were supposed to be *partners* and co-own the movie theater—"

Esther gasped. "You're kidding!"

I got Esther up to speed regarding the partnership agreement I had found in the office at Christian Cinemas, and how Matthew had signed it but Bobby had not, and as the first warning bell rang and children filled the hallways and filtered into our classrooms, I quickly told Esther the broad strokes of what Rachel had explained to me over dinner.

"So, Matthew did a total 180 as a result of Bobby changing his mind about co-ownership," Esther surmised.

"It could be more complicated than that," I allowed. "According to Rachel, it was more like Bobby was the one who did a 180. Initially, the movie theater was supposed to play secular, blockbuster films like any old movie theater. It was Bobby who changed his mind and only wanted to present Christian films. Matthew didn't think that would be smart financially, and because they didn't see eye-to-eye, Bobby ditched Matthew altogether and proceeded with his Christian movie theater vision."

She took all of the information in and wondered, "If Matthew killed Bobby, he might not have been doing Samantha's bidding, but rather his own."

The second warning bell sounded, indicating that classes should begin momentarily.

"If he did," I said quickly, "it could be extremely difficult to prove. I can only imagine how many protestors will be ready to provide Matthew with an alibi."

Esther and I were huddled so closely, that we didn't realize Matthew had walked up to us until he said:

"Ladies?"

"Oh!"

My heart leapt up my throat and Esther clutched her chest for the near heart attack he had caused her.

"Would you like to sign the petition?" he asked, offering us the clipboard.

Esther became tight-lipped, shrank beside me, and shook her head, declining.

"Think about what you're doing, Matthew," I said after refusing to sign the petition. "Rachel Harder is now a widow, and you want to put her out of business just because her late husband wouldn't let you co-own that very same business?"

Behind the bookish glasses he wore, a dark glimmer filled his eyes.

"What you're doing isn't right," I told him in no uncertain terms, "and we both know Samantha wouldn't be capable of this level of antagonism against Christian Cinemas without your help."

"If you're not with us," he darkly warned me, "then you're against us."

I didn't take heed of Matthew's warning, nor did I understand that he had issued me a straightforward threat, until I crossed the school parking lot at the end of the day and discovered the rear tires of my car had been slashed.

CHAPTER NINE

OVERWHELMED, I STARED at the two rear tires of my sedan, as I crouched behind my car.

Had there only been one flat tire, I might have been able to chalk my bad luck up to an accident, such as driving over a nail at some point. But both tires were deflated, and when I applied pressure to the rubber near the hubcap of one of the tires, the rubber split, exposing a deep slash.

I had one spare tire in my trunk, but even if I was capable of changing a tire myself, which I wasn't, I would still only be able to solve half of the problem. I needed a second tire and someone to put both tires on my car, and this needed to happen in the span of fifteen minutes or else I would be late for rehearsal at the church.

Already feeling cold, as snow fluttered down, the only solution I could think of was to call Alan.

I bit my mitten and pulled it off my right hand, freeing my fingers to place a call to Alan on my cell phone.

Pressing my cell to my ear and listening to the ring tone, I glanced around the dusky parking area. I felt uneasy. I strongly suspected that Matthew had slashed my tires, but I told myself not to jump to conclusions.

"Penny?"

"Alan!" A sting of tears filled my eyes, I was so relieved to hear his voice boom through the line. "I need help! I have two flat tires and I'm supposed to be at the church for rehearsal."

"Where are you?"

Unlike the last time I had called my husband in a frantic tizzy about murder weapons, this time Alan didn't send his subordinates.

In a matter of minutes, the familiar sight of Alan's pickup truck growled into the school parking lot. The truck's windshield wipers kept the glass clear of snowfall, and there was Alan behind the wheel.

He pulled to a stop next to my car and climbed out.

"I think this was done on purpose," I told him as he joined me at the rear of my car.

"That possibility crossed my mind when you said you had *two* flat tires," he mentioned. "Do you have any idea who would do such a thing?"

As we both crouched down and I showed him one of the slash marks in the rubber, I explained, "I really hope I'm wrong, but I think it could have been Matthew, the science teacher."

Alan had not been expecting that. We stood up, and he asked, "The goofy-looking guy who teaches earth science?"

Alan had met Matthew more than a handful of times over the years when he had accompanied me to school functions and events.

"I found out that Matthew was supposed to co-own the new movie theater, but at the last minute, Bobby didn't sign the partnership agreement, which essentially cut Matthew out of the business."

Furrowing his brow at me, he didn't look pleased.

"I wasn't snooping."

"You were sleuthing," he corrected, which sounded like an accusation.

"I don't want to be late for rehearsal," I said, changing the subject. "This is our first rehearsal on the real stage that Dad built in the sanctuary—"

"I'll drive you over," he offered, coming to my rescue in the exact manner I had hoped. "Then I'll come back and get some new tires on your car. I should have your car all good to go by the time you're finished with rehearsal tonight."

I smiled from ear to ear. "Please don't drive off after you drop my car off at the church, though. Come inside and check out how our rehearsals are going."

He chuckled and touched eyes with me before opening the passenger side door of his pickup truck for me to climb in.

"I wouldn't want to spoil the performance by peeking at the children rehearsing."

Buckling up, I told him, "Stopping in will hardly spoil the show."

He shot me a crooked grin and shut the truck door for me, then after making his way through the snow, he climbed up behind the wheel and we drove through the heart of town to Hopeful Heart Ministries where hopefully Ashley was warming the kids up with a fun game that wasn't as politically charged as 'duck, duck, goose.'

Dusk turned to darkness. Conflicting feelings bubbled inside me. Alan had blabbed to my father about the fact that he had been living at a motel, which I took as a betrayal. And yet, whenever I was with Alan, all I wanted to do was curl up in his arms and forget about every argument we had ever had.

Alan was sure to pull the truck up to the church walkway so I wouldn't have to trek through the snow farther than necessary.

"Thanks so much again," I said. "See you soon?"

We locked eyes. There always seemed to be so much unsaid between us, and this moment was no exception.

He nodded and the slightest grin formed on his handsome face.

I climbed out, knowing that if I lingered, we would only end up arguing. I started through the snow.

As soon as I came into the vestibule, I stomped snow off my boots, freed myself from my winter coat, hat, and mittens, and pulled my sequin cap onto my head. This one was a classic, Christmas-red color.

In the sanctuary, I found Ashley had control over the children, who were playing a game of Simon Says.

I got situated in the front pew, closest to our brand-new Christmas pageant set where the kids were squatting, jumping, and tapping their heads whenever 'Simon' told them to.

During this round of the game, 'Simon' was Nathan, the eleven-year old Wise Man who had yet to perfect his lines and blocking for the big moment he would give baby Jesus the gift of gold during the live performance.

Having settled, I was able to focus on the kids. Ashley was standing behind Nathan and using grand gestures to enhance all the commands that Nathan, as 'Simon,' was giving the group.

I noticed that the other older boys were intentionally *disobeying* Nathan. They looked cross. As the game progressed, whenever Nathan told the group to jump, using the 'Simon says' command, the boys didn't move. According to the rules of the game, the only way to lose would be if a player performed a command even though 'Simon' didn't specifically say, 'Simon says' first. This meant that even though the older boys were disobeying, they didn't have to sit down.

I wondered what their obstinacy was all about, and by the looks of it, Nathan did, too.

Color rose in Nathan's cheeks when one of the older boys named Andy blatantly refused to perform a command.

From out of nowhere, Nathan charged at Andy, shoved him, and kicked him in the shin before Ashely or I could get a word in.

"Hey!"

I jumped up from my seat, and Ashley immediately began pulling the boys apart, but they tangled into a pretzel on the stage floor that neither of us could separate.

"You're supposed to do what I say!" Nathan raged, throwing punches and kicking awkwardly, as Ashley and I tried to pry the boys apart.

"Stop it!" Ashley yelled.

"Remember to be Christ-like!" I shouted, but Andy and Nathan were determined to make each other suffer.

"Your dad killed him!" Andy shrieked. "Everyone knows it!"

Horrified, I yelled at the top of my lungs, "Let go of each other right this very minute or both of you will be expelled from the Christmas pageant!"

Though both boys threw a few more punches to appease their pride, they untangled and I pulled Andy to one end of the stage while Ashley pulled Nathan to the other end.

I took Andy by the shoulders. He fought to catch his breath. Tears spilled down his cheeks, but as I gave him the once over, I was relieved to discover he wasn't bleeding or bruised.

"What in the world was that about?" I asked him, as Ashley did similarly with Nathan at the other end of the stage and the rest of the children looked on in fearful silence. "Why were you boys fighting?"

Andy frowned and folded his arms.

"Andy," I warned.

"Nathan's dad told Bobby that he was going to kill him, and then a week later, Bobby was dead!"

From the other side of the stage, Nathan shrieked, "My dad didn't kill him!"

"Yes, he did!" Andy insisted. He was utterly irate over his suspicion that Nathan's father had killed their beloved basketball coach.

"What are you talking about?" I questioned, turning Andy so that Nathan couldn't distract him.

"It's true! Everyone at basketball practice saw! Nathan's dad charged into our practice one night and got into an argument with Coach Bobby. He said he was going to kill him!"

Furious, Nathan shouted at Andy, "That doesn't mean my dad did it!"

"Yes, it does!" cried Andy, and soon all of the children were crying and nodding in bizarre agreement that Nathan's dad must be the murderer. "And now we don't have Bobby or basketball! Everything's ruined!"

Ashley and I locked eyes. We were both thinking the same thing. What chances did we have of getting through the play rehearsal this evening if all the children thought Nathan's father had killed Bobby Harder?

✝

AS ASHLEY DID what she could to direct the Christmas pageant rehearsal without one of the Wise Men, I met with Nathan's parents, William and Cathy-Ann Farber, in the fellowship hall.

I had called them immediately following the fight between Nathan and Andy. Cathy-Ann had answered the phone. She hadn't sounded shocked to hear that Nathan had gotten into a fight, and had offered to come to the church right away with her husband, William.

Nathan was seated at one of the tables near the bookshelf on the far side of the fellowship hall, which afforded William, Cathy-Ann, and myself some privacy.

Sullen, he flipped through a book and awaited his punishment.

I hadn't organized this meeting to punish him, however. I only wanted to find out what could be done to help Nathan cope with Bobby Harder's death. I also wanted to find out why all the other eleven and twelve-year old boys were convinced that Nathan's dad, William, had killed their beloved basketball coach.

"Is the other boy okay?" asked Cathy-Ann, genuinely concerned for Andy's welfare.

Cathy-Ann was a short, mousy-looking woman with honey-blonde hair and an overall competitive air to her personality. At forty-years old, she was a real 'soccer mom' when it came to supporting Nathan's interests, and she dressed the part. Whereas her husband, William, was the polar-opposite.

"Andy wasn't seriously hurt," I assured her. "The boys have always been friends and gotten along, and I'm sure they'll patch things up in no time. But I have noticed Nathan's behavior has changed since Bobby was killed. At Walnut Mountain Middle School, he has become the class clown, which hasn't been disruptive, per se, but it's not in his natural character to act out like that for attention."

"I'll have a stern talk with him," William offered. "We've noticed the same changes in Nathan's attitude, but we were hoping for the best."

He glanced at Cathy-Ann, but she didn't return his gaze. The married couple seemed distant from one another, and it wasn't just the fact that their chairs were three feet apart. Cathy-Ann looked closed off from William. Everything about her body language was turned away from her husband, including the direction of her crossed legs and the tilt of her head.

I wondered if Cathy-Ann felt that she had married beneath herself. She was an attractive woman who kept herself fit and trim. William, by contrast, was short, portly, and balding. He worked as a dentist on Lake Way and had done a great job on my new dental fillings a number of years back.

Leaning in and using a discreet tone so that Nathan wouldn't overhear me, I mentioned, "I've been hoping for the best, too. Of course, Nathan is going to need time to mentally process and mourn the death of his basketball coach. But your son is dealing with more than mourning. You see, the other boys have ganged up on him."

Cathy-Ann's eyebrows knit together as though this was news to her.

William asked, "Why have they been picking on him?"

"Let me preface this by promising that I plan to speak with the other boys and their parents about the matter. The other boys should not blame Nathan for what happened to Bobby, period. But at the moment they believe that you..."

"That I what?" asked William.

"That you killed Bobby."

Cathy-Ann pressed her mouth into such a firm line that her pink lips practically disappeared.

William froze, which wasn't the reaction I had expected.

Again, William looked at his wife, but she denied him any acknowledgement.

I offered, "Kids can be cruel and they also have wild imaginations. Like I said, I'm planning on talking to Andy's parents, as well as the parents of the other boys. But before I do, is there anything I should know? Mr. Farber, Nathan and Andy both mentioned that you got into a verbal altercation with Bobby at one of the basketball practices... Could you tell me about that?"

"I lost my temper," he admitted. "The timing was unfortunate and now that I think about it, it doesn't surprise me that the kids would jump to childish conclusions—"

"It's a private matter," interrupted Cathy-Ann as she stood up from her chair. "William and I will speak with Nathan so that he knows he must behave at school and at the rest of the rehearsals this week."

As Cathy-Ann crossed the fellowship hall and told Nathan it was time to go, I was tempted to ask William what Bobby had done to provoke William into confronting him that night at basketball practice. But William had turned austere and I knew I wouldn't get an honest answer out of him.

We both rose from our chairs. William buttoned his winter coat and I held the fellowship hall door open for all three of them to exit into the vestibule.

"Will you be able to manage the rest of the rehearsal this evening without Nathan?" William asked.

"We'll be fine, as long as Nathan is with us for the rest of the week," I said. "He really has been doing wonderfully as one of the Wise Men, and I'm so glad to have him in the Christmas pageant."

Cathy-Ann helped her son bundle up and then steered Nathan out into the blustery cold. William followed after them, and I returned to the sanctuary where Ashley had been leading the play rehearsal like a pro.

✝

AN HOUR LATER, the children were stumbling through a full run of the play. Ashley and I were seated in the front row. Whenever one of the kids said, 'line!' Ashley would shout the line and the child would repeat it. All told, the kids knew more than half of their lines and most of their stage blocking.

I heard the sanctuary door creak open behind me and glanced over my shoulder to find Alan slipping into the back of the church.

He pulled his winter hat off his head and ran his fingers through his dark hair, smoothing the cowlicks down.

I waved at him to come sit next to me, but he shook his head and gave me a wave.

"I'll be right back," I whispered in Ashley's ear.

She didn't take her eyes off the kids on stage as she nodded.

I made my way down the aisle and joined Alan at the back of the sanctuary.

"Come take a look at how the play is going," I quietly said.

"Your father did an exceptional job with the stage set," he said, impressed, as he drank in the sight of Dad's hand-carved woodwork. He cut his twinkling blue eyes to me and said, "Your car is good to go, but—"

"Let's talk in the vestibule," I whispered when Ashley glared at us over her shoulder.

Alan had a loud, booming voice.

Once we entered the vestibule, I closed the double-doors of the sanctuary so that Alan and I could speak at a normal volume.

"Thank you so much for getting those tires replaced," I said with a smile, as a strong urge to hug him came over me.

"I don't want you staying at the cabin all by yourself."

My smile drooped. Alan stared down at me with an air of authority that I didn't like.

I told myself to keep hope alive and asked, "Are you saying you're going to come back home?"

"I'm saying you have to stay with your parents—"

"Not this again!"

"Penny," he warned.

"I'm not a child, Alan, for God's sake!"

"I need you to stay with Lucas and Dottie until I find whoever slashed your tires. I spoke with Matthew and got a very bad feeling, but that doesn't mean that someone else didn't do it. Right now, I'm looking at Pastor Peter for the murder. I know you've been sleuthing and asking him questions, too. He could have slashed your tires as a result. Either way, you won't be safe at the cabin all by yourself."

"Alan—"

"This isn't up for debate, Penny."

"You know what, Alan," I said, losing my temper as well as control over the volume of my voice. "I wasn't going to say anything or confront you, but you leave me no choice. The only reason I have a real problem with you insisting I stay with my parents is because you have been sowing discord between me and my parents."

He made a face at that. "Sowing discord?"

"Yes, sowing discord. You have been talking about me behind my back to my dad—"

"This again," he balked, rolling his eyes.

"Yes, *this* again!" I sarcastically agreed. "But *this* time, you went too far, Alan. You told my dad that you've been living in a motel? How could you?"

Like a deer in headlights, he didn't move a muscle. Then, a healthy amount of guilt rose up in his face. His countenance fell and he looked down.

"The fact that you're temporarily living in a motel is such a private matter, Alan, and I trusted you to keep it private. But you didn't do that. You told my dad, and now you expect me to stay at my parents house? Do you see the position you've put me in?"

Whatever guilt he had been feeling disappeared. He straightened his spine and suddenly looked two inches taller.

"I have a right to confide in my closest friends about the difficulties I'm facing. Your father happens to be my best friend and I'm not going to apologize for seeking his wisdom and advice regarding what has been going on between you and me. If you don't like it, then that's too bad. I'm your husband and if I tell you that you're in danger and you have to stay at your parents house, then that is what you're going to do, Penny, and you aren't going to argue."

I stopped arguing. I didn't say a word. I could have made the irrefutable point that if Alan moved back into our cabin, then I wouldn't be alone or in danger, but I held my tongue.

He checked his wristwatch and said, "When will you be finished with rehearsal?"

"Look, Alan, you win. I will drive myself to my parents' house after rehearsal."

"No, you won't," he told me frankly, "because I didn't bring your car here. It's already at your parents' cabin."

"Wow, you really don't trust me at all, do you?"

He gazed into my eyes and said, "Nope."

That made two of us.

CHAPTER TEN

THE FOLLOWING MORNING at dawn, after sleeping well in my childhood bedroom and filling a thermos with freshly brewed coffee that I sweetened with cream and sugar, I started through the knee-high snowdrift behind my parents' cabin.

The air felt a bit warmer than it had been, or perhaps the trek towards the river was warming me up. Either way, I was happy for the peaceful morning.

As I came to the snowy riverbanks where three creeks converged into a river, the golden rays of the sun pierced through the mountains, brightening the white landscape all around me.

There I stood, watching the babbling waters rush by.

I had the sudden urge to pray, and so I did.

I prayed for forgiveness and self control. I prayed for Rachel and for her loneliness. I prayed for Alan and his investigation. I prayed for the murderer and for whoever had slashed my tires, whether that was the same person or not. And lastly, I prayed for Walnut Mountain and for the people who were being pulled further and further apart each day. A house divided against itself cannot stand, and I feared that if the residents of this town became further divided, attacking one another in order to impose their differences on each other, then Walnut Mountain wouldn't last very long.

"There you are!"

I glanced over my shoulder and saw my mother trekking through the deep snow with the sunlight in her eyes.

"Did you see the cardinal?" she asked as she joined me on the snowy riverbank. "I've been keeping the bird feeder full on the deck, and every morning a cardinal comes by for breakfast."

"I must have missed him," I said. "I've seen blue jays in the fir trees."

"I live my life in perpetual awe of the beauty here," she said, glancing up at the sky and drinking in the sights of the mountains, the creeks and river, and the full expanse of the snowy landscape stretched out before us. "Your father and I are glad to have you here with us, Penny."

I sighed.

She said, "I know it's only temporary—"

"Alan will catch the killer and then we'll be back at our cabin," I agreed, but my mother was keen to my lies.

"Honey—" She stopped herself when I shot her a warning glance. Then she proceeded with caution, "I would love nothing more than for you and Alan to restore your marriage and live together in your cabin. I really would."

"Sometimes I doubt that."

"Hey, now. Don't doubt me. I *do* want you to have a happy, healthy marriage. But I can't say I'm upset that you're staying here with me and your father for a few days."

She studied me for a moment as I drank hot coffee from my thermos, then she asked:

"Who do you think slashed your tires? The killer?"

"I don't know. At first, my gut told me Matthew had slashed my tires, and I thought he might have killed Bobby. But now I'm not so sure."

I had been wrestling all night with the urge to speak privately with Cathy-Ann, Nathan's mother. She had seemed closed off and disconnected from her husband William when I had spoken with them in the fellowship hall. I believed the children and believed that Nathan's father had threatened Bobby by saying the words, 'I'll kill you.' I had a hunch that under the right circumstance, Cathy-Ann might open up to me about the real conflict between William and Bobby Harder.

All this was to say that I no longer believed Matthew had murdered Bobby at the movies. But that wasn't to automatically say that Matthew hadn't slashed my tires. Even Alan strongly suspected Matthew at this point.

My mom asked me, "Can I have a taste of your coffee? It smells delicious."

I grew tense. I knew she didn't trust me, and I knew what she was doing, but I passed the thermos to her. She wasn't going to taste liquor in my coffee. Despite my close brush with falling off the wagon, the fact of the matter was that I hadn't. Since the accident, I hadn't touched a drop of alcohol. I honestly wondered if the accident I had caused the last time I had really overdone it with drinking would ever be behind me. Would my family ever truly forgive me if none of them could seem to forget?

After taking a little sip, my mom smiled, asked me which roast I had used, and drank a big gulp.

"Alan wants me to go to some kind of AA program at the church," I told her, even though it was obvious she already knew. If Alan had confided in my dad about every last thing, surely my mother was up to speed. "For the record, I need to be able to move on. A program like that is going to force me to live in the past."

"I don't know about that, Penny," she replied, choosing her words very carefully. "It might be wise for you to participate in a program that will hold you accountable, at least for a little while."

"You want to talk about 'accountability'?" I challenged. "Why is no one holding Alan accountable?"

She furrowed her brow, unable to understand my point. "Alan didn't do anything."

"Yes, he did, Mother."

"What are you talking about?"

I was talking about the truth, but I wasn't sure I should go there. Painting my husband in a negative light was the wrong thing to do. My actions were my own fault. I knew and accepted that. But Alan had played his role in the night of the accident.

That being said, I wasn't going to betray Alan in the same subtle manner that he had betrayed me by confiding in my parents matters that were private and should have been kept between Alan and me.

So, I said this instead, "Alan is an enabler. This isn't to cast him in a bad light. Alan is the closest thing to perfect that I have ever seen with my own two eyes. But there's a specific type of person who marries an addict. If I'm an alcoholic, then Alan is an enabler. End of story."

✝

AS LUCK WOULD have it, after teaching at Walnut Mountain Middle School all day, I arrived at Hopeful Heart Ministries early for rehearsal and was able to catch Cathy-Ann Farber as she dropped Nathan off.

Ashley was already in the sanctuary, greeting the kids that filtered into the church and getting them settled with a warm-up game of charades, while I hung back in the vestibule, helped the children out of their winter coats, and made sure everyone took off their snowy boots before they entered the sanctuary.

I neared Nathan and Cathy-Ann, smiled down at the boy, and said, "You did very well in class today. I really appreciated your cooperation during the group work we did, and I'm glad you're here to participate in rehearsal this evening."

He looked up at me with his boyish face, slightly skeptical of the praise.

"What do you say, Nathan?" Cathy-Ann pushed.

"Thanks?"

I smiled and suggested, "Why don't you go on into the sanctuary and join the game of charades. Ashley is going to get things started for the first ten minutes, and I'll be in shortly after that."

Having taken off his winter coat and snowy boots, Nathan hopped into the sanctuary and tugged on Ashley's arm when he reached her, eager to play with the other kids.

"Thank you so much," I said to Cathy-Ann, as I closed the double-doors of the sanctuary. "Nathan was on his best behavior today, and after I spoke with the other boys and their parents today during the lunch period, all the kids seemed to get along just fine. But if you notice Nathan expressing any issues with the other boys, please let me know, and I'll do the same, of course."

"I definitely will." Cathy-Ann pulled her knit hat off her head and fluffed her honey-blonde hair, as she added, "We've had our fair share of challenges at home, and this was before Bobby was killed."

I could tell that she had just revealed the tip of the iceberg, and I sensed that she was itching to vent.

"I'm a very good listener," I assured her, inviting her to go on. At first, she hesitated, so I mentioned, "I know what it's like to have a rift at home."

Her mouth quirked into a funny smile. "I thought 'the

Matchmakers' had a perfect home life, or at least that's the rumor."

"The rumors are flattering," I admitted. "My husband and I don't have children, so it's easier for us to hide our problems."

She relaxed and a friendly connection formed between us. Then she widened her eyes, leaned in, and whispered:

"Bobby came on to me."

I was instantly thrown for a loop. I had not seen that one coming at all, and it made me wonder if I had heard her correctly.

"I'm sorry, did you say that Bobby *came on to* you?" I questioned.

She nodded. "And my husband, William, found out."

"Really?" I asked, mentally working as hard as I could to comprehend the dynamic. "When did this happen?"

She sucked in a deep breath, taking a moment to mentally pull the pieces together so that the story she told would make sense, or so it seemed to me.

"William rarely dropped Nathan off or picked him up from his youth basketball practice. Oftentimes, I would stay at the courts and watch Nathan at practice. Bobby was always friendly with me, just like he was friendly with the other moms and dads. I mean, Bobby had to have been the nicest guy in the world."

"Oh, I know," I agreed wholeheartedly. "Bobby was the nicest guy in the world."

"Absolutely!" she sang without holding back. "But then, one evening I showed up extremely late to pick Nathan up. I totally lost track of time, then I hit traffic, and then I had car trouble on the road. I mean, it was one of those instances when one bad thing set off a chain reaction of frustrating inconveniences.

"Anyway, I ended up getting to the basketball courts twenty minutes late. The only people at the court were Bobby and Nathan. As soon as I opened the glass door of the building, Nathan sprinted out from the lobby and jumped into my minivan. Of course, I didn't rush off. I went inside the lobby to apologize to Bobby.

"Looking back, I really wasn't thinking," she added before a faraway look filled her eyes. "I should've known better than to find myself *alone* with a man in a dimly lit lobby. Plus, I was wearing leggings and a thin tee shirt under my coat, which hardly left much to the imagination."

"And he made a move on you?"

"He did, and it should have been nothing more than an adult mistake, but Nathan saw us. He was so confused that he asked his father about it, which of course, set William off. William jumped to his own conclusions, and he tried to restrain himself. But before long, he showed up at basketball practice to confront Bobby."

"Oh, my goodness," I breathed, "and all the boys saw the confrontation…"

"Obviously William didn't kill Bobby, but from the kids' perspectives…"

"Yes, I understand how it must have looked to them," I agreed. I had a hard time completely believing Cathy-Ann, and as a result, I couldn't stop myself from asking, "Was William at the movie theater that night?"

She stared at me for a long moment and said, "Why would you ask me that, Penny?"

✝

EVEN THOUGH I HAD planned to go to my parents' cabin after rehearsal, Esther called me and asked if I would join her at Christian Cinemas for a special film screening.

"Special film screening?" I asked as I climbed into my car, turned the engine, and cranked up the heat. "I didn't think Rachel was planning on showing any movies until after the New Year."

"All I know is that Daniel invited me to a special film screening tonight at Christian Cinemas…"

"Okay…?" I said when I thought she would tell me more.

Suddenly, her voice sounded frazzled through the line. "He's really freaking me out."

"Daniel is?"

"He has been looking at me strangely and acting aloof. Plus, remember how we ran into him at that men's boutique when I was Christmas shopping?"

"Yeah…?"

"Well, I found out that he bought a *suit* that day. A three-piece suit!"

"Do you want me to ask Alan to conduct a full investigation?"

"Penny!"

I teased, "The mystery of Daniel and the three piece suit—"

"Not funny! I'm seriously freaked out! I think he bought the suit to impress another woman! He probably wants to break up with me! You have to come to the movie theater and be my emotional support!"

"I'm on my way," I promised, but when I arrived at Christian Cinemas, Esther wasn't waiting out front.

The glass entrance doors were locked.

I turned to find my cell phone in my purse, thinking I should give Esther a call, but then Rachel hurried through the movie theater lobby and let me in.

"Goodness!" she exclaimed, as the incoming wind blew her long black hair off her shoulders. "Come inside! You must be freezing!"

In the lobby, I asked, "You've planned a special screening?"

"Not exactly," she said, her eyes bright and her mood upbeat. "Daniel contacted me to see if he could rent the main auditorium for a private screening."

As we crossed the lobby, there wasn't a single soul but the two of us, and it didn't sound like there was a big crowd in the movie theater, either.

Sure enough, when Rachel led me into the auditorium, the entire screening room was cool and empty.

"Do you know what movie Daniel is screening tonight?" I asked, realizing that this was all highly mysterious.

Perhaps Esther wasn't wrong to feel freaked out.

"I don't know anything. Daniel asked to be let into the projection room and handled everything himself."

"Where is Daniel?"

"He's in the projection room and Esther has yet to arrive," she explained. "In fact, I thought you were her. Daniel didn't tell me that you were coming."

"Daniel probably doesn't know because Esther invited me last minute," I told her, as we sat in the third row from the front. Since I had Rachel to myself, I had to ask her about the confrontation between William and Bobby that the boys had blown out of proportion...

All I could think was, maybe the boys *hadn't* blown the situation out of proportion.

"You're doing so well," I began. "I wouldn't want to bring up a difficult subject, but do you know a man named William Farber?"

Rachel took a moment to consider the name.

When his name didn't seem to ring a bell, I added, "William is married to a woman named Cathy-Ann. Their son, Nathan, was in Bobby's youth basketball program."

As soon as I said Cathy-Ann's name, Rachel's inky eyes widened with recognition.

"I know Cathy-Ann," she said, but then quickly clarified. "I don't *know* her, know her. But Bobby told me about her."

A strange look of contempt came over Rachel's otherwise beautiful face, and she told me:

"Cathy-Ann threw herself at Bobby."

"Threw herself at him... sexually?"

Rachel pushed her dainty eyebrows up to her hairline and shot me a look that said it all.

"Every chance she got," she added.

My jaw dropped. "I spoke with Cathy-Ann not even an hour ago, and she said that it was *Bobby* who had come on to *her*."

"Bobby would never," she insisted. "She said that? What a liar! No, it was Cathy-Ann who was practically sexually harassing Bobby at just about every basketball practice."

"He told you this?"

"Eventually, yes. She was really bothering him and embarrassing him. It damaged our marriage in fact, because it was difficult for me to fully believe and fully trust Bobby. You have no idea, Penny. Once the trust broke down between us, the emotional state I was living in basically drove me to drink, or at least want to. It was awful."

"Huh," I said, pondering all she had said.

I could have asked her more, but the sound of someone entering the movie theater stole our attention.

I turned. In the entryway of the auditorium stood Esther.

"Hello?" she said, squinting through the dimly lit movie theater to see who was there.

Rachel and I stood up, and I said, "It's just me and Rachel."

Rachel told us both, "I'll leave you two and see where Daniel is at. Enjoy."

She made her way up the aisle and smiled at Esther as they passed one another.

Esther reached me. Rachel closed the auditorium doors on her way out.

"What in the world could all of this be about?" asked Esther, as she unbuttoned her winter coat.

She wore a white feathery chemo cap and when she removed her coat, I saw she had a beautiful pearl-colored dress on.

"You look lovely," I said, beaming a smile. "Look at you!"

"Daniel told me to wear white," she said, as a frown of horror filled her worried face. "I'm really freaked out!"

The dim lights went out.

Esther and I locked eyes.

The movie screen flickered as the film projected onto the silver screen.

Esther and I simultaneously dropped to our seats, grasped hold of each other's hands, and stared wide-eyed and breathless as the film that was beginning to play.

Music poured out through the speakers and Daniel filled the screen.

As soon as we saw that he was wearing a three piece suit, we touched eyes, surprised, then quickly returned our attention to the screen just as Daniel, looking directly at us from the silver screen, said:

"Esther, the day I met you, I knew I was experiencing a miracle. My whole life, I have prayed to find a woman like you, but the Lord saw it fit to put me through trials and tribulations, to strengthen me, and to help me to become the kind of man who might be worthy of a woman like you. Not only have I been specially prepared, having been put through the spiritual fire of surviving cancer, but I know in my heart that he has perfected you by way of the same spiritual trials and tribulations. You are my best friend, my first love, and my better half, and I hope to continue this spiritual journey with you, on earth as it is in heaven, until the very end. Esther..."

Tears had welled up in my eyes so badly that I didn't immediately realize Daniel had emerged from a door to the left of the movie screen.

Wearing the same three-piece suit, he came out, crossed in front of the screen, and turned up the aisle, coming to Esther, who stepped out into the aisle to meet him.

Daniel took her by both hands.

I gasped and Esther blurted out a crying laugh of joy and disbelief, as Daniel lowered down onto one knee.

"Will you spend the rest of your life with me, as my wife, Esther?"

Though her knees were wobbly, she cried out, "Yes! Yes, Daniel,

I'll marry you!"

He sprang up and lifted her in a hug, kissing and twirling Esther, as I clapped and proclaimed:

"Hallelujah!"

Once again, I had made a lasting match that would end in marriage, but all I wanted was to find my own happily-ever-after with my husband, Detective Match.

CHAPTER ELEVEN

WHILE ALAN WAS INVESTIGATING Matthew's culpability in relation to the murder as well as my slashed tires, I couldn't stop thinking about Cathy-Ann Farber.

According to Cathy-Ann, Bobby had made an inappropriate move on her. Her son, Nathan, had witnessed the indiscretion, told his father, William, and William had confronted Bobby at one of the basketball practices.

However, something wasn't adding up.

Rachel had contradicted Cathy-Ann's account, flipping the dynamic between Bobby and Cathy-Ann on its head. As far as Rachel understood, it had been *Cathy-Ann* who had been coming on to Bobby.

So, who was telling the truth? Cathy-Ann Farber or Rachel Harder?

Bobby Harder had looked as though God Almighty had carved him out of marble. He was practically a Greek god. Easily the most attractive man in the country, if not the world, as evidenced by his long career as an international high fashion model. He had married a model. Rachel possessed otherworldly beauty, and whenever the gorgeous couple had been together in public, the electric love between them had been palpable.

And yet, Bobby had *come on to* Cathy-Ann?

Cathy-Ann?

Really?

The more I thought about it, the more I doubted that Bobby had crossed an inappropriate line with Cathy-Ann. But then again, I also knew that sexual harassment wasn't about looks. It was all about power. When I considered the contrasting testimonies from the standpoint of power, taking 'looks' out of the equation, then I had to admit that Cathy-Ann could be telling the truth.

But whether Cathy-Ann or Rachel were correct about what had transpired between the 'soccer mom' and the 'Greek god,' none of that mattered if it wasn't connected to the murder.

When I had asked Cathy-Ann if William had gone to the movie that night, she hadn't wanted to admit the truth. But when I had pressed her, she had come out and told me, yes, William, Nathan, and she had been in the theater auditorium and had fallen asleep just like everyone else.

This told me that it was possible William had killed Bobby.

But had he?

Or had Matthew Chapman?

Or had Pastor Peter?

Perhaps Vince Salisbury had fooled us all, and he was the killer...

It seemed that the longer the killer remained free at large, the more potential suspects there were, surfacing to the forefront of my secret, sleuthing investigation.

I found it sad and strange. Bobby Harder had been the nicest guy in the world, and yet, four men had plausible motives to kill him.

There was another aspect that saddened me, as well—a running theme I couldn't help but notice that was cutting through this entire story.

Distrust between spouses.

A cold rift had divided Cathy-Ann and William.

The trust between Rachel and Bobby had been shattered thanks to Cathy-Ann.

Worst of all, Alan and I had been estranged for months and drifting further and further away from one another with each passing day.

And all of this was happening during Christmas time...

I sucked in a lungful of air, pulled the keys from the ignition of my car, and climbed out of my car, stepping into the crisp winter evening.

Ashley and I had arranged to meet at the gazebo in the heart of Walnut Mountain in order to do some last minute shopping and buy the rest of the props that were needed for the Christmas pageant.

The gazebo sparkled with little white lights. I passed Santa Claus, who was ringing a bell for the Salvation Army, and dropped a few dollars into his red kettle, then ascended the gazebo steps.

Ashley was hopping around with a to-go cup of coffee in her mittened hands.

"I'm here!" I sang out.

"Can you believe how cold it got?" she asked. The tip of her nose was red and her teeth were chattering. "I even braved Morning Glory and faced the wrath of Dex to get this coffee, because I knew the only way to combat the freezing temperature would be to drink hot liquids non-stop!"

"The wrath of Dex," I laughed, as we left the gazebo, crossed the street, and started along Main Street towards the craft store.

"You think I'm kidding?" she teased, letting out a little laugh. "I dread encountering him."

I stole a glance at Ashley and caught sight of the grin she was trying to suppress.

I pulled my mitten off my hand and found the list of props in my coat pocket.

"There are only a handful of items we need," I said, skimming the list to refresh my memory. "We should be able to get most of the props in this store."

Opening the door for Ashley, we entered the warm craft store, which smelled of cinnamon and nutmeg. Christmas music was softly playing, and there were many shoppers browsing the shelves and aisles, picking out Christmas presents for their families and loved ones.

Ashley took the list, read through the itemized props, and I followed her down one of the aisles where we were sure to find colored construction paper, glue, glitter, and little cardboard boxes, all of which we needed in order to make the 'gifts' that the Three Wise Men would give to Mary and Joseph for the Lord. In rehearsal, the kids had been practicing with plastic cups, but they needed the real performance props during the last few rehearsals to get comfortable.

As she browsed through the different shades of glitter, Ashley remarked, "Having the Christmas pageant on Christmas Eve is going to be so sweet. Your husband is coming, right?"

A smile formed on Ashley's face from ear to ear.

"I believe so, but the police station keeps him pretty busy, so we'll see."

"He's so handsome," she commented. "How did you snag him?"

That was the million dollar question, wasn't it?

"Some things are just meant to be," I told her. "I didn't snag him and he didn't snag me. Alan and I are supposed to be together, and therefore we are."

Two seconds after the statement left my mouth, I believed it was true.

"Wow," she said.

"When you meet 'the one,' there's no fighting it," I added.

Ashley grew quiet and thoughtful. "I feel like all I do is fight."

I wondered what she meant specifically. "Well, don't," I suggested lightheartedly.

She sighed. "Forcing some things and resisting others is my nature," she admitted. "I'm controlling. I'm afraid it's my Achilles' heel."

"We all have weaknesses," I assured her. "But our weaknesses aren't meant to be fatal flaws. Remember, the Lord said, 'My grace is sufficient for you, for my power is made perfect in weakness'."

Ashley furrowed her eyebrows and frowned, as she said, "I don't know what that means."

"Oftentimes, I don't know what that means either," I said and we had a bittersweet chuckle. "But then I have moments of clarity, and I understand that my weakness helps me realize that I can't rely on myself, and that I must depend on God. I must draw close to the Lord and follow him, and God's power will save me from myself, from those very weaknesses that might otherwise destroy me."

Ashley stared at me for a long moment, while what I had said worked its way down through all the layers of her psyche.

"I think I'm in love with Dex," she realized.

"You are," I said.

"I am," she agreed and then a huge grin formed on her face.

As we continued our shopping, I felt uplifted. Romance was blossoming between Ashley and Dex. Daniel had proposed to Esther a few days ago in the most romantic way I had ever seen.

Love would always lead the way. There was hope for all of us.

Including me.

✝

I FELT INSPIRED TO surprise Alan. I didn't want to be lumped into the camp of couples that couldn't repair the rifts caused by their differences. I wanted to live securely on the side of love, hope, and romance.

Alan loved me. He couldn't stay away for good, and he couldn't keep his hands off me whenever we were alone. I felt determined to mend our marriage, so after quickly stopping by my cabin to get dolled up, I mustered every shred of courage I possessed and drove out to the motel where my husband had been living for the last four months.

I had never visited Alan at the Nutcracker Motel, and I never before had a reason to go there. Of course, ever since Alan had moved into the motel, I had daydreamed about showing up for this and that reason, but had never gone through with the idea.

This time, I had a good reason to show up.

It was Christmas time, and enough was enough. My husband and I should be together.

Located on the outskirts of Walnut Mountain, the Nutcracker Motel was a quaint, one-story structure that looked more like a ski lodge than a truck stop.

As I pulled into the snowy parking lot, I didn't see Alan's pickup truck, which didn't surprise me. It was only a little after 8 pm, and I imagined he was wrapping things up at the police station for the evening.

I parked in front of the motel office, slung my purse over my shoulder, and used the sun visor mirror to quickly check how I looked. I wasn't wearing a winter hat, and the way I had styled my chin-length auburn hair was holding up. I dabbed a bit more gloss on my lips and then climbed out of my car and entered the motel office.

"I'm Detective Matchmaker's wife," I told the clerk, a mild-mannered young man who was wearing a red Santa hat and reading a comic book.

It took a second before he realized who I was talking about. "Oh, you mean Detective Match?"

It took all the strength I had not to roll my eyes.

"Yes, he's my husband. I was hoping to surprise him…"

"He's been staying in Room 3," he said as he stood and found a spare room key hanging on the wall where there was a grid of keys laid out in numerical order.

One of the things I loved most about living in Walnut Mountain was that it was a safe, small town, and people trusted one another. I didn't have to bribe or threaten the clerk to let me into Alan's room.

He offered me the key, smiled, and said, "Merry Christmas."

"Merry Christmas to you, too," I said before heading back out into the blustery cold.

When I reached Room 3, I scanned the parking lot for Alan's pickup truck once again. He definitely wasn't here, which was good. It would give me a chance to get comfortable and really surprise him.

I keyed into the motel room. The warm air inside smelled like Alan, and a feeling of longing came over me.

I stomped the snow off my boots outside, then stepped in and closed the door behind me.

Once I had turned on the lights and taken off my boots, I glanced around the simple room, which was larger than I had expected.

There was a queen-size bed in the middle of the room, a couch and coffee table across from a full entertainment center, and a desk, on which Alan had organized his papers and files. The bed was made, and the room was clean and tidy overall.

I removed my winter coat and hung it in the closet. I had decided to put on a long-sleeve, knit dress that flattered my figure. With my knit tights and jewelry, I felt good about my appearance.

I took a slow lap around the room, coming to the desk, where I discovered a Bible was lying open.

It made me smile.

Alan had been so busy at the police station that he had only been able to attend church sporadically. But that didn't mean he was falling away from the Lord. One of the things I loved most about Alan was that for as long as I had known him, he had never stopped seeking God's face.

I felt a pinch of guilt.

I shouldn't have told my mother that Alan was 'an enabler.'

On the one hand, it was true that my husband did have forgiving, optimistic characteristics that had unintentionally enabled my ability to minimize and justify my relationship with alcohol.

But on the other hand, it had been wrong of me to speak badly about my husband, period.

I told myself I needed to repent from that kind of behavior.

The open Bible caught my attention and the bold-faced chapter heading jumped out.

"Joseph and Potiphar's wife," I said, reading the chapter heading out loud.

In this particular chapter of Genesis, one of the youngest Israelites, Joseph, was sold into slavery by his older brothers, who were jealous of him. Joseph ended up serving a high-ranking Egyptian official named Potiphar. Because the Lord was with Joseph, Potiphar was impressed with everything Joseph did and soon Joseph was put in charge of Potiphar's entire household and all that Potiphar owned.

I sat down at the desk, engrossed in reading about Joseph.

"Now Joseph was well-built and handsome, and after a while Potiphar's wife took notice of Joseph," I read out loud, leaning into the pages and absorbing every word. "And Potiphar's wife said, 'Come to bed with me!' But Joseph refused..."

Day after day, Potiphar's wife lusted after Joseph for his good looks and begged him to go to bed with her, but every day Joseph refused.

I continued reading farther down the page, "One day, he went into the house to attend to his duties, and none of the household servants was inside. She caught him by his cloak and said, 'Come to bed with me!' But he left his cloak in her hand and ran out of the house."

I looked up and leaned back in my chair, remembering the full story.

What happened next in the Bible passages was that Potiphar's wife told her husband that Joseph had tried to force himself upon her. She used the torn piece of his cloak as evidence. As a result, Potiphar threw Joseph in prison...

Potiphar had believed his wife without question, and had ruined Joseph's life as a consequence.

I wondered...

Why was my husband, Alan, studying this portion of the Bible? Did it relate to the murder?

Maybe it did and maybe it didn't, but I didn't wait for my

husband to return to the motel room to find out.

CHAPTER TWELVE

THE DAYS LEADING UP to Christmas Eve were a blur of play rehearsals, gift shopping, and running around Walnut Mountain to spend as much quality time as possible with my friends.

Rachel was having her ups and downs, mourning Bobby yet carrying on with the movie theater. Esther and Daniel were madly in love and inseparable, which only made me miss my husband terribly. Ashley was a ball of nerves and had been avoiding Morning Glory to avoid Dex, terrified of the romantic revelation that had dawned on her. And it seemed no matter where I went around town, I ran into Matthew and Samantha. The blossoming romance between them was strengthening in direct proportion to Rachel's determination to open Christian Cinemas for business in early January right after the New Year.

All the while, Alan continued investigating the murder of Bobby Harder, giving heed to the strong possibility that whoever had killed Bobby might have also slashed my tires.

Though patience was required, I stayed at my parents' cabin as Alan had insisted, which gave me time to reconnect with my mom and dad, learn more about my Grandmother Mable, and contemplate the mysterious reason why the Bible in Alan's motel room had been opened to the story of Joseph and Potiphar's wife.

When the night of the Christmas pageant finally arrived on Christmas Eve, I delighted in dolling myself up. I wore a forest-green dress, high-heel boots, jingle bell earrings, and a red Santa hat.

My parents, Dottie and Lucas, looked festive as well, and we all drove over to Hopeful Heart Ministries in Dad's pickup truck, which had the most trustworthy winter tires out of all of our vehicles. Walnut Mountain was expecting a big snowstorm this evening, but we were all praying that the falling snow wouldn't start accumulating until after the Christmas pageant had ended and the congregation had safely returned home.

The church twinkled as Dad pulled into the parking lot. He had helped Pastor Peter string lights around the trim and the steeple of the church, and also the nativity scene. Even the little stone pillar that Pastor Peter had stacked weeks ago sparkled with white lights.

Parishioners made their way up the walk and into the church, which was aglow with soft interior light.

My heart swelled with the hope, awe, and wonder of Christmas, and my spirit felt alive and grateful.

Families were taking photos in front of the outdoor nativity scene that Dad had built, as snow fluttered down all around them.

After climbing out of the pickup truck, I was eager to find Ashley inside to make sure that the props were set for the play, but my mother stopped me from hurrying off.

"Penny, let's take a family photo in front of your father's nativity scene," said Dottie. She smiled from ear to ear, proud of Lucas's artistry. "This is beautiful!"

As she neared the hand-crafted stable, one of the families that had just had their photo taken stepped away. The wooden camels, donkeys, and sheep were dusted with a thin layer of white snow, which caused them to sparkle like ice under the twinkling lights.

Pastor Peter seemed to be in charge of taking everyone's photo. My father greeted him with a handshake then handed the pastor his cell phone, while Mom and I gathered around the wooden statues of Mary and Joseph. When my father joined us, we smiled at the cell phone camera in Pastor Peter's hands.

"Merry Christmas!" we shouted in unison, smiling wide just as the camera's flash went off.

My mom gave me a hug and told me to break a leg, even though she knew I wasn't performing in the play, and my dad gave my shoulder a pat.

"Merry Christmas, sweetheart," he said, as he hugged me.

Unless Alan came tonight, I didn't see how my Christmas would turn out very 'merry,' but I hid all signs of pessimism from my face, and told him I would find him and Mom after the play.

Inside, the vestibule was wonderfully crowded with parishioners who were hanging their coats and greeting one another near the refreshment table where hot coffee, hot chocolate, and Christmas cookies were available to anyone who wanted to warm up from the cold.

As I took off my winter coat and found a spot on the rack to hang it up, I peeked into the sanctuary, which was full of Christian residents, excited to watch the Christmas pageant and eager to worship the Lord's birth.

Gloria Davis let out a joyful exclamation and threw her arms around Esther, pulling her in tight and congratulating her on her engagement, while Hank and Daniel shook hands.

My parents slipped past me into the sanctuary, followed by Pastor Peter.

Deeper in the church, I spotted Vince Salisbury and his four boys. Cathy-Ann and her husband, William, were also present, though they didn't look especially happy to be in each other's company. Even *Samantha* was here...

Samantha?

I did a bit of a double-take and then saw Matthew approaching her with two hot coffees in his hands. He gave Samantha one of the steaming cups and she flashed him a thousand watt smile.

Huh, I thought to myself. Maybe she *wasn't* using Matthew. Maybe she genuinely liked him. Maybe, just maybe—and *hopefully*—Samantha's heart would open to Christ and she would put a stop to all the antagonistic protesting she had been at the helm of for weeks.

I began to make my way down the aisle of the church, crossing through the sanctuary. Ashley and the children knew to meet behind the beautiful stage my father had built, in the backstage area.

As I neared the foot of the wooden, hand-crafted scenery, squeezing my way through members of the congregation who were hugging each other and wishing their neighbors merry Christmas, I realized Rachel Harder had come!

She was sitting in the front pew all alone and looking a bit down, though she wore a beautiful purple dress that accentuated the allure of her inky eyes and high cheekbones.

"Rachel! I'm so glad you made it!" I said as I came to sit next to her. There were only about ten minutes before Pastor Peter would begin the Service by announcing the Christmas pageant, but this was the first time Rachel had returned to church since Bobby's murder and I wanted to make sure she felt comfortable and at home. "Merry Christmas, how are you?"

I gave her a little hug and she mustered a thin smile.

"I'm okay," she said. "I couldn't stand the thought of being all alone on Christmas Eve."

"Of course," I agreed.

I was about to say more when Vince Salisbury approached with his boys.

"Merry Christmas, Penny," he told me before glancing at Rachel with his steel-blue eyes.

She smiled up at him, and if I wasn't mistaken, there appeared to be a connection between them. Rachel invited Vince to sit next to her and Vince's boys piled onto the pew around them as soon as I got up and excused myself to join Ashley and the kids.

Before I disappeared around the corner of the scenery into the backstage area, I glanced over my shoulder at Vince and Rachel. There was clearly a bond between them, and I wondered if they had formed a connection as widow and widower since each of them had lost their spouse, or if something else had occurred...

Backstage, all the kids were dressed in their costumes and looked amazing. Ashley was putting the final touches on the children playing the angels by dabbing their cheeks with sparkles and adjusting their golden pipe cleaner halos. She was also—very much to my surprise—in the throes of a heated yet low-key argument with *Dex*.

Ashley's cheeks were flushed red and it wasn't because she was too warm.

She looked furious and glared at Dex every chance she got, as he hovered over her and maintained his stance that all *systems* in the United States, whether run by the government or not, had to collapse.

"That's insane!" Ashley hissed at Dex, as she sent one child on his way and pulled the next towards her for sparkles. "If you collapse all the systems we have in place, you'll collapse *all of civilization*."

"You think that's a bad thing," he argued, "because you lack vision and an adventurous spirit!"

"I do not lack an adventurous spirit!" she shot back, squaring her shoulders at him and getting in his face.

So passionate was their whispering argument that neither noticed I had slipped backstage.

Nathan neared me and said, "They've been at each other's throats since I got here."

"Is that so?"

He screwed his face up and asked, "Who is he?"

I whispered, "He's the barista from the coffee shop, Morning Glory."

That made as much sense to Nathan as the feud that had been unfolding between Ashley and Dex in the first place.

Dex stepped in even closer to Ashley and said, "Overt government control is not the answer!"

"I never said it was!" she fired back, coming nose to nose with him.

"You look really pretty!"

"Don't change the subject!"

"I'm not! You always look really pretty!"

"I do?"

"Yes!" he growled.

They stared at each other, wide-eyed and breathless for a beat, and then Dex took hold of Ashley's face and kissed her.

I had seen this coming from a million miles away.

All of the kids cringed and whined, "Ew!" as the passion between Dex and Ashley turned from hostile to romantic. They kissed, entwining their arms around one another.

"Alright, everyone, that's enough!" I said, wrangling the children.

Dex and Ashley eased off of one another, but Dex stole a few more kisses and pecks, while Ashley floated back to planet earth.

"Dex," I began to suggest, "you might want to claim your seat out there. The church is getting crowded."

He gazed deeply into Ashley's eyes. "I'll see you after the play."

"Mmm-hmm," she murmured, drifting somewhere between Cloud 9 and reality.

"Bye, Dex," I said, prodding him along.

"Wow," said Ashley with a dopey grin on her face once Dex had returned to the pews.

Mrs. Matchmaker has done it again! I thought to myself, as I gathered the children into a circle.

"Hold hands, everyone," I whispered. "Let us pray that we will each do our best to honor our Lord and Savior as we perform the Christmas pageant this evening."

As I led the prayer, I inwardly hoped that Alan would catch the killer in time to spend Christmas with me tomorrow, yet deep down, I knew that if I didn't uncover who had murdered Bobby Harder at the movies, then it was possible no one ever would.

✝

AS THE CHILDREN performed the Christmas pageant play, I stood near the sanctuary wall and watched, having a vantage point to see the kids on stage as well as the audience of parishioners in the pews.

The performance went off without a hitch. The children remembered their lines and blocking, and everyone in the audience loved the show.

When it came time for Nathan and the other Wise Men to present the baby Jesus with three gifts of gold, frankincense, and myrrh, each one spoke his lines clearly and on cue.

I could not have been prouder to see the good fruits of everyone's hard work.

By the time the play was over and all the kids filled the stage to take their final bows, I felt tears well up in my eyes. I had always loved children. I wanted a little boy or a little girl of my own.

As the entire congregation clapped and cheered for the wonderful performance, I glanced across the church at all the familiar faces and looked for my husband.

But he wasn't here.

He hadn't made it in time to see the Christmas pageant.

I snuck a peek at my cell phone, hoping that Alan might have at least sent me a text message.

He hadn't.

On stage, the children made their way into the wings, disappearing out of view just as we had rehearsed all week.

Ashley and I met the children backstage, and as we congratulated them with hugs and high-fives, there came a commotion from out in the sanctuary.

A bad commotion.

An argument that sounded like a bad fight.

"You never apologized for what you did!" yelled a man.

Confused at the sudden argument unfolding in the church, Ashley and I locked eyes.

"I've graciously allowed you to bring your boys to church, and yet you never apologized!" the man continued yelling.

The yelling man was Pastor Peter, I realized. I recognized his angry tone of voice, but it took me a moment to place the other man who was responding to the pastor's many accusations.

"I didn't do anything wrong!" said the other man.

"You don't think it's wrong to deface private property?" the pastor snapped, irate.

"You should have taken it up with Bobby when you had the chance!"

Now it made sense. Pastor Peter was arguing with Vince Salisbury.

As I darted out from backstage, the pastor yelled, "Bobby was responsible for doing what he did, and you're responsible for what you did!"

"You killed him, didn't you?" Vince yelled, pointing his finger in Pastor Peter's face.

The entire congregation was stunned, but no one more so than Rachel.

Her jaw dropped and she gasped, "Pastor Peter would never harm Bobby!"

"No?" Vince challenged. "Look at him! He's practically foaming at the mouth, he's so furious about his precious stone pillars!"

Rachel addressed the pastor, questioning, "You didn't kill Bobby, did you?"

Pastor Peter was at Vince's throat, and now Rachel was at Pastor Peter's throat. All three of them began arguing, blaming one another and pointing their fingers in each other's faces.

This wasn't a scene for children, so I asked Ashley to usher the kids over to the fellowship hall. A few parishioners slipped out the back with them, not desiring that their blessed Christmas Eve should be spoiled by the dramatic uprising that was unfolding at the front of the sanctuary.

That being said, Matthew and Samantha drew closer, as did my parents, Esther, Daniel, and others who wanted to see if this Christmas Eve confrontation would lead to a killer confession.

Cathy-Ann and William Farber, however, did not sneak off,

even though their son, Nathan, tugged at Cathy-Ann's arm to leave.

The way Cathy-Ann was *glaring* at Rachel gave me pause.

The petite 'soccer mom' had contempt written all over her glaring face. Rachel, on the other hand, was a vision of beauty and emotion, despite the sudden rage that consumed her.

It was then that I recalled how deeply Bobby was beloved by everyone in Walnut Mountain…

…and soon I had an epiphany that had everything to do with Joseph, Potiphar's wife, and the murder of Bobby Harder.

Chaos completely broke out, as Cathy-Ann threw herself into the argument, accusing *Rachel*, of all people, of being the *reason* Bobby had been killed.

"What?!" Rachel shrieked, radically offended that Cathy-Ann had the audacity to assume such a thing. "I loved my husband! Bobby was my entire world! I didn't kill him! I wasn't even at the movie theater that night! My God, how dare you, Cathy-Ann!"

Stepping between Rachel and Cathy-Ann, I raised my voice and shouted, "Enough! Stop accusing one another! None of you are innocent! Not a single one of you! Any of you could have killed Bobby thanks to your dark, selfish motives!"

I directed my point to Vince, Pastor Peter, and Cathy-Ann, though Rachel wasn't exempt. Of course, Rachel didn't have a twisted, selfish motive to kill her husband. But I was all too aware of what wrestling with a drinking problem did to a marriage. Just as I had been damaging my relationship with Alan, Rachel had been inadvertently killing Bobby in a way, as a result of turning to alcohol to soothe her anxiety.

"No one believes that Rachel had a thing to do with Bobby's murder," I went on, "but the rest of you should all take a good, hard look at yourselves. You might not have been the one who strangled Bobby, but every one of you had it in you to do the deed."

I approached Vince Salisbury whose boys had left the sanctuary with Ashley a moment ago.

"At first, I suspected Vince—"

He objected, "I didn't kill Bobby—"

"But you could have! You footed the bill, paying for expensive materials to construct Bobby's black wrought iron fence, and when it came time for Bobby to pay you, he refused. Withholding thousands of dollars from you right before the holidays had put you in a difficult financial position. What were you going to say to your four sons if they asked you why there were no Christmas presents this year?"

Vince shrank, turning solemn. "Thank God, it didn't come to that," he said.

"If you had killed Bobby," I went on, speaking sympathetically, "it would have made sense. It wouldn't be right, but people would understand, because the motive would have been logical. However, I knew that you didn't kill Bobby, and the reason you didn't kill him was because more than anything you wanted to receive the money he owed you. There would have been no sense in killing him, because dead men don't write checks."

Pointing the finger of blame, Pastor Peter suggested, "Vince could have killed him anyway for revenge."

"You could have, too, Pastor," I shot back fearlessly, as I neared him and continued to explain how they all had motives to murder Bobby. "We all have come to understand your devotion to God. We all know how deeply you love the Lord, and that you cherish the spiritual insights and revelations you've received over the years. What most people don't know, and what I didn't know, was that you commemorate your spiritual revelations by building stone pillars, most of which happened to be on Bobby's property."

"Bobby and I came to an agreement!" he barked as though I had poked a festering wound that refused to heal.

"You did," I agreed. "But your agreement couldn't prevent a terrible misunderstanding—"

"It wasn't a 'misunderstanding'!" he told me, as he charged at Vince, preparing to let the man have it.

Thinking fast, Matthew stepped in front of the pastor and placed his palm against Peter's chest, holding him back from taking a swing at Vince.

"Whoa, Pastor!" said Matthew.

Pastor Peter yelled at Vince, "You should have never taken it upon yourself to install Bobby's fence wherever you pleased! If I regret anything, it's that I shouldn't have focused my anger at Bobby! I should've come after you!"

"Yet you *did* focus your anger at Bobby!" I yelled. "Bobby's lack of oversight and his lack of keeping tight control and watch over Vince's work resulted in the destruction of your irreplaceable stone pillars. That must have broken your heart, Pastor. It must have felt as though Bobby had carelessly trampled over, not only the pillars, but also the love you carry for the Lord in your heart."

"It killed me," he admitted. "It was as though he had attacked my very faith, or my very own soul."

"I understand that," I told him, "which is why I truly believed that you were the one who had killed Bobby Harder at the movie theater. But I know you. Though you're human and though you can be unforgiving, I *do* know you well enough to trust that you are not a killer. You would never take a man's life no matter what he's done. You're a God-fearing individual and you live by the 10 Commandments."

"Thank you, Penny," he said, the anger having left him.

"Ever since Bobby was murdered," I went on, "I kept returning to the likely theory that the person who killed Bobby must have really hated him and everything he stood for. Given the fact that Bobby was the nicest guy in the world, I couldn't fathom who would despise him. Then it occurred to me. Only someone who didn't know him could despise him. And that's why, from Day One, I have always suspected that one of the protestors snuck into the movie theater that night and committed the murder."

As soon as I mentioned the protestors, Matthew and Samantha shrank. Samantha folded her arms and glared at me. Matthew's bookish glasses magnified the guilt in his eyes.

"None of the protestors knew Bobby," I continued. "All they knew was that Bobby was in the throes of opening a Christian movie theater and they didn't want that movie theater to ever see the light of day. When the theater opened, the protestors shifted their objective. They couldn't stop the movie theater, so they decided to stop the man responsible for the movie theater in the hopes that the theater itself would shut down once Bobby was dead."

Samantha screwed her face up and stated, "Everyone who was protesting the movie theater that night was *outside*, Penny. No one went inside to watch the movie or to kill Bobby."

"I thought the same thing, until I discovered the partnership agreement between Matthew and Bobby."

This was news to Samantha. "Partnership agreement?" she asked, confused. "What are you talking about?"

"Didn't you know? Matthew was going to co-own the movie theater."

She turned to Matthew and asked, "You were?"

"It's not what you think—"

"But you created the Walnut Mountain Warriors website for me months ago..." she said, thinking out loud. "You've been against Bobby and against his Christian movie theater... haven't you? Why would you want to co-own the theater? Why would you want to go into business with the enemy?"

Matthew stammered and began groveling, "It wasn't supposed to be a *Christian* movie theater, Samantha. Bobby went back on his word! He broke our deal! He refused to live up to his agreement with me. He didn't sign the contract—"

"And you were mad enough to kill him for it," I interjected.

Samantha softened from head to toe and melted into Matthew's arms. "You killed Bobby for me?"

Horrified, and yet clearly turned on, Matthew began stammering even worse than before, desperate to insist he hadn't killed Bobby, while at the same time basking in Samantha's affection.

"I would kill anyone for you, Samantha," he said, swooning.

"But you *didn't* kill him," I informed everyone. "As much motive as Matthew had to kill Bobby Harder, he wasn't the one who committed the crime."

"Then who did, Penny?" asked Esther, who had been listening, enthralled, from the sidelines where she was standing next to Daniel and my parents.

"I'll tell you who killed Bobby Harder," I announced.

A hush fell throughout the sanctuary of the church.

"It was Potiphar. But Potiphar would have never sentenced Joseph to the most severe punishment had it not been for Potiphar's wife and her lie!"

As soon as I said it, I locked eyes with Cathy-Ann. She knew exactly what I was talking about, but no one else did.

"You see, Potiphar loved and respected Joseph," I went on, "just like William Farber loved and respected Bobby."

In an instant, all eyes were on William, but not everyone understood the comparison between the dentist and the Biblical story.

"Cathy-Ann and William first met Bobby when their son Nathan began attending the youth basketball program that Bobby coached. Bobby loved those kids, including Nathan, and all of the boys loved him, too. Because Bobby was truly a servant and mentored the kids, he earned William's respect. And he also earned Cathy-Ann's unwanted attention."

"How dare you!" sneered Cathy-Ann. She looked about ready to strangle *me* to death. "Don't you say another word!"

Rachel couldn't hold her tongue. "You were coming on to my husband! He politely tolerated your relentless sexual advances, and it was tearing our marriage apart!"

Everyone around them gasped.

"Cathy-Ann, you know what you did!" I asserted. "When Bobby rejected you, you ran to your husband, just like Potiphar's wife ran to Potiphar, and you *lied* about what had happened between you and Bobby. Bobby hadn't tried to force himself on you. It was the other way around, but when you made Bobby out to be some kind of attempted rapist, William took matters into his own hands!"

Rachel gasped and stared wide-eyed at William Farber. "It was you?"

"I only meant to confront him!" cried William. "That's why I showed up at Nathan's basketball practice that night! I only wanted to confront him and tell him to stay away from my wife!"

"William, don't!" yelled Cathy-Ann.

"But he laughed!" he went on. "Bobby actually *laughed*, and then he made my wife, Cathy-Ann, out to be some kind of lustful harlot! The way he spoke about my wife… I couldn't let it go. It infuriated me and I became obsessed with him. I tried to stop myself from fantasizing about killing him, but I couldn't! Then, the night of the movie screening, it was as though the stars aligned in my favor! If everyone hadn't fallen asleep at the movie, I could have never strangled Bobby from behind."

Again, everyone in the sanctuary gasped at William's harrowing confession.

"But everyone *had* fallen asleep that night," he concluded. "I acted on the opportunity, and took his life."

I felt eyes on me and glanced over at the entrance of the sanctuary where the double-doors had been open. Alan was standing in the open doorway with three police officers. He held a pair of handcuffs in his hands.

I didn't know how long Alan had been listening, but he offered me the faintest smile.

Then he ordered his men to move in.

The police officers walked briskly down the aisle, making an authoritative beeline for William Farber. Cathy-Ann began shrieking. Rachel was hit with a wave of emotions and cried with relief. Vince Salisbury, Pastor Peter, and Matthew Chapman all looked sheepish, guilty with their own culpability even though none of them had acted on their urge to murder Bobby.

"William Farber," said Alan as he handcuffed the killer. "You're under arrest for the murder of Bobby Harder."

The police officers escorted William up the aisle, removing him from the church, as Cathy-Ann scurried after them, crying and insisting that Bobby had deserved it.

In the vestibule, Ashley was protectively gripping Nathan's shoulders, but Cathy-Ann took hold of her son and together they hurried out into the snowy night.

"I just have one question," I said, turning to Alan. "Who slashed my tires?"

Alan didn't have to answer me.

Matthew sighed and shuffled towards me. "I panicked, Penny."

"You slashed my tires?" I was stunned.

"I was terrified that you would expose the partnership agreement and Samantha would find out and hate me," he confessed, as he held his wrists out for Alan to handcuff him and haul him into the police station. "I deserve to be locked up."

It was Christmas Eve. I didn't want anyone else locked up. I just wanted to go home with my husband and have a merry Christmas.

"Tell you what," I began proposing. "Reimburse me for the cost of the new tires, and we can put the whole thing behind us."

He offered me a humble smile and said, "Deal."

Alan put his arm around me and quietly suggested, "Now that the killer has been caught, how about you and me go home for Christmas, just the two of us?"

I could have leapt for joy, I was so happy. Tears filled my eyes but I blinked them away, as my parents looked on, grateful for the Christmas miracle they knew was occurring to mend my marriage.

"I would love that," I breathed, as I looked up at him.

"Me, too," he softly said, and then he kissed me.

✝

ALAN AND I LEFT THE church separately that night. While he briefly returned to the police station to oversee processing William Farber's arrest, I tidied up the sanctuary and fellowship hall, making sure that everything would be in order for the Christmas Service the following day.

To my surprise, by the time I arrived at the cabin, Alan was already there. I parked my car next to his pickup truck in the snowy driveway and entered the warm house, feeling grateful, relieved, and elated, among a whole host of excited emotions.

This was the beginning of the rest of our happy life together, I thought to myself, as I hung my coat and hat, and removed my winter boots. Surely, Alan was ready to come home for good. We could work on our marriage and rebuild trust, and hopefully—*God willing!*—we could work on getting pregnant. and finally start a family.

I stepped into the living room and couldn't believe my eyes. There was a fully decorated Christmas tree standing at the side of the room with wrapped presents beneath! Alan had strung lights along the ceiling, and Christmas music played faintly through the speakers. The wood burning stove crackled with fire, and Alan had placed scented candles on the coffee table in front of the couch.

When did he have time to do all this? I wondered, as my heart swelled with joy.

"Merry Christmas, Mrs. Matchmaker."

I grinned from ear to ear, hearing my hot husband's deep, sexy voice behind me.

I whipped around just in time to catch a kiss.

His warm mouth smooshed against mine. I melted into his arms. I could feel his heartbeat, we were pressing so tightly.

It was as if he couldn't get enough of me, and I certainly couldn't get enough of my husband!

At long last, all the mistakes, all the distrust, and all the hurt feelings vanished.

There was only love between us!

Marrying Alan was the most important 'match' I had ever made…

…and our love was here to stay!

I let out a little yelp of surprise, as he scooped me up in his arms.

Alan started carrying me towards the stairs.

"Where are you taking me?" I asked.

"To the bed!"

I swooned, nearly fainting…

Had the heavens opened up? I heard a chorus of angels singing 'Hallelujah' and their song resounded all night, as my husband and I reached new heights of marriage bliss!

☦

BUT THE FOLLOWING morning, after I had showered and wrapped myself in a robe, the worst misunderstanding slammed into what should have been a perfect Christmas day...

… and everything changed in an instant.

I returned to the bedroom.

Alan was seated on the bed.

He looked pale and forlorn.

Beside him was the box of alcohol that Rachel had given me.

Alan stared at me with his blue eyes as if I was a stranger.

"I found your stash under the bed," he said in a small voice that broke my heart.

All I could think to say was, "It's not what you think."

A split second after I said it, I realized I had made a huge mistake.

THE END

CATHERINE GIBSON

POISONED AT THE PICNIC
(The Matchmaker Murders, Book Three)

CHAPTER ONE

"MY NAME IS PENNY, and I struggle with alcohol addiction."

It had taken three and a half months, but I could finally admit that I had spent years secretly struggling with a drinking problem.

"Hi, Penny!" replied the other members of this humble addiction recovery program.

We were seated on chairs in a circle in the fellowship hall of Hopeful Heart Ministries.

A gorgeous Catholic woman named Jessica Saxon ran the Celebrate Recovery program here at the church.

Jessica kept a close eye on her stopwatch and an even closer eye on me, as I began sharing during my allotted five minutes.

As my sponsor, Jessica watched my every move. She constantly texted me. She called me at least five times a day, and otherwise treated me as a ticking time bomb that could explode any second if I was left unsupervised.

To say that she wasn't my favorite person would be putting it mildly. But I appreciated how much she cared about my sobriety.

Unlike Alcoholics Anonymous, Celebrate Recovery was a Christ-centered addiction recovery program that addressed a wide variety of addictions.

Our tight-knit group not only included recovering alcoholics like myself, but also people who were determined to overcome all kinds of addictions, from compulsive overeating to codependence to shopping addiction. The program was still anonymous, but the members were never expected to identify with their addiction. Instead we would say we're *overcoming* our *struggle* with our given *issue*, which I liked.

I touched eyes with my sponsor, Jessica, and continued sharing, "Now that it's springtime, I've been feeling especially optimistic. I haven't been stressed out, and I'm getting along with my parents again. My husband, Alan, continues to be a rock in my life. I can see how Alan discovering that box of alcohol on Christmas morning really was the best thing for me."

Seated across the circle from me was Rachel Harder, another recovering alcoholic. Her husband, Bobby, had been murdered last year in his movie theater, Christian Cinemas. The box of alcohol that had turned my night of bliss with Alan into a morning of mourning had really belonged to Rachel.

"At the time, I felt devastated," I went on. "But if that hadn't happened, I wouldn't have joined this program."

I let that hang for a moment, feeling proud that at long last I was once again the woman Alan had married.

As I smiled, enjoying my victory as much as the sweet spring air that was breezing through the open windows, I glanced at the other group members—my true companions on this journey of recovery and self-discovery.

Next to Rachel was Hailey Wexler, a young waitress who worked at Fancy's restaurant. Hailey struggled with a shopping addiction.

Then there was Hailey's friend, Sue Ellen Grossman, a tender-hearted young woman with short, curly, blonde hair and the most unusual addiction out of the entire group. Sue Ellen was recovering from what she referred to as a *rescuing* addiction. Simply put, she had rescued over twenty cats, and her life had become *unmanageable* because of it. She was my favorite waitress at Charming Diner. But often she felt distracted at work, swallowed in worries about how her furry friends were getting along at home.

In my estimation, Sue Ellen's need to rescue could have been a virtue instead of a vice, but only time and the Lord's guidance would tell.

Jessica Saxon frowned at me, her dainty eyebrows knitting into a hard line.

Jessica didn't like it when I indulged in quiet moments of heartfelt connection during my five minutes.

I quickly concluded, "Thank you for listening."

Everyone replied, "Thanks for sharing!"

Next Pastor Peter Peterson, who was seated to my left and struggling with one heck of an anger addiction, began his allotted five-minute share time.

Jessica started the timer and relaxed her demeanor.

She ran a tight ship. Dressed in tight clothes. And reminded me of a ballerina despite her big hair. Jessica oozed perfection, but there was something oppressive about it. Like every breath she took was measured and every move she made was calculated.

Not quite a ballerina, she owned Angel Arts & Crafts at the corner of Main Street and Walnut Way. She painted in her spare time, and had overcome literally every addiction under the sun—alcohol addiction, nicotine addiction, prescription drug addiction, regular drug addiction, compulsive overeating, compulsive undereating, compulsive shopping, and codependence. She had even overcome a compulsive gum-chewing addiction.

I didn't trust her...

...which was why I hadn't opened up to her about *everything* I had been going through.

It's not that I didn't trust her because she used to have so many addictions. And it wasn't like I didn't trust her because of her immaculate appearance—her chocolate-brown hair and perfect porcelain doll face. She looked like an angel, and Lord knew she was trying to be one.

But *that's* what I didn't trust.

I didn't trust her perfection because it came with a holier-than-thou attitude.

And I definitely didn't trust the pressure to confess that she had been putting on me since day one. Celebrate Recovery was an anonymous program. Everyone in the group was sworn to secrecy, Jessica included. But she still wanted *me* to tell my friends, colleagues, and extended family that I was an alcoholic. I wasn't going to do that. My best friend, Esther, didn't know about my drinking problem, nor did the other teachers at Walnut Mountain Middle School where I worked as a Language Arts teacher. I was determined to keep it that way.

Which was why I hadn't told Jessica the story about the night my drinking had gotten *way* out of hand.

I feared that if Jessica knew the truth about the *accident* I had caused that one time I really *had* drank *way too much*, then she would put so much pressure on me to 'come clean' to 'everyone in my life' that it would only drive me to drink.

I wasn't about to let that happen.

I still had my secrets.

I kept them buried.

But little did I know that with time every secret of mine would surface...

✝

AFTER STANDING IN a circle, holding hands, and reciting the serenity prayer, our Celebrate Recovery meeting dispersed, and I left Hopeful Heart Ministries, stepping out into the sunshine of a beautiful Saturday afternoon.

Across from the church was a white gazebo, which sat in the very center of Walnut Mountain. Today, the honky-tonk band, Jail Bird, was playing music on the gazebo. Picnic tables spanned the grassy knoll, and every resident of Vermont who loved my parents gathered around the buffet tables where burgers and barbeque were just begging to be devoured.

It was my parents' 50th anniversary celebration. Dottie and Lucas Hawkins, otherwise known as the best mom and dad a girl could ask for, had made their marriage work for half a century. And the whole town had come out to celebrate their shining example of true love in an otherwise twisted world.

I had been sure to dress appropriately for the blessed occasion. I wore a flowing, flowery sundress, wedge-heel sandals, and a fashionable chemo cap with a huge sunflower on the side.

Carefully crossing the street as cars rolled by, I spotted Esther and her fiancé Daniel, who I had matched last autumn. Esther was also wearing a chemo cap, hers with sequins, even though her black, wispy hair had grown out. She had survived cancer last year and was in remission, but our habit of wearing head coverings was one we weren't about to give up.

"Penny!" Esther threw her arms around me, giving me a big hug. She was still frail as a bird yet more radiant than ever. "Did you just come from church?" she asked, curious about what I might have been doing there.

"I'm helping out with the upcoming Easter service," I said, deciding it wasn't a *total* lie.

Easter was right around the corner and I was on the decoration committee.

Daniel gave me a little squeeze, which wasn't easy with the plated burger in his hand. "This is a great turn out! Great band, too! Honky-tonk is my favorite!"

I was about to agree when I felt the familiar sting of watchful eyes on me.

I glanced over my shoulder.

Jessica Saxon had locked her distrusting sights on me, as she headed my way.

Oh, for Christ's sake!

I hadn't invited her.

I tried not to let my spirits falter as I welcomed her into the conversation.

She regarded Esther and Daniel with a cool air of suspicion as she greeted them.

Esther quickly offered, "Can I get anyone a wine spritzer? I was about to grab one myself!"

Jessica frowned and then glared at me with disapproval. "Penny and I will help ourselves to soda when we're thirsty, thank you."

Ever since Jessica had become my 'friend,' Esther had grown somewhat used to Jessica's overbearing nature.

I, on the other hand, had not.

A sharp edge of worry cut through my chest whenever my sponsor behaved like this. Sooner or later, I feared, Jessica would spill the beans about my recovery. Attempts to control me like this were a dead giveaway that I was in the throes of overcoming alcoholism, or was I being paranoid?

"Mrs. Matchmaker!" sang Gloria Davis as she pressed her full figure through the crowd. "What a lovely party!"

I had successfully matched Gloria with a surly attorney last year, who very unfortunately was murdered shortly thereafter. Gloria had ended up reuniting with an old flame, Hank, who was playing bass guitar with Jail Bird as we spoke.

Before I could catch up with Gloria, Jessica hissed at me, "Penny, I think we should speak privately."

Esther screwed up her pretty face at that, and Gloria and Daniel exchanged a look of confusion, as Jessica took me by the arm and led me away from my friends.

"It's my job as your sponsor to support you," she hissed

through her teeth when we reached the refreshment table. "My responsibility is to make sure you don't expose yourself to any triggers!"

"My friends aren't triggers—"

"This is a party where alcohol is being served!"

"I don't feel tempted to drink—"

"Why didn't you tell me about this? Why didn't you invite me? I can save you from putting yourself in a bad position—"

"Jessica, with all due respect—"

"This is a *family* event, Penny," she went on, snapping at me in hushed tones as guests streamed past us. "For people like you and me, being around family is the biggest trigger of all!"

Whether or not I needed to be saved from the temptation to drink was up for debate. But I definitely needed someone to save me from my sponsor's smothering version of support.

Luckily, my prayers were answered when my parents, Dottie and Lucas, swooped in with hugs and happy faces.

"You look beautiful," my mom exclaimed, giving me a big squeeze that melted the anxiety in my heart. "Hello, Jessica."

"Mrs. Hawkins," said Jessica cooly.

"Oh, please, how many times do I have to tell you to call me Dottie!"

My mom gave Jessica a hug, while my dad steered a tailored-looking thirty-five year old man towards me. It took me a second, but then I beamed the biggest smile, recognizing him.

"Patrick!"

"How're you doing, Penny?" he said, thrilled to see me.

Patrick was my cousin from my mom's side of the family. He lived in Industry City with his sweet wife, Margot, and their three children. I rarely saw him. He had made a name for himself as a successful real estate agent, and he never failed to send Alan and me a Christmas card every winter.

"Are Margot and the kids here?"

"No, they couldn't make it, unfortunately," he said, as a gloomy look came over him.

"That's too bad," I sympathized.

Patrick's gloom darkened even more when he noticed Jessica, who had inched away. He did a bit of a double-take seeing her, and when I glanced at Jessica, she turned white.

"Pardon me," I quickly offered. "Patrick, this is my friend,

Jessica."

He swallowed the lump in his throat and sort of stammered, which was odd. But Jessica's reaction was even stranger. She barked something about needing air, even though we were standing outside in the freshest air in Vermont.

Jessica turned on her heel and took off like she was fleeing the scene of a crime.

I didn't care why she had left, I was just happy she had.

Making excuses came naturally, so I said, "She hasn't been feeling well."

My dad, Lucas, added, "She's unwell in general. Don't take it personally, Patrick."

"Not at all," he breathed, still looking like he'd seen a ghost.

Lucas told me, "Honestly, Penny, I know she's your friend, but what do you see in her? She's very controlling."

"Very controlling," my mother echoed, shaking her head. "And she doesn't go to church."

"She goes to *her* church," I pointed out. "She's a Catholic."

Dottie shrugged like she would never be able to make sense of it. Patrick recovered from whatever had rattled him. And the conversation turned to cheerful topics.

A moment later, I glanced across the grassy knoll, and there he was.

The handsomest man in Walnut Mountain.

Alan Matchmaker had arrived.

✝

MY DREAMBOAT HUSBAND peeled his sunglasses off his face and locked eyes with me. A grin tugged at the corner of his mouth, giving me a twinge of hope that I might get lucky tonight.

As he made his way through the picnic tables where people were devouring burgers and tapping their feet to the honky-tonk music, I excused myself from conversing with Cousin Patrick and my parents, and ventured to meet Alan halfway.

Alan had been promoted to a detective position last year. He'd solved two murders in two months. Everyone in Walnut Mountain was grateful for Alan. He had caught the killers! Hopefully, no one else would ever get murdered in our cozy neck of the woods.

"Aren't you a sight for sore eyes," he said, as he pulled me in for a smooch.

There wasn't a day gone by that my heart hadn't melted for my husband. He just did it for me! Even though our marriage was on the mend, I still desperately wanted him to move back home to our cabin.

I savored the kiss.

"Are you planning on spending the night?" I whispered as he released me.

"Penny," he warned.

I told myself not to feel dissatisfied with the progress we had made. Alan was thrilled I had enrolled in the Celebrate Recovery program and that I had a sponsor. It had helped build a foundation of new trust between us. But I wanted more. I wanted my *husband*. I wanted *all of him*.

Boldly, I decided to push, "Springtime is all about new beginnings and fresh starts…"

"Let's enjoy your parents' anniversary and see how the day goes," he suggested.

"Do you have to go back to the station?" I asked, not loving my sudden insecurity.

"Can we just enjoy the moment? Have you had a burger yet?"

As I tried to keep our conversation quiet, I told him pointblank, "I want you to come home."

"There are too many memories in the cabin," he shot back.

He had sounded definitive.

My heart sank.

"Does that mean you're *never* coming back?"

"Don't put words in my mouth, and don't jump to conclusions," he sternly warned. He let out a breath, letting the tension go, and asked, "Is Jessica here?"

I scowled.

"She's your lifeline, Penny. You do whatever she tells you to do. Do you understand?"

"I have been," I seethed.

Speaking of the devil, Jessica interrupted us, shattering our privacy as well as my sanity!

Classic Jessica.

"It's so nice to see you, Detective Match," she said, offering Alan a lukewarm smile that was far from friendly.

Alan was blind to her cold demeanor, however. All he could see was how, as my sponsor, she was keeping me sober. Frankly, I thought Alan was giving her far too much credit. I hadn't had a single slip up since I had chugged Holy Communion wine last autumn, which was hardly a big deal.

Jessica asked me, "How are you *feeling*?" as if I was about to fall off the wagon.

"I *feel* fine, Jessica."

"Because there's no shame in leaving the party," she added.

"I'm not going to leave the party."

Alan reinforced Jessica's sentiment. "If being around alcoholic beverages is too much—"

"It's not too much," I promised.

Jessica and Alan shared a look of concern between them. It bothered me how they were on the same page and apparently reading an entirely different book than me. The story of my life was *not* all about my former drinking problem!

Excusing myself, I headed towards the buffet table, which wasn't far.

Esther and another teacher from Walnut Mountain Middle school, Harriet, were helping themselves to wine spritzers. Harriet taught Art with Janice, who was also at the picnic.

Jessica was hot on my heels when I reached the table.

Esther and Harriet must have seen the look on my face, because Esther's eyes widened and Harriet was standing ready.

Harriet handed me a plate of desserts and whispered, "For Jessica."

I passed the plate to my sponsor—"Hungry?"—just as Esther handed me a soda with the same idea.

I passed the soda to Jessica, who began to gulp it, angrily. She shoved a cupcake into her pretty mouth next.

Esther winked at me and whispered, "That ought to shut her up."

Harriet was an ordinarily upbeat woman with a zany artist's mind, but whenever she saw Jessica coming, her mood soured. So, I didn't blame her when she slipped away from us and got lost among the dancers who were enjoying Jail Bird's honky-tonk set.

I decided I had to put my foot down with my sponsor. I wasn't going to let Jessica's overbearing nature spoil my time at the anniversary picnic.

"Esther, would you excuse us?" I said.

When Esther had, I turned to address Jessica and give her a piece of my mind.

But without warning, she grabbed her stomach and keeled over.

"Jessica?"

Her porcelain doll face scrunched into a grimace. She dropped to her knees and then took a face dive onto the grass.

"Jessica!" I screamed.

"Oh, my God!" exclaimed Esther, as she rushed over.

I crouched and brushed the immaculate chocolate-brown hair away from my sponsor's neck.

I hoped for the best but feared the worst as I touched her neck, praying I would feel a pulse.

There wasn't one.

Jessica Saxon was dead.

CHAPTER TWO

THE WALNUT MOUNTAIN police station was not where I imagined I would end up after my parents' 50th anniversary celebration, but here I was, tucked in an interview room with my husband. He wasn't acting very 'husbandly.'

At the moment, he was strictly 'Detective Match.'

I had never been on the *suspect* end of his piercing blue gaze.

I kind of liked it.

"Tell me everything you can remember, leading up to Jessica's death," he said.

He wasn't recording the interview. He didn't pick up the pen and notepad that were on the desk between us. But it was obvious he planned to find clues.

"What do you mean, Alan? We were both talking to Jessica," I reminded him.

"Then you walked away and she followed you."

"To the refreshment table, yes," I allowed.

We stared at each other for a beat. Across the street from the police station, guests of the picnic were lingering and talking about Jessica's shocking death. Through the open window of the interview room, I could hear their attempts to make sense of what had happened, though the hum of their confusion sounded muffled from where I was sitting.

"I handed Jessica a soda and a plate of desserts," I went on, trying to be helpful and trying even harder not to be distracted by my husband's dashing good looks.

Alan was a woodsy, rugged man. He looked even better than

usual at the moment, now that he was giving me the third-degree.

Wait a second, was Alan giving me the third-degree? Did he suspect me of foul play?

My eyebrows shot up to my hairline.

"Was Jessica murdered?"

He pressed his mouth into a hard line.

"Was she?" I pushed, stunned. "I thought she choked on something, or maybe had a heart attack, though both seem peculiar."

"You know I can't divulge any details about the crime—"

"Crime?!"

"It looks like she was poisoned."

Suddenly, it hit me why I was being questioned. If Jessica had been poisoned...*to death*...that meant that she had to have eaten something poisonous. And I had definitely handed her soda and desserts...

"Alan, you can't possibly think I had anything to do with—"

"I just want to hear from you exactly what happened."

"Well, for the record, I didn't invite Jessica to the picnic, and once she had arrived I wasn't with her the entire time."

"Everyone knows she sticks to you like glue, Penny."

He must have noticed my sudden terror at being treated like a criminal, because he quickly offered:

"I don't think you poisoned her. Trust me. But someone at the picnic must have had it in for Jessica. All we know at this point was that she ingested *something* poisonous. We have yet to find out what the actual poison was."

"She could've eaten the poison long before she keeled over," I suggested, thinking out loud.

"That's true," he agreed. "Once we know what specific poison killed her, we'll have an idea of whether it instantly took her life or whether it was a kind of poison that would take ten or twenty minutes to do its deadly work. For now, I only need to hear *your* story."

Esther came to mind. I felt fiercely protective. Harriet had been at the refreshment table, too. But I wasn't going to sit here and incriminate my own friends and fellow teachers. Besides, what if someone else had *poured* the soda or *baked* poison into the cupcake and cookies? What if that person had calculated every move? What if they had supplied Esther and Harriet with the poisonous item with perfect premeditated planning?

"There were a lot of people at the refreshment table," I finally answered. "There were people I know, like Esther and Harriet."

I winced, having named my friends, but pushed myself to go on.

"And there were other guests, like my cousin Patrick, additional friends of my parents, and even Mom was nearby."

Alan sighed. He didn't write any of those names down.

Instead, he told me:

"I need at least one valid lead, Penny. I really don't want that to be you."

"I don't want that to be me, either!"

Chief Pepperdine barged into the interview room, startling me so badly that I exclaimed:

"Sergeant Pepper!"

The chief was a towering mountain of a man with salt-and-pepper hair, a leathery face, and a voice so booming it could cause an earthquake.

He directed his anger at Alan and barked:

"Detective, you can't question your own wife! What's gotten into you? Have you lost your mind?!"

Faster than a heartbeat, Alan stood.

"Penny did nothing wrong, Chief! She didn't poison Jessica Saxon!"

Gauging the look on my husband's face and how he planted his fists on his hips, and the fact that he continued arguing—he didn't back down even for one second—I suddenly realized that Alan had been far more husbandly towards me than I had initially thought.

By interviewing me himself, he thought he could protect me.

"This is completely out of line, Matchmaker!" boomed Sergeant Pepper. He tempered his emotions long enough to tell me, "Penny, would you please excuse us?"

"I'm free to go?"

"For today," he allowed, giving me a hard look before returning his attention to Alan.

As I slung my purse over my shoulder and slipped out of the interview room, the chief and my husband *really* got into it. Everyone in the police station heard them, and I wouldn't be surprised if people outside did as well.

I walked through the station where there were a few desks for the police officers that worked in Walnut Mountain. Officer

Jeremiah and Officer Charles, who we all called Chuck, were interviewing guests of the picnic.

In the waiting area at the front of the police station were even more picnic guests, seated on chairs and looking forlorn. There were a lot of familiar faces, and a few people I didn't recognize.

I guessed the word had gotten around that Jessica had *keeled* because she had been *killed*.

And townsfolk were lined up to give statements and help Alan catch the killer.

I paused in the waiting area, taking a moment to find my cell phone in my purse. I had named Esther during my interview, and though I absolutely doubted that Alan would proceed to investigate my best friend, I wanted to give her a heads up and see her if I could.

As I composed and sent a text message to Esther, Officer Chuck grumbled his way from his desk to the front counter to deal with the phones. They had been ringing off the hook. I would bet money that the incessant callers were news reporters. Walnut Mountain was too small to have a television news station, but the county wasn't. Our sleepy little town in Vermont had been 'put on the map,' as they say, thanks to the murders last year. If word of another murder had *really* gotten out, then the news media was going to want stories to print and broadcast.

Chuck looked overwhelmed. His sandy-brown hair was cowlicked as though he had already raked his fingers through his hair about a million times, feeling beside himself. He grabbed the phones, two at a time, and stated, "No comment," as fast as he could. Then returned one phone after the next with a slam, but the calls kept coming.

My gut told me he needed rescuing. Sue Ellen came to mind. But my train of thought was broken when my cell phone began vibrating with an incoming call.

Esther's name and number flashed across the screen.

✝

"JESSICA WAS MURDERED?" asked Esther, horrified.

"Poisoned."

"At the picnic?" she breathed, her big brown eyes widening.

We strolled along Main Street, heading towards Morning Glory for a late afternoon cup of coffee.

Despite the warm, breezy weather and sunshine, there was tension in the air. Pedestrians weren't smiling. Residents seemed disturbed. Everyone must have known about the murder.

Thinking out loud, Esther commented, "Jessica wasn't particularly well-liked. I mean, everyone loves her store, Angel Arts & Crafts, but she's not a member of Hopeful Heart Ministries."

"She attended her own church," I said, but I had to admit that I didn't necessarily *know* that Jessica had been a church-going Catholic. I only assumed so based on what she had told me.

"Even so, Penny," she went on. "Who even really knew her? I didn't until you became friends with her. And once you had, I honestly couldn't understand why. She was very controlling."

"I think that's why Alan wanted to question me."

"Does he think *you* killed her?" she whispered, as she pulled the entrance door to Morning Glory open.

"No, not at all," I quietly responded as we made our way to the counter.

We put our conversation on hold as we ordered two coffees. Gloria, who owned the coffee shop, wasn't behind the counter, but Dex was. I had successfully set Dex up with my sweet stage manager last Christmas, and the love birds were still going strong.

"Anything else?" Dex asked us, as he pushed his long hair out of his eyes.

"The coffees are perfect, thanks," I told him, giving him cash and dropping the change into the tip jar.

As we turned to leave, my cousin Patrick entered the coffee shop. He looked frazzled, sweaty, and more pale than he had at the picnic.

"Patrick," I said, getting his attention. "Did you meet my friend, Esther?"

Distracted, he barely shook Esther's hand, while Esther mentioned they had already met earlier at the picnic.

"Are you okay?" I asked him.

"I need the restroom," he mumbled.

As soon as I pointed to show him the men's room, he darted off.

"That was strange," I said to Esther.

"Do you think the police questioned *him*?" she asked me, as we started off down the sidewalk.

"I don't see why they would."

"I don't see why they'd question *you*," she pointed out.

"Me, neither," I agreed.

My friend stiffened as we walked, fell silent for a tense moment, then blurted out:

"You don't think Alan will question *me*, do you?"

I tried not to wince, pained with guilt that I had mentioned Esther and also Harriet to Alan back at the police station.

"If he does, it won't be because he thinks you're a suspect," I promised.

"Oh, I'm so nervous, Penny!"

"Why on earth would you feel nervous?"

"Because!" she crumbled, unable to contain herself.

I took her coffee from her so she wouldn't drop it. She slapped both hands over her face to cover her tears.

"Esther, what in the world is wrong?"

"It's the wedding! Oh, God! Daniel is the most important, most meaningful thing that's ever happened to me! I'm terrified that something will go wrong! What if the wedding doesn't happen? I'm a nervous wreck, worried that we won't get married!"

She was spiraling… badly. I had been best friends with Esther long enough to know that she harbored deeply-seeded fears. She had developed a strange belief that if she loved something too much or if life got too good, something would come along to ruin it. This fear was the result of the fact that her life had been turned upside down a year ago when she had been diagnosed with cancer.

But it was *only* a fear. And fears *weren't* premonitions.

She had survived cancer, and she would survive this.

I pulled her in and gave her a good hug, careful not to spill our coffees.

"Nothing, and I mean nothing in heaven or on earth, will prevent Daniel from marrying you," I told her, praying to high heaven I was right.

"What if I'm accused of murder? What if I'm arrested? What if I go to prison for a crime I didn't commit?"

"That's not going to happen," I insisted, as I held her even more tightly.

"It isn't?"

"Never in a million years," I promised.

I couldn't help but wonder, however. Why was Esther so afraid that the police would think she had poisoned Jessica Saxon?

✝

ONCE I HAD CALMED Esther down, we walked to the late Jessica Saxon's craft store, Angel Arts & Crafts. Going to the craft store had nothing to do with my growing curiosity about who might have killed the pushy Catholic, and everything to do with the upcoming Easter service at Hopeful Heart Ministries.

I wanted to buy some Easter decorations for the church, and I wasn't about to part ways with Esther when she was in such a state of anxiety.

Helping her to take her mind off the murder, I changed the topic to the happier subjects of Easter and her wedding.

"You're going to be the most beautiful bride, Esther," I said, as we meandered down one of the aisles.

I carried a shopping basket that I had already filled with Easter decorations—plastic vines and white lilies, colorful plastic eggs for the children's Easter egg hunt, and a large 'He Is Risen' banner for the church vestibule.

She sighed, feeling noticeably better, and thanked me.

"You've been such a big blessing to me, Penny, the way you've been helping me plan the wedding."

"I'm so happy for you. I'm practically overjoyed. Don't blame me if I cry my eyes out at the wedding," I said, sharing a moment with her in front of the angel displays at the front of the craft store. "No one deserves to have marriage bliss more than you do, Esther."

She smiled and her eyes welled up with tears of affection.

She really was my best friend.

"I just pray," she said softly, "that my marriage with Daniel can be as loving and strong as yours is with Alan."

I tried not to let my own smile falter.

If only she knew the mess I had made of my own so-called 'happily ever after'...

...but I wasn't about to let Esther find out.

I would do anything to prevent my best friend, and everyone else in this town for that matter, from ever knowing the truth.

Glancing through my shopping basket, I concluded, "I think I have everything I came in here for."

We headed towards the register where Hailey Wexler, recovering shopping addict, appeared to be buying *way* too much *stuff*.

Two Angel Arts & Crafts shopping bags at her feet were full of items, and the sales girl behind the counter was still bagging the rest of Hailey's purchases into three more large bags.

I touched eyes with Hailey. She shrank with guilt. But I wasn't about to say a thing. I had been sworn to secrecy along with all the other members of Celebrate Recovery. Whatever was going on with Hailey was between Hailey, her sponsor, and God in heaven. Period.

Once Hailey had paid, collected her many shopping bags, and headed for the door, I set my basket on the counter and found my wallet in my purse, as the sales girl scanned the items.

Esther remarked, "That's a beautiful painting. How much is it?"

She was referring to the large painting that hung on the wall behind the cash register. The painting depicted an ethereal, feathery angel flying through heaven. The color palette included shimmery pastel hues.

It was gorgeous!

The sales girl glanced over her shoulder at the painting and smiled.

"That one isn't for sale," she said. "It won the Angel Art Award. See?"

She pointed to a huge, golden trophy that was resting on a display shelf behind her.

She added, "Jessica submitted the painting earlier this year and won. The Pembroke Pines Foundation awards one winning artist with a big grant each spring. The money would've totally changed Jessica's life, if she had lived to use it."

CHAPTER THREE

THE FOLLOWING MONDAY MORNING, I pulled my car into the school parking lot, took my usual spot, and flung my purse over my shoulder.

As I walked, I slipped a lavender, knit chemo cap onto my head that matched the long, flowing dress I wore.

Fluffy clouds eased across the clear blue sky.

Walnut Mountain Middle School was tucked in the woods. Walnut trees surrounded the schoolhouse and playgrounds. This time of year, the trees blossomed with giant, green walnut husks that looked exactly like tennis balls. And when the nuts inside were ready, the green balls would drop.

As I made my way into the little brick building, I heard the soft thuds of those round walnut husks plopping onto soggy grass and warm mud.

A yellow school bus growled behind me, making a hard turn off of School Street and angling into the parking lot.

When the bus came to a stop, children poured out. They looked like little marching turtles with their heavy backpacks.

I noticed nearly all of the students were wearing the same yellow tee-shirt.

Smiling to myself, I read the slogan across one of the kid's shirts—*He Is Risen*.

Easter certainly was around the corner!

I had worked as a teacher at the middle school for as long as I could remember. I absolutely loved it here, especially on days like today when most of the students proudly displayed their Christian faith on their clothing. But I had recently gotten in the habit of trying to say *goodbye* to the place in my heart.

My biggest dream was to have a baby with Alan. I was fast approaching 41 years of age, but the ticking biological clock hadn't run out yet. It wasn't too late to start a family, it wasn't! As my mother Dottie had been telling me lately, it ain't over til it's *over*.

Once the baby arrived, assuming Alan and I could get pregnant, I knew I wanted to be a stay-at-home mom, at least for a little while.

Alan and I weren't out of the 'rocky marriage' woods yet. But I had the highest faith that my big dream would one day very soon become a big reality.

Esther was already at the schoolhouse door when I reached the building.

"Morning, Penny!"

She wore a blue chemo cap on her head that had beautifully embroidered blue jays. Very fitting for spring!

"You seem in a good mood," I observed with a smile, glad to see she had overcome her anxiety from a couple days ago.

"I'm keeping my eye on the prize and ignoring everything else!"

"Me, too, Esther," I said with a determined smile. "Me, too."

Having entered the building, we rounded into the teachers' lounge where Principal Garth Longchamp sat in a huddle with the Art teachers, Harriet and Janice. They didn't touch their steaming coffees. They were too engrossed in an intriguing conversation.

Other teachers occupied tables. Rather than focusing on their lesson plans for the day, it sounded like everyone was murmuring about the recent murder.

Esther and I joined the science teacher, Matthew, at the coffeemaker, and helped ourselves.

Matthew was a bookish man who loved chess, loved the Lord, and very unfortunately, loved Samantha, the Social Studies teacher.

I didn't approve of their relationship.

I could've matched Matthew with any number of wholesome Christian women from Walnut Mountain. But he had never indicated he was looking...

"I'm concerned about Samantha," said Matthew, stealing my attention from my creamy coffee.

Esther asked, "Why, Matthew?"

Before he could respond to her, the Computer Science teacher, Timothy, shuffled over and asked him:

"How's Samantha holding up?"

Matthew let out a long sigh, pushed his glasses up his nose, and replied, "She's too strong for her own good, but that's not necessarily a *good* thing."

"Did something happen to Samantha?" I asked, confused.

Matthew looked surprised for a moment. Then he told me, "Her best friend was murdered."

Esther and I exchanged a glance. We were thinking the exact same thing.

Either someone else had been murdered in Walnut Mountain…

…or Samantha and Jessica had been best friends.

I hadn't known.

And frankly, if I had, I might not have asked Jessica Saxon to be my sponsor.

Matthew went on to explain to Timothy, "Instead of mourning, Samantha has *really* thrown herself into her activism."

Oh, God, no…

"How so?" asked Timothy.

Samantha's hair-brained political activism had been poisoning the minds of the teachers and students alike. Her liberal, progressive ideologies antagonized the Christian faith that Esther, myself, and others at the school shared. And it wasn't a fair fight. As the Social Studies teacher, Samantha was allowed to introduce her ideas by weaving them into her curriculum. Esther and I, however, were prohibited from voicing our Christian perspective to the students.

Answering Timothy, Matthew said, "She spent the weekend channeling her bitter emotions into a new project, which she referred to as 'bringing down Easter'."

"What the hell does that mean?!" Esther blurted out, irate.

Suddenly, all eyes were on Esther. The teachers' lounge fell into a hushed silence.

I expected to hear a pin drop.

But instead, I heard the distinct *clicks* of Samantha's very high heels, as she swayed her way into the teachers' lounge.

Samantha stopped in the middle of the room, curving her hip and striking a severe yet sultry pose. She took a mean moment to glare at each and every one of us with her sharp, green eyes. Her tight, form-fitting dress left little to the imagination, as did the clipboard in her hand.

"Attention, everyone!" she announced, even though she had

already stolen our undivided attention. "I have a very important petition we all *must* sign."

Principal Longchamp frowned.

Steam was shooting out of Esther's ears and Samantha hadn't even explained her agenda yet.

"It is utterly offensive," Samantha began, speaking in a loud, authoritative tone, "that no one was *with me* when I *insisted* that we prevent our students from printing those highly discriminatory 'He Is Risen' tee-shirts!"

I grabbed hold of Esther before she could take a running swing at Samantha.

I whispered in my friend's ear, "Longchamp will shut this down, don't worry. Samantha's going to be in big trouble for this."

"I hope so," she grumbled.

"Well!" Samantha barked as a snide smile spread across her full, glossy lips. "I just saw our students in the hallway wearing the very tee-shirts I tried to warn you all about!"

Principal Garth Longchamp slammed both fists against his table as he stood.

"Samantha! In my office, now!"

"You can't silence me, Garth!" she argued. "I have rights!"

As Garth started through the teachers' lounge, angling to collect Samantha and her clipboard, she shouted:

"Sign the petition to *ban* the students from wearing religious clothing at school!"

Nearly all the teachers rolled their eyes.

Samantha kept chanting, "Sign the petition! Sign the petition! Sign the petition!" as our trustworthy principal came nose-to-nose with her.

"My office! Now!"

Scowling, Samantha stuck her nose in the air, tossed her beautiful blonde hair off her shoulder, and turned on her very high heel. Following after Garth, she clicked her way out of the lounge, all the while shouting at us:

"There's something wrong with your *brains* if you can't see how important this is!"

Esther grumbled under her breath, "There's something wrong with *Samantha's* brain if you ask me."

I happened to agree.

But more than anything, what seemed wrong to me was the fact that I hadn't known Samantha and Jessica had been so close.

It worried me.

☦

"PENNY, IS NOW a good time?" asked Harriet in-between First and Second Period.

"Of course!" I said, as I tucked my lesson plan into a binder.

Students streamed down the hallway. Most of them wore their 'He Is Risen' tee-shirts, though Samantha's disapproving glances had pressured some of the students to either put on their spring jackets to cover the Christian slogan or turn their tee shirts inside-out.

This time of year, Harriet always wore bright spring sweaters, long bohemian skirts, and thick clogs on her feet. Her short, spiky hair was an artistic eggplant-purple color.

We walked against the current of middle schoolers, making our way into the Art Room where Janice was pouring paint onto palettes for the next class.

I smiled at Janice, as I followed Harriet through the room to a large supply closet.

"I was able to get the artwork here from my studio at home when my hatchback sedan was running," Harriet explained, "but recently my car has been in the shop."

The moment I saw her artwork, I gushed, "Harriet! These are breath-taking!"

Propped against one of the shelving units were three large paintings. The artwork was under glass, matted, and framed. But that wasn't what made them so stunning.

Each had perfectly preserved butterflies!

Over the years, Harriet had mastered her unique artwork. She was more than a painter. She had also learned how to humanely collect real butterflies and keep them alive. When they died, she preserved their brittle bodies and then incorporated them into her art.

There were Monarch butterflies, Black Swallowtail butterflies, and even the most rare Menelaus Blue Morpho butterflies used in each of the framed paintings.

"These are going to look gorgeous at the church for the Easter

Service," I complimented.

"You're too sweet, Penny," she said humbly.

Furrowing my brow, I realized, "They're probably too big to fit in my car. Do you have a tape measure?"

As Harriet found a tape measure on one of the shelves and handed it to me, she said, "Shoot, I was afraid of that."

"It's okay," I promised. "I can borrow my husband's pickup truck."

I measured the dimensions of the first painting since all three were the same size. The artwork stood at a whopping 54 inches, which was 4 ½ feet! And it was nearly as wide.

"Yes," I decided, as I recoiled the tape measure and handed it to her. "I'm sure I can borrow Alan's truck."

"I'll wrap them in thick, bubble wrap and moving cloth," she mentioned.

The warning bell rang, indicating that Second Period would start in five minutes.

"I can't thank you enough, Penny."

"It's my pleasure, believe me!"

"You're sure Alan won't mind?" she questioned.

"He won't mind at all," I assured her.

Harriet turned gloomy and suggested, "Maybe you shouldn't tell him you're helping *me*."

"Don't be silly," I said. But then I quickly wondered, "Why shouldn't I tell him?"

She grew tense. "He really grilled me the other day about Jessica's murder."

I offered her a sympathetic smile and placed a warm hand on her shoulder.

"He grilled me, too, Harriet. He's determined to grill everyone til we're all crispier than a well-done burger."

She chuckled at that and seemed to relax.

"I have to get to my classroom," I gently told her. "Talk soon!"

☦

I KNEW I WOULD BE late for Second Period when I heard the bell ring again.

I rushed up the hallway. My classroom door was closed, which was odd.

As I pulled the door open, I found Samantha standing in front of my desk with her horrible petition in hand.

Oh, no she didn't!

"No one's asking you not to be Christian," she carried on, berating my students. "But don't you think that keeping your religion *to yourself* is the right thing to do?"

"Samantha," I warned.

She didn't even acknowledge my presence.

"Do you have any idea how *hateful* Christianity is to *marginalized* people?" she balked, as if she had come face-to-face with a room full of little devils. "Take off those tee-shirts!"

Little Peter's glasses fogged up with tears. And though Nathan's lower lip was trembling, his folded arms told me that he would die before he would remove his 'He Is Risen' tee-shirt.

"Samantha!" I yelled, losing my temper.

I held the door open and pointed for her to get out.

"Leave at once!"

"Each of you should ask yourself why you don't mind *hurting people's feelings*—"

"At once, Samantha!"

She shot her cool gaze at me.

"Not until you sign my petition," she negotiated.

My eyebrows shot up to my hairline and I felt my cheeks turn bright red.

As if!

"I could have you fired for this," I threatened.

Samantha was not intimidated. Quite the opposite, in fact, she tossed her blonde hair and laughed.

Outrageous!

She clicked her way across the wooden floor, towered over me, and held out a pen, presenting me with the petition.

"Sign it, Penny."

"No," I growled.

"Did your brain stop working?"

"Did *yours*?"

"If you don't sign this," she warned, "I'll make you regret it."

As strong as I tried to sound, my voice turned to a thread, as I told her, "I doubt that."

She smirked. "Have it your way."

Samantha swayed her way around me, and as she left my classroom, I loudly said the most offensive thing I could think to say:

"God bless you."

She stopped and glared at me over her shoulder.

"In Jesus' name," I added, glaring at her even harder.

Samantha shook her head and disappeared down the hallway.

And I shook my head, too, as I disappeared into a fear-stricken panic about what that woman might do to make me regret standing up for my students and myself.

✝

"PRINCIPAL LONGCHAMP!" I blurted out the moment I found him in the teachers' lounge after my Second Period class had gotten out.

Garth was filling his thermos at the coffeemaker.

I tried not to make a scene as I neared him.

Other teachers occupied the tables. Esther clutched her cell phone to her ear, using the break to take a personal call. If every teacher was present, I didn't notice. Samantha was out of control, and whatever Garth had told her in his office hadn't prevented her from making more than half of my students cry.

"Samantha *really* crossed a line with me," I told him with as much composure as I could muster.

Concern was written all over Garth's face. He twisted the cap of his thermos on then locked eyes with me over the rims of his spectacles.

"I know she's gotten out of hand," he agreed.

"She has more than 'gotten out of hand'," I insisted. "She tried to guilt my students into taking their tee-shirts off, and then she pressured me to sign that petition of hers, and—"

"Penny, I'm on your side," he assured me. "Not only did I give Samantha a warning, I also filed a report with the Vermont State Board of Education. For now, I can't do more than that. I have to let the bureaucratic process unfold."

Esther floated over. She looked as concerned as Garth.

But when Samantha breezed into the teachers' lounge and made a beeline for the coffeemaker as if I didn't exist, Esther turned cross.

As Samantha poured herself a mug of coffee, she very nonchalantly commented:

"Penny's just mad because her serious drinking problem ruined her marriage."

I froze.

She smiled at me and asked, "Isn't that right, Penny?"

My blood ran cold. I felt the color drain from my cheeks.

Esther screwed her face up. "Penny doesn't have a drinking problem."

"Oh?" replied Samantha. "Then why is her husband living in a motel?"

I breathed, "*What?*"

My mind started racing. Samantha's threat. Her friendship with Jessica, my *sponsor*. All the pieces shuffled through my brain. The room started spinning.

I didn't even hear Esther defend me. She called Samantha crazy, but the snide Social Studies teacher insisted it was true.

"Penny has the strongest marriage of anyone in Walnut Mountain!" said Esther, furious.

"That's not what I heard," Samantha cooly retorted as she stirred her creamy coffee.

Esther looked at me. "What is she talking about?"

I was speechless.

"Penny?"

If Jessica hadn't already been murdered, I could've killed her with my bare hands for this.

Esther asked, "Are you and Alan separated?"

I was too furious, too *humiliated* for words.

"Oh, dear," said Samantha, smirking at Esther. "Did Penny not tell you? How strange that a devout Christian would end up being a total liar."

It was then that I realized everyone in the teachers' lounge now knew.

All eyes were on me.

Penny Matchmaker.

The woman who had made over a dozen successful love matches.

The woman whose marriage everyone envied.

The woman who had been living a lie.

CHAPTER FOUR

PASTOR PETER PETERSON INVITED all of the Celebrate Recovery members to a last-minute meeting at Hopeful Heart Ministries.

He was furious Jessica had been murdered.

Who would run our meetings now?

When I arrived at the Fellowship Hall, Rachel Harder, Hailey Wexler, and her best friend Sue Ellen Grossman were carrying tables to the back of the room and arranging chairs into a circle.

I lent a helping hand, as other members spilled in from the church vestibule.

All of Walnut Mountain had been swallowed in the cool darkness of a quiet spring night, but it didn't compare to the blackhole everyone had been pulled into as a result of Jessica's untimely demise.

"I haven't been able to stop buying things," Hailey discreetly confessed to Sue Ellen, as they got situated next to one another in the circle.

Rachel sat next to me. Her black inky eyes appeared darker than ever.

"I feel like I could fall off the wagon any second," she told me, as she tucked her black hair behind her ears.

"We have to take things one hour at a time," I suggested, not that I was an expert on the subject.

Sue Ellen wedged her tote bag between her feet. She seemed preoccupied with her bag and kept peering down at it. She wore her Charming Diner uniform, which was a blue 1950's style diner dress.

It had a collar, buttons down the chest, and a flared skirt. Given Sue Ellen's short, curly, blonde hair, she looked like someone James Dean would want to seduce.

She also looked worried.

Pastor Peter started the meeting.

"I didn't want any of us to have to wait until Saturday for the scheduled Celebrate Recovery meeting. Surely, we've all been badly affected by Jessica's murder. Penny worse than anyone—"

"I haven't been affected worse than anyone else," I objected.

"Please, Penny!" he snapped, losing his temper. "Don't interrupt me! The last thing I need is a relapse!"

I was taken aback, but held my tongue.

Besides, could I really argue with him? A fiery ball of rage had been burning in the pit of my stomach ever since Samantha had humiliated me in front of Esther and the entire teaching staff earlier that day. I had been exposed as a hypocrite. I could barely stand to look at myself in the mirror.

"I've been flying off the handle left and right," he went on. "My wife, Sharon—God bless her soul!—has been a saint to put up with me. Of course, I want the killer caught. But more than anything, I want the stability and structure of Celebrate Recovery to continue. I can't bear to live without it."

Everyone nodded their heads in emphatic agreement.

"None of us can afford to discontinue this program," he warned us.

Again, we all agreed wholeheartedly.

"Jessica ran our meetings," he reminded us. But what the pastor said next shocked everyone. "I can't run Celebrate Recovery."

"Who's going to run it?" Sue Ellen blurted out, concerned.

Members murmured among themselves, overcome with anxiety.

"I'm sorry, but I can't!" he insisted. "I have to focus on Hopeful Heart Ministries, my Sunday sermons, and being a good husband at home, which I've been failing at miserably."

As if Pastor Peter's attitude was contagious, one member after the next insisted that *they* couldn't run the meeting either.

The room was filled with an uproar of frustration.

Meow.

"What was that?" I wondered. "Quiet!"

The members fell into a hush.

Meow.

Sue Ellen froze. Her eyes widened, and her mouth pinched into a guilty pucker.

Meeeooooow.

A white, fluffy kitten poked its cute face out of Sue Ellen's tote bag.

She groaned. "I had a relapse!"

"Oh, Sue Ellen," I said, my heart bleeding for her, as she pulled the latest cat she had rescued out of her bag.

"I couldn't resist!" she explained, desperate to be understood. She cuddled the kitten and tears welled up in her eyes.

"I couldn't resist, either," Rachel blurted out. "I drank last night!"

"I punched a wall!" yelled Pastor Peter. "And it felt great!"

"People! People! Quiet down!" I shouted, as everyone confessed to having fallen off their own personal wagons in the last day or two. "We obviously need to share! I'll start the clock!"

I found my cell phone in my purse, opened the timer app, and told Sue Ellen:

"Since we're all going through a lot, let's each share for *ten* minutes. We'll start with you, Sue Ellen, and go around the circle clockwise."

Sue Ellen wiped the tears from her eyes and began to share the story of finding and rescuing Faith, her new kitten. Faith curled into a ball on her lap and was soon purring.

About an hour later, everyone had shared for ten minutes, including myself, and it was time to conclude the meeting.

I hadn't meant to take charge of matters. I certainly hadn't meant to fill Jessica's shoes. But after we stood, held hands, and recited the serenity prayer, all of the members unanimously agreed that I should be the new leader of Celebrate Recovery.

"Oh, don't be ridiculous!" I told Rachel, who clutched my arm and was pleading with me to accept the position.

"Out of all of us, you're the only one who didn't fall off the wagon!" she pointed out.

"You got the meeting under control tonight," Hailey added.

Pastor Peter humbled himself and told me, "We need you, Penny."

I looked around at all their hopeful faces.

I felt like the last person in the world who should *run* an addiction recovery program.

But how could I refuse?

"Okay," I agreed.

Everyone cheered and patted each other on the back.

Rachel pulled me in for a big hug, and soon all of the members had piled onto me, hugging and pressing in—a giant ball of hopeful addicts with a little Faith on the side.

Meow!

✟

TWO STEAMING MUGS of diner coffee sat on the table between Esther and me.

"Penny, why didn't you tell me?"

Esther's huge brown eyes were filled with sympathy. But I knew she felt betrayed also.

She had texted me, asking me to meet her at Charming Diner. It had been *easy* enough to walk from Hopeful Heart Ministries after the impromptu Celebrate Recovery meeting, not that I had *wanted* to.

I wasn't especially eager to face the music.

I shrugged, stared down at my mug of coffee, and admitted:

"I didn't want to be a burden?"

"Is that the truth? Or are you guessing?"

Neither, I thought to myself. I was lying.

But the truth had already come out thanks to Samantha. I might as well address it.

Words wouldn't come.

Esther said, "I'm so confused by all of this. You hardly drink, Penny."

"I know, but Alan tells me I'm an alcoholic," I said with a shrug.

She blinked.

"If I'm being honest here, Esther, the fact of the matter is that I was in denial about my drinking. I didn't think it was a problem. Frankly, neither did Alan until…"

"Until what?" she asked on the edge of her seat.

She leaned in even farther, overcome with curiosity.

I shook my head.

"Like you said, I hardly ever drink. But there was one time I sort of overdid it. It was *nothing*, though," I lied, then quickly compromised. "I really don't want to talk about it, but let's just say, the night I *did* have a bit too much alcohol Alan saw me in a new, unflattering light. And he moved out."

"My God, Penny," she breathed. "When was this?"

"Last year," I told her, as I glanced around the diner, making sure no one was eavesdropping.

The diner was packed. Every vinyl booth was full of families or couples on dates. Waitresses wearing blue 1950's style dresses jotted down burger orders and refilled their customers' mugs with piping hot coffee.

Our waitress, Sue Ellen, was flitting around the diner, tending to the many demands of her section.

"*When* last year?" Esther pushed.

She wanted to know how long I had been keeping secrets from her.

"It was around this time last year," I admitted.

Her dainty eyebrows shot up to her hairline where her embroidered chemo cap hugged her forehead.

"Please don't look at me like that," I begged her.

"I'm just so sorry that you've been all alone, carrying such a heavy hardship this whole time."

"It hasn't been that bad, Esther, really," I promised. "It's not like Alan walked out of my life. We've been seeing each other the whole time, as you know. I completely stopped drinking. We're fine. And our marriage will be fine."

"Are you sure?" she asked, unconvinced.

"I need you to believe me," I said. "I need you to believe *in* me."

She nodded, fully understanding.

I loved her fiercely for it.

I straightened my spine, drew in a deep breath, and smiled.

"What I need most right now," I went on, "is to focus on happy things and to look forward to life."

She bucked up and offered me a little smile.

Then she totally shook off the doom-and-gloom that had resulted from my secrets-and-lies. She beamed a huge smile at me and gushed:

"I picked out my wedding dress!"

"You did?" I said, eager to leap into the new topic of conversation.

"Yes! It's gorgeous! I have photos in my cell phone, but let me visit the ladies' room first!"

Esther excused herself from the table and shuffled off through the busy diner, just as Sue Ellen swooped in, holding a pot of steaming coffee.

"Are you ladies ready for dessert?" she asked, as she filled our mugs.

Knowing Esther like the back of my hand, I ordered a chocolate mousse for her and a slice of warm cherry pie for myself.

"You're a real lifesaver, Penny."

"Oh, hardly."

"I mean it. We all need you. And you're so strong, my God," she said with more awe and wonder in her voice than I deserved. "While everyone else in the group is falling apart, you're selflessly committed to helping us. It's Christ-like. You're a real inspiration."

I couldn't bear to hear even one more compliment.

Luckily, Esther returned.

But *very* unluckily, Sue Ellen wasn't done praising me.

"Everyone at the recovery meeting is grateful for you, Penny."

"Recovery meeting?" Esther asked as she slid into her side of the booth.

I groaned and buried my face in my hands.

Sue Ellen gasped.

"I'm so sorry! I totally forgot!"

"You're in a recovery program?" Esther asked me.

"It's supposed to be *anonymous*." I shot Sue Ellen a look.

She winced, embarrassed.

"That's great, Penny!" said Esther.

"I'll be right back with your dessert order," Sue Ellen said sheepishly before slipping away.

"Don't be embarrassed," Esther said, encouragingly. "It's wonderful that you're getting help!"

"Thanks," I grumbled.

"Oh! Is *that* how you knew Jessica?"

"Yes, but—"

"Oooooh," she breathed, mentally putting the pieces together. "Was Jessica your *sponsor*?"

I groaned.

"That explains *so much*, Penny!"

Esther was a lot smarter than she may have looked. But I had always known she was brilliant. She taught mathematics, after all, and could do long equations in her head.

I, on the other hand, could barely leave a decent tip unless I used a calculator.

Momentarily puzzled, she asked, "But how did *Samantha* find out about your drinking problem and your ruined marriage?"

I didn't exactly love her choice of words, but the question was valid.

"Apparently, they were friends."

"Oh, right!" she suddenly remembered. "Matthew said Samantha should've been mourning her best friend's death, but instead she had—"

"Turned into a social justice monster," I supplied.

"Why would she be friends with Samantha?" she wondered. Esther was a bit of a sleuth investigator, herself. "Samantha can't stand Christians, and didn't you say Jessica was Catholic?"

"I have no idea why they were friends," I said, equally baffled. "But Jessica had the same pretty, perfect, pushy personality as Samantha, you know? Maybe they were two peas in a pod."

"Wait a second!" she blurted out. She gasped, and her jaw dropped. "Did Jessica *tell* Samantha *all that stuff about you*?!"

"Please keep your voice down," I whispered, as I worriedly glanced over my shoulder and around the diner.

"She broke confidentiality?"

I nodded.

Esther's mouth was still hanging open.

"What a b—"

"Esther!"

She pressed her mouth into a hard line. "I never liked her."

"Frankly, neither did I."

Esther fell into contemplative silence, trying to figure a thing or two out in her fast-working mind.

Then she started mulling over the details, "Jessica was in your alcohol recovery program. She was your sponsor. And now she's dead…"

I loved Esther. But I couldn't let this conversation go on. I chose my words carefully.

"The program *is* supposed to be anonymous, so while I really appreciate your enthusiasm—and you *know* I love you—I'm going to have to set a boundary and ask that we not discuss this at all."

"Good for you, Penny! Learning to set boundaries is one of the most important things that a recovering alcoholic can do for themselves!"

Again, I groaned and buried my face in my hands.

All I wanted was to keep one secret to myself, but they had all come to light.

As the world's greatest best friend, however, Esther had no problem changing the subject. She pulled out her cell phone and started showing me photos of her wedding dress. Sue Ellen returned with our desserts. I was ready to get lost in the conversation. Focusing on Esther's upcoming wedding would provide me with the perfect mental vacation I needed!

But my mental vacation was quickly replaced with an actual nightmare.

My husband Alan entered Charming Diner with Police Officers Chuck and Jeremiah.

They looked like they were here to conduct official police business…

…and they were heading straight for our booth.

Esther glanced over her shoulder to see what had stolen my attention.

She let out a horrified yelp, locked eyes with me, and exclaimed:

"They're here to arrest me!"

"What?!" I blurted out.

"I've been obsessed with the idea of getting framed for murder and not being able to marry Daniel because of it, and now look at what's happening!"

I didn't think Alan was marching through the diner to arrest Esther.

But then again, I didn't think he was marching through the diner to arrest me, either.

And I was wrong.

"Penny Matchmaker?" he barked, as if he had just caught a perp and wasn't addressing his wife of twenty years.

"What's gotten into you, Alan?"

Police Officers Chuck and Jeremiah fanned out, I guessed so that I wouldn't be able to make my getaway, while Alan took me by the arm and said:

"We need to talk, downtown."

Downtown?

"Do you mean at the police station?" I asked before dryly

adding, "The police station is across the street, Alan."

"Let's go," he said, as he steered me up the aisle.

Esther shouted:

"Are you arresting her?"

She tried to follow after me, but Officer Jeremiah held her back.

The bad news was that all the customers who had been eating at Charming Diner probably assumed I was getting arrested.

But the good news was that I suddenly knew the next 'match' I would make!

This occurred when Alan escorted me past the hostess stand where Sue Ellen was watching me, horrified. I noticed that Officer Chuck couldn't take his eyes off Sue Ellen.

Would the cat rescuer and the man who needed rescuing make a good match?

CHAPTER FIVE

ALAN HAD LEFT HIS pickup truck idling in front of Charming Diner. He helped me into the passenger's seat and shut the door.

Officers Chuck and Jeremiah climbed into the police cruiser behind Alan's truck.

"That reminds me," I said once my husband had hopped into the driver's seat and we pulled out into the street. "Can I borrow the pickup truck sometime this week?"

Alan shot me a look, as he turned onto Main Street.

The police station was up ahead past the library.

"I need to help Harriet move her artwork from the school to the church before Easter," I explained.

"There's been a serious development with the investigation, Penny."

"How serious?"

"We're going to have to ask you some hard questions—"

"I'm obviously not under arrest, Alan. You know I didn't poison Jessica."

"Can you please focus on the seriousness of the situation?"

"Is that a 'no' regarding the truck?"

"You can borrow the truck," he allowed, as he squeezed the brakes, rolling slowly towards the police station.

I would've thanked him if I hadn't been immediately distracted.

Outside the station house, a cluster of news reporters crowded the entrance. There was a television crew filming a reporter. Photographers took photos of me, the flashes of their cameras practically blinding me, as they rushed towards the truck.

"My goodness!"

One of the news reporters slammed into my window and shouted:

"Penny Matchmaker! Do you know who murdered Jessica Saxon?"

"Dang," Alan grumbled as he eased on the gas and kept driving. "We'll have to go in through the back."

"Do they think I had something to do with Jessica's death?"

"Don't worry about them. They're just after a story. Reporters have been swarming the police station since yesterday," he said, as we drove around the corner and came to the private parking lot behind the station.

He threw his truck into Park and killed the engine.

"I won't be able to interview you, Penny," he explained. He unbuckled my seatbelt then his own. "Chief Pepperdine won't allow it. So, one of the police officers is going to ask you a few questions. Don't be intimidated. Just answer honestly."

"Who do you guys suspect poisoned Jessica?" I asked.

Alan held my gaze for a long moment.

He brushed his hand across my cheek tenderly.

Searching my eyes, he leaned in.

When next he kissed me, I melted, closed my eyes, and yearned to be alone with him in our cabin.

"Ready?" he asked.

He didn't wait for my reply, but rather climbed out of the truck, rounded to my side, and opened the passenger's door for me.

"It'll be okay, Penny. Just tell the truth."

As he walked me into the rear of the police station, I got a very strange feeling.

What on earth did he think I knew that I hadn't already told him the first time I was interviewed?

Phones were ringing off the hook. Chief Pepperdine barked at one of the police officers. The station house felt chaotic.

Alan pushed the interview room door open for me and called Officer Chuck over.

The room was as bare as ever, but the window was open, allowing plenty of fresh spring air to breeze in.

Chuck entered the room, eased the door closed behind him, but he didn't shut it all the way.

I sensed more than saw Alan lurking on the other side of the door that had been left ajar.

"Have a seat, Penny," said the police officer.

I sat down and found it impossible to get comfortable.

Chuck raked his fingers through his sandy-brown hair, while he poured over the contents of the file he had brought with him.

Fast approaching middle age, Chuck had accomplished a lot as a Walnut Mountain police officer. But from where I was sitting, he had accomplished virtually nothing in terms of his love life.

What good was having a great job, owning a house, and being a fit, handsome man, if you came home to an empty house every night?

Once he organized his thoughts, he lifted his nose from the manilla filing folder, and said:

"At the picnic, you handed Jessica a soda and a plate of desserts, correct?"

"That's right," I answered.

"And you said that Harriet and Esther were the ones who supplied you with those items?"

I didn't like the implication.

"Yes, but she could've eaten or drank something prior to that," I argued. "Someone else could've poisoned her."

"Do you remember who handed you what item?"

He held a pen, ready to make note of my answer.

I didn't want to give it. I didn't want to be helpful if it meant the police were going to focus on my friends.

"Penny?" he prodded me.

"Who do you think killed Jessica?" I countered.

"Please answer the question and don't make this harder than it is."

I could tell that Chuck didn't like the position he was in, but I didn't feel so sorry for him that I would incriminate Esther and Harriet.

"I don't remember," I finally said.

He narrowed his green eyes at me.

"Chuck, I think we both know that Esther didn't poison Jessica. She survived cancer and finally got her life back. Why would she risk losing it all over again by going to prison? And Harriet didn't even know Jessica or have history with her, as far as I understand."

Chuck obviously didn't want this fight. Alan had clearly pressured him.

He ran his big hand down his face, coming to his senses.

Then he confided in me, speaking in a low tone.

"Alan's gone off the deep end," he whispered. "We're grasping at straws hoping to find the long one. It's investigations like these that make me wish I had chosen a different line of work. Walnut Mountain never has serious crimes, and when I became a police officer in this town, I didn't anticipate murders, reporters, or pressure. Frankly, I just want a pension, a cozy home with a few cats, and a good wife."

Sue Ellen came to my mind.

He sighed then asked:

"I'd like to get you out of here quickly. Can you give me *anything?*"

"I'm Mrs. Matchmaker," I said proudly. "I can give you a shot at love."

"Really?" he asked, his voice full of hope.

Alan slipped into the room and closed the door behind him.

"Officer Charles," he seethed, speaking through his teeth. "Have you forgotten the objective?"

I asked, "What's the objective?" as Chuck popped off his chair, making room for my husband to take over.

Alan kept his voice down, but his intensity was higher than ever.

"Who handed you the soda and who handed you the plate of cupcakes and cookies?"

The killer must have poisoned one of them, but the killer wasn't one of my fellow teachers.

"I don't remember," I lied.

Alan stared at me for a long moment and said:

"You might not know your friends as well as you think."

"What is that supposed to mean?" I demanded, "*Which* friend?"

"Jessica had become a strong presence in your life, Penny. I know she wasn't always easy to tolerate. She had been taking up a lot of your time. Time you ordinarily would've been spending with Esther."

I gasped.

"Are you crazy?!"

I didn't like how calm Alan was as he continued:

"We know that Jessica betrayed you—"

"You *what?*"

"And we know how much Esther loves you. She would protect

you from *anything*, Penny. She would go to *any* length to keep your heart safe—"

"Esther didn't do anything!" I insisted.

"Penny, we know that Jessica broke sponsor confidentiality. Samantha was here earlier—"

"Samantha!" I hissed.

It was bad enough she had tried to destroy my life by ruining my reputation at school and humiliating me as a result of exposing the lie I had been living. But now she was trying to ruin Esther's life?

Alan went on to put the puzzle pieces in place, but the overall picture was wrong.

It had to be!

"Esther was jealous of Jessica. And if that wasn't bad enough, she then discovered Jessica had betrayed you by telling Samantha your secrets. In an attempt to protect you and put a stop to Jessica's blabbing, she killed her."

"There's no way that's true, Alan! You've gone mad!"

"I've never been more sane in my entire life."

"But you know Esther," I pointed out. "You've known her for years."

I expected to at least see some remorse on his face. But he looked determined. Satisfied with his keen investigative skills.

I hotly argued, "If anyone had a motive to murder Jessica, it was me! She was overbearing. I never had a second to myself—"

"Penny, that's enough!" he barked.

"She knew all my secrets," I went on, "and she constantly pressured me to admit to everyone that I'm an alcoholic! If anyone benefitted from her death, it was me!"

"Enough, Penny!"

Flashes of light poured into the interview room through the open window.

Chuck rushed over to the window and yelled, "Hey!"

Alan was on his feet in a blink.

"Reporters!" said Chuck.

"Get 'em!" Alan ordered, and Chuck raced out of the room.

"Damn it, Penny! Who knows what they heard you say!"

☦

THE NEWS REPORTERS had heard me say *a lot*, but I wouldn't know the full extent of it for another hour when the 11 o'clock news came on.

For the time being, Alan had convinced me to spend the night at my parents' cabin.

"I don't want you to worry about Esther," he said, as we drove through the long, winding back roads, heading towards my parents' place.

I glared at him from the passenger's seat with my arms folded.

My current strategy with my husband was to stonewall him.

He hadn't noticed.

"I'll bring your car here later tonight so you can get to work tomorrow morning," he offered.

Thanking him was the last thing I was planning to do.

"Penny?"

I touched eyes with him.

"You need a new sponsor."

"No, I don't."

He grinned at me. "Thought you could stonewall me, huh?"

"Congratulations, Alan, you got me to respond."

"Look, Penny, you have to admit that Jessica was good at her job."

"She told Samantha literally everything I had told her in confidence!"

"Okay, so aside from violating the secrecy rule," he allowed, "she kept you sober."

"*I* kept me sober, Alan."

"You've made such progress—"

"You don't know the half of it!"

"You need a new sponsor," he insisted.

"I'll have you know that *everyone* at Celebrate Recovery *unanimously* appointed *me* to be the new leader of the program."

"They did?"

"Yes!" I stated proudly. "Even Pastor Peter."

"Is that so?"

"Yes, it *is* so," I said hotly. "I was the *only* one at Group that didn't fall off the wagon after Jessica died. The *only one*, Alan!"

"Really?" he questioned.

"Why does that surprise you?"

"It doesn't."

"It shouldn't," I said with a huff.

"It doesn't," he promised.

My parents' cabin came into view through the walnut trees. At the end of the long, winding driveway sat my childhood home. The windows were aglow with lights and a stream of smoke trailed from the chimney.

The stream of smoke called to mind the biggest mistake I had ever made in my life.

The reason Alan had decided to move out this time last year.

The reason I had started living a lie…

I pinched my eyes shut for a moment and shook my head, as we drove up the driveway.

Alan pulled the pickup truck right in front of the cabin door since there were too many cars in the driveway.

I recognized Daniel's pickup truck, which told me Esther was inside. And Cousin Patrick's sedan was there as well.

Alan shoved the gear shifter into Park and focused on me.

"Just think about it, alright?" he said softly. "Having a sponsor is always a good thing."

I looked at him for a long moment.

The memories came rushing back.

The wine.

My delusions of grandeur, thinking I could cook my handsome husband a five course meal.

The nerves and jitters I had felt. The *second* bottle of wine I had started working on. The blurry vision. The bad decision to lie down *just for a minute* while my culinary foray into mastering buttermilk fried chicken sizzled on the stove…

I cringed at the memory.

"It was an accident," I breathed. "I didn't mean to fall asleep on the couch that night."

"Hey," he said softly, noticing the tears in my eyes.

"I didn't mean to start a fire," I whispered.

I was overcome with hard emotions.

If Alan hadn't come home that night when he had, the grease fire could've engulfed the whole house with me in it.

But my husband *had* shown up that night. He had fought his way through thick smoke. He had beaten the grease fire down with wet towels. He had saved my life.

And he had never looked at me the same since.

It had taken a couple thousand dollars to repair the kitchen.

I still didn't know what it would take to repair our marriage.

In a small voice, Alan said, "I know you didn't mean to start the fire. But it happened."

"When are you going to forgive me?" I asked. "When are you going to come home?"

He leaned back, resting his head on the headrest.

"I'm figuring it out," he murmured. He held my gaze for a moment after that and added, "You're just going to have to trust me."

I helped myself out of the truck, shut the door, and flung my purse over my shoulder.

It was a very long walk into the house.

When I entered my parents' cabin, the familiar scents of cedar, cinnamon, and the wood-burning stove gave me hope.

Alan loved me, and I loved him. Somehow, we would eventually be better than ever. Or at least that was what my heart told me. Deep down I knew that the Lord spoke to me through my heart.

"Penny!"

My mom found me in the vestibule.

I set down my purse on the entryway table just in time for my mother to grasp me in a horrified hug.

"I'm fine, Mom."

"Are you? Esther's here! She said you got arrested at Charming Diner! Has Alan lost his dang mind?"

As my mom kept at my heels, I came into the living room where Esther and Daniel were seated across from my dad. Cousin Patrick was slumped on the loveseat. Everyone sprang to their feet when they saw me, except for my cousin, who anxiously watched the muted TV.

I announced, "I'm okay. I wasn't arrested."

"Oh, thank God!" Esther exclaimed, hugging me.

My father, Lucas, echoed the sentiment. He pressed his meaty hands together in prayer, looked up, and thanked the good Lord in heaven.

My mom said, "Let's get that spring chill out of your bones with some hot cider."

She disappeared into the kitchen.

"Alan simply had a few more questions for me, that's all," I promised as we all sat down around the living room.

Esther stared at me with wide, nervous eyes.

"What questions?" she asked with trepidation.

I loved her too much to worry her with the truth. She had survived so much in the past year. I wasn't about to tell her that all her fears were coming true. That Alan suspected her of murder. That her upcoming wedding really *was* in jeopardy.

It was then that I decided *I* would solve the case of who poisoned Jessica Saxon at the picnic. Esther obviously hadn't, and I wouldn't stop until Alan agreed.

"What questions did Alan ask you, Penny?" my dad asked when I hadn't answered Esther the first time.

Dad's hair was especially red in the living room light.

Mom returned with a steaming mug of cider for me.

I clutched it in my hands and began explaining:

"They honestly don't have any valid leads."

Patrick immediately turned his attention from the TV to me. He looked interested. He didn't even blink.

"Jessica was poisoned, as we all know," I went on. "Alan just wanted me to list all the food items that I saw Jessica eat."

Esther still seemed tense, but Daniel put a comforting arm around her.

Patrick appeared jumpy, I realized. Was he sweating? His forehead was beaded with sweat and he looked a bit pale. Haggard, in fact.

Was he *on* something?

"Penny's on the news!" Esther blurted out.

My dad grabbed the remote control and unmuted the TV.

Patrick planted his elbows on his knees, leaning forward with his eyes locked on the news story.

"Jesus," my dad muttered under his breath.

Lucas had never been one to take the Lord's name in vain, but this was a much called-for exception.

The news footage showed me in the passenger's side of Alan's pickup truck as it rolled slowly along the curb.

An off camera reporter yelled:

"Penny Matchmaker! Do you know who murdered Jessica Saxon?"

From the couch, my mom told my dad, "Turn it up, Lucas!"

He turned the TV volume up as far as it would go just in time for all of us to hear…

My voice?

Closed captions played across the bottom of the screen for the hearing impaired, as a recording of my voice played:

"If anyone had a motive to murder Jessica, it was me! She was overbearing. I never had a second to myself. She knew all my secrets and she constantly pressured me to admit to everyone that I'm an alcoholic! If anyone benefitted from her death, it was me!"

I gasped!

A polished news anchor filled the screen. He had a grim frown on his neatly shaven face.

Shaking his head, he stated, "That was Penelope Matchmaker's voice you just heard. Complicating matters is the fact that she's the wife of the lead detective who's investigating the murder. The plot could not be thicker."

"It certainly couldn't, Michael," said his co-anchor, Diane. "This twisted tale is still developing, and though our sources claim Mrs. Matchmaker is the prime suspect, the police have yet to confirm."

"Turn it off," my mom yelled. "Turn it off, I can't bear this another second!"

My father fumbled with the volume but soon the TV went dark and the living room was quiet.

Mom was beside herself.

"I didn't do it," I told her.

I knew that she didn't think I had.

But the current circumstances still broke her heart.

From the loveseat, Patrick turned his sweaty face to me and said:

"Jessica deserved to die."

A shadow cut across his face, as he darkly added:

"I hope she's in hell."

My dad was ready to chastise him for his very un-Christian attitude.

But Patrick began gasping for air.

"Patrick?" Lucas asked, alarmed.

"Someone get him a glass of water!" my mom cried, and Esther ran into the kitchen.

My dad rushed over to Patrick and tried to hold him up, but my cousin clutched his chest and collapsed.

"I think he's having a heart attack!" my dad yelled.

Daniel sprang to call an ambulance. Esther returned with a glass of water but didn't know what to do with it. My mother shrieked to high heaven and began praying over Cousin Patrick's slumped body.

As for myself, I watched the commotion and had to wonder.

Why would my cousin think that Jessica had deserved to die?

CHAPTER SIX

COUSIN PATRICK WAS RUSHED to Mercy Hospital, located in Industry City.

I piled into my dad's pickup truck, squeezing in-between my parents.

My dad, Lucas gripped the steering wheel so tightly as he drove that his knuckles were as white as Mom's hair.

As we rode in tense silence, following the ambulance, my mom, Dottie, clutched her Christian cross necklace. Her lips moved with prayers, but she didn't make a sound.

The ambulance's red, flashing lights illuminated our worried faces.

I prayed, too, but was often distracted by what Patrick had said.

Why would he hope that Jessica was in hell? Why did he think she had deserved to die?

They didn't know each other...

...or did they?

When the ambulance swung into the emergency port, Dad pulled the pickup truck up to the hospital's emergency entrance.

"I'll find you inside," he told us, as Mom and I hopped out.

We jogged into the emergency room.

Mom stumbled over her words. The nurse at the emergency admissions desk had to slow her down.

"Patrick O'Brian," I said, telling the nurse my cousin's name. "He just arrived in an ambulance."

The nurse got straight to work, collecting information from me and coordinating with the E.R.

"Was it a heart attack?" I asked. "Is he okay?"

"We don't know just yet," she said. "You can have a seat in the waiting area. We'll update you as soon as we can."

The waiting area was crowded, and Mom seemed too anxious to sit, anyway.

We stepped away from the admissions desk just as Dad spilled into the hospital, having parked his truck.

"Lucas!" my mom cried, getting his attention. "He's barely thirty-five. What could've caused him to collapse?"

Holding my mom, he said, "I don't know, but he hasn't looked well in general for the past day or two."

I had noticed the same thing.

"He was sweaty and a little jumpy," I agreed.

"We'll have to wait to see what the doctors say," he concluded.

My mother was suddenly overcome with a fresh wave of grief.

"Margot and the children!" she exclaimed as soon as Patrick's family came to mind. "Penny, would you call her?"

"Of course," I said.

I found my cell phone in my purse and pulled up Margot O'Brian's number, as I eased away from my parents to concentrate on the call.

When I sent the call through, it rang and rang and rang. And then the outgoing answering machine message began to play.

"You have reached the O'Brians!" sang the entire family in a chorus. Then each member of the family said their own name, starting with Patrick.

"Come on, come on," I grumbled, waiting for the sound of the *beep*.

I didn't have Margot's cell phone number, so leaving a message on their home answering machine would have to do. I chose my words carefully. I didn't want to alarm the children. Finally, I recited my cell number and told Margot to give me a call as soon as she could.

An E.R. doctor found my parents. My mom waved me over. There was an update!

Quickly, I called Alan first.

He picked up.

"Penny?"

"Alan!"

"Try not to freak out about the news," he advised, assuming

that the 11 o'clock story about me being a murderer was why I had called.

"Patrick collapsed at the house!"

"What?"

"We brought him to Mercy Hospital," I told him. "The doctor is speaking with Mom and Dad now."

"What happened?"

"I don't know. It might have been a heart attack. I'll call when I can!"

I hung up and joined my parents just as the doctor led them into a quiet corner of the triage unit where Patrick was lying on a hospital bed.

His hair was damp with sweat and his face was pale. But other than that, he looked okay.

Patrick had given the doctor permission to tell us what had happened to him medically. But as the doctor explained how Patrick had suffered a mild heart attack, he never stated *why*.

"When can we bring him home?" my mom asked.

Both of my parents followed the doctor out. He closed the curtain, giving Patrick and me privacy. As he answered my parents' questions, they made their way back to the waiting area, their voices disappearing as they went.

I neared Patrick, sat on the bed, and gave his hand an affectionate squeeze.

"We were really worried about you."

"No need to worry," he said, as a thin smile spread across his dehydrated lips. "I'm fine."

"I called Margot and left a message," I told him.

He sighed and ran his hand down his face.

"I wish you hadn't," he murmured.

Taken by surprise, I asked, "What do you mean?"

He shook his head. He had no intention of telling me.

"When can I get out of here?" he asked, changing the subject.

I didn't know. "I think Mom's finding out right now. I can see?"

"Thanks," he replied in a flat tone without looking at me.

I stood, but I had to ask:

"Patrick, should I not have called your wife to tell her you had an emergency?"

Quickly back-pedaling, he said, "You did the right thing. Really, thanks so much."

He was a really good liar.
I would know.
So was I.

I pulled the curtain aside, padded through the emergency room, and found my parents in the waiting area.

"When can we bring him home?"

My dad told me, "They want to keep him for a few hours at least."

"He's not going to like that," I realized.

On the other side of the hospital entrance came Alan.

The glass doors whooshed apart and he breezed into the waiting area.

His blue eyes were dead-locked on me.

Alan greeted my parents, warmly hugging my mom and shaking my dad's hand.

Taking me by the shoulders, he asked, "Are you okay?"

"Mm-hmm," I replied, nodding my head.

"It was a mild heart attack," said my father, filling Alan in with the details.

A hard look came over my husband.

He didn't agree.

"I believe the killer struck again," he said darkly. "Or tried to."

"What?" my mom breathed.

My dad blurted out, "That explains it! Why else would a young, healthy man have a heart attack?"

"The doctor didn't say Patrick had been poisoned," I pointed out.

My dad corrected me, "The doctor didn't have to state the *cause* of the heart attack."

Even so, that didn't sound right to me. How could poison that had killed Jessica only have caused a heart attack for my cousin?

Alan took me by the arm and pulled me aside.

"Penny," he said, speaking very quietly. "Patrick collapsed at your parents' cabin?"

"Yes."

"Was Esther there?"

"Alan!"

"Was she?" he pushed. "She was, wasn't she?"

I refused to admit it.

"Penny," he warned.

I hissed through my teeth:

"Why would Esther want to kill my cousin?"

"That's for me to investigate."

We stared at each other for a long moment.

Then he told me, "I'm going to take your silence as a 'yes'."

"Fine, Alan. Yes, she was there. Do you know who the prime suspect is as far as *all of Walnut Mountain* is concerned? Hmm? Do you?"

He rolled his eyes. "That'll blow over in two seconds."

"Will it?" I challenged him. "That news story made me look like a murderer, and frankly, Alan, it made you look like a damned fool!"

"Lower your voice!"

"I don't know who killed Jessica, but it wasn't Esther. If you do *anything* to jeopardize her wedding day, then I'll…"

I shook my head at the situation, fearing the worst, and at Alan in general, but I couldn't finish the threat.

What was I going to do? Tell him I would never forgive him? Tell him I would never speak to him again if he ruined my best friend's chances at marrying the man of her dreams?

"Excuse me," he said. He pulled me in, kissed my forehead, and told me, "I have to ask Patrick a few questions."

I watched my husband flash his badge at the nurse behind the admissions desk. The nurse immediately escorted Alan into the emergency room. I remained standing where I was.

I refused to entertain even a single suspicion that my best friend in the world was a killer on the loose.

I heard my cell phone ringing in my purse.

"Thank God," I breathed.

It was Margot, Patrick's wife.

"Margot!" I said, answering the call. "It's Penny!"

"I know it's you, Penny," she said in a heavy voice. "I'm the one that's calling."

"Right," I murmured, embarrassed. "I'm a little frazzled. Patrick has been admitted to Mercy Hospital in Industry City."

Patrick, Margot, and their three children lived in Industry City, so I expected Margot to tell me she's on her way.

But she didn't interrupt. In fact, she didn't say anything at all.

"Margot?"

"I'm listening," she cooly replied.

"The doctors say he had a mild heart attack."

She snorted out a little laugh.

"I can give you the address of the hospital," I offered.

I only heard breathing on the other end of the line.

"I'm sure that if you and the kids come—"

"I'm not going to come to the hospital, Penny."

It occurred to me that my marriage might not be the only one that was on the rocks...

"Why not?"

She had nothing to say other than, "I appreciate the call."

I felt suddenly protective of my cousin. He'd had an emergency. He could've died.

He needed his wife!

Didn't Margot understand the importance of *marriage vows*? She had promised to stand by her spouse *in good times and in bad*, for *better* or *worse*!

"Listen Margot, the fact of the matter is that a woman was killed at my parents' 50th anniversary picnic. My husband is investigating the murder and he believes that the killer tried to take Patrick's life, too. I don't see how Patrick would have known the victim, Jessica Saxon, but—"

"Jessica Saxon!" Margot blurted out, as if she knew the name.

"Yes—"

"Jessica Saxon the artist?" she guessed.

"Ah, she was a bit of a painter," I allowed. "She owned a craft store—"

"Jessica Saxon, who looks like a porcelain doll, with chocolate-brown hair, and—"

"You know her?"

"Someone killed Jessica Saxon?" she said and laughed. "Good!"

I didn't know what to say, so I went with, "I'm glad to hear you're not torn up about it..."

"It's late, Penny. I don't want to wake the kids."

"Margot—"

"Take care."

She hung up before I could ask her how she might have known Jessica.

As I made my way back to Patrick's curtained room in the triage unit, I recalled how Patrick had seemed to recognize Jessica the day I had introduced them at the picnic. Patrick had stammered and turned white as a ghost seeing her, and Jessica had literally turned on her heel and walked away.

Patrick must have known Jessica, because his wife certainly did…

"No one poisoned me, Detective!" Patrick yelled, as I pulled the curtain aside and stepped into the tight quarters.

"You don't know that!" Alan hotly retorted. "We need to ask the doctors to take blood and run tests to see if there's any poison in your system!"

"I wasn't poisoned!" my cousin insisted, getting worked up.

Worried to the bone, my mom pleaded, "Alan, you're upsetting him! He needs to stay calm so he doesn't have another heart attack!"

Alan ignored her and threatened Patrick, "You will submit to a blood test or else I'll have you arrested for obstruction of justice!"

"I have a drug problem!" he blurted out.

We all fell silent.

"I did too much, alright?" he added, slumping into a slouch of shame. "This has happened before. No one tried to kill me… except me."

After a long moment, he admitted:

"I need help."

✝

"MY NAME IS Patrick, and I'm a drug addict—"

I lovingly pointed to the card I had supplied my cousin with.

"Oh, pardon me," he said. "My name is Patrick, and I'm *struggling* to *overcome* a drug addiction."

"Hi, Patrick!" everyone at Celebrate Recovery replied.

"You have five minutes," I gently reminded him, as I started the timer. "I'll warn you when you have half a minute left."

"Thanks, Penny," he said, touching eyes with me.

We shared a moment of connection, and then Patrick shared his story for the next five minutes in the fellowship hall of Hopeful Heart Ministries.

I listened closely. But he didn't mention his wife, the state of his marriage, or any stress factors in his life. Instead, he focused on trying to make sense of his long-standing relationship with drugs. Why he felt he needed them. And how he imagined he would carry on in life without them.

It wasn't my place to judge, however. He was at liberty to talk about whatever he wanted to. The most important thing I could do was be supportive and connect him with another Celebrate Recovery group in Industry City so that he would be able to continue to get the help he needed when he returned home.

I also planned to find a Christ-centered therapist for him, one that specializes in drug addiction and rehabilitation.

When his time was wrapping up, I whispered, "Half a minute."

He finished his point and thanked everyone for listening.

"Thanks for sharing!" we all said in unison.

Hailey shared next. She hadn't engaged in any compulsive shopping recently. Proud of herself, she mentioned that she had been most tempted to 'buy everything in sight' the day after she had watched me 'getting arrested' on the news. But she had overcome the urge.

In fact, most of the other members of Celebrate Recovery used their five-minute share time to talk about how triggered they had felt as they'd learned I had probably killed Jessica.

All I could do was frown until it was my turn to share.

"My name is Penny," I began, "and I struggle with alcoholism."

"Hi, Penny!" they sang.

"I'm going to use my five minutes this evening to promise all of you that I did not poison Jessica at the picnic. That horrible news story was a giant misunderstanding."

I went on to get a number of frustrations off my chest, but I was careful about what I shared and what I kept to myself.

My biggest source of anxiety was the fact that my husband was convinced Esther was the killer. But I didn't breathe a word about it to the group. The last thing I wanted was for anyone here to suspect Esther.

I concluded sharing, and since I was the last one to speak, we all stood, held hands, and recited the serenity prayer.

Rachel and Hailey began putting the fellowship hall back in order. As they carried tables and arranged the chairs, I said hello to Sue Ellen. She was wearing her Charming Diner uniform, so I knew she would be heading to the diner for her shift in a moment.

"Penny, we're all so relieved to hear you weren't arrested that night," she said. "We can't afford to lose you as our group leader. I'm so happy you didn't kill Jessica."

"So am I."

She opened her tote bag in front of me. "See, no cats."

"You're doing great," I said with a smile. "Sue Ellen, you're not seeing anyone, are you?"

I had quite a reputation as a matchmaker, so she instantly had an idea about where I was going with this. A glimmer of interest flashed behind her small, green eyes.

"I'm not seeing anyone," she told me, as her eyebrows floated up to her curly, blonde hairline.

"I'd like to set you up with someone."

"You would?"

"I think the two of you might hit it off."

Her smile faltered and she turned gloomy.

"I have *a lot* of cats, Penny."

"He likes cats," I said brightly.

She munched on her lower lip, thinking, then said:

"Men who like cats don't always like *cat ladies*."

"You're not a cat lady," I promised her.

Her eyes widened and went white all around.

"I'm *definitely* a cat lady."

Optimistically dismissive, I told her, "You're sweet and beautiful and lovable! Plus, the guy is *really* cute. And he has a great, stable job. He's very responsible. He's looking for something serious. I think you'll like him. What do you say?"

✟

DEEPLY PROUD OF Cousin Patrick for taking the first big step in the recovery process, I invited him to Charming Diner after the meeting.

We decided to walk from the church to the diner since it was such a beautiful spring night.

Strolling along Main Street, Patrick told me how hopeful he felt. He almost wished he didn't live in Industry City. Walnut Mountain had stolen his heart.

Thud.

"What was that?" he asked, slowing his step and looking off into the shadowy grass.

I hadn't heard it.

Thud, thud... Thud.

"There it is again," he said. "You don't hear it?"

Thud.

"Oh! Those are walnuts."

"Walnuts?" he asked, confused.

"It's walnut season," I explained as I started across the cool grass. "Come, I'll show you."

I walked across the grassy expanse that separated Hopeful Heart Ministries from the library.

A huge walnut tree stood, looming over the side of the library. On the grass beneath it were dozens of round, green, fuzzy walnut husks.

I picked one up and handed it to him.

"There's a ripe walnut inside."

"This is a walnut?"

"It's a walnut husk," I clarified.

"It looks like a tennis ball."

"Everyone says that."

"Man," he remarked, as he looked at the round walnut husk in his hand. "This must have been a great place to grow up."

We continued on our way, reminiscing about childhood memories and what it had been like for me growing up in quaint, sleepy Walnut Mountain. Patrick tossed and caught his walnut husk, as we walked.

When we reached the diner, Sue Ellen smiled from behind the hostess stand. She sat us in her section and poured two steaming mugs of coffee for us. There was cream and sugar on the table, so we helped ourselves.

"You know, I really cherished the times I visited you, Dottie, and Lucas when I was growing up," Patrick commented, as he stirred a second packet of sugar into his creamy coffee. "It was only a handful of times, but I remember every visit."

"Me too," I said, sharing the nostalgia for a moment.

"I once visited Grandmother Mable, you know," he said from out of nowhere.

"Oh?"

I was surprised he had uttered her name so cavalierly. In the Hawkins household, Grandmother Mable was *never* spoken of.

"You did?"

He nodded and smiled to himself, as a memory washed over

him.

"I don't know what made me think of her. Well," he said with a shrug. "Obviously, addiction runs in the family."

Patrick kept the volume of his voice low, as he explained:

"I have my *problem*, and you have yours."

I couldn't disagree.

"And Grandmother Mable had *hers*," he added.

"She had a drinking problem," I recalled. "But I thought she overcame it."

"As far as I know, she did," he agreed.

Our Grandmother Mable had lost her marriage because of her addiction to alcohol. Those were different times back then, and she couldn't face the shame that had come with being divorced. She had moved to Paris, running away from her problems, but not herself.

In Paris, she had become something of a sleuth investigator. I honestly didn't know much about it. But my mother had alluded to the possibility that my grandmother's hobby of solving crimes in Paris had ultimately gotten her killed.

"I visited her in Paris once."

"You did?" I asked, highly interested.

"I was *very* young. Mom and Dad brought me, and I stayed with Grandma Mable while they toured the French countryside for about a week. I loved Paris."

"My parents never talk about her," I told him. "All I know is that she was murdered?"

"My parents and I are convinced she was. But according to her death certificate, she died of alcohol poisoning."

"But she had stopped drinking," I said.

"She had been sober for years, as I understand," he confirmed.

"Why does everyone in our family think she was killed?"

He gulped his coffee, leaned in, and asked:

"Have you ever heard of the Eiffel Tower Murders?"

I was intrigued, but I hadn't.

"When Grandma Mable was living in Paris," he began, "there was a serial killer on the loose. The killings were soon referred to as the Eiffel Tower Murders. Mable put the Paris police to shame, because she was the one who caught the killer."

"Really," I breathed.

He nodded. "Yes, it was headline news all over the Paris newspaper. Then, Mable was found dead. If you ask me, someone in the Paris police department did it. Someone high up who was embarrassed. Or maybe it was a conspiracy of many police officials working together to take her out and cover it up. All I know is that my gut tells me she didn't fall off the wagon and drink herself to death after becoming a national treasure in France, you know?"

I mulled that over, as I sipped coffee.

"People like us have to be careful," Patrick began to conclude. "When everyone knows you have an addiction, they'll automatically believe that you died of an overdose, even if you've had decades of sobriety under your belt."

How dreadfully ominous!

No wonder my mother had been worried sick about me.

She feared I would end up like my grandmother.

And for a split second, so did I.

Sue Ellen swooped in with her notepad, ready to take our orders.

Feeling hungry, I told her I would have the Midnight Breakfast, and Patrick ordered the Classic Burger.

As Sue Ellen jotted down our drink order next, I saw Officer Chuck enter the diner alone.

It was divine timing!

"Excuse me a moment, Patrick," I said, as I slid out of the booth.

I took a gentle hold of Sue Ellen's arm like an old friend and whispered:

"He's here."

"Who's here?" she asked.

I steered her up the aisle towards Chuck, who looked dashing in his policeman's uniform.

"The fellow I'd like you to meet," I told her.

"Oh?"

Chuck was waiting at the hostess stand.

He couldn't take his eyes off Sue Ellen as we approached.

Sue Ellen blushed.

"Chuck, I'd like you to meet my friend, Sue Ellen," I said, making casual introductions. "Sue Ellen, this is Charles Abel, but everyone calls him Chuck."

Sue Ellen's sweet voice was full of cautious optimism when she asked him:

"I hear you like cats?"

CHAPTER SEVEN

SPRING WAS IN the air!

And so was love!

Nothing made me feel cozy and content like making a successful match!

Not that I wanted to count my chickens before they had hatched, but I had a warm-hearted feeling that Sue Ellen and Officer Chuck had *really* hit it off.

I had good instincts about these things.

When I had introduced them at the diner, the mutual interest between them had been palpable. Sue Ellen's cheeks had flushed pinker than an April rose. And Chuck had adorably straightened his spine and planted his fists on his hips while talking with her.

Thanks to my being an expert in male body language, I knew that Chuck had instinctively done this to make himself appear larger, and therefore more virile, to Sue Ellen, similar to how male peacocks flaunt their feathers to attract a mate.

I hadn't needed to facilitate their conversation too much. But at one point I had nudged them along by mentioning the upcoming Easter Service at Hopeful Heart Ministries. Chuck had jumped at the chance to accompany Sue Ellen, and once their date had been locked in, I had returned to the vinyl booth where my cousin had been entertaining himself with his cell phone.

In the days that followed, I reminded myself of Sue Ellen and Chuck's budding romance whenever stress tried to seize me.

I avoided Samantha at school even though she hadn't exactly given up her political crusades. Instead of spending time in the teachers' lounge during our breaks, Esther and I sat outside in the sunshine where walnut husks fell and plopped onto soft grass.

I had become something of a state-wide celebrity thanks to the developing news story that had made me out to be a killer. I couldn't control the newspaper articles that were printed about me nor the Channel 9 news updates that were being broadcast. But that didn't stop my mother from quietly blaming me for the grief she had been suffering because of it.

Dottie was terrified I would end up like my grandmother, taken out in such a way that it would look like my own fault. Cousin Patrick's dark comment about how *people like us* needed to be careful had chilled me to the bone. Was that what my mom was truly worried about?

I tried not to think about it.

In fact, there were *many* things I was trying not to think about, including...

Who had killed Jessica?

Why did Alan *really* suspect Esther?

What evidence did he have on my best friend?

And how in the world had *both* Patrick and his wife Margot known Jessica Saxon?

Neither had been especially torn up to learn of her murder...

...but *why?*

Could Cousin Patrick have poisoned Jessica at the picnic?

Could he have offered her a poisoned drink, or strategically placed a snack just in time for her to pick it up and pop it into her mouth?

The fact of the matter was that Jessica could've been eating this and that all throughout the celebration, so why had Alan become fixated on investigating only the edible items that I had handed to my sponsor?

Dang, I was doing it again!

I shook all thoughts of murder and suspects from my head, and pulled Alan's pickup truck around the side of the brick schoolhouse where there was an entrance close to the art room.

As I came to a stop and threw the truck into Park, I reminded myself to focus on what mattered in life.

I turned off the engine, left the key in the ignition, bowed my head, and folded my hands in prayer.

"Lord, I want to give Alan a baby. I'm begging you to inspire his heart and compel him to come home. I want my life back. I want it all. I'm praying and asking and pleading with you, Lord. This Easter, as we commemorate your resurrection from the tomb, I ask that you resurrect my marriage from the grave. I can't live this dead life anymore. Please."

I fought a sting of tears that were trying to well up in my eyes.

Sniffling, I glanced at myself in the rearview mirror, making sure I didn't look sad.

I adjusted the sequin chemo cap I was wearing, this one was a beautiful spring-green color that complimented my red hair and matched my breezy dress.

Then I climbed out of the pickup truck, dropped the tailgate, and found Harriet in the Art room storage closet where she had wrapped her butterfly artwork in bubble wrap and protective cloths.

"Penny, you're here!"

"I'm here!" I said with a smile.

Coordinating with Alan to get his truck had taken me less time than I had thought. My own car was currently parked behind the police station. Alan had left his keys in the truck, so I hadn't even needed to find him in the station or deal with news reporters who were still in the habit of clogging the front entrance.

Harriet pushed her eggplant-purple hair off her forehead. Her hair was less spikey today. She began thinking out loud.

"We'll need to carry each piece vertically through the doorways. They're pretty heavy, but I got them here myself."

"Between the two of us, they should be light and easy," I agreed.

Together, we lifted the first wrapped painting, carried it vertically through the storage room door, and then eased it horizontally as we carried it through the Art room.

When we reached the Art room door, we lifted the wrapped painting vertically again, and kept it that way, as we quickly crossed the hallway and exited the schoolhouse.

I had already laid a number of thick, woolen blankets in the truck bed.

Harriet and I angled the wrapped painting horizontally once again and carefully slid it onto the bed of the truck.

We took a moment to catch our breath after that.

Then we proceeded in the same manner, as we carried the other wrapped paintings out and laid them on top of each other in the truck bed.

"Hallelujah!" I cheered, pushing the tailgate up to close the hinged door.

After we had climbed into the pickup truck, I took one of the Morning Glory coffees that I had gotten on the way and handed it to Harriet.

"For you, my lady," I said.

"Coffee!"

As Harriet took a little sip—her black coffee was still piping hot!—I grabbed the other to-go coffee from the cup holder and enjoyed a couple gulps. Mine was creamy with just a hint of sugar.

"To the church!" I announced.

"Actually, can we go to my house first?" asked Harriet.

She shrank with embarrassment and added:

"There's one more piece of art that I'd really like to see at the Easter Service."

"Oh?"

"I got so inspired this past week, I started working on another painting with butterflies. I wasn't sure why I was making it at first. Honestly, I think I needed to throw myself into an artistic project to take my mind off of things..."

"I know the feeling," I said, as I started the truck and began driving through the parking lot towards School Street.

"When I finished the piece last night, my heart told me that the giant painting is meant for Hopeful Heart Ministries. I might even donate it so that it can have a forever home at the church."

"That's so sweet of you, Harriet!"

She shrugged. "I feel a little embarrassed, because if I had left all my artwork at my house, you could've just picked it up there, and we wouldn't have to make two stops."

"Oh, don't be embarrassed. If I had to drive all over Walnut Mountain collecting your artwork, I wouldn't complain. Look at all this springtime beauty!"

"You're the best, Penny."

"Hardly," I said with a smile.

Harriet lived in a single-story bungalow cabin that was located on the eastern foothills of Walnut Mountain, the very mountain after which our town had been named.

As I steered the pickup truck up her muddy, steep driveway, falling walnut husks thunked against the roof of the truck as well as the hood.

"The paintings!" I gasped, worried that a falling walnut husk might crack the glass panes.

"The bubble wrap and cloth will keep them safe," she assured me, but I wasn't so certain.

She directed me to pull around and back in so that the rear of the truck would meet the closed garage door.

"Perfect," she said, as she jumped out.

I followed after her.

She opened the garage door. Sunlight bathed her garage which she had converted into a home art studio.

It smelled of paint, turpentine, and other scents I couldn't identify. There were countless canvases, works-in-progress art pieces, easels, and palettes of paint.

One of the tables contained Harriet's butterflies in various stages of the preservation process.

I was fascinated.

"This is the piece I've been working on all week," she said. As I neared her, she mentioned, "It'll take me a few minutes to get it wrapped up."

"Oh, Harriet! You've outdone yourself!" I exclaimed when I saw the painting.

Larger than the other three that had been loaded into the truck, her final piece was nearly as tall as she was. And it was almost *all* butterflies. Having chosen each butterfly carefully for its color and shape, and having arranged those butterflies perfectly, the overall image she had created was of our Savior's serene face!

"This is phenomenal!"

Graciously, she smiled and bowed her head.

"You're too kind."

"You're being far too humble, Harriet! My God! This is gorgeous! Our congregation will love it!"

We got to work wrapping the massive painting in several sheets of thick bubble wrap. Next we covered it five times over with all the protective cloths that Harriet owned.

When all was said and done, we muscled the gigantic artwork out of the garage and onto the other wrapped paintings in the bed of the truck.

Catching my breath, I wiped my brow and fanned my dress to get a little air on my skin.

"To the church!" Harriet said enthusiastically.

Given the distance, I didn't think I would make it.

"That coffee has caught up with me," I said.

"You can use my bathroom," she offered. "Go in through the door in the garage. To the right is the living room and on the far side is the bathroom."

"Thanks," I said, as I made a beeline.

"Take your time!"

The bathroom was easy enough to find. I relieved myself, washed my hands, and gave myself the once-over in the mirror.

I remembered my prayer and reminded myself:

"I have asked. Now my job is to believe that I have already received."

I pinched my eyes shut, sucked in a deep breath, and searched with all my might to find within my heart a mustard seed's worth of faith.

When I found it, I opened my eyes, threw the bathroom door open, and started across the living room.

That's when I noticed…

In the corner of the room stood a painting on an easel.

I hadn't seen it on the way in.

But now, the painting caught my eye…

…because it looked ruined.

What had once probably been painted angels was smeared and streaked.

As I neared the ruined painting, I saw that the canvas had been slashed, too.

There was a manila filing folder resting on the easel.

I opened it to find an application of some kind.

I began reading.

"Pembroke Pines Foundation," I murmured as I skimmed the form. "Angel Art Award…"

It was a submission form.

I stared at the ruined painting then re-read the document that Harriet had filled out to submit her painting.

The foundation's name was ringing a very distant bell in my mind, but I couldn't place where I had heard of that award before.

Why did the 'Pembroke Pines Foundation's Angel Art Award' sound so familiar?

✝

"ALL OF MY DREAMS are coming true, Penny!" sang Esther as she twirled around the living room of my cabin.

She was wearing her wedding dress and smiling from ear to ear.

The pearl-white wedding dress had a mermaid cut that accentuated Esther's modest curves. The lace bodice sparkled, and the hourglass shape hugged her thighs and dramatically flared at the knees.

She looked like an enchanting princess and I couldn't have been happier for her.

There was only one thing that was out of place.

"Esther," I said tenderly, as I approached her.

"Don't you love it, Penny?"

As sensitively as I could, I told her, "You look beautiful, and I think it's time to say goodbye to the chemo cap."

"Huh?" she replied.

Her hand floated up and touched the gray, knit chemo cap on her head.

She wasn't bald any more. Her hair was no longer patchy. At this point, her chemo caps were a kind of security blanket. They looked great, but in a sense, they were holding her back from fully embracing being the strong, healed woman she had become.

"Your hair has grown in," I reminded her. "You're healthy, and I think a white, lace veil would be best for your wedding day. What do you think?"

"Oh, I don't know, Penny..." she said in a small voice.

"May I?" I asked, as I took the white veil from its box on the couch.

She grew nervous, but allowed me to remove her gray chemo cap.

She touched the back of her head and said, "It's still kind of thin. I've been using castor oil and taking vitamins. It's helped a little."

"Let me see," I said as I stepped around her. Her dark brown hair was a bit thin, but she had grown enough length that I thought it wasn't noticeable. "Your hair looks good, Esther. And the veil will prevent anyone from scrutinizing your hair."

"You think?"

I gently brushed my fingers through her hair, giving her locks some shape. Her hair was very wispy, but I knew that hair spray would add texture and volume on the big day.

I carefully bobby pinned the veil to the top of her head, having gathered the hair on the crown of her head, though there wasn't much.

As the veil spilled down the back of her head, I swept her longer bangs aside and tucked them behind her ear.

Then I took a few steps back and marveled at my work.

Her eyes widened.

"Do I look okay?" she asked.

"You look more than 'okay'," I promised her. "You look like a beautiful bride."

"Oh, Penny!" she cried, as she threw her arms around me, she was so overjoyed. "I hope you're not lying to me!"

"You know I would never lie to you!"

We hugged it out.

"Try not to cry," I teased. "We don't want your dress stained with tears!"

Releasing me, she said, "I can't wait for the wedding! I wish it was tomorrow! I'm so anxious to get married. I feel like I'm holding my breath!"

Suddenly, Alan burst into the cabin.

"Penny!" he barked, as he stomped through the vestibule. "Is Esther here?"

He came into view, entering the living room.

He held a pair of handcuffs in his hands.

Esther gasped and turned whiter than her wedding dress.

"Alan!" I yelled, fearing the worst. "Esther didn't do it, and you know it!"

As if her nightmare were coming to life, Esther shrieked and asked:

"Has Alan been investigating me?!"

"Not at all," I told her, though my gaze was locked on Alan whose gaze was locked on me.

"Penny," he growled.

He charged at me, using long strides, and when he reached me, he cupped the back of my head, pulled me in, and planted the biggest kiss on my mouth.

Coming up for air, he told me, "I miss my wife," and then

smashed his lips against mine again.

"Oh, my," said Esther, as my husband and I started making out. "I'll get changed and see myself out..."

Esther disappeared into the bathroom.

I didn't know what had gotten into Alan, but I liked it!

"Esther's no longer a suspect," he told me as he searched my eyes and drank in the sight of my ravished face.

"Am I?"

"No," he growled before diving into my neck with a hungry smattering of kisses.

"Then what were the handcuffs for?"

"Dramatic effect."

"It worked."

He grinned at me and said:

"You ain't seen nothing yet."

CHAPTER EIGHT

THE SUN WAS SHINING in the clearest blue sky I had ever seen.

Birds chirped, as butterflies fluttered around the flowery bushes outside of Hopeful Heart Ministries.

The sight of the white church with its tall steeple filled my heart with warmth this fine Easter morning.

I entered the church with my parents amid a stream of parishioners.

Everyone was dressed in their Sunday-best for the holiday. My dad, Lucas, had even thrown on a brown suit and ran a comb through his thick red hair to make himself look more presentable. Mom and I wore long, summery dresses, and our heads were covered, Dottie's in a straw hat and I was wearing a lovely yellow chemo cap that matched my ballet flats.

Along with the rest of the decoration committee, I had put a great deal of time, effort, and care into decorating the church.

The vestibule had been transformed with the decorative vines and white lilies I had purchased at Angel Arts & Crafts. Harriet and I had hung the large 'He Is Risen' banner I had bought above the entryway of the sanctuary.

Yet the crown jewel of all the Easter decorations was Harriet's *Savior* masterpiece.

The *Savior*, artfully constructed with butterflies, was hanging on one of the walls in the sanctuary.

Parishioners clustered around the giant work of art, marveling its glory. Though Harriet hadn't signed her name on the painting or told anyone outright that she had created the masterpiece, word spread quickly through the congregation that the *Savior* as well as the other butterfly paintings were hers.

People patted her on the back, offered her compliments, and otherwise regarded her with awe and wonder.

I found Harriet, gave her a hug, and said:

"Happy Easter!"

She returned the sentiment and we exchanged pleasantries, as my parents sat in the front pew.

Esther and Daniel arrived, happy and in love.

Gloria and Hank settled in their seats.

My favorite barista, Dex, held his girlfriend Ashley's hand, as they started down the aisle, looking for a good place to sit.

Even Rachel Harder and Vince Salsbury, who had taken a shine to one another, having bonded over their shared grief at surviving their spouses deaths, were canoodling together in the church.

It seemed every couple I had successfully matched was present, ready to worship the Lord with grateful hearts.

I hadn't picked a pew, nor had I sat down.

Rather, I worked hard to temper my emotions and not let my hopes soar too high.

I didn't know if Alan would make it to the Easter Service.

I only knew that I desperately prayed he would.

With Esther off of the suspect list, there was more pressure than ever on Alan.

He hadn't disclosed to me who he might be investigating now.

And I hadn't thought to ask him the night he had come over, flashing handcuffs and setting my heart on fire.

We had spent the night together in a kind of bliss-filled haze.

That night, I had given myself the gift of forgetting he had moved into a motel. I had pretended we had always been perfect, and always would be. As if I had never drank a drop of alcohol in my life. As if I had never fallen asleep while the kitchen caught fire. As if Alan had never had to battle flames to save my life, only to never look at me the same again after that.

By the time I had woken up the next morning, memories of our passion lingering in my mind, my husband had already driven off to the police station, leaving me with a smile on my face and an Alan-shaped hole in my bed.

I told myself to find a spot in one of the church pews before they all filled up.

"Penny, sit with us!"

I turned to find Sue Ellen. She was tucked closely next to Chuck, and they were holding hands!

Squeezing in, I gave Sue Ellen a little hug and shot Chuck a smile.

From the pulpit at the front of the sanctuary, Pastor Peter greeted the congregation, and soon the Easter Service was in full swing.

I never stopped hoping that Alan would show up...

✝

MY PARENTS hosted Easter lunch at their cabin.

A decent portion of the congregation had been invited, but few arrived. After what had happened at Dottie and Lucas' 50th anniversary picnic, no one could really blame the parishioners for declining to attend another picnic where poison might be on the menu.

It ended up being an intimate group of friends and family. They came straight from Hopeful Heart Ministries to my parents' cozy neck of the woods.

Patrick hadn't come to the Easter Service, but he was making himself useful now, manning the grill and stacking a huge mountain of cooked burgers on a tray.

My mom was on the deck where she had set up the refreshment table. There was an assortment of beers, wine coolers, and wine, as well as non-alcoholic options available. Mom helped our guests get drinks, and she mingled with our extended family who, like Patrick, had planned to head home after Easter.

"I could use a little room, Penny," said Patrick, as he slid a freshly cooked burger on top of the current mountain of burgers he had been working on. "Could you move the cooked burgers?"

"Of course," I said.

There was a buffet table where other picnic foods had been placed along with condiments, bags of buns, and disposable plates and utensils.

I first made a little space on the buffet table and then carefully began carrying the tall stack of cooked burgers across the grass.

Most of the guests were on the deck having drinks even though

Dad had set three picnic tables near the buffet table.

I held my breath. My arms burned, the plate of cooked burgers was so heavy.

They smelled delicious!

Almost there…

Finally, I set the steaming burgers on the buffet table and let out a rocky breath.

I hadn't dropped them, phew!

It was then that I suddenly realized all the guests were staring at me with their jaws hanging open.

No one moved a muscle.

I blinked, confused.

"What?" I asked.

My mom looked white as a ghost.

My dad breathed, "Penny, don't move," but I didn't hear him.

Cousin Patrick froze.

Again, I asked, "What?" and let out a little laugh.

ROAR!

Hot beast breath hit the top of my head, blowing my red hair against my cheeks.

I whipped around, coming face to face with…

A bear!

"Ah!" I shrieked.

The bear roared in my face!

Standing on its hind legs, the black bear was at least six feet tall!

I was pinned between the towering bear and the buffet table!

But then!

To my surprise!

From out of nowhere!

Alan dove between me and the bear, shoving me sideways to save my life!

I spilled across the grass.

"Penny!" cried my mom from the deck.

The bear took a swing at Alan as it fell forward, coming onto all fours.

Everyone gasped.

Alan drove his fist against the side of the bear's head, stunning it.

I scrambled to my feet and was about to sprint for the cabin, but bear cubs were trotting around the picnic tables.

The next thing I knew, Alan wrapped his arm around my waist.

As he began running with me, weaving in-between baby bears to get to the deck, the mother bear shook off the blow, sat down at the buffet table, and started eating the burgers!

Alan and I scrambled up the stairs after Patrick.

When we reached the top, my dad pulled us into the safety of the deck…

…while the family of bears devoured our Easter cookout.

As my parents squabbled about what to do, our guests used their cell phones to record videos of the Easter bears.

Alan held me in his arms.

"Are you okay?" he asked, catching his breath.

"I think so."

My heart pounded in my chest.

Alan brushed my hair from my cheeks.

"I'm never going to let you out of my sight again," he said before giving me a kiss.

I knew right then and there that my prayers had been answered.

My husband was coming home.

✝

"TWO PICKUP TRUCKS is more than enough, Lucas," my husband told my dad after we had parked at the motel where Alan had been living. "The biggest hassle will be breaking down the home gym equipment."

Located on the outskirts of Walnut Mountain, the Nutcracker Motel was a quaint, one-story structure that looked more like a ski lodge than a truck stop.

My dad grabbed his tool kit from the bed of his truck and followed Alan into Room 3, and I was right behind them.

I honestly could not stop smiling.

At long last, after struggling and praying and struggling even more, I was finally getting what I had been deeply craving for nearly a year.

Never again would I wake up alone in a cold cabin.

Never again would I have to put on a brave face while I lied through my teeth about how my marriage was doing.

And never again would I jeopardize the love of my life for a drink.

I was standing at the precipice of the kingdom of heaven…

My hand was on the plow…

…and I refused to look back.

Alan had kept his motel room neat and tidy.

My dad examined the exercise equipment that Alan had gradually accumulated over the months. The men assessed and strategized the most productive way to break down the home gym so that the pieces would fit into the truck beds.

As they got to work, I found two suitcases in the closet and opened them on the bed.

I packed up all of Alan's clothes, cramming them into the first suitcase. When I was certain nothing more would fit, I carried that suitcase out to Alan's pickup and flung it into the truck bed.

I used the second suitcase for my husband's toiletries and other items he had stuffed into the nightstand drawer.

There was a desk in his motel room, as well, which he had been using whenever he'd investigated on his own time after hours.

The desk was one area of the room that *wasn't* neat and tidy.

There were a number of manilla filing folders, some open, some closed. Their edges were tattered as if Alan had thumbed through them a hundred times.

I glanced at Alan and my dad. Dad was nearly upside down, trying to unscrew the bottom rack of what appeared to be a jacked up power trainer. Frankly, I didn't know what it was or how you were supposed to use it. All I knew was that all 6' of my husband's physique had looked rock hard and rippling the other night, like his body had been chiseled out of marble.

They were grunting and cursing, trying to dismantle the thing.

I peered down at the open filing folder on his desk. The tab of the folder had a printed name.

O'Brian.

That was my cousin's last name.

My breath hitched in my throat and I swallowed hard.

The document on top was a divorce decree.

The plaintiff listed on the front page was Margot O'Brian.

Margot had filed for divorce?

I felt terribly for Patrick, as I mulled that over.

No wonder she hadn't come to the hospital when Patrick had suffered a heart attack.

His prior drug use would've been a reason for Margot to reach the end of her rope and want to end the marriage.

But why would Alan have collected my cousin's divorce decree as part of a murder investigation?

"Son of a biscuit!" my dad barked after a loosened rack bonked him on the head.

Alan really let the curses fly after that, and soon both men were sweating and using every swear word in the book.

"Language!"

"Sorry, Penny!" they replied.

I turned back to the paperwork and folders on Alan's desk. What did Patrick and Margot's divorce have to do with Jessica Saxon's murder?

I recalled the night of the news broadcast that we had all watched at my parents' cabin. Patrick had chilled me to the bone when he had said that Jessica had deserved to die.

Margot had also known Jessica somehow, or at least that was the clear impression she had given me during our brief phone call...

She, like Patrick, had also regarded the fact of Jessica's murder as good news.

How did they all know each other?

And could their association have ended in murder?

I needed to pack up Alan's files.

As I did, stacking them neatly and clearing the motel desk, I told Alan and my dad that I would be outside in the truck.

Considering how they had barely made a dent in breaking down and packing up the home gym equipment, I was guaranteed plenty of time to read through Alan's files while I waited.

✝

CANDLELIGHT DANCED across the dining room table, as Alan and I sipped chilled sparkling cider out of champagne flutes.

The romantic lighting had complemented the romantic, three-course dinner I had cooked without burning the house down.

"That was delicious, Penny," he said, as he blotted the corners of his mouth with a fancy cloth napkin that I had folded into the shape of a swan earlier. "Ah, it feels good to finally be home again. I knew this day would come."

He took my hand in his.

Happy tears stung my eyes, but I blinked them away.

"You look beautiful," he told me.

Clumsily, I replied, "So do you."

Alan was wearing a simple black tee shirt and blue jeans.

I, on the other hand, had gotten dolled up in a sexy cocktail dress, wondering all the while how it might have come to be that even *dresses* were designed for *drinking*.

I was about to clear the plates from the table, but Alan wouldn't let me.

He was on his feet in a dash, piling the plates and collecting the dirty napkins.

I enjoyed another sip of my sparkling cider until he returned from the kitchen where he had set the plates in the sink to soak in soapy water.

"Shall we get comfortable in the living room?" I suggested.

I had placed scented candles across the wooden coffee table. Alan lit them all and then kneeled in front of the wood-burning stove.

As he started a romantic fire to ward off the early spring chill in the air, I sat on the couch and drank in the sight of my victory.

Our victory.

We had survived the worst.

Only good times were ahead of us.

Our marriage was perfect once again.

When Alan joined me on the couch, I asked:

"Any fresh leads?"

He narrowed his twinkling blue eyes at me and shot me a funny smile.

"Penny," he warned.

"Any suspects?" I pushed.

He tucked a lock of my red hair behind my ear.

"Now that I'm home," he began to explain as he caressed the side of my neck. "I'm going to have to set a boundary with you. You know I can't discuss the details of my investigations."

"That makes sense," I allowed, knowing full well I could *seduce* information out of him, if not bait him into divulging by luring him with information of my own. "But I know things, too."

"You do, do you?"

"Mm-hmm." I nodded, trying not to get distracted by the kisses

Alan was planting on my neck.

If I didn't know better, I would have guessed that Alan was trying to seduce me into not minding being seduced!

"I think my cousin knew Jessica."

His lips went slack against my neck, and he pulled away to look at me.

"Really?" he said, interested.

"He said she deserved to die—"

"When was this?"

"When we were all at my parents' cabin the night of the news broadcast. And when I called Margot from the hospital, she indicated that she *also* knew Jessica. Let me tell you, she sounded *happy* that Jessica had been murdered."

Alan ran his thumb across his bottom lip, falling into deep thought.

"Have you looked into Patrick at all?"

He locked eyes with me.

He knew what I was doing.

And he knew that I knew he knew.

But he didn't warn me 'not to go there' by saying my name in that distinct tone of his like he usually did.

"I haven't been able to talk to Patrick," he told me.

Thinking out loud, he added:

"Maybe I could use your help."

CHAPTER NINE

"MY GOODNESS, Alan!"

"Sorry," he said, as he shoved his hand even farther down the front of my blouse.

"Buy a girl a drink first!"

He glared at me halfheartedly.

"Too soon to crack jokes?" I teased.

"The microphone isn't staying put," he complained, as he fished around for it in-between my boobs, feeling the tiny bulb he had lost. "Got it."

I smiled at him. "We can do this all day, babe."

"Ha, ha," he replied dryly.

We were seated in the back of a white delivery van that was parked in an alley between Christian Cinemas and a little gift shop. Beyond the gift shop was Morning Glory, where I was about to meet my cousin Patrick.

The white van didn't belong to the Walnut Mountain Police Department. It was actually Gloria Davis' Morning Glory delivery van. As a classic delivery van, there were no windows in the back, which made it the perfect surveillance van for Alan.

Officers Chuck and Jeremiah were crammed in the back with us.

They had set up their recording and surveillance equipment, and were sitting on little stools with headphones on their ears.

As soon as Alan taped the microphone to my bra, he began running sound checks with Chuck and Jeremiah.

During his first night home at our cabin, Alan and I had

discussed the criminal investigation, which had both surprised and delighted me. Technically, he shouldn't have disclosed *anything* to me about the murder. But once he had warmed up, he discovered that he liked bouncing his ideas off of me and gaining my input.

Did we think that Patrick had definitely poisoned Jessica?

Not necessarily.

But we had agreed that he was worth looking into.

Patrick and his wife, Margot, hadn't finalized their divorce yet. Margot had filed for the divorce and Patrick had yet to sign the papers.

If I hadn't gleaned from both Patrick and Margot that they had known Jessica and didn't particularly care for her, Alan might not have proposed this sting operation to me.

We didn't expect to record a confession, but we were erring on the side of caution. If I went into the coffee shop to talk to my cousin without wearing a wire and he *did* end up confessing to me for the purposes of unburdening his soul, then Alan would be left kicking himself.

Officer Jeremiah said, "The mic's working. She's good to go."

Officer Chuck shot me an encouraging look to stiffen my resolve.

"You know the plan, right?" my husband asked me as he held my shoulders, preparing to send me out.

"I'll walk to Morning Glory while you guys drive down the rear alley and park behind the coffee shop," I answered, reciting the steps we had worked out. "I'll sit down with Patrick at the quietest table and get him to start talking about his marriage."

I would also open up to Patrick about my own marriage history, which should encourage him to confide in me about what happened with Margot, and how it might relate to Jessica.

Alan reminded me, "If he doesn't bring up Jessica on his own—"

"Then I'll ask him pointblank about her," I supplied.

"Exactly."

Alan gave me a kiss on the forehead, and Officers Chuck and Jeremiah wished me luck.

Alan popped the back doors of the delivery van open.

I hopped out, and as I made my way out of the alley, Alan and the police drove up behind Morning Glory and got into position.

I had to admit to myself that I felt uneasy about taking

measures to catch my cousin. But the fact of the matter was that I honestly suspected him. If he truly had taken Jessica's life, then he needed to come clean and face justice.

I had barely emerged from the alley and turned up Main Street when I saw a group of news reporters clustered outside of the coffee shop.

Groaning, I kept my head down and tried to hurry towards Morning Glory, but they recognized me and began snapping photos and shoving their padded microphones against my mouth.

"Penelope Matchmaker, is it true that the murdered woman, Jessica Saxon, was your Alcoholics Anonymous sponsor?"

Horrified, I blurted out, "What?!"

I shouldn't have responded at all!

I told myself to keep shouting, "No comment!" as I pressed through them, but what came out of me was a garbled mess of mutterings and shocked gasps.

I couldn't *not* listen to their offensive questions.

"Many of the recent murder victims in Walnut Mountain have been individuals that you set up on dates," another reporter stated, as he punched his padded microphone into my eye, having aimed for my mouth but missed. "Why does your matchmaking seem to end in murder, Mrs. Matchmaker?"

"NO COMMENT!"

I spilled through the glass entrance door and my cousin Patrick caught me.

"Patrick!" I gasped, feeling relieved.

The relief faded the second I remembered what I was there to do.

"The weather forecast should've said it would be sunny with a chance of a *sh*—"

"Language!"

"—*storm*."

"Pat," I warned.

"Sorry," he apologized, as he flashed me a sideways grin. "The reporters have been getting on my nerves."

"Have they been questioning you, too?"

"Me and everyone else in this town," he surmised, as he kept a protective arm around me and brought me to the counter. "They're harassing just about everyone that tries to go into Angel Arts & Crafts."

"What do you know about the craft store?" I asked, trying to see if he would admit he knew Jessica, who had owned it.

Don't push too hard, Penny! I warned myself.

Patrick hadn't even heard me, though.

He smiled at Dex, who was working behind the counter.

"Sorry about the reporters," said Dex as he tossed his sandy blonde hair out of his eyes. "Gloria asked the police to do something about them, but apparently they have a right to stand on the public sidewalk."

"It's alright," I told him. "We'll live."

"They're not allowed to take photos of anyone inside the coffee shop," he explained. "So, if any of them do that, let me know and I'll call the police."

"Thanks," I said and then ordered the usual.

Patrick asked for a large coffee and a raisin bagel with strawberry cream cheese. We stepped aside for the next customer to place their order, and waited for ours in the meantime.

My cousin leaned into my ear and told me:

"I can't thank you enough for inviting me to those *meetings*. I feel so much better now that I'm cleaning up my life. I hadn't realized how dark things had gotten in my world. It might sound crazy to hear, but Jessica's murder was the best thing that's ever happened to me in my life."

My eyes widened with interest.

Thank God I was wearing a wire!

I hoped that Alan was recording every word of this!

Before I could ask Patrick specifically what he had meant by that, Gloria came out from the bakery with our orders on plates, though the coffees were in to-go cups.

"Let's pray Alan catches the killer soon," she said, "so those news reporters will leave town."

"Amen," I agreed.

Patrick and I found a quiet table in front of the windows and got settled.

He smiled at me again, looking bright-eyed and bushy tailed. Compared to the sweaty, haggard man that had first come to Walnut Mountain over a week ago, my cousin truly did seem healed, healthy, and refreshed.

"Penny?"

"Yes?"

"I want to ask... if you would be willing... Would you be my sponsor?"

For the second time since entering the coffee shop, I froze. My eyebrows shot up to my hairline.

"Would you?" he asked when I hadn't responded.

I was wearing a wire! Sponsors were sworn to secrecy! If I said 'yes,' I would be committing a betrayal of astronomical proportions! I would be worse than Jessica! And what would Patrick do to me if he ever found out? My God, *if*? Of course he would find out! Alan was waiting in a van right now, listening in and ready to pounce!

"I'm honored you would want me to be your sponsor, Patrick, but you live in Industry City and I live here—"

"We could do phone calls and video chats," he suggested, glowing with the bright future that he thought he still had.

"I don't know," I said, feeling uneasy.

"It would give me a chance to confide in you, Penny. Even right now, I have a burning desire to tell you my deepest, darkest secrets. But I can't do that unless you're my sponsor. I need to *know* you'll never tell a soul about the things I want to share with you."

I swallowed hard. My heart was racing. Did he want to confess to murdering Jessica?

And if so...

...could I betray my own cousin worse than Jessica had betrayed me?

I drew in a long breath and hoped to high heaven I wouldn't regret this...

"Yes," I finally said. "I'll be your sponsor."

A huge wave of relief washed over him.

He leaned in.

I leaned in, too.

"I had a one-night stand with Jessica Saxon," he whispered.

"No!" I breathed.

We both glanced around the coffee shop to make sure no one was eavesdropping.

"This was a month or so back," he went on. He cringed and shook his head at his mistake. "It was all because of the drugs. I was such a mess, Penny. And you're my lifesaver now. I want to forget the past."

"You will," I assured him. "With time, you will. But for now... How did you meet her?"

"We met at an art opening at one of the galleries in Industry City. She was beautiful, as you know. She looked stunning that evening. There was wine and cheese and music and art. I was taken with her, caught up in the magic of the night.

"She told me she was an artist. She had smart things to say about the artwork that was on display. Penny, when I went out that evening to the gallery, I had taken off my wedding band."

"Oh, Patrick."

"I had never before cheated on Margot. But I had a feeling about that night. And the moment I saw Jessica, I knew I was going to see where the night might take us."

I gulped my coffee and munched on my buttered croissant, as Patrick divulged precisely where his night with Jessica Saxon had gone.

"As a realtor, I have keys to all of the properties I'm trying to sell. Well, after Jessica and I had gotten tipsy on wine at the gallery—"

"Jessica doesn't drink. She's a recovering alcoholic. She was my sponsor," I said, interrupting again and again.

"The 'Jessica' I met that night was not the same 'Jessica' you knew, Penny."

"She's been my sponsor since New Year's."

"I met her a month ago, and let me tell you, she knew how to handle her liquor and that's not all she did that night," he said.

I was stunned, and the shock didn't wear off.

"She didn't know anything about me when I brought her to one of the high-rise condos I was trying to sell. It was fully furnished. I led her to believe I was a bachelor that lived there. We drank more, did recreational drugs, and had a wild night.

"But the next morning, when the stark light of day brought me back to reality, I felt awful. I was full of remorse, but Jessica woke up full of happiness. She thought we would spend the day together. Penny, she thought we would *be* together."

"Oh, poor Jessica."

"I told her the truth right then and there. She was immediately furious. She threatened to ruin my life. And, long story short, she did."

"She told Margot?"

He nodded and added:

"Margot filed for divorce."

Even though I knew that, I pretended I didn't and guessed:

"That's why Margot and the kids didn't come to my parents' 50th anniversary picnic?"

"I didn't expect to run into Jessica at that party," he admitted. "If she had told me she was from Walnut Mountain, I would've remembered and I wouldn't have come here."

Patrick had a solid motive to kill Jessica, but he hadn't confessed to poisoning her...

I had to ask him.

Whispering, I said, "Did you poison her?"

"She made good on her threat to ruin my life, Penny. But—"

"Patrick O'Brian!" Alan yelled as he charged through the coffee shop with police officers. "You're under arrest for the murder of Jessica Saxon!"

†

"I CAN'T BELIEVE Patrick was the killer," Esther said as we strolled through Angel Arts & Crafts.

She held a shopping basket on her arm. She needed to buy decorative candles for the wedding reception among other last minute ideas.

"Do you think he came to your parents' anniversary picnic just to murder Jessica?" she asked.

"No, that's the thing," I said, overcome with the same bad feeling that had been nagging me ever since Alan had hauled my cousin away in handcuffs two days ago. "He told me that Jessica never mentioned she was from Walnut Mountain. He said he wouldn't have come to the party if he had known."

"So, it was an impulsive murder," she concluded. "An act of passion."

I shook my head, entirely bothered.

"Poisoning Jessica took planning," I said, thinking out loud. "The killer had to either mix poison into a cupcake, cookie, or the soda that was given to Jessica."

"What are you saying, Penny?" asked Esther, suddenly concerned.

"Patrick had the motive to kill Jessica," I agreed. "But something isn't right. How could he have poisoned her? I was standing right there when they 'met' at the picnic. I saw the look on Patrick's face. It was like he had seen a ghost. He was *surprised* to run into her..."

"Alan arrested him," she reminded me.

"But Patrick hadn't confessed."

Esther looked deeply disturbed. Then a massive sense of resolve changed her countenance. She straightened her spine and told me:

"The killer has been caught. Alan came home to you."

"Yes, he did," I confirmed, and I had to smile.

"See? All is right in the world. I'm getting married, Penny. The wedding is just days away. Nothing is going to ruin my big day!"

With that, she turned on her heel and started down the shopping aisle, heading for the registers at the front of the store.

Esther was right, I told myself. All *was* right in the world. I had my husband back and my best friend was getting married.

I wasn't about to let anything spoil how far we had come.

But when I joined Esther at the front of the store and saw the trophy that Jessica had won for her angel painting, the nagging feeling returned.

The engraved placard on the foot of the trophy read:

Jessica Saxon, Winner of the Angel Art Award, Pembroke Pines Foundation.

Then I remembered...

Harriet's destroyed angel painting surged to the forefront of my mind.

I had seen it on an easel in her living room.

It had been smeared and slashed.

She hadn't submitted it, but I had seen the submission form on the easel as well that day.

"Penny!" Esther barked, ready to leave the craft store.

My petite friend was becoming a bit of a bridezilla!

"Coming!"

CHAPTER TEN

HARRIET'S CAR WAS STILL in the shop. She needed help transporting her artwork home from the church. Of course, I said I would help.

With Patrick sitting in the police station jail, all of Walnut Mountain felt safe and was breathing easier. The latest killer had been caught. And best of all, news reporters were no longer crawling all over town and harassing every passerby they saw.

Which meant that breezing into Morning Glory was once again a true delight.

Behind the counter, Gloria and Dex poured coffees and bagged pastries, as the line of customers inched along.

When it was my turn, I ordered 'the usual' plus an additional coffee for Harriet who was waiting for me at the church.

"Can you believe your cousin was behind the poisoning?" Gloria asked me, as Dex handled my order.

"No, I can't," I answered frankly.

Her eyebrows knit together. She pushed her big hair off her shoulders then planted her hands on her tremendous hips.

I was familiar with that *look*.

"Penny," she sighed, though she felt endeared. "You're not thinking about *meddling*, are you?"

"He's my cousin," I said with a *can-you-blame-me?* shrug. Besides, she had started it by bringing up the subject. "He didn't have time to plan, not to mention that he didn't even know that Jessica lived in Walnut Mountain."

"You only know what he told you," she pointed out, which was valid. "I heard that Patrick had been having an affair with that woman."

Word certainly got around town when the town was as small as ours.

"It was a one-night stand," I informed her.

With motherly love, she informed *me*, "It's over, Penny. The bad guy is in jail. And we all have a wedding to look forward to."

"We certainly do," I agreed, as Dex placed my bagged order on the counter. "Thanks for the coffee."

Dex had wedged the to-go cups into a cardboard carrier.

I picked up the carrier and bag, elbowed my way through the glass door, and walked to Alan's pickup truck that I had parked along the curb.

After climbing in and getting situated, I drove up Main Street, used the roundabout at the gazebo, and pulled up to Hopeful Heart Ministries, angling the rear of the truck as close to the church entrance as I could.

I found Harriet inside. Pastor Peter Peterson was helping her wrap the last butterfly painting in thick cloth.

"Good morning, Pastor," I said with a smile, as I handed Harriet her coffee.

"Lifesaver as always, Penny," said Harriet, who was eager to get more caffeine into her system.

She blew on her coffee, took a sip, and suggested:

"Give me a minute to catch my breath and we can start taking the wrapped paintings out."

Pastor Peter had barely said hello. He was still wrestling with the painting they had been working on. He seemed annoyed if not angry, and I hoped he wasn't struggling with his addiction to anger.

Under her breath, Harriet told me, "He's been in quite a mood."

"Nice of him to help, though."

"Certainly," she agreed.

It was *very* nice of the pastor to help, because the fact that he was lending a hand made carrying Harriet's three paintings to the truck fast and easy.

In no time, Harriet and I were on the road, her precious artwork safe and secure in the bed of the pickup truck.

"You must feel so relieved, Penny."

I knew what Harriet was referring to, as we traveled through the heart of Walnut Mountain, making our way to the foothills where

Harriet lived.

I had been all over the news as a prime murder suspect, but now that Patrick had been arrested, I was off the news-media-hook.

"I'm having mixed emotions, honestly."

"He's your cousin," she said, understanding. "But he obviously did it."

There was nothing *obvious* about Patrick's culpability. I wondered why Harriet thought there was.

"I'm just praying that everyone will move on from this," she added.

I wondered why Harriet was so eager for everyone to move on.

And I wondered many more things about Harriet, as I drove us along winding, rural roads.

I kept my ruminations to myself, however, gulped my creamy coffee, and steered the truck up the steep incline of Harriet's driveway.

After backing up towards the garage, I threw the truck into Park, killed the engine, and climbed out.

I unhinged the tailgate, while Harriet opened the garage door and also the door that led to her living room.

Together we made fast work of carrying her paintings, one after the next, all the way inside.

Harriet had cleared one of the living room walls and had nailed small, metal, painting-hangers into the wall.

We unwrapped the paintings and hung them on the metal hangers on the wall.

"They look beautiful," I said, drinking in the sight once all three butterfly paintings had been hung.

"Thank you, Penny."

"Have you ever thought about selling your artwork?" I asked, as I glanced around the living room.

"Oh, from time to time I *do* sell my paintings," she said, but I was distracted.

The ruined angel painting that I had seen on an easel in the corner of the room was gone.

It gave me pause.

The easel wasn't there either, and in their place was a tall potted plant.

Why would Harriet have moved the slashed painting?

The only answer that came to mind was that, unlike the last

time I had been here and she had only expected me in the garage, this time she had known I would be in the living room to help her hang the paintings.

"During the summertime, I sell my artwork at craft fairs all throughout Vermont," she went on. "But it's only a hobby. I would need a significant amount of money if I wanted to focus on being a true artist."

"Like if you were to receive a grant from an art foundation?" I asked.

The Pembroke Pines Foundation was fixed at the forefront of my mind.

"Yes, exactly," she said cheerfully.

"Have you ever submitted artwork to get a grant?"

She turned a bit gloomy.

"From time to time I have," she said.

"Any luck?"

"Not yet."

"Jessica won an award, you know," I said as casually as I could.

Harriet's eyes darkened, but her demeanor was steady.

"Oh? I wasn't aware."

Something told me that she *had* been aware, but I filled her in anyway.

"I wasn't aware either until I was at Angel Arts & Crafts a few weeks ago and saw Jessica's trophy. She received an artist's grant from the Pembroke Pines Foundation. Sadly, she was never able to use the funds. She submitted a gorgeous angel painting. It's hanging on the wall behind the registers at the craft store. The grant she won was called the 'Angel Art Award,' if I'm not mistaken."

The color had drained from Harriet's face. Was she furious? Jealous? She appeared to be *seething* with emotion, but it was just under the surface of her tolerant expression.

"It's no wonder Jessica won," I went on, hoping to provoke Harriet into telling me the story of why her own submission had been destroyed. "She really perfected the art of painting angels."

"She was talented," Harriet agreed dryly. "But she sabotaged herself."

"What do you mean?"

"I'm really not one to speak ill of the dead, Penny. But Jessica could've really gone somewhere as an artist. She never did, because of her drinking and drugging. She was more dedicated to living a wild artist's *lifestyle* than she was to seriously becoming a successful artist."

"You must have known her more than I realized," I commented.

"She was jealous of me," she hotly replied. "I had no problem excelling with my art. After art school, I even went to Europe to study painting. Jessica never went anywhere. And yet, we both ended up coming back to Walnut Mountain. I never became a famous artist, you know? I told Jessica several times not to be envious of me, but she was. She never let it go, not that we really saw each other often or were close. I kept my distance from her. When I needed art supplies, I never went to Angel Arts & Crafts, that's for sure."

She seemed to get lost in a memory and it couldn't have been a good one.

Finally, Harriet said, "She became obsessed with me, Penny. At one point, the police got involved…"

A faraway look filled her eyes.

"Harriet…?" I breathed.

"No!" she blurted out, shaking the memory off. "I don't want to talk about this! She's dead, and we can all move on, thank God!"

"Harriet, why are you getting so upset?"

Tears began streaming down her face, but all Harriet wanted was for me to leave.

"Thanks for your help, Penny. But I'm going to have to ask you to go. I'll see you at the wedding."

✝

THERE WAS more to the story.

My gut told me there was *way* more to the story of Jessica, Harriet, and the Angel Art Award.

If the police had gotten involved at some point, then there would be a record of what had happened.

It was times like these that I was very glad for my matchmaking hobby. Many happy couples in Walnut Mountain felt indebted to me for having introduced them to the love of their life. And I knew of one such individual who just might feel so grateful to me that he would be willing to do me a favor.

The trick would be going unnoticed... by my husband.
I doubted Alan would appreciate me poking around.
He thought the case was closed.

At least I had a reason to swing into the police station once I drove back to town. Alan needed me to return his pickup truck, and I had left my car at the station anyhow.

I just needed to be careful, clever, and most importantly, calculated in terms of how I proceeded.

News reporters occupied the sidewalk in front of the police station, though there were fewer of them than there had been since the murder.

It wasn't terribly surprising. Patrick was inside the jail, after all. He hadn't confessed outright and he hadn't had a bail hearing. The reporters must have been hungry for a new story to print.

I sucked in a deep, fortifying breath, preparing for the worst and praying for the best.

Then I climbed out of my husband's pickup truck and walked as fast as I could through the news reporters.

They were on me like white on rice, and before I knew it, I had been swallowed in a tsunami of microphones, flashing cameras, and questions I didn't want to answer.

"Mrs. Matchmaker! How do you feel knowing your cousin was arrested?"

"Did you know Patrick O'Brian had killed Jessica Saxon?"

"Were you covering for your cousin, Mrs. Matchmaker?"

"No comment!"

I slammed against the entrance door and tumbled into the police station, as cameras flashed behind me.

But I was safe inside.

Pushing my hair out of my face, I straightened the sky-blue chemo cap I was wearing and otherwise got my bearings.

Alan was nowhere in sight and neither was Chief Pepperdine, which told me they might be meeting in the chief's office. His door at the back of the station was shut.

Officer Chuck was behind the front desk. Next to him was Officer Jeremiah, but he was speaking with a resident.

Just my luck!

Chuck smiled at me, looking dapper in his policeman's uniform. "Are you here to see Alan?" he asked.

"No!" I blurted out. Calming myself, I tried that again. "No,

Chuck. But there's something I'd like *you* to do for me."

"Anything, Mrs. Matchmaker," he agreed, as a huge grin spread across his face. "I'm having the time of my life with Sue Ellen. She's quite a girl."

"Isn't she?"

"She has a *lot* of cats..." he added, his eyes widening at the fact.

"You love cats," I reminded him, hoping it was true.

"I love Sue Ellen," he countered.

"Really?"

I was thrilled.

"I'm thinking of asking her to marry me—"

"Chuck, that's fantastic news! I'm so happy for you!"

"You don't think it's too soon?"

"Never put love on hold, Chuck. Life's too short."

He had a think on that, then muttered:

"I have to figure out how to 'cat-proof' my house..." A moment later, he snapped back to reality and asked, "What can I do for you?"

I glanced through the police station. My husband was still out of sight and beyond earshot, if he was there at all.

Leaning towards Chuck, I quietly explained:

"I'm interested in finding a police report, but I'm not certain one exists."

"Oh?"

"Did Harriet ever file any kind of police report that mentioned Jessica Saxon?"

He narrowed his eyes at me, full of suspicion.

"Oh, don't give me that look," I balked. "I introduced you to your wife."

"She hasn't said yes yet! Penny, I haven't even proposed!"

"Keep your voice down," I hissed, as I stared at Sergeant Pepper's closed office door. I was certain Alan was in there. "Chuck we both know that filed police reports are a matter of public record."

"We both know that Alan's not going to like it if you dig up anything that muddies his case."

"His case is closed, as far as he's concerned."

"Until Patrick is sentenced, Alan's going to keep pushing."

"Chuck," I warned.

"Alright," he agreed. "I'll print out the arrest record."

"Arrest record? Who was arrested?"

He sighed and said, "Jessica."

"Harriet had Jessica arrested?" I questioned. "Chuck, wouldn't that give Harriet a motive? What if my cousin didn't do it?"

"Hold your horses."

He put his hand up, found the record in the computer, and sent the job to print.

When a few sheets ejected from the printer behind the front desk, Chuck stapled them together, and handed the report to me.

"I was the arresting officer that night, Penny."

"You were?" I breathed.

"Long story short, Jessica broke into Harriet's garage and destroyed a work of art. Harriet called us, we arrested Jessica, and that was that."

I flipped through the report and said:

"Thanks, Chuck."

"Don't tell Alan I gave that to you."

"I wasn't planning on telling Alan anything," I said with a wink, as I folded and tucked the police report into my purse.

I was about to turn on my heel and leave, but instead I asked:

"Can I speak with Patrick?"

"He's meeting with his attorney."

"Here?"

"They're over on Lake Way, actually, at Walnut Mountain Legal: Cranston, Downes and blah, blah, blah, attorneys at law, esquire and yadda yadda."

I chuckled and teased:

"Alright, don't hurt yourself."

"They might as well have printed the entire alphabet on their awning," he said, rolling his eyes.

"Thanks again, Chuck. You're the best!"

I was out the door in no time, and I would've heard Chuck call after me if it hadn't been for those noisy news reporters.

From inside the station, Chuck yelled:

"Alan's the one who brought Patrick there!"

But I didn't hear him.

✝

I JUMPED IN MY car, found my key in my purse, and fit it into the ignition.

After starting the engine and buckling up, I pulled the police report out of my purse and read the details of Jessica's arrest. The third page included a black and white photograph of Harriet's slashed angel painting, the one I had seen in her living room.

I glanced up from the report, trying to fathom all that I had read.

"Oh, Harriet," I said under my breath. "Could you have taken Jessica's life?"

The law firm, located on Lake Way, sat on a curved block with other professional offices. There was a dentist's office, an accounting firm, and a realtor, Vermont Realty, in addition to the newly branded Walnut Mountain Legal.

I found a parking spot and prayed that I would be able to speak with Patrick.

Alan might be convinced that Patrick was guilty. But Patrick's defense attorneys might be able to cast reasonable doubt if I could get this police report into their hands.

As soon as I entered the law firm, a perky receptionist greeted me.

She had neatly styled hair and pink nails, and she smelled of strawberries and hairspray.

"Would it be possible for me to speak with Patrick O'Brian? I'm his cousin—"

"Penelope Matchmaker," she guessed accurately. "I recognize you from the news. Your husband's a real dreamboat!"

"Thanks."

"You know, all the attorneys here had a betting pool going about when you'd give us a call!"

"What in God's name are you talking about?"

"You were brave not to call a lawyer while this entire town thought you killed that woman!"

"Is that a compliment?"

"Are you really a matchmaker?"

"It's a hobby—"

"Does your husband have a *twin*? Because I'd love for you to set me up!"

I scraped together every shred of patience I had and for the second time asked the receptionist:

"May I please speak with Patrick O'Brian?"

"He's meeting with Downes Senior and Junior," she told me. "But I can ring them and see."

"Please do," I said. "I have information that might help my cousin's defense."

The receptionist tucked her office phone between her cheek and her shoulder, and spoke with whoever had picked up on the other end. I took a slow lap around the waiting area, and looked out the huge bay windows. Beyond the street outside was a lake. Sunshine sparkled off the water.

"You're in luck, Mrs. Matchmaker," said the receptionist.

A moment later, I followed the receptionist through the law firm.

I recognized Gregory Downes, a young attorney who I had met last autumn when Edgar Swaine had been murdered. He was standing with his father, Jeffrey Downes, in front of a conference room. The door was open, and Patrick was seated inside.

The receptionist announced my arrival and introduced me to the attorneys, but I was too anxious to see my cousin.

"Penny!"

"Patrick, I'm so terribly sorry you've been arrested!" I exclaimed, as I rushed towards him.

He pulled me into a big hug.

He wasn't mad at me?

I was ready to apologize to him! I could've poured my heart out until there was nothing left inside!

But he started thanking me!

"Once again, Penny, you've saved my life!"

"I have?" I said, surprised.

The receptionist closed the door, giving us privacy, while the attorneys talked outside the conference room.

"When I got arrested, I won Margot back!"

"You did?"

He beamed with joy, as he explained:

"She saw me on the news, getting arrested, and she drove straight to Walnut Mountain. She said it was the most romantic thing I could've ever done for her—"

"Get arrested?"

"No, kill Jessica," he said, grinning from ear to ear. "With Jessica dead, Margot was able to fully forgive me. She's willing to totally forget the one-night stand. You've given me my life back, Penny!"

"But Patrick, you might go to prison…"

"Margot's in the ladies' room. She's going to be overjoyed to see you!"

"Patrick," I said. "I know you didn't do it. You couldn't have."

He grew serious.

"It doesn't matter, Penny. Margot thinks I killed Jessica, and she loves me for it."

"But you didn't kill her—"

"Don't you dare ruin this for me," he warned. "For the sake of my marriage, don't you dare take this away from me."

"This is crazy, Patrick! If you go to prison, you won't have Margot, and worse. The real killer will still be on the loose!"

He took me by the shoulders and promised:

"I won't go to prison. A jury will never convict me. My attorneys assured me of that. But I need Margot to continue to believe that I killed Jessica out of love for Margot and our marriage. I need this, Penny!"

I was stunned. Had he gone mad?

"Don't say a word," he warned. "You betrayed me once, and it ended up working out in my favor. But do not betray me again."

"Okay," I breathed. "I won't."

Just then, the conference door opened.

Margot O'Brian stood on the other side.

She was a trophy wife, through-and-through, with her trim figure and polished style.

"Penny!" she sang in a melodically soft and high voice. "I'm so sorry I couldn't make it to your parents' anniversary party!"

Yeah right, I thought to myself as I hugged her.

I bet she would've loved to see my cousin kill Jessica Saxon that day.

There was only one problem with that.

Patrick hadn't poisoned anyone at the picnic.

After catching up with Margot and asking about the kids—the children were staying with Margot's parents in Industry City—I excused myself and found Patrick's attorneys, Jeffrey and Gregory Downes, near the receptionist's desk at the front of the law firm.

If nothing else, I could give them the police report. Bringing up another potential killer in court could help a jury to not convict my cousin. Not that I wanted things to go that far.

"Mr. Downes?" I said, as I neared Downes Senior. "I have

something that I believe will help Patrick's defense."

But just as I pulled the police report out of my purse and offered it to Gregory Downes, Alan appeared out of nowhere and grabbed my wrist.

"Alan!"

"What's this?" he asked, taking the report from me.

He glanced over the report then locked his steely gaze on me and asked:

"Are you trying to sabotage me?"

CHAPTER ELEVEN

"I'M SO EXCITED for the wedding, Penny! I don't see how I'll be able to concentrate on my classes today," said Esther, as she poured herself a mug of coffee in the teachers' lounge.

I gulped my own coffee and asked:

"Is there anything you need me to help you with after school today?"

The wedding was tomorrow. The ceremony would take place at Hopeful Heart Ministries with Pastor Peter officiating. Esther had booked Fancy's for the reception afterwards since Jacque Vique's restaurant had a dance hall as well as an outdoor patio.

"I don't believe so."

We stepped away from the coffeemaker so that other teachers could get their morning fix of caffeine.

The lounge was filling up. Principal Longchamp was reading the morning newspaper, as always. Harriet breezed in with a bagged breakfast from Morning Glory.

I kept my eye on her.

It was entirely possible that suspecting Harriet of being the real killer was a waste of time. But the more I thought about it, the more certain I became that Patrick would go to prison if the real killer wasn't caught. He was innocent, but I didn't trust that a jury would be able to see that.

I had felt deeply for him when he had begged me not to tell Margot the truth.

He had made a mistake that night with Jessica.

I knew what it was like to make a mistake and regret it.

And I knew what it was like to love your spouse fiercely and fight like hell to win them back. Now that Patrick had restored his marriage, I wasn't about to mess with that.

But I also wasn't about to let him go to prison for a crime he hadn't committed.

I had to catch the real killer. Alan certainly wasn't going to, since he thought he already had.

The last thing I wanted to do was jeopardize my own marriage, however.

I would never want to sabotage my husband's investigative accomplishments.

It pained me that he had accused me of such a thing.

I needed to be careful, discrete, and unrelenting.

I was distracted when I heard one of the teachers gasp and mutter:

"Oh, Samantha!"

Samantha had just swung into the teachers' lounge on her very high heels. She was wearing a baggy tee-shirt over her pink, tailored dress, which wasn't at all her usual style.

She was ready for a fight.

When Esther read what Samantha's tee-shirt said, Esther was suddenly ready for a fight as well.

"What's the matter?" Samantha asked with a snide smirk on her face. "I thought wearing tee-shirts was fine and dandy at this school."

It was then that I saw the writing on the front of her shirt.

The only thing that rose on Easter was a religion that ended up killing millions of people over the course of 2,000 years.

Samantha catwalked a few steps then turned as if she was modeling at the end of a runway.

When she turned on her very high heel, Esther and I realized that the back of her tee-shirt was even worse than the front.

Christ is a Killer!

Esther was seething beside me. Her chest heaved and her delicate hands balled into fists.

"Take it off, Samantha," she growled through her teeth.

"Never! You people refused to sign my petition to have tee-shirts like this banned!"

Even Matthew, who was undeniably in love with Samantha, began pleading with her to stop this.

Principal Longchamp pushed out of his chair and barked: "My office, now!"

"You people and your Christian hypocrisy have been giving me migraines all year!" she complained. "Now I'm playing by *your* rules and you don't like it?"

Again, Esther yelled, "Take off that shirt, Samantha!"

"You've made your bed," she yelled back, "and now you'll lie in it!"

Esther must have seen red and gone into a rage-induced fugue, because before I knew it, she took a running leap at Samantha and tackled the blonde harder than a linebacker trying to block a winning pass.

As they tumbled and tangled on the floor, Esther throwing punches and Samantha shrieking, Principal Longchamp and Matthew rushed to pull the women apart. The teachers' lounge flew into an uproar of gasps, as Esther yanked Samantha's tee-shirt so far up her chest that she was able to start choking her with it.

"Take it off, Samantha!" she yelled.

Samantha wheezed out:

"Never!"

Finally, Longchamp pulled Esther off of Samantha. Matthew tried to get Samantha breathing. The woman gasped and coughed, as Matthew freed her neck from the shirt.

Samantha rubbed her throat then pointed her finger at Esther.

"I want her arrested!" she said from the floor. "You're going to jail, Esther! I'm pressing charges!"

✝

ESTHER SAT BEHIND bars in the police station jail, her face long and pale.

She had a few scratches thanks to Samantha's long, manicured nails, but other than that the majority of her wounds were in her heart.

"I can't believe I attacked Samantha," she murmured with a far-away look in her eye. "I'm supposed to get married tomorrow."

"She really crossed a line," I said to comfort her.

"I couldn't control myself." Esther shook her head. "What is Daniel going to think?"

"Everyone makes mistakes," I offered from where I was standing on the other side of Esther's jail cell. "He'll forgive you."

She didn't look so sure of that.

"You've got to get me out of here, Penny."

"I'll see what I can do," I promised, knowing that it just might take a miracle.

The jail sat across from the interview room where I had spent too much time recently. I walked from the little hallway and came into the back of the police station.

Samantha saw me and glared. She was seated on a chair next to Officer Jeremiah's desk. He was taking her statement.

What a mess.

I passed Chief Pepperdine's office and swung into Alan's small office.

Alan was behind his desk, engrossed in a phone call.

He touched eyes with me as I eased the door closed behind me.

When he wrapped up his call and returned his phone to its cradle, I asked:

"Well?"

"Everyone wants this to go away, trust me."

"Does Samantha?"

He shook his head *'no,'* which didn't surprise me.

Alan stood, rounded out from behind his desk, and put his warm hands on my shoulders.

"I'm taking care of it," he told me.

"Alan, if Esther doesn't get married *tomorrow*—"

"She will," he assured me, as he pulled me in and hugged me. "Who knew Esther had it in her."

"It was surreal, Alan. She had superhuman strength."

"Well, she must really love our Lord."

A quiet knock came at the door and Chief Pepperdine swung in and closed the door behind him.

Alan kept an arm around me.

"I just spoke with the county district attorney," he told us. "After the media circus we barely survived due to the murder, no one wants more press in Walnut Mountain. The D.A. doesn't want us pursuing this."

"What about Samantha?" I feared. "What does she want?"

"Will she drop the charges?" Alan asked on my behalf when Pepperdine fell into deep, strategic thought.

"She won't need to," he explained. "As long as Esther signs a guilty plea right now for the assault, I can process the paperwork right away, and she'll be released. All that matters is the paperwork. No one needs Esther to sit in our jail cell and no one in the district attorney's office wants her to see the inside of a courtroom to state her plea."

"Esther can leave today?"

"As long as she pleads guilty and signs some papers," Pepperdine confirmed.

"Thank God!" I burst into tears of relief.

"What about a punishment?" Alan asked.

"There doesn't have to be one," said Pepperdine. "I'll make the *entire* issue go away."

"This won't come back to bite us in the behind?" Alan questioned.

"I'm not about to do this everyday," he allowed. "But I've done this before. The victim is never happy about it. But when I see a woman like Esther who has committed a crime of passion, I don't have the heart to ruin her life over it."

"Thank you! Thank you!" I exclaimed as I threw my arms around the chief. "Thank you, Sergeant Pepper!"

He chuckled, surprised, as Alan asked him:

"When have you done this before?"

"That's the irony," he replied. I let him go and looked up at him through tears of gratitude, as he went on. "The last time I did some fast filing in order to quickly release a criminal… It was for Jessica Saxon. She broke into someone's house and damaged the homeowner's property. If I hadn't helped Jessica get out of that jam, however, and if she *had* gone to prison, she might be alive today."

"You let Jessica go after a break in?" Alan asked.

"I released her an hour after she got to the station."

I knew Pepperdine was referring to Harriet's home and the slashes that Jessica had used to destroy Harriet's artwork.

What I hadn't known after talking to Chuck and reading the police report was that Jessica had essentially gotten away with it.

That must have infuriated Harriet.

But could it have driven the art teacher to kill?

As Alan handled the paperwork with Esther, I was asked to wait at the front of the police station.

Officer Jeremiah and Officer Chuck were stationed behind the front desk.

Samantha was having an angry phone call in the waiting area.

At first, I assumed she must be talking to an attorney perhaps to file a civil lawsuit against Esther. But as I passed by her and sat down on one of the chairs, I realized that her phone call sounded far more personal.

Maybe she was complaining to a friend about how she had been attacked at school...

"The migraines aren't from that!" she snapped at whoever she was talking to on her cell phone. "These are *aggravation* migraines! No one at Walnut Mountain Middle School understands how *critical* it is to educate the students about the greater social issues of our modern times!"

She listened for a moment then hissed, "I don't care if politics aren't your area of expertise! I don't have a brain tumor! There's nothing wrong with my brain! It's these *teachers* I work with! If anyone's brain isn't working properly, it's *theirs*!"

Brain tumor?

"I don't care where you got your medical degree," she barked. "It should be revoked if you think I have brain cancer! Good day, Ma'am!"

Samantha hung up and whipped her cell phone into her purse.

We locked eyes.

"What are *you* looking at?" she snapped.

"Oh, Samantha," I breathed, overcome with compassion. "You have cancer?"

A hard look came over her. Her eyes filled with tears and her lower lip quivered.

But she forced herself to steady her resolve and barked:

"What do you care?"

✝

"BRAIN CANCER?" ESTHER asked from the other side of the table.

We were sitting in a vinyl booth at Charming Diner, two steaming mugs of coffee between us.

Dusk settled over Walnut Mountain. Beyond the diner windows, Main Street sat under a purple sky.

Esther had been released from the police station jail, having signed her name under a guilty plea.

"A brain tumor would explain Samantha's personality changes," I mentioned.

"She has gotten worse," Esther agreed. "More intense."

"And I've found her in the ladies room at school several times, groaning with migraines," I added, putting the pieces together.

"Poor Samantha."

I felt as pained as Esther looked.

"I was so mad at her," I said. "When I saw how heartless and cruel she could be, blabbing all my secrets in the teachers' lounge…"

I shook my head at how upset I had been.

"But now," I went on, "I don't want to be angry at her. I don't want to harbor hatred in my heart."

"Oh, God, I don't either," said Esther. "Penny, I really went to a dark place when I was sitting in that jail cell. I was furious at Samantha for that tee-shirt, but my God, the fury turned to rage when I was in jail. On the inside, I wasn't even remotely Christian."

"Me neither."

We sat for a moment, feeling the full weight of our error.

"I'm going to forgive her," I decided.

"Me, too," said Esther. "I'm going to forgive her and love her as she is. Do you think she'll forgive me?"

I thought about it, leaned across the table, and said:

"I have an idea."

✝

SAMANTHA LIVED IN a two-story, brick Colonial House not far from the heart of Walnut Mountain. From the outside, her home looked elegant with potted flower beds at every window and huge, blooming lilac bushes lining the walkway.

At this hour, now that the sun had long since set, the house was aglow with interior lights. Likewise, the brick walkway leading up to the front door was illuminated with a row of lights.

I pulled up along the curb in front of the house. Esther sat in the passenger's seat and stared at Samantha's home. Neither of us had been here before, but her address had been easy enough to obtain from the teachers' contact sheet.

Esther drew in a deep breath and told me:

"My feelings for Samantha have completely changed. All I want to do is love her."

"I truly believe that what we're about to do will be the first step in the direction of real and lasting friendship."

We smiled at each other and climbed out of my car.

When we reached the stately front door, I grabbed the shiny, metal door knocker and pounded it a few times.

Esther held our peace offering in her hands. It was tucked in a gift bag.

The distinct sounds of Samantha's high heels clicked on the other side of the door, growing louder, and then she opened the door and saw us standing with big, friendly smiles on our faces.

She frowned.

"What the hell are you two doing here?"

Esther began:

"Samantha, I'm deeply sorry that I attacked you earlier today. I had no right, and what I did was completely inexcusable."

She seemed to soften. "Well, you pled guilty, so..." she shrugged.

"I won't put any pressure on you to forgive me, but I hope that with time you will."

Samantha didn't seem especially touched.

"Whatever," she said.

I wasted no time saying, "I also want to put all tension and animosity behind us, Samantha. We haven't always gotten along—"

"We've literally never gotten along, Penny."

"I'd like to change that," I said with a little smile. "Which is why..."

Esther and I looked at each other.

It was time.

She handed Samantha the gift bag.

I continued, "We would really like to be friends."

Samantha screwed her face up as she pulled a red chemo cap out of the gift bag. The cap was the fanciest one we could find. It had red feathers and a beautifully twisted knot at the side.

"Is this what I think it is?" she groaned.

We exclaimed:

"Welcome to the Chemo Club!"

"Jesus Christ," she muttered.

Language!

Samantha glared at me, "Is this about the phone call you heard me have earlier?"

Esther grabbed her heart and said:

"I know what you're going through, Samantha, and I'm here for you. We both are."

She rolled her eyes.

"I don't have a brain tumor!"

"Yes, you do," Esther said gently as she pulled Samantha in for a hug despite the woman's resistance. "And it's going to be okay."

Samantha pried Esther off of her.

"Seriously," she insisted. "I don't have a tumor. The nurse that told me I did made an administrative error. My actual doctor called me back after that and said so."

"You don't have cancer?" Esther asked, a bit disappointed.

"No!" said Samantha, exasperated. "My birth control pills got all effed up, and the hormones were giving me migraines, that's all!"

I placed a comforting arm around Esther.

"Now, would you please leave me alone?" Samantha snapped.

Esther and I looked at each other.

We were both thinking the same thing.

"We're glad your health is fine," I told Samantha. "But you're still in the club."

"Penny never had cancer," Esther mentioned. "Yet she wears her chemo cap every day."

"Keep it," I said, referring to the red chemo cap in her hands. "It'll look beautiful on you."

Samantha rolled her eyes, muttered *'Christians!'* under her breath, and slammed the door in our faces.

Esther looked up at me and said:

"I think that went well."

✝

THAT NIGHT, I parked in the driveway and entered my cabin, relieved that Samantha didn't have cancer and even more relieved that tonight I was coming home to my husband.

"I could get used to this," I said with a smile, as I smelled Italian food.

After setting my purse down in the vestibule, I rounded into the kitchen where dinner was on the stove. The burners were on low, keeping the delicious food that Alan had made warm.

"Honey, I'm home!" I called out, as I made my way out of the kitchen and up the stairs.

I heard the shower running and Alan said:

"I'll be out in a few minutes!"

"Take your time!"

In our bedroom, I pulled the chemo cap I was wearing off my head and fluffed my hair. Debating whether or not to change out of my sundress, I sat on the bed and kicked my sandals off to get more comfortable.

I heard a buzzing sound behind me.

Alan's cell phone was vibrating on his nightstand.

I leaned over and grabbed his cell, but didn't recognize the number.

"Alan, your phone is ringing!"

"What?"

"Should I answer it?"

"What?" he replied and then I could've sworn he said either *yes* or *please do...*

"Hello?" I said after accepting the call.

"This is Mindy from Vermont Realty, is Alan Matchmaker available?"

Vermont Realty?

"No, but I'm his wife," I said, highly curious.

"We're just calling to let Alan know the funds cleared escrow and he can move into his new home any time. The keys are here at the realty office."

I felt my heart plummet into my gut.

New home?

My voice was like wind over reeds as I said:

"Thanks for letting us know."

Alan had bought a new house?

What about our cabin?

What about *me?*

Suddenly, my worst fears took hold and I felt like I couldn't breathe.

Was Alan planning on leaving me for good?

CHAPTER TWELVE

THE NEXT MORNING, I found a handwritten note where my husband should've been.

Sunlight streamed through the window, as I took the note from Alan's pillow and read:

I'll meet you at the church. Have to go to the station for a bit.

I couldn't imagine why Alan would have to go to the police station early on a Saturday morning when he had a wedding to get ready for.

Then I remembered...

Vermont Realty.

The house he had bought.

Oh, God.

Last night, I had been too scared to tell Alan that a realtor had called to let him know he could move into his new *house*. Instead, I had panicked and deleted the realtor's phone number from the call history in my husband's cell. When he had emerged from the bathroom with a towel wrapped around his waist, I hadn't mentioned the phone call. And when he had asked me what I had been shouting about, I had lied, saying I had wanted to know what he'd cooked for dinner.

Was that where Alan had disappeared to? Maybe Mindy from the realtor's office had emailed him as well...

I groaned, covered my face with both of my hands, and permitted myself to wallow in despair for an excruciating moment.

How much faith could my husband have in our marriage if he had secretly bought a *house*?

"Lord, get me through this day," I prayed.

I reminded myself that God would be my strength. He always had been and he always would be. I couldn't let myself panic, because if I did, I would spiral out of control.

It was Esther's big day.

She needed me.

As I pushed myself out of bed, poured a mug of coffee in the kitchen, and hopped in the shower, I forced myself to focus.

But by the time I arrived at Hopeful Heart Ministries and found Esther in the fellowship hall that had been reserved for the bride, my crumbling marriage was all I could think about.

"I think Alan's leaving me!"

"What?"

Esther was seated at a desk in the corner of the room. There was a large, portable, vanity mirror on top of the desk. She turned her attention from blotting gloss onto her lips and looked up at me.

"He bought a house!"

"He did *what?*"

"A realtor called his cell phone last night and I picked up," I explained, as I began pacing in my peach colored, patent leather heels. My long, chiffon dress kept getting in the way, however. It was impossible to blow off steam while dressed in formal wear! "What if he leaves me, Esther? What if he's planning on filing for divorce?"

Esther was on her high heeled feet in no time.

Her pearl-white wedding gown swished, as she grabbed me by the shoulders and slapped me clear across the face.

I was stunned.

She slapped me again and yelled:

"Snap out of it!"

My cheek smarted, but I had to hand it to her. It had done the trick.

"Penny, you know I love you," she said, calming herself down and taking me by the shoulders again, this time gently. "I'm not going to let you self-destruct."

"Thanks," I said, meaning it.

"The last thing you need to do is jump to conclusions," she wisely advised. "If Alan bought a house—"

"He did!"

"Listen to me!" she yelled. She might as well have been ten

times her natural size. "You've survived a lot. I have, too. You taught me the importance of setting all fears aside and taking a chance on love. That's what I did. And now, that's what you're going to do. For today, you're going to forget about that other house, and you're going to have a great time at my wedding."

Deep down, I felt terrified of losing Alan. At the level of my bones, I feared that he would never see me as a mother after what I had done when I had gotten drunk one night and nearly burned the cabin down. My worst nightmare had always been that Alan would never find it in his heart to forgive me, and that he would eventually leave me.

But fear was not my friend.

Esther was.

"Okay," I breathed.

"Okay, good," she said softly. "You're not thinking about drinking, are you?"

I shook my head.

"No, not at all."

"Good," she said.

She offered me a reassuring smile then asked:

"How do I look?"

✝

I TOOK ESTHER'S advice as wholeheartedly as I could, found a seat in the church among the other wedding guests, and only looked at my cell phone three times to see if Alan had texted.

He hadn't.

And he still wasn't here.

Harriet and practically all of the teachers from Walnut Mountain Middle School were in attendance. Matthew had been invited, of course, since he was a member of the congregation. It was no surprise that his date for the wedding was Samantha.

She looked beautiful.

This was a happy occasion, and as the ceremony got underway, I truly was able to suspend my fears and get swept up in the spirit of holy matrimony.

Pastor Peter stood at the front of the church. The handsome groom, Daniel, was dressed in a tailored suit and standing beside the pastor. Soon a string quartet began playing Pachelbel's Canon in D Major, alerting the congregation that the bride was about to walk down the aisle.

Daniel's eyes misted over with tears.

Everyone turned their heads to watch Esther, who was being escorted by her sweet dad to be given away.

She looked angelic. The white, lace veil spilled down her back. Her dark hair was shiny and healthy beneath the lace.

Esther's dad kissed her on the cheek when they reached the altar then he stepped aside, and Daniel took his bride's hands.

Both Esther and Daniel had written their own vows. Their love was palpable. And before long, they each said, "I do," and slipped a wedding band on the other's finger.

Everyone cheered and clapped and sprang to their feet when the newlyweds kissed.

No one was more enthusiastic than me.

But Alan never showed up.

✝

THE WEDDING RECEPTION was held at Fancy's, the fanciest restaurant in all of Walnut Mountain. It was also where Edgar Swaine had been murdered in the men's room last autumn, but I tried not to think about that, as I arrived with the other guests.

The owner, Jacque Vique, had done a wonderful job working with Esther to transform the dining room for the reception. The dance hall beyond the large dining area had a DJ and a long bar where guests were served cocktails, beers, and a wide variety of wine.

I mingled with my fellow Christians and teachers. I danced with Esther. I spent time with my parents. They were doing a soldierly job of not feeling down about Patrick, who hadn't even had a bail hearing yet.

We slipped outside to the patio where other guests of the wedding were getting some air, smoking cigars, and otherwise enjoying the fine weather as dusk gathered across the sky.

"Penny?"

I turned from conversing with my parents to find Harriet on the patio.

She wore a long, eggplant-purple velvet dress, an exquisite butterfly brooch pin on her chest, and a look of remorse on her face.

"Mocktail?" she said, offering me a mixed drink. "It's non-alcoholic. The bartender said it's a 'Can't Elope' because it's made with cantaloupe juice. All the drinks have clever names."

"Funny," I said, taking the drink from her.

The mocktail was fizzy and had a salted rim, and there was a skewer of various fruit, including cantaloupe, laying across the top. It was too pretty to drink!

I used the skewer of fruit to stir the drink, as Harriet mentioned:

"I also don't drink alcohol."

I felt embarrassed. Samantha had certainly blabbed to all the teachers that day, *hadn't* she?

"I used to be in A.A.," she went on. "But then after a number of years, I really didn't need the program anymore. I can come to events like these and not even feel tempted."

I held her gaze for a moment, as her expression drooped and she said:

"I feel terrible about rushing you out of my house the other day."

"Oh, that's okay, Harriet," I told her, not wanting any conflicts at the wedding reception.

"No, I mean it, Penny. I shouldn't have been rude to you. Not after you helped me transport my paintings."

"Well, thanks for the apology," I allowed. "But really, it's okay."

"Do you like the drink?" she asked, smiling at me.

I hadn't even tasted it yet.

She gulped her own mocktail and said, "Mmm, yummy! Go on, try yours!"

I lifted the glass to my mouth, but then I got a good look at the butterfly brooch she was wearing, and I had to ask her:

"Goodness, Harriet! Is that one of *your* butterflies?"

"It is," she said. Her previously pleasant expression darkened over.

"It's so shiny! It's not delicate?"

"Not too delicate, no."

"How do you preserve the butterflies like that?" I asked, genuinely curious. I lifted my mocktail to my mouth again, but then lowered the glass as I added, "How do you get them to appear so shiny?"

"It's a two-step process," she said, mildly annoyed. "I have to use a chemical, but you wouldn't want to hear about that. It's boring."

"Not at all! I'm interested!"

Through gritted teeth, Harriet suggested:

"Why don't you drink your mocktail, Penny? It's really good. You'll like it."

I lifted the glass to my nose.

"Smells good," I agreed.

"It definitely is."

Again, I brought the mocktail to my lips.

But when Harriet said, "Drink up," I suddenly got a very bad feeling.

Harriet had been the other person at the refreshment table the day of Jessica's murder. Harriet had handed me cupcakes and cookies to give to Jessica. Of course, someone else could've given Jessica a poisoned drink or cookie that day when I wasn't looking... but still...

I lowered the glass from my mouth.

"Exactly *what* chemical do you use to preserve your butterflies, Harriet?"

The tension rising between us was thick.

"Why do you ask?"

"Why do you want me to drink this, Harriet?"

A slight smirk spread across her face.

"I'm just being friendly," she said.

"I saw the police report," I told her. "I know what Jessica did to you. And I know that even though she was arrested, she was never really punished. You could've won a lot of money if you had been able to submit your painting to the Pembroke Pines Foundation. But because of Jessica, you weren't even able to apply."

Harriet glared at me. Her chest rose and fell, as she sucked in hard, emotional breaths.

"She never even saw the inside of a courtroom!" she yelled, furious.

The nearby guests turned to see who was yelling.

"Her so-called punishment was to write me a check for the cost of materials!" Harriet yelled. "I poured blood, sweat, and tears into my painting! It had taken me *months* to paint! And all Jessica had to do was write a check for the *cost of materials*?! That painting was priceless!"

"So, you killed her," I surmised.

Suddenly, Alan burst outside onto the patio, having charged through Fancy's. Officers Chuck and Jeremiah were at his heels.

With his gun drawn and aimed at Harriet, Alan yelled:

"Freeze!"

Harriet shrieked and the next thing I knew, she smacked the mocktail out of my hand.

The poisonous liquid rained over the patio and the glass shattered against the polished stone floor, destroying all evidence that Harriet had tried to kill me.

She took off running.

The police officers raced after her, as Alan holstered his gun and found me.

Harriet kept scrambling away. She was wobbly and slow moving in her heels, but she managed to push through the other guests, making her way towards the darkness of the grassy hills behind the restaurant.

But when Harriet's high heel landed on a round, slippery walnut husk, she lost her balance!

"Whoa, whoa, whoa!" she yelled, as she slipped and slid, one foot then the next landing on the round husks.

Officers Chuck and Jeremiah were gaining on her.

Just as Harriet's feet flew out from under her, the police officers caught Harriet before she could take a bad spill across the grass.

"I think she was trying to poison me," I told Alan. "She handed me a mocktail."

"Did you drink any?"

"No," I said, feeling shaken up.

"It was formaldehyde," Alan told me. "The poison that killed Jessica Saxon."

"*That's* what she used to preserve her butterflies! Formaldehyde," I said. It all made sense now.

"I was able to put the pieces together when Sergeant Pepper said that he had released Jessica quickly after her arrest. Penny, if you hadn't obtained that police report…"

Was Alan about to *thank me* for poking around?

"I had to get a warrant this morning for Harriet's home studio," he explained. "We found formaldehyde there. I never would've missed Esther's wedding otherwise."

"What about Patrick?"

"He's free to go. He's with Margot. We let him out as soon as we found Harriet's canisters of formaldehyde."

Officers Chuck and Jeremiah held onto Harriet's arms. They had handcuffed her. As they hauled her across the patio, she cursed up a storm, shouting:

"Any one of you would've killed her, too, if she had done to you what she did to me!"

Alan cupped my cheek.

I stared up into his blue, twinkling eyes.

"Penny, I know we're ready to take the next step. But there's something I need to show you first."

✝

"KEEP YOUR EYES covered," said Alan, as he helped me out of the passenger's side of his truck. "Are your eyes closed?"

"Yes!" I said.

I had kept my eyes closed the entire drive from Fancy's to wherever we were now.

My peach-colored patent leather heels soon struck a brick walkway.

"Keep them closed!"

"For God's sake, Alan, I am!"

The cool evening air smelled of freshly cut grass and lilac bushes.

Where the heck had he taken me?

He held my shoulders, standing behind me, and positioned me *just so*.

Then he said:

"Okay. You can open your eyes."

I lowered my hands and gasped, smiling from ear to ear when I saw a large, two-story cabin.

"Penny," he said. "I want this to be our new home. The cabin where we'll have our children. I want us to start a new chapter of our lives together *here*. There are too many memories in the old cabin. I want us to move on. Forget the past. And stay focused on our happy future."

"Oh, Alan!" I exclaimed as I threw my arms around him. "I love it!"

He kissed me, swept me up in his arms, and said:
"It's baby making time!"

THE END

ABOUT THE AUTHOR

Hi, I'm Catherine Gibson! I write fun, witty, cozy mysteries, because that's what I love to read! My stories feature lovable Christian sleuths, quaint storybook towns, and murder motives you won't find anywhere else! In my spare time, I attend ballet classes, whip up fragrant batches of homemade soap, hang out on the beach, and spend time with my twin sister after church.

Discover more of my books at www.MysteryRoyalty.com

Copyright © 2024
Published by: Mira Gibson

All Rights Reserved. This book or any portion thereof may not be reproduced or used in any manner whatsoever without the express written permission of the publisher except for the use of brief quotations in a book review. All characters appearing in this work are fictitious. Any resemblance to real persons, living or dead, is purely coincidental.

For questions and comments about this book, please contact www.mysteryroyalty.com